To Beryl

The Hidden Crown

Northland: 1166

Happy reading and
"Waes hael!"

David M

The Hidden Crown

Northland: 1166

David Haworth

**TOP HAT
BOOKS**

Winchester, UK
Washington, USA

First published by Top Hat Books, 2013
Top Hat Books is an imprint of John Hunt Publishing Ltd., Laurel House, Station Approach,
Alresford, Hants, SO24 9JH, UK
office1@jhpbooks.net
www.johnhuntpublishing.com

For distributor details and how to order please visit the 'Ordering' section on our website.

A CIP catalogue record for this book is available from the British Library.

Design: Stuart Davies
www.stuartdaviesart.com

Printed and bound by CPI Group (UK) Ltd, Croydon, CR0 4YY

We operate a distinctive and ethical publishing philosophy in all
areas of our business, from our global network of authors to
production and worldwide distribution.

In memory of my father and Anne

Characters

Pre Conquest

Edwine	A northern earl, brother of Morcar
Harald Hardrada	King of Norway
Harold II	King of England
Morcar	A northern earl, brother of Edwine
Tostig	Brother of Harold, exiled Earl of Northumbria
William	Duke of Normandy

Ængland

Adelise	The orphaned granddaughter of King Æthelgar
Æthelgar	The dying King of Ængland
Edgar	Earl of East Anglia
Ceolwulf	Son of Edgar, the Earl of East Anglia
Cinedred	Wife of Edgar, the Earl of East Anglia
Eadric	Archbishop of Cantwaraburg
Godric of Waneting	Archbishop of Westmynster
Hereman	Earl of Grantbrygscir
Leofwin	Earl of Suthseaxe
Ricmund of Readinga	A loyal thegn to Swegen, nicknamed 'Eoten' – the Beast
Swegen	Earl of Berrocscir, the Ænglisc king's nephew

Northland

Arnewulf	An Ænglisc-born abbott in Jorvik
Biarni	A villager in Midelesby

Egbrand	A shepherd from Catune
Galinn	Jarl of Northhymbre
Hakon	King of Northland
Herri	Jarl of Westmoringaland
Hrafn	Captain of the city guard in Jorvik
Ivar	Jarl of the East Thrith of Jorvik
Knut	A Northlandic prince, son of King Hakon
Leif	Kirkby's huskarl captain
Sigtrygg	Archbishop of Jorvik
Sluta	A huskarl in Kirkby Kendale
Sorli	Thurstan's friend and fellow huskarl
Svarðkell	Jarl of Suthribel
Thurstan Ælfsson	A young huskarl, a cavalry solider, stationed in Kirkby Kendale
Vinder of Kirkby	Sheriff of Westmoringaland

Scotland

Cyneburga	Ænglisc born wife of Prince Malcolm, aunt to Adelise.
Eadgyð	Adelise's lady-in-waiting
Kenneth	A Scottish prince, young son of Prince Malcolm
Malcolm	A Scottish prince, son of King Duncan III
Tola	Daughter of Eadgyð

Prologue One
14th October 1066
Senlac Hill, near Hastings

King Harold II lies dying on a battlefield. An arrow has pierced his eye, fired from an invading Norman's bow. Having witnessed the death of its leader, his army begins to rout. The Duke of Normandy, William the Conqueror, has achieved victory in the Battle of Hastings.

Harold had waited all summer for the anticipated invasion from Normandy, but the Channel's infamous weather had prevented the duke from crossing the sea.

On the 8th August, Harold sent home the fyrd, the raised army composed of conscripted men. They had given their two months of service and the harvest was due.

Then, much to his surprise, an invasion did happen – but from the north. King Harald Hardrada of Norway landed twelve thousand men on the north east coast. The legendary Hardrada, the most feared warrior in Europe, had a surprise ally – Tostig Godwinson, Harold's own brother.

Tostig had once been the Earl of Northumbria. Through his greed and cruelty, he had alienated the northern nobles to such an extent that Harold had been forced to exile his own brother or risk civil war. Now he was back for revenge and alongside him the ambitious Norwegian king, who desired England for his own.

Together they beat the brother earls, Morcar and Edwine, at the battle of Fulford on the 20th September. Harold force-marched his army up to near York in just four days, recruiting men wherever possible. On the 25th September, Harold defeated the recuperating Norse army, taking them by surprise at the Battle of Stamford Bridge. Harald Hardrada was killed by an arrow through the throat; the body of Tostig was never found.

Then came the news Harold had been dreading. The wind had finally changed and William of Normandy had landed on the south coast. Gathering the remains of his exhausted army, Harold marched back down the length of the country to face the Norman invader.

His army took up an advantageous position on top of Senlac Hill, but at the first sign of victory, the fyrd broke rank to chase fleeing Normans. This division of his army proved decisive and the mounted Norman cavalry chased the English down and slew them.

Now Harold lies dying in a pool of his own gore. William, the Normans and the feudal system they bring with them are set to dominate the country for centuries to come.

And the last thought that goes through Harold's mind is that it could have all been so different.

"Ex parvis sæpe magnarum momenta rerum pendent"
"...The course of great events often depends on the smallest of things..."

-Titus Livius

Prologue Two
20th September 1066
Fuleford, near Jorvik

King Harold II lies dying on a battlefield. An arrow has pierced his throat, fired from an invading Norseman's bow. Having witnessed the death of its leader, his army begins to rout. The King of Norway, Harald Hardrada, and Tostig Godwinson have achieved victory in the Battle of Fuleford.

Harold had waited all summer for an anticipated invasion from Normandy, but the Channel's infamous weather had prevented Duke William from crossing the sea.

Then, on the 7th August, the wind changed.

William crossed the channel and landed on the south Ænglisc coast. Harold's full-strength army, including the conscripted men of the fyrd, met William head on at the Battle of Pefensea. Harold's numerical superiority counted for much and the Normans' one clear advantage, their cavalry, became bogged down in the fields that had been churned into mud by recent rains. The invading Norman army was routed, William's body was never found. The nation defended, Harold sent the fyrd home and returned to the capital, Winceaster.

Then, much to Harold's surprise, another army invaded. Harald Hardrada landed twelve thousand men on the north east coast. The legendary Hardrada, the most feared warrior in Europe, had a surprise ally – Tostig Godwinson, Harold's own brother. Tostig had been the Earl of Northymbre, a nobleman from Wessex imposed upon the North in an attempt to keep the unruly local lords under some sort of control.

Yet this was a region that only a generation before had been an independent Anglo-Norse kingdom. The northern lords had not taken kindly to yet another Godwinson being made earl, as all his brothers had been in other parts of the country. Through his greed and cruelty, he had ended up alienating the local noblemen to such an extent that Harold had been forced to exile his own brother or risk civil war. Now Tostig was back for revenge and alongside him the ambitious Norwegian king, who also desired the kingdom for his own.

On the 20th September, Harold's exhausted army met the awaiting Norsemen. Harold had force-marched his men up to near Jorvik in just four days, recruiting wherever possible along the way. The Ænglisc army was reinforced by the northern earls, Morcar and Edwine, but the Battle of Pefensea had taken its toll.

The battle started well for the Ænglisc, but their tiredness soon showed and fatigue set in. The Norsemen, led by their fearsome axe-wielding leader, started to press home their numerical advantage, showing no mercy.

Now Harold lies dying in a pool of his own gore. Earl Edwine takes an arrow through the eye and falls. Morcar, his brother, retreats from the field and sends a message to Hardrada that he will parley with the Norse king on the condition he will speak with Hardrada, and Hardrada alone.

And the last thought that goes through Harold's mind is that it could have all been so different...

One hundred years after the Battle of Fuleford...
7th April 1166
Grarigg, Westmoringaland, Northland

The two riders crested the hill and looked down into the wide, fog-smothered valley. From the top of the ridge, they could only see the very highest branches of the nearest trees. The rest of the landscape was swathed in a blanket of grey. They spurred their mounts forward and started to descend slowly towards the small village of Grarigg. The village should have been around a mile from where they were.

"Where are the others?" the younger of the two men asked. The six-man patrol had drifted apart climbing the final hill before the valley had opened out.

"Don't worry, Thurstan, they can't be far," his companion replied, gently pulling his horse to a halt. "Ahey there!" he shouted through cupped hands. His voice sounded oddly loud, yet muffled in the silence, as if all the noise of his cry had stayed with them. He waited several seconds then called again.

"Should we wait for them or press on?" Thurstan asked. He glanced around, trying to make out any figures in the distance. Water droplets ran down the nosepiece of his helm and dripped onto his short beard. Wiping them away with his glove, he too cupped a hand to his mouth and shouted. This time they heard a distant shout in reply, although it was not clear from which direction it came.

"We might as well press on to the village," Sorli, the older rider, replied. Wrapping his green woollen cloak around him, he urged his horse forward. "There's no way of knowing where they are in this weather, but at least they know we're still here. God awful Northlandic weather."

"And the weather in Norway is wonderful by comparison, I

imagine," Thurstan said, grinning.

"It is compared to this. This is a good day by Northlandic standards," Sorli grumbled. He had been born across the sea, in the old country, and despite having lived in Northland for the best part of ten years, still moaned about the weather.

Thurstan Ælfsson, however, had been born and raised in Northland. He had only ventured outside its borders once, and even that was just to the Scottish border town of Penrith. His father was a merchant in Lonborg whose Anglo-Norse family had been living in Westmoringaland for at least three generations before the conquest. His mother, on the other hand, had been born in Norway and like so many over the last hundred years, had moved to Northland as a child, her family having heard about the abundance of farming land found across the North Sea.

"Come on, and watch your footing," Sorli muttered, kicking his mount forward.

They reached the bottom of the hill, where the fog was at its thickest, and rode towards where they believed the village ought to be. The previous week, a farmer from Grarigg had come to petition the sheriff in Kirkby Kendale with a story of wolfheads menacing his village. The wolfheads were a mixture of outlawed men and bandits from both Scotland and Northland; men who had killed, men who had lost land or had forfeited a debt. In many cases though, they were simply violent men who preferred stealing and killing to farming.

Reports of the wolfheads attacking isolated farms were common enough, but Grarigg was near the main road from Kirkby to Penrith, one of the most important trade routes from Scotland to the rest of Northland and Ængland beyond. The threat to important revenue if banditry was allowed to go unchecked was too great, however insignificant the plaintiff. Somewhat reluctantly, the sheriff had sent out a party of six of his household soldiers, his huskarls, to investigate.

Sorli and Thurstan rode slowly through the open fields towards where they imagined the village to be. Sorli had been there twice in the last year to assist tax collectors and was fairly confident of its whereabouts, using the faint sun as a guide. Thurstan had only been riding with the other huskarls for six months and until today, had never needed to use his sword. The thought of any fighting, albeit with a few ragged wolfheads, armed with no more than pitchforks or scythes, made his mouth go dry and his palms twitch.

"We should be there by now," Sorli announced suddenly. He stopped his horse and stood up in the stirrups, the sound of his mail hauberk against the sword at his side seeming unnaturally loud.

"There, I can see a spire, I think." He spurred his horse forward into a trot and Thurstan dutifully followed him. They arrived at the outlying buildings of a village that was little more than a few houses, a church and an inn. Even though the fog had muffled all sounds, the village seemed eerily quiet.

"Hello?" Sorli called again, this time trying to attract the attention of any of the villagers. The huskarls rode slowly along the mud track that ran between the wooden houses, to where the blacksmith's forge stood next to the inn. There was no sign of any activity at all, apart from a black cat that ran out from between two of the small wooden buildings and quickly disappeared into the gloom.

Sorli jumped down from his horse, his boots making a dull splash in the mud, and tied his horse's reins to the one of the open-fronted smithy's posts. He walked over to the forge, held his hand over the remains of the charcoal, and then stuck his hand in the ashes. "This hasn't been lit in days. It's stone cold."

Thurstan swallowed deeply and glanced around him. He had imagined that his first fight would have been against an opposing army on a bright sunlit battlefield, where everyone would be clearly marked out with colourful shields; not chasing ghosts in some deserted village. "Perhaps they all fled to Kirkby?" he ventured, although he didn't sound convinced by his own theory.

"Surely we would have met them on the way? Besides, if a blacksmith was going to abandon his smithy, surely he would have taken his tools with him." Sorli waved at the assortment of hammers and mallets hanging on the back wall of the building. "Let's check the inn."

"You don't want to wait for the others?" Thurstan immediately regretted the question and its inference of cowardice on his part.

"If there were wolfheads waiting to jump on us, Thurstan, they would have done it by now," a smiling Sorli replied.

Thurstan dismounted, tied his horse next to his companion's and walked over to the inn. He pushed the door open and stepped into the deserted building. The smell of stale ale and rotting food assailed his nostrils. On several of the low tables in the small timbered room were unfinished wooden pots of ale, one or two of which had been knocked over. Two plates of half-eaten food were sitting on another table, flies busily crawling over the dried mash of vegetables that had constituted someone's unfinished dinner. Sorli touched Thurstan's elbow, causing him to jump. Without speaking, he pointed to a point on the floor by the bar. The earthen floor was covered in rushes, but one patch was noticeably darker than the rest and receiving considerable attention from the already busy flies.

"Blood?" Thurstan whispered. Sorli shrugged and moved to the door. They walked back outside into a fog that still showed no sign of abating, even though a slight breeze was gradually starting to pick up. Sorli stared into the distance and without turning to Thurstan, slowly unsheathed his sword. Needing no prompting, the younger huskarl did the same, the sword feeling unusually heavy in his clammy, gloved hand. The silence was broken by a raven, cawing as it flew overhead and away from them. The sudden noise of something other than themselves sent a shiver down Thurstan's spine. They walked towards the small church whose spire Sorli had seen through the fog. As they grew nearer to the only stone building in the village, they could hear the sound of more ravens.

"There's a small orchard behind the church, where they keep pigs and apple trees, if I remember rightly," Sorli said. He walked though the small graveyard that ran down one side of the church.

"The blessed church of St Hild and our Lord Jesus Christ," Thurstan read the inscription from above the church door. Sorli smiled nervously and pointed his sword at one of the gravestones that, alongside the inscribed crucifix, also had several runes scratched across the bottom, presumably added at a later date by a relative, beseeching Odin to protect their loved one.

"You can never be too sure," he snorted and crossed himself. Old habits died hard in the countryside. The village priests were often a little more tolerant than their city-based counterparts of their flock's fairly loose interpretation of the Christian faith, mixing it, as they often did, with the older religions.

Sorli climbed the small wall at the end of the churchyard and strode into the orchard, unslinging the small circular shield from his back. The thick fog limited his vision to tree trunks just a few feet away, the tops of their branches invisible to him, like mountain peaks in the clouds. Thurstan clambered over the small wall, stumbling as he landed on the soft ground. From a distance a shout came, the voice instantly recognisable as that of Leif, the captain of the patrol.

"We're in the orchard," Thurstan shouted, unsure as to whether his voice would carry back. He turned and hurried to catch Sorli up. Sorli had halted further ahead, his sword lowered. Brushing low wet branches out of his face, Thurstan walked quickly over to a small clearing where Sorli stood, his hand raised, signalling him to stop. A pig's carcass lay on its side, its body cut open from neck to tail down one side and left to rot.

Several ravens hopped around the carcass, picking here and there at the darkening flesh and spilled innards. Sorli breathed deeply through his mouth, trying to not let the smell of decomposing pig into his nostrils any more than necessary.

"Desperate men would take a pig. They would eat it, use it, not kill it for game," he said, staring at the dead animal. Thurstan stepped back from the smell that even on this cold morning emanated from the pig's body like a pungent miasma. He felt a large branch knock against his shoulder, which he pushed away from him, only to have it swing back against him again.

"There you are!" Leif shouted, appearing from out of the fog. "I can't even see the end of my own beard in this. Dear Christ, where is everyone?" He walked towards the two younger men and then stopped dead in his tracks before reaching the pig. "Thurstan," he said, his eyes focused on something past the young man's shoulder. "Step towards me."

"What is it?" Thurstan answered, slowly stepping forward. He looked at the older man, who raised an arm and pointed at the tree behind him. Slowly turning around, Thurstan looked up and saw that it had not been a branch brushing against his shoulder. It had been a foot. A grey wrinkled foot, attached to a body hanging from a tree. The fog started to lift, revealing several more gently swinging shapes throughout the orchard, and Thurstan suddenly realised where all the villagers had gone.

Oxnaforda, Ængland

Æthelgar of Wessex, son of Tostig II, King of Ængland and Kernow, was dying. For the last three months, he had been confined to his bed in the castle that his grandfather had built at the end of the last century. In the winter of the previous year, he had started complaining of a severe stomach ache that the royal physician had initially diagnosed as indigestion. This sort of thing was quite common, he had been assured, simply resulting from over-indulgence during the festive period.

Yet things had not improved in the new year; his stomach had swelled grotesquely and started to discolour, despite the constant poultices, potions and bleedings applied by his physician. When they had all failed, the incompetent doctor had been put to death and Æthelgar had taken to his bed for the final time.

Now the king lay in his draughty bedchamber, surrounded by several of his closest earls and servants. Outside a gale howled, causing the wooden shutters to clatter and the tall candles that dimly lit the sickroom to splutter and flicker. A young maid mopped the dying monarch's forehead with a damp cloth, aware that the gazes of many of the kingdom's most important men were upon her. The current royal physician, a hollow-cheeked man only too aware of his predecessor's fate, listened to Æthelgar's shallow breathing. He leant in close to his chest, then turned to the assembled noblemen and shook his head.

"He hasn't long, my lords. I think it's time you fetched the archbishop," he said sadly. A servant boy, who was standing in attendance, nodded quickly and left the room. Æthelgar arched his back, gasping shallowly and tried to speak to the physician. "Try not to talk, my lord; save your strength for making your peace."

The Archbishop of Westmynster was waiting in a side chamber, where he had changed into his robes after having arrived only an hour before. By rights, the leader of the Ænglisc church, the Archbishop of Cantwaraburg, should have administered the last rites to the king, but the storms across Ængland had delayed his arrival. Godric, the Archbishop of Westmynster, had been tending to his family's estates near Waneting and had been less than half a day's ride away. His superior's misfortune had gifted him the most important political duty a churchman could perform, short of crowning a new monarch. He would hear Æthelgar's last confession and confirm his nominated successor.

The common expectation was that the throne would pass to Æthelgar's nephew, Swegen, Earl of Berrocscir. Godric had made it his business that the Swegen was aware of his presence. Since the moment that the king's only son and direct heir, Edmund, had been lost in a storm in the Channel four years previously, Godric had known that Swegen would be a man to get on his side. Æthelgar's only other direct descendant, his nine-year-old granddaughter Adelise, was far too young to take the throne, and even with a steward, a little girl was surely never going to be left in control of the Ænglisc kingdom.

It was Swegen who had practically been running the kingdom for the last six months, and it was Swegen who had ruthlessly put down a peasant uprising against the latest shipbuilding tax in the Mercian shires the previous spring. True, the dying king and his nephew did not see eye to eye; Æthelgar could be such a stubborn old mule at times, but it would be madness to nominate anyone else as heir. Besides, in the ambitious Swegen, Godric saw a kindred spirit; a man with plans for an expanding, modern Ængland, who currently felt shackled by old, traditional views. It was Swegen who had wanted to promote Ængland's expansion into Cymru, to the west, but the elderly king had held him back, favouring trade and friendship, even when the resources were there for the taking. If Ængland felt bound by the century-old Morcar Oath not to expand to the north, then surely Cymru was the logical alternative.

Likewise, Godric's repeated requests for greater independence in Westmynster had fallen on deaf ears. Westmynster and the neighbouring city of Lunden were the powerhouses of Ængland; the kingdom's capital may have been Winceaster and the Church may have considered Cantwaraburg as its home, but everyone knew that Lunden was the nation's real heart. The monarchs were happy to use his cathedral for their coronations and let the Archbishop of Cantwaraburg perform the important ceremonies there when it suited them, like someone renting a tavern for a birthday celebration, but then refused to grant Westmynster the power it truly deserved.

Well, Godric thought, *tonight that may all well change.* A knock at the door was followed by an apologetic-looking servant waddling in with his head bowed, like some idiot dog.

"It's the king, my lord. The physician says he hasn't long to go, you should come quickly," he gabbled. Godric nodded and walked out of the chamber. He strode down the stone corridor, past the hanging tapestries of previous monarchs; St Edward the Confessor, Ælfred the Great, Tostig I and II. *You may be kings,* he thought, *but tonight, I am the kingmaker.* Coming to the antechamber, a man dressed in an expensively ornate tunic greeted him with a solemn, if somewhat exaggerated bow of the head.

"My lord Archbishop," the man said gravely, though his blue eyes shone brightly.

"My lord Earl of Berrocscir," Godric replied, aware that the attending earls, thegns and servants also present in the antechamber would expect no less formal a greeting between two such men. They stared at each other for what seemed to be a moment too long, but exchanged no words. The following hour would determine each man's long-term future more than any other moment so far in his life.

"After you, my lord," Swegen said, holding the door open, this time barely containing the anticipation in his voice.

Godric flattened his robes with his hands, took out his rosary beads and stepped into the room. The assembled earls stiffened noticeably and stood back to make room for the churchman. Swegen followed him in, nodding in greeting to the other earls. Outside, the wind howled around the stone tower, causing a young serving girl to hurriedly relight the candles that were blowing out every few minutes. Godric cleared his throat and started reciting the Latin rites he had said many times before, but that were now taking on such significance. Æthelgar's eyes flickered, possibly in recognition, but Godric could not be sure if it was of him or the words. Once finished, the archbishop cleared his throat and addressed Æthelgar directly in Ænglisc.

"My lord King, it is your servant, the Archbishop of Westmynster, by your bed. Our Lord God is soon to call you to His side," Godric said, his voice quiet but clear. Æthelgar's eyes stopped flickering and appeared to focus on the archbishop.

"I should like that very much," he said through dry, cracked lips. "I would like to see my wife and son again." His voice rasped, each word coming with a stilted breath. "Is my grand-daughter here?"

"No, my lord, you sent her to live with her aunt in Scotland last year." Godric looked around the room with an expression of pity that he might have otherwise used when speaking to an elderly relative. "You thought it important that she spend time with her family in Carleol, away from the politics of court."

"So I did, so I did," Æthelgar replied airily, then gasped as another ripple of pain racked his body. For a while he lay still, not moving a muscle, to the point that Godric leant across to put an ear to his mouth. "She's a good woman, a good woman," Æthelgar said suddenly, causing Godric to recoil quickly. "Cyneburga, that's her name. Her mother's sister, married to a Scottish prince, Malcolm, I think, lives in..." his voice trailed off and he sank back into silence.

Godric glanced around and felt a slight twinge of panic. If Æthelgar's wandering mind could not give him an answer, the whole succession would be thrown into doubt. In truth, Ænglisc kings were never directly elected by their predecessors, but nominated and then confirmed by a council of wise men, a witenagemot. The wise men in effect were just the major noblemen, who in Godric's experience were hardly ever wise, and members of the clergy. If the dying king nominated a chosen heir, then the process was little more than a formality; if not, or the nominated successor was challenged, then it could take months.

"My lord, have you anything you wish to say before you leave this earth?" Godric prompted Æthelgar, who appeared to have fallen unconscious. *God help me if it's already too late,* he thought to himself.

Æthelgar's eyes flicked open and for once seemed lucid and focused. He turned his head, looked at Godric, and grabbed him by the wrist. The frail arm still had a surprising amount of force in it.

"Bring me my sword," he said in a stronger, if still croaking voice. "I shall not meet my maker without my sword."

Godric waved at the Earl of Suthseaxe who was holding Æthelgar's favourite sword. He was not quite sure how the king had a favourite sword, or why he still held on to the archaic tradition of dying with one in his hand, given that Æthelgar had hardly ever seen battle. He had been a solid administrator and a competent orator and had seen the country through two successive bad harvests ten years before, but was by no means renowned for his prowess in the field. The king was king though, and a dying king had his last wishes granted.

"Here you are, my lord," Godric said. He lay the sword down on the bed next to Æthelgar and pressed the pommel into his palm. Æthelgar gripped the hilt and then, much to the surprise of those assembled in the room, raised himself onto his elbows. The sheets pulled tight across his horribly distended stomach and the pain was visible on Æthelgar's face, but he looked around the room and stared into the eyes of each nobleman present.

"I name as my heir…" he announced suddenly, surprising the very people who had been waiting many hours to hear such an announcement. Godric glanced towards Swegen who was staring intently at his uncle. "I name as my heir, my grand-daughter Adelise. She is my blood and she shall be your queen. You shall swear loyalty to her person and throne. I name Swegen, Earl of Berrocscir, as her guardian and steward until she reaches the age of eighteen, or until she is found a suitable husband, whichever occurs first; something I also charge you with, Swegen."

The assembled nobles murmured in surprise, though none dared articulate anything aloud. Godric looked up and stared at Swegen, who had turned very pale. His Adam's apple was bobbing up and down rapidly. He stepped forward, his mouth open, ready to say something, but Godric almost imperceptibly shook his head, his hand very softly waving him back.

"Your nephew is here, my lord, standing next to you," Godric told the dying king.

"I can see him, Bishop," Æthelgar replied curtly. The archbishop bristled at this lesser title, intentional or otherwise.

"And you know where you are?" Godric tried, probing the unlikely avenue of a mental incapacity to choose the heir.

"I know full well where I am, Godric of Waneting," Æthelgar replied sourly. "Come here, Swegen." He raised a gaunt, yellowing hand and beckoned his nephew over. "Do you promise to adhere to my will, to protect your queen and to protect her body and throne? Do you accept the duty I have laid upon you?"

Swegen glanced at Godric again, who this time remained impassive. "I do," he finally managed.

"Then swear it. On oath, swear it to me." Æthelgar lowered

his hand, adorned with a simple gold band and offered it to Swegen. The earl looked around the room briefly, aware that all eyes were upon him. He stepped forward, knelt and kissed the dying king's ring.

"I swear it, my lord," he whispered, then stood back from the bed.

Godric closed his eyes and offered a prayer, that to others in the room may well have seemed one of thanks. On the final amen he opened his eyes again and looked down at the bed, where Æthelgar was staring directly at him. He shuddered, but was fearful that averting his gaze would cause offence. When the king did not blink for several seconds, Godric realised that he would blink no more. He stepped forward and placed his ear to Æthelgar's mouth. He delicately pressed the dead king's eyelids closed and murmured a small prayer in Latin before turning to the assembled noblemen.

"The king is dead, my lords, did..." Godric paused. He had been about ask whether anyone had seen whether Æthelgar had died before Swegen had kissed the ring, but he thought better of it, aware of the insinuation that any question might provoke. "I name Princess Adelise the nominated heir to the throne, and Swegen, Earl of Berrocscir as her guardian." He spoke the words calmly, keeping the ever-growing sense of outrage and disappointment at bay. "Might I humbly suggest that Carleol be let known immediately and to summon all the earls, so that a witenagemot may confirm her succession? Given the circumstances, that perhaps might be..." Again, he trailed off, but the proposal that the kingdom's earls and most senior clergy should hold a council was greeted with murmurs of assent.

Swegen coughed and stood up for the first time since kissing the dying Æthelgar's signet ring. He straightened his tunic out and turned to the assembled audience.

"Go back to your shires and let your people know that the old king died well and with dignity. We shall convene here in two weeks, within this castle. Let messengers be despatched immediately to those earls not present here today, summoning them. We shall hold a witenagemot to decide how best to interpret our king's last wishes. Tomorrow we can discuss the details, but for now, my lords, if I may pay my last respects to my king and uncle."

Swegen ushered the earls out of the room, along with the now redundant physician and even the crying servants. The room was left empty, save for the corpse, Godric, the Archbishop of Westmynster and Swegen, Earl of Berrocscir; the second most important clergyman and the second most important member of the royal family in the kingdom. The large wooden door was closed heavily and Swegen turned around and strode over to the archbishop, ignoring the cooling body on the bed.

"So then, Godric, what are we going to do now?"

14th April 1166
Kirkby Kendale, Westmoringaland, Northland

Thurstan scooped water from a butt in the bailey courtyard and soaked his face and hair. He had been in a cold sweat since waking at first light. The anticipation of the upcoming raid had kept him suspended between excitement and gut-wrenching fear. He inhaled deeply, the smell of horses, baking bread and the smithy's coals mingling together in a combination of odours he had come to associate with riding out on patrol.

"You've missed a bit," laughed Sorli as he walked past, carrying a saddle to his mount. Thurstan turned, momentarily startled out of his own world, and grinned weakly back. A wave of nausea welled up – was it really excitement? Today was the day he would strike the wolfheads down, slicing down from horseback swiftly and efficiently, earning the thanks of the sheriff and the praise of his fellow huskarls. He smiled at the thought; alternatively, it could also be the day that a glancing blow from a lucky spear thrust could knock him from his horse, leaving him to be gutted like a caught fish. Thurstan's mouth went dry and he stuck his entire head under the water.

"I wouldn't do that if I were you. I pissed in there this morning," Sorli said, walking back to collect his round shield and spear from a stable boy. Thurstan smoothed his wet hair back and gave a genuine laugh. Although he imagined that Sorli would not describe him as a friend, Thurstan certainly considered him as the nearest thing he had to one in the fort. He was too young, too inexperienced to be liked by the older huskarls.

Huskarls were employed full time by the jarls to maintain law and order or to provide military service in times of war. Unlike their southern neighbours in Ængland who would conscript most of their army from the farmers and freemen, Northland's shires each maintained a sizeable standing army. The King of Northland retained two thousand or so soldiers in Jorvik alone, of whom less than a hundred were nominated to act as his personal bodyguard, the Royal Huskarls. To be one of the king's select huskarls was to be recognised as one of the finest warriors in Northland. It was an ambition that Thurstan had secretly harboured for many a year; an ambition that had made him grateful not to have been the eldest of his merchant father's sons, obliged to inherit the family business.

"When you've finished making yourself beautiful, Thurstan, we'll set off, eh?" Leif shouted from across the courtyard, just loud enough to embarrass him in front of anyone in earshot. Thurstan's appearance was a constant source of amusement to the others; he wore a short beard with no moustaches that others took for a vain affectation. The truth was that his moustaches would simply not grow on his top lip, despite his beard being thick enough on his chin, but he was much happier to let his peers think it was an intentional fashion than an inability.

Thurstan grabbed his helmet, forcing it onto his wet hair, wiping the water off the inside of the nosepiece. He tied his scabbarded sword around his waist, pulled on the leather gauntlets that were reinforced with small metal plates, giving the riders a flexible grip, and walked over to the stables. The other men were now mounted and smirking at him. He ignored the usual comments, most of which he knew were born out of an envy of his family's relative fortune.

Most of the shire's huskarls were traditionally recruited from experienced fighters, but there had been no major wars for over ten years now and as such, men of experience were growing fewer. As a result, Thurstan's father's money had been quite effective in convincing Vinder, the Sheriff of Westmoringaland, that a boy who could already ride and hold his own in tavern brawls, could be taught to fight as a soldier.

As a younger brother, Thurstan was destined not to inherit the family business and the church was no place for a boy with dreams of charging into battle alongside his king.

His father had been able to provide him with a fine horse and the best leather armour; items that would normally be provided by a jarl or sheriff for service, but rarely owned. Their grandfathers used to talk of times of when horses and weapons would be taken as spoils on raids, but now they would be have to be earned through service and hard work.

Thurstan's family's wealth had not made him popular, it was true, but there was another reason the older huskarls resented him: Thurstan was fast. It was grudgingly accepted that his reflexes and agility were among the finest in the garrison. These were things that a man was born with, not bought or learnt. His skill with a blade had quickly been recognised and it had only lead to more resentment, it seemed. Yet the practice ground was still the only place his skill had been tested. Thurstan was only too aware that he had still not yet wielded a sword against a real foe in battle.

He mounted his dark bay mare and patted its neck in the hope that the animal would not sense his nervousness. He had named the beast Svarnat, meaning 'black night' in the Saxon-Norse mix that was the Northlandic dialect. He had hoped that perhaps giving the horse such a name would convince people that it was black and not the very dark brown it actually was. All it seemed to do was just provide another reason for mockery. Svarnat bristled at his clumsy clambering and stepped nervously about the stable, the lad holding her bridle trying to keep out of reach of the horse's head.

Another boy passed up to Thurstan the small shield to be slung over his back using a leather strap and then finally, the gungar, the war spear that had become a staple part of the mounted huskarls' weaponry. It was said that any fool could ride a horse, a soldier could throw a spear, but only a true Northlandic huskarl could lance a man from horseback with a thrown gungar. Thurstan slid the spear behind his cloak, into the leather bands that held it securely to his back, ready to be grabbed with one hand when charging. It was another weapon with which his ample practice ground skill contrasted with his inexperience, having never used it in anger.

"Right then, ladies, let us ride out," Leif shouted to the horsemen. The silver-haired captain rapped Thurstan twice on the helm as he rode past in what he liked to think of as amicable disapproval. "Come on, son; let's go lose your battle virginity." Leif barked a laugh to himself and kicked his heels back. The fort's gates were opened and the thirty horsemen rode out through Kirkby Kendale, towards the valleys to the north where the wolfheads' den was reported to be.

Kirkby was the largest town between Scotland and Lonborg, Westmoringaland's principle city. As such, it was responsible for all military and judicial matters for the rugged, mountainous lands between the River Lon and the Scottish border. In truth, this part of Westmoringaland was really under the control of Vinder, the sheriff, who was second only to the jarl in authority for the shire. Jarl Herri spent most of his time to the south, in Lonborg, nearer the main roads to the other Northlandic shires, meaning the duty of administrating the more remote areas around Kirkby fell almost completely under the control of Vinder.

Riding single file at first, through the town's narrow, muddy streets, the huskarls spread out to five abreast once they were into the open countryside. They followed a cart track that would struggle to be considered a road, towards Grarigg, the village that had been the site of the massacre the week before. That had been done, it was said, as a warning to other settlements that tried to enlist the sheriff's help. The riders rode mostly in silence, with one of the few topics of conversation being the identity of this latest band of wolfheads.

"It'll be the Scots, no doubt, you mark my words," a large,

bearded huskarl named Sluta opined. He had a loud, deep voice and was more than happy to share his opinions with others, whether they wanted to hear them or not. Thurstan had tried to stay clear of him for the first few months, but Sorli seemed to enjoy arguing with him. Thurstan and Sorli, unusually for huskarls, could read, a trait that only aroused suspicion in riders like Sluta. Sorli enjoyed nothing more than antagonising the older riders, something Thurstan desperately tried to avoid and something he was sure would get his friend into serious trouble one day.

"Ha! Christ, Sluta, why would you think that?" Sorli laughed.

"They've been raiding since before you were born, lad, since our grandfathers' time. They would take this land tomorrow, if they thought they could keep it. It'll be them, just you see," Sluta snapped back. Sluta liked to refer to Sorli as 'lad', despite only being ten years older, much to Sorli's annoyance.

Sorli sniffed. "Maybe they were Scots, Sluta, maybe they weren't. Though if they were, then they were probably Ænglisc three generations ago and Northlandic two generations ago. Hell, our grandfathers weren't exactly shy of raiding and laying waste to the odd village or two, were they?" This brought a ripple of nervous laughs from a few other riders. "It's not as if the Scots are invading, is it? There's a slight difference between the King of Scotland going to war with our king over a shire or land and some hairy-arsed vagabonds torching a village. What does it matter where they are from? An outlaw is an outlaw, like a farmer is a farmer and a whore is a whore. Doesn't matter if he's Scottish, Northlandic or Ænglisc. If he takes a dump in your bed, it still stinks. The wolfheads around here are probably both. They don't care where each other are from or where you're from. They steal, they kill and we have to stop them and at the end of it, the rich land owners are still rich land owners."

He's gone too far, Thurstan thought. This was not the audience for one of his usual ale-fuelled rants. Sluta was not a bad man, but some of his views irked Sorli beyond belief, and Thurstan had the impression the feeling was reciprocated. They were not views shaped by bigotry or hatred though, or at least Thurstan liked to believe, but just views Sluta had inherited from his father or drinking companions.

"If it makes you feel any better, Sluta," Sorli sighed, "Just pretend that they're Normans."

Sluta sunk into a silent, foul sulk for the rest of the ride. About a mile before Grarigg, the riders veered off down a small valley to the north, in the bottom of which a small settlement called Hvinfell nestled, in the shadow of a large hill of the same name. The eastern side of the hill was covered in woodland that for the most part was untouched by the locals.

Three days previously, a report had come in of smoke being seen one clear night coming out of the forest and the next day several campfires were found, only recently extinguished. Given that all the inhabitants of the small valley knew the activities of each other, Vinder had surmised that the wolfheads' base had been found. Reluctant to send foot soldiers into the woods, the huskarls were to scout around the forest and confirm the wolfheads' presence; and if at all possible, exterminate them.

The riders arrived at the southern tip of the woodland and halted, taking thirsty sips of water from their leather pouches as the morning grew warmer. Thurstan looked up towards the end of the valley where the hamlet sat quietly. He could see a couple of white chickens milling around against the mud-coloured huts from half a mile away, but no villagers. The woods, though, were alive with birdsong and it seemed hard to believe that a shadowy death could be waiting inside. Leif stood in his stirrups, spat into the wind and turned to the huskarls.

"We'll split into three groups, two to skirt either side of the woods and one to stay here. If you see or hear anything, you come back here and report to me, is that clear? If there are any problems, you sound the horns. I do not want ten men going in alone – if we see anyone, we regroup and then attack." He sank back down into his saddle and sighed. "I'll stay here in the first group. The rest of you get going." The riders closest to Leif smiled at the prospect of what could be quite an easy morning for them.

Thurstan and Sorli's party turned their horses and started to climb around the southern edge of the forest, up the hill. At regular intervals, they would stop, dismount and venture a few yards into the trees, checking for any sign of human activity. Never venturing far though, their sightings were limited to the occasional squirrel and a solitary badger.

"This is a waste of time," Sorli muttered bitterly after an hour. "Why bother sending us if we can't even go in?" They had reached other side of the forest and were now waiting, expecting to see the other party at any time. A few of the riders had dismounted, whilst the others rested on their pommels, thoroughly bored by the morning's excursion.

"Because we can be in and out and back at the fort within a day," replied Emund Blacktooth, the reason for his nickname obvious as he spoke. "The sheriff doesn't reckon on more than a dozen outlaws, reckons we can ride them down, even in the woods." He sniffed, walked his horse into the shadows of the first trees and then cupped his hands. "Hello!" he bellowed, his cry answered by a host of birds taking flight from out of the trees.

"Christ, Emund, keep it down," Thurstan said.

"What's wrong, Ælfsson, still pissing your breeches from last week? They say you positively shat yourself when you saw the dead bodies," Emund chuckled.

"No more than you would have done too," Thurstan replied, not at all in the mood for confrontation this morning. Emund hollered again, then dismounted. He walked over to a broad-trunked oak and started to urinate loudly.

"This is my impersonation of what Thurstan will do when he meets the wolfheads," he laughed, much to the amusement of the other riders.

"Leave it, Emund. I crapped my breeches too when I saw that orchard. That is not something you want to see every day, believe me," Sorli said. He removed his helm to wipe his brow on the back of his glove.

"Whatever you say, Sorli, whatever you girls say," Emund sneered. Having finished relieving himself, he turned to walk back towards his tethered horse. He breathed in deeply to prepare to holler again, opened his mouth, but the words never came.

Thurstan heard a choked gasp come from Emund and looked round to see a look of confused anguish come over the huskarl's face. A gore-covered arrow head was protruding out of Emund's mouth, fired through the back of this neck, leaving him gargling and choking on his own blood. Thurstan stared in horror, watching Emund weakly raise a hand to touch the arrow before sinking to his knees and keeling over before he could reach it.

Thurstan thought for a moment about dismounting, seeing whether there was anything he could for his fellow huskarl, but the thick jets of dark blood pumping out onto the dry leaves told him all he needed to know.

"Shite!" Sorli swore, leapt up from the log he had been sat on, and scrambled onto his horse, leaving his helmet on the ground. "Back down to Leif, quickly!"

Thurstan stared into the forest beyond where Emund's twitching body lay and could make out dark shapes moving rapidly towards them. Five, six at most? Certainly no horde.

"Come on, Thurstan!" Sorli shouted. Thurstan kicked his horse and followed the eight remaining riders back down the hillside, towards Leif and his men.

"We could have taken them," Thurstan shouted as they slowed to a trot, nearing the base of the hill. He had said it as an opinion, but had come out sounding more like a question.

"You can't know that, Thurstan," Sorli answered. "You saw

what, half a dozen men? Who's to say there weren't ten others a few yards behind them? What did they look like?"

"It was hard to see. Kind of ragged, no mail as far as I could see. One or two may have had a scythe, a staff or two, but naught to be too scared of," Thurstan replied.

"That was a fine bow shot, if that was meant to kill," Sorli reminded him.

Thurstan shrugged. "Should we blow the horn yet?"

"Aye, we'll be in range. Blow it now," Sorli called out, having assumed unspoken command of the group. One of the riders placed a horn to his lips and let out a single, shrill call. At the bottom of the valley, Thurstan could see Leif's group of men stir. They turned their mounts towards them and started to ride over, but in no great haste.

At almost the exact same moment, a small movement caught Thurstan's eye. A flash of light from his right and Thurstan instinctively ducked as an arrow passed just inches over his head. A second later, a group of at least twenty men emerged from the trees to their right. No band of desperate vagabonds in rags these, but men in leather armour armed with maces, swords and one shaven-headed man swinging a giant two-headed axe. One rider went down immediately, his horse's legs taken by the giant axeman. Another fell with two arrows to his chest, falling from his horse, only for his feet to be caught in his stirrups and be dragged along, his head smashing against the ground repeatedly.

Thurstan pulled hard to his left to avoid a spearman and unsheathed his blade. *So this is it,* he thought, *now it is time to kill.* He raised his sword and wheeled Svarnat round. The spearman crouched, waiting for Thurstan to ride down onto his blade. Thurstan kicked his heels back and charged straight at the tangled-haired wolfhead. The two men's eyes interlocked and for a moment he saw himself impaled on the spear, wriggling and struggling, slowly being eviscerated. It was going to happen, his worst nightmare; the gutted fish. Then, in the blink of an eye, it was all over.

At the very last moment, just as Svarnat was on the man, Thurstan shifted in his saddle as far left as possible. His right arm flicked out, the swordpoint danced in the sun and cleanly opened the spearman's neck from ear to shoulder. A fine spray of blood misted the air, the wolfhead dropped his weapon and Thurstan had killed his first man.

Shocked, Thurstan hauled on his reins and wheeled Svarnat around. The five riders that had outrun the ambush slowed to wait for Leif, who was now charging up the hill with nine other riders in tow.

Thurstan turned in the saddle to see another spearman jab towards Sorli. The huskarl tried to avoid the spear but the tip caught him just above the knee and the momentum of the galloping horse tore the blade through his thigh and into the horse's flank. Sorli screamed in pain and fell from his horse, the force of the impact on the ground smashing his shoulder and causing his left arm to flail uselessly at his side.

Thurstan watched all of this in slow motion. He was aware of ever more wolfheads appearing from the trees, trying to encircle him; he was vaguely aware of the approaching Leif, but knew he was still some distance off. He kicked his heels into Svarnat's flanks and turned back to where his friend lay on the damp grass.

Sorli rolled onto his front, scrabbling onto one arm, but he could not stand. Looking around him, Sorli knew instantly that he would not be able to escape.

"Run, Thurstan, run!" Sorli screamed. Thurstan rode forward, returning to help his friend, but then stopped in his tracks. The giant axeman that had floored the horse, reared up behind the bareheaded Sorli, bellowing like a hamstrung ox. Thurstan grasped the gungar from his back but his movements were slow, as if he were underwater. Arrows were dropping around him, but Thurstan was oblivious to them. From somewhere behind him he heard a shout from Sluta urging him to go on, but he had no idea what 'go on' was intended to mean at that moment.

"Thurstan, go!" Sorli screamed. Thurstan glanced behind him, looking for Leif, but he was still too far away. He turned back, pulled his arm back to throw the gungar, but as he let fly the axeman brought his huge blade down, shattering Sorli's skull, cleaving it almost in two down to his brow, sending flecks of brain and bone into the giant wolfhead's tangled beard. Thurstan's gungar hung in the air for what seemed an eternity. Then, whatever magic had been suspending time suddenly evaporated and the world became a blur of events. Thurstan's spear caught the axeman full in the chest and the sound of screams and hooves filled his ears as Leif and the other horsemen charged by and ran down the ambushing wolfheads.

Thurstan was left alone, still stood in his stirrups, staring at the ruined body of his friend, tears coursing down his face, a silent scream filling his open mouth. He had failed his only friend; torn between saving himself and saving Sorli, he had done neither.

15th April 1166
Theodford, East Anglia, Ængland

Edgar, Earl of Anglia, was a sick man. Despite his protestations that it was naught but a passing ailment to his wife and his physicians, he was sick. The late King Æthelgar, the Lady Cinedred had been quick to point out, had gone from a hearty man to withered corpse in a matter of months and her husband had been ill for some weeks now. She had almost taken the news that had arrived three days previously as an omen, as if Æthelgar's death proved her point that her husband should seek help.

Edgar had been feeling nauseous nearly constantly and awoke most nights in a fever. Worst of all, over the last two weeks his skin had started to bruise at the lightest touch. His physician argued that this was simply a symptom that Edgar had 'too much blood' in his veins and needed bleeding. Edgar had seen enough battles in his youth to know that a man could never have too much blood, and in his veins it should stay. He did agree, however, with his wife on one point; a sick earl was a vulnerable earl. He had been unable to travel to Oxnaforda the fortnight before to pay homage to his dying king and even though his absence had been understood, it would have been noted by many people.

Now he had been summoned to attend the witenagemot for the royal succession and he knew he could not miss it. The earldom of East Anglia was the largest in Ængland; it had escaped the fate of most other earldoms after the conquest of King Tostig Godwinson a hundred years previously. Tostig had not trusted most of his earls not to raise armies against him and had split the existing earldoms into their component shires, making sure no single earl became too powerful. East Anglia had escaped that fate, largely because one of Tostig's brothers, Gyrth, had been the earl at the time.

Now the large, arable-rich earldom was looked at greedily from Winceaster and Earl Edgar was viewed with mistrust. Unlike many of the Ænglisc earls, he maintained a relatively large standing army and navy; his explanation was that East Anglia bore more than its fair share of raiders and attacks from across the sea, which although true, did little to appease suspicions in many other earls' minds.

Moreover, Lady Cinedred was a cousin, albeit not a closely related one, to the late king. Although many thegns and earls could also claim some familial link to the royal family, those close to the throne always viewed any other possible claimant with a fair amount of dislike. Princess Adelise had even stayed in Theodford Castle for six months after the death of her parents, before being sent to Carleol, which had added weight to the arguments of those who thought East Anglia had too much influence in the kingdom. Now that the succession was to be discussed, a non-appearance by Earl Edgar could be easily misconstrued by those happy to spread malicious rumours.

"You cannot go, father, not in your state," the voice of Edgar's son, Ceolwulf, was pleading.

"I cannot afford not to go. What message would it give about East Anglia? That it is indifferent to the kingdom's future? That its earl is too weak? There are many at court who would dearly love our new monarch to remedy that. No, my son, I must go," Edgar said, clasping his son's shoulder.

They were sitting in front of the large fire in his longhall, the only other stone building apart from the keep in Theodford not owned by the Church. Edgar had been spending more and more time in front of the large fire in the room that was normally used for entertaining groups of guests. Despite the warm spring weather of the last week, he had found himself increasingly feeling the need to sit near the fireplace, when he wasn't gripped by a feverish sweat.

The hall was more or less deserted at this hour, with most of the serving staff having retired to their quarters, save for a few maids attending to the earl's wife. Over the past few weeks, the Lady Cinedred had become used to Edgar preferring to sit next to the fire rather than in his private quarters. To fill her time she had started a small tapestry showing a scene from the battle of Fuleford, to celebrate its centenary.

"Then let me come with you, if not instead of you," Ceolwulf said. In the far corner of the room, Cinedred looked up from her embroidery. She had not wanted either of her men to go, let alone both of them. When she had asked her son to speak to his father, this was not what she'd had in mind.

Ceolwulf leant closer to his shivering father. "If you go, I will follow you anyway."

She sighed, recognising the stubbornness that her son had inherited from his father. His sense of loyalty was definitely his father's, although his occasional impetuousness she suspected came from her side. In the firelight, he could have easily been Edgar thirty years ago – his blond hair falling loosely past broad shoulders, ice blue eyes offset by dark eyebrows and beard. It was an Edgar that was barely recognisable now – gaunt and pale, with ever darker rings under his eyes. The last thing he needed now was a four-day ride to Oxnaforda.

"Could Ælfric not go instead?" she asked loudly, not attempting to hide the fact that she was listening in to the two men's conversation. Ælfric was her younger brother, a powerful thegn in his own right who owned lands in the south of the earldom.

"No, no, that would not do. With all due respect to your brother, it would be better to send no-one at all than a thegn," Edgar said, with a dismissive wave of his hand. "My mind is made up; I will go. Ceolwulf must stay here in my place. That is my final word." With that, he slapped the arm of his chair and stood up quickly.

"As you wish, father," Ceolwulf said, turning to the fireplace. For a moment Edgar opened his mouth as if he were about to say something, but he was suddenly overcome by a hacking, grating cough. When after several seconds he didn't stop coughing and started to double over, Ceolwulf sprang up and took him by the shoulder, forcing him back down into his chair. He grabbed a mug of weak ale that was on the nearby table and put it to his father's lips. He waved it away and pressed a small square of linen to his mouth, the coughs finally subsiding. When he took the cloth away, it was covered in dark blood. Father and son looked at each other, the mug of ale slowly passed over in silence.

"Are you feeling well, Edgar?" the Lady Cinedred called from across the hall.

"He's fine, mother," Ceolwulf replied, without taking his eyes off the cloth.

Edgar stared at his hand for a moment more, then turned to his son and spoke quietly. "You shall come with me to Oxnaforda, but you will accompany me only. For your own benefit it would be best if you do not attend the witenagemot."

"Please credit me with some sense, father," Ceolwulf protested.

"Court is a nest of vipers, Ceolwulf. Smiling vipers, waiting for the wrong word or deed."

"I know, I know. I don't see what risk there is, I mean, the Earl Swegen seems a good enough man, doesn't he? I know you don't see eye to eye but if Adelise is deemed too young, he wouldn't make such a bad king."

"An opinion that should be kept to yourself, whether it be right or wrong." Edgar sighed and threw the bloodied linen onto the fire. "The Earl Swegen is a charming and good man when it suits him. The trouble with the Earl Swegen is when he decides not be charming or good. Through no fault of his own, he lost his father when he was young, which is hard for a boy, I admit that. Since then though, no-one has ever told him 'no'. You will see in

Oxnaforda the earls and thegns that support him and you will see his close friends. Then you will notice that they are one and the same and if you are outside that circle, then you probably don't exist in his world." Edgar sank back into his chair and breathed deeply.

"Then he isn't to be trusted?"

"No-one is to be trusted. For the time being though, it would appear that Princess Adelise is to be our queen and he will act as guardian."

"Then why summon us all to a witenagemot so urgently?"

"Who knows? Protocol? To keep an eye on us? To annoy me?" Edgar stroked his moustaches. "The fact remains that even if Swegen is not to be king, he will effectively rule the kingdom for the next five years at least, unless Adelise can be married off young. For that he will need the support of the earls, including those that do not particularly like him. He knows we were close to the late king, God rest his soul. If we are seen to approve of him, it will go some way to gaining the trust of others. I don't know what they're playing at in Winceaster, it may just all be for pomp and show. Whatever it is, any suspicions you have, you keep to yourself, if you must insist on coming with me. "

"I promise that if I come with you, I shall hold my tongue. Anyway, I have to make sure you don't dawdle in the whore-houses, for mother's sake," Ceolwulf grinned.

Edgar sighed and gave a small cough. "We will have to be back for month end; there is much to do. We need to visit Gipeswic port, the northern tower here needs strengthening and we need to oversee the coins being restruck at Ælmham, especially after what happened last time; many things, many things." He closed his eyes and it appeared to Ceolwulf that his father might have dozed off again. The fire crackled, the wolfhound stretched out by Edgar's feet yawned and Ceolwulf turned to stare into the fire. One of the serving girls stepped out of the shadows, offering to refill Ceolwulf's flagon of ale, but he waved her away distractedly. When Edgar started to snore, Ceolwulf stood up and walked over to his mother. He gently took her hand in his and kissed her cheek.

"I'll look after him, mother, don't worry," he said, looking at her worried eyes.

"It's not just him I worry for," she said, touching his hand lightly. "Remember, the earldom comes before personal issues. Don't be quick to anger or praise. And do not anger the future king."

"The queen, you mean," Ceolwulf corrected her.

"We shall see," she replied with a smile, the corners of her eyes wrinkling into the crows feet that grown more apparent in the last few months. "Good night, son."

"Good night, mother." Ceolwulf stood up and walked out of the hall, pausing only to thank one of the prettier maids, before shutting the heavy door behind him. The flames in the hearth flared for a moment in the rush of air, then settled down, leaving Cinedred to her tapestry. She sighed and unpicked the last two hours' worth of work; she just couldn't quite get the death of King Harold right.

Kirkby Kendale, Westmoringaland, Northland

The rain clouds that had drenched Kirkby during the night were now moving off to the east, carried by the wind that was blowing through the rolling valleys of the borders. From the stone walls that encircled the bailey and hillfort in the centre of the town, sentries gazed towards the purple-green mountains of the north and west, the tallest of which marked the Scottish border. When they weren't looking out for invasions that never came, they stared off to the greener valleys of the south for messengers and traders who did come, but only slightly more frequently.

On mornings such as these, when the fog of a previous night's drinking filled his head, Thurstan often walked beyond the town gates and into the fells that surrounded Kirkby. It had been one of the first mornings of the year that he had not felt the need for a cloak at dawn; he found that walking up hillsides would soon warm a man though, much quicker than waiting for the sun to heat the valley. The views of the rolling fells and dales from the summit were an antidote to the poison his fellow huskarls were brewing for him in the hillfort and inns of Kirkby. Since the death of Sorli, his fellow huskarls had all but stopped speaking to him; Captain Leif had even offered him three months' wages to leave Vinder's service and return to Lonborg.

Walking back through the gates of the fort, Thurstan replayed the events of his friend's death over and over in his mind. Could he have saved Sorli? Should he have reacted quicker? If he had just ridden on with the other riders, would he still have been held responsible? Yet the outcome would have been the same. Sorli would have still died and Thurstan cursed himself for worrying as much about his companions' opinion of him as his friend's life.

Lost in thought, Thurstan walked past the fort's bakery and blacksmith, wafting a blade of long grass he had picked from the hillside. Sidestepping chickens that were free to wander around the fort's courtyard, he headed towards the stables. Although the stableboys did a fine job of tending the horses, Thurstan still liked to groom Svarnat whenever possible. It gave him time to think; the rhythmic, monotonous combing and brushing relaxing his mind to the point where he could mull things over rationally rather than the usual maelstrom of thoughts that assailed him whenever he was left to his own devices.

Thurstan was quite surprised therefore to see Sluta and two other huskarls in leather uniform when he walked into the stables. He checked his step and kept his head bowed, not wanting to catch their gaze and feel obliged to speak to them. Sluta had been facing away, his two companions slouching in an empty stall, but as Thurstan walked past, they suddenly straightened up. Thurstan knew immediately he was in trouble; Sluta and the company he kept did not pay social visits to exchange pleasantries.

"Thurstan, my dear brother," Sluta said with a warmth that he hardly tried to pretend was sincere. "Where are you going?"

"Svarnat," Thurstan replied, looking Sluta straight in the eye, slowing his pace but not wanting to stop to speak his fellow huskarl. If Sluta's mouth spoke of being friends, then the rest of his face quite clearly showed that he was anything but.

"No, you're not." Sluta shot an arm out and blocked Thurstan's way. Looking beyond him, Thurstan could see that the rest of the stables were empty. The stableboys had no doubt been told to make themselves scarce for twenty minutes. From behind him came the noise of the stable doors being closed. Thurstan turned to see a fourth companion, a skinny dark-haired man that he recognised as one of Sluta's drinking companions, barring the door. Thurstan thought for a moment about asking Sluta to let him through, but he already knew it would be of no use. The four men had not come here only for a polite request to change their plans. He was going to be beaten, the intention was clear; the only question was who would strike the first blow.

"Why do you stay, Thurstan? You don't belong here. Your friend Sorli didn't belong either, and he ended up with his head split in two," Sluta smirked. "You know I'd happily take that mare of yours off your hands. I might even pay for her, if you're lucky."

Thurstan was not listening though. Nothing he could say would make any difference at this point. He was not trying to stare Sluta down in a show of bravado or a misplaced sense of masculinity. He was already in a world of his own, one of distances, angles and time. He was aware of Sluta's mocking comments, but he wasn't taking any notice; instead, he was judging the gap between himself and the two huskarls slowly approaching him from behind. He knew them less from patrols and more as companions of Sluta in the alehouse. One stood the same height as Thurstan, the other around three inches taller, and if he remembered rightly, favoured his left hand, at least for drinking. In the stall to the right, just behind him, about four foot away, no more, was a pitchfork used to change the horses' bedding.

The smaller, dark-haired man was more of an unknown quantity, although Thurstan had once seen him dance a blade between his fingers at a blur, one drunken night. He had a slight limp Thurstan had noted, possibly a defect from childhood, possibly a wound, but one that had perhaps caused him to compensate whatever speed he had lost in his legs with sharp reflexes. The right foot, Thurstan thought to himself, just as Sluta grabbed him by the throat.

"Are you even listening to me, you little prick?" Sluta spat in his face.

"No," Thurstan replied simply.

Thurstan seized Sluta's wrist with one hand and slammed his other against the man's elbow. There was a sharp crack and Sluta howled in surprise and pain, immediately releasing his grip.

Thurstan spun to his left, already raising his arm and blocked the incoming left fist of Sluta's taller companion. Grabbing his shoulder, Thurstan placed a boot on the side of the stall and launched himself over the surprised huskarl, springing around him before slamming a fist into the back of his head, causing the big man's knees to buckle.

Before the huskarl's body had hit the floor, Thurstan had turned to face his third assailant. The man was carrying a cosh, a small bag filled with wet sand, which he swung wildly at Thurstan's face. Thurstan simply sidestepped to his left before landing a punch squarely in the man's face. He was faintly aware of a loud click as the man's nose broke, but he was now more concerned with grabbing the pitchfork in the stall.

The last assailant, the dark-haired stranger, was still waiting by the door. He was not charging in, but biding his time; he had seen his three companions floored in seconds. Sluta was back on his knees, trying to grab the bottom of Thurstan's tunic. A quick kick behind him and Sluta went quiet. The last man stepped forward, unsheathing a knife and Thurstan threw the pitchfork. It landed in the earth floor, right between the approaching man's feet. The man stopped dead in his tracks, the trembling fork handle just inches from his face. Thurstan stepped forward and gave a swift kick to the man's right leg. He howled and dropped to clasp his knee, before Thurstan delivered a sharp blow with his elbow to the man's crown and he fell silently to the floor.

Time and sound returned to Thurstan's world – the whole fight had been over in less than ten seconds. He looked at the four prone bodies on the floor, staggered to one of the empty stalls and vomited what little breakfast he had eaten earlier. From outside the stables he could hear someone banging on the door. Quickly wiping his mouth with the back of his sleeve, Thurstan stumbled over to the stable door and lifted the wooden bar. The door swung outwards and Captain Leif strode in, two huskarls flanking him.

"What the hell is going on here?" he shouted, as he immediately spotted the four men lying in various states of consciousness around the stable floor. Stablelads standing with their ears to the closed stable doors had been a sure sign that something had been going on, and Leif's suspicions had been confirmed. He did not need an answer, as this kind of confrontation had been growing ever more inevitable over the last two weeks. Impressed as he was with the skill that Thurstan must have shown, the knowledge that the boy was just ostracising himself more and more from the group tempered any satisfaction.

The two huskarls, short swords drawn stepped towards Thurstan, but Leif waved them back. He looked the young man up and down, his dark hair lank and stuck to his forehead with sweat, flecks of vomit trapped in the ends.

"They attacked you?" the captain asked, his voice neutral. Thurstan just nodded. "Your horse is untouched?" Again, Thurstan nodded, his eyes glancing towards the two huskarls hovering behind the captain. Leif glanced at Sluta, who was slowly starting to come to with small whimpers. The barest flicker of what might have been interpreted as a smirk passed his lips. "I think we're done here," he said. "Get back to your quarters, boy, we'll speak in the morning."

Without saying a word of explanation or thanks to the captain, Thurstan walked out of the stables, pausing only at a butt by the smithy to splash water over his face. He washed his bloodied knuckles, rubbing at the scuffed white skin where he had caught one of the men's armour. He could not remember which one now, it was already all a blur. He stood up straight and arched his back until he felt a small click between his shoulders.

Smoothing back his now sodden hair he walked across the outer courtyard of the bailey towards the long wooden thatched building that most of the younger huskarls used as sleeping quarters. A spearman walking towards the gate stepped back out of his way, his expression a mixture of respect and dislike.

This is the way it is going to be then, Thurstan thought to himself. *Either I get myself killed because I am disliked, or make them dislike me even more because I won't let them kill me.* No matter what he did, how hard he tried, every day that passed seemed to be a day further away from realising the dream of becoming a fighter, a warrior, a respected huskarl.

The others seemed content enough to do exactly what was expected of them, with the minimum of fuss; regular patrols with an occasional skirmish; and they were accepted and liked. Thurstan's dream of emulating his forefathers' bravery and glory was turning sour, and it was a spiral downwards over which he felt he had no control. He had been sure he was destined to drink and laugh with companions in alehalls, sharing in battles and victories; not stabbed in the back on a cold fell somewhere in the border country.

He stopped outside the wooden door to the huskarls' quarters. He didn't want to see the other huskarls now, he didn't want to tell them what had happened, neither as a victim nor as a victor. He walked around the side of the building and sat down on the damp earth, his back against the timber wall. From here, the bailey courtyard sloped away to the east and he could see over the top of the palisade to where a distant grey shape marked another line of mountains. The sun had disappeared again behind a newly arrived wall of dark clouds from the west. He watched the shadow it cast race away across the landscape, covering fields and hedges in a black curtain. From somewhere within the quarters he could hear men's laughing mixing with the excited shriek of a girl, who was no doubt enjoying copious amounts of mead, amongst other things. He was aware of heavy raindrops starting to fall around him into the earth, the wind picking up again and a dog barking in the town beyond the walls.

I am not meant to be here, he thought, *this is not how my life is meant to be.* Blocking out the sounds of other people enjoying themselves, he closed his eyes and fell asleep.

21st April 1166
Oxnaforda, Ængland

Ceolwulf rode through the giant stone gateway into the courtyard of Oxnaforda Castle. A page ran across to him, taking the reins of his horse. Ceolwulf jumped down from his bay mare and turned to his father, who was riding in behind him. The four-day journey had taken its toll on Edgar and he looked worse than at any point during the last two months. Yet he had refused to travel in a carriage, wanting to ride into Oxnaforda on his own horse. Edgar turned slowly in his saddle and stepped down out of the stirrups, refusing the assistance offered by his son. He wiped away the sweat that had made his hair lank during the morning's short ride and took a pot of spiced wine that been brought out by a serving girl to the newly arrived guests. He took a deep gulp and nodded to his son.

"Drink up," he said. "It's going to be a long day."

Ceolwulf took a pot and sipped tentatively, sniffing at the unusual spices. He squinted up at one of the three huge towers that formed part of the walls and keep. The stone castle of Oxnaforda was far larger than that of Theodford; the smallest of the three towers was almost as large as the keep back home. Everything in Oxnaforda seemed to be made of stone – the castle, the city walls, and most of the major buildings – even several private houses. The Earl of Oxnaforda nominally owned this, but the royal family had traditionally used the castle as a second seat of government. The keep's famed, spacious round hall was ideal for the gemots where matters of national importance were discussed. Ceolwulf had visited once before, but was still impressed with the scale of the building.

He gave his wine back to the girl, almost untouched, and joined his father. The two men, their horses led off to the stables, strode towards the large keep in the far corner of the courtyard.

The Great Hall on the second floor was a large round room in which most of the kingdom's earls and bishops had assembled. Cushioned wooden benches were in semi circular rows around half the room, the other half taken by a raised dais where Swegen and the senior clergy would sit, with space for any speaker from the audience to stand and give a speech, should he so desire. Narrow high windows behind the dais illuminated the room, with ornate candlesticks dotted around the room and a central brazier for light and warmth in the evenings. The gemot was planned to last two days and it was expected that the first day would go on past nightfall, at least.

Edgar and Ceolwulf had been amongst the last to arrive and took a bench at the back. They left their weapons in an antechamber, in accordance with ancient custom. The only weapons inside the room were the large broadswords of the royal guards, whose weapons, along with their full face helmets, were mostly for ornamental show, rather than practicality. Edgar's armed escort had been made to wait in the castle bailey, along with those of the other earls, and he did not doubt they were already playing dice or sampling the liquid delights of the castle's brewery.

A blast of a hunting horn opened the proceedings, followed by a lengthy sermon by Eadric, the Archbishop of Cantwaraburg, half in Ænglisc, half in Latin, with no discernible reason for using one language or the other at any given point. He gave thanks to God for receiving the soul of good King Æthelgar and then blessed the gemot. Several earls then took it in turn to stand up and address the witan, delivering eulogies to the late King Æthelgar. The more florid and lavish the praise, the less important the earl, it seemed; as if his own importance to the king had to be elaborated on.

Edgar remained seated; the wave of nausea that had beset him as he had entered the hall was showing no sign of abating. After an hour of speeches, the subject moved onto Æthelgar's funeral. Most of the details had already been decided privately – the tradition had recently been to hold the late monarch's funeral the day before the coronation of the new one. Westmynster Cathedral had been the venue for the last two occasions and there was no reason not to choose it for this one. All this was accepted, but protocol dictated that each aspect of the arrangements was proposed and agreed upon, even if just for show.

"The king's body will be taken from Oxnaforda to Winceaster, then onto Lunden where it will lie in state. He will then be interred in Westmynster Cathedral, next to his father and son, God rest their souls," Eadric announced. This was met with a murmur of approval; this was the way it was normally done. Æthelgar's body had already been prepared and interred within a wooden coffin within days of his death, due to the time it could take to organise the coronation. As soon as the body reached Lunden, it would be interred in the stone tomb already engraved with his name; but he would not be considered to have been formally laid to rest until the state funeral. "The ceremony," the archbishop continued, squinting at a scroll of parchment, "shall be performed by myself, along with the assistance of the Archbishop of Westmynster." He turned and nodded benevolently at Godric, who in turn nodded back.

"Like two vipers in the same nest," Edgar muttered to Ceolwulf, who even at the back of the room, could sense the forced cordiality between the two archbishops.

Discussions continued into the afternoon until Eadric brought up the subject of the succession and the coronation. Normally, if the king died without a direct heir, then the witan would deliberate, sometimes for weeks, months even, on who his successor would be.

Æthelgar, however, had nominated his heir. Just not the one most people had expected. The only man who could realistically challenge the succession was sitting on the high stage now, gazing at the rambling Archbishop of Cantwaraburg.

Swegen looked every bit a future monarch; a rich ermine-collared cloak draped across his shoulders and a coronet of fine silver on his head. Eadric finished muttering through the formal procedures before turning and gesturing towards the man the nation had expected to become king.

"My lords, the Prince Swegen," a young page announced. This raised cheers from half the room and raised eyebrows from the other half.

"Prince now, eh?" Edgar said to Ceolwulf. "Ah well, who's going to stop him?" There were no other male heirs, or at least none with as strong enough a bloodline to challenge him on appointing himself prince.

Ceolwulf stared at the usual gaggle of braying cronies and spotted an unusually tall man, hugely muscled with a large scar down one side of his face. In the midst of Swegen's usually finely attired and vain companions, the giant man seemed quite incongruous.

"My lords, my lords, please," Swegen said to those assembled earls who were still cheering him. "I fear that some vicious rumours have been circulating over the last month. It gives me no pleasure to have to discuss the death of my uncle, but let me be clear. He was lucid and clear of mind at the end. His nominated heir is my cousin Adelise and I must urge us all to rally behind her and support her as our queen. I know there are some who have suggested that perhaps I ought to be crowned…"

"Only your friends, Swegen," Edgar grunted, quietly enough that only Ceolwulf heard.

"But my lord King Æthelgar's words were clear. I will support my cousin, Princess Adelise, and let no man stand against her. Does any man here declare against her for the succession to the throne?"

The room was silent; even Swegen's most ardent supporters would not say a word.

"Then may God praise Queen Adelise." A cheer went up from

the assembled earls.

"That all seemed a bit too easy. What's he up to?" Edgar whispered to his son.

"Maybe he is sincere, father. The man has been nothing but genuine so far," Ceolwulf replied, to which his father did not even respond, save from an expression of disbelief.

"Then we are left with a task no more difficult than to plan the return of Queen Adelise back to Winceaster and to plan her coronation. It has already been suggested by my lord archbishops that the coronation take place three weeks from today." Swegen smoothed down the front of his tunic with his palms and continued. "Word has already been sent to Carleol informing them of the death of King Æthelgar; King Duncan of Scotland has already promised an armed escort for the queen back from Carleol to Penrith. All that remains is to request safe passage through Northland, to which end I must appeal to one of you noble lords to travel to Jorvik immediately. Obviously, we would expect some Northlandic hostages in return to guarantee her safety."

"I hadn't realised how much would have been decided before we even got here," Ceolwulf whispered to his father. "I thought we were here to discuss such things."

"You'll soon learn how much of this is actual discussion and how much is just for show, once Swegen and the bishops have finished planning," his father replied.

Godric coughed, attracting the attention of the newly proclaimed prince. "My lord, many here may be wondering, and rightly so, why Adelise does not travel by ship, from the Carleol Firth down to Ceaster, thus avoiding the need to travel through hostile country?"

"By hostile I assume you mean the terrain and risk of banditry; let us not besmirch our Northlandic cousins, Archbishop," Swegen said smiling. "The archbishops and I discussed the matter together and agreed that given the recent bad weather, and Adelise's understandable reluctance to sail on water, following the loss of her parents, the safest and kindest way to return her home would be over land." This was met with murmurs of agreement and understanding.

Swegen clasped his hands together and scanned the room until his gaze fell on Edgar and Ceolwulf. "My lord Earl Edgar of East Anglia, I wonder if you would do us the honour of travelling to Jorvik to request the safe passage of our queen?"

"My lord?" Edgar replied neutrally, quickly lowering the bloodstained rag of linen he had been using to wipe the corners of his mouth.

"I would think that for such an important duty as speaking to the King of Northland, we should grant the duty to our most powerful earl? I am sure the negotiation of hostages and safe passage will not prove too onerous, will it?" Swegen asked.

Edgar quickly gripped Ceolwulf's arm just as his son was about to speak out in protest.

"It shall be an honour, Prince Swegen," Edgar said, his voice flat.

"Excellent," Swegen replied, his eyes shining. "Excellent."

The two men held each other's gaze for some moments before Swegen clapped his hands and turned back to face the archbishops. "I should think that the details of the coronation can perhaps be discussed in length tomorrow," he said, picking up a goblet of wine and sipping slowly. "We can move on to other matters for the remainder of the day, before the culinary splendour that will be the feast this evening."

The rest of the afternoon was filled with various discussions on shire governance, approvals for more roaming courts and a dispute on the inheritance of the earldom of Herefordscir between the twin sons of the late earl, one that Swegen unusually suggested be settled by trial by combat; a practice more common to the continent than Ængland.

Ceolwulf, however, barely registered any of it. He sat staring at his father, who was struggling to stay awake, his eyelids continually drooping and snapping open. The afternoon sun, that was streaming in through the narrow, high windows and the spiced wine that was being continually passed around were certainly not helping matters, but Ceolwulf sensed his father's fatigue was not due to either. His father would not now even to speak to him in a whisper, save for an instruction to wait until afterwards before discussing the gemot.

When the day's proceedings were finally called to a close, the Earl of East Anglia and his son left quickly, without speaking to anyone else and retired to lodgings in one of the smaller towers of the castle. Edgar slumped immediately onto a large bed; one of the boys brought with them from Theodford removed his boots. Ceolwulf shut the heavy wooden door and turned immediately to his father.

"Don't tell me," Edgar pre-empted him.

"You cannot go," Ceolwulf said, regardless.

"I know that."

"You are sick, father."

"Swegen knows that."

"So why send you?"

"Precisely because of my sickness, I would guess. I have no idea what the scrote is up to, but he would dearly love me to either fail or to stand up in front of the entire witenagemot and tell all the other assembled earls that I am too weak to travel on behalf of our new queen. I will have to go."

"You will not let me go on your behalf? He wouldn't know or care."

"I have no doubt that whatever we do, Swegen will have someone happily report it back to him, be it here or Jorvik."

"He has that much power?"

"It's not a question of power. All he needs is just one person to report. To find one such person in Jorvik is not a problem. The bishops too, will have plenty of correspondence between each other, I am sure. Why send hundreds of men anywhere when one letter between two people can do just as much damage? Not that any of this matters; I am sure he will want to send some of his men with us to Northland."

"So we just go?"

"Yes," Edgar replied. He lay back on the bed, his forearm shielding his eyes and thought for a moment. "We'll go tonight," he said quietly.

"What?"

"There's nought to stop us, and we cannot be faulted for keenly following Swegen's instructions. That way we have an extra day and can leave before we get saddled with a gaggle of Berrocscir's men."

"And you, are you in any state to travel?" Ceolwulf asked, sitting down on a low wooden chair, pinching the bridge of his nose. There was a familiar sense of inevitable defeat about this conversation with his father.

"Son, I am sick, possibly dying. One day more or less in this castle will not change that," Edgar replied, in a rare admission of his own illness.

"So we ride tonight?" Ceolwulf asked. His father nodded. "Then I shall inform our riders. We will purchase supplies on the way; if we go, then we go immediately, before Swegen decides on some extra burden to place on us." He waved a hand at the serving boy. "Eastmund, go tell Captain Osberht that we plan to leave this evening. Get our horses ready and wait for us in the stables. Do not tell anyone else what we plan to do, do you understand?" The boy nodded and quickly left the room. Ceolwulf went to the bed and knelt beside his father. "Just promise me one thing. If you are too sick to continue, that you will let me go in your place?"

Edgar sighed and closed his eyes. "If it gets too much, you will be the first to know. All I ask is that we are seen to leave together. God bless you, Ceolwulf," he placed his hand on his son's head. "If this had been my father and me, I'd have had his earldom in the blink of an eye," he chuckled, which caused him to cough again. "Just give me an hour's rest, and then we'll be on our way."

Ceolwulf stood up, and quietly walked over to the other side of the room, where he collapsed onto a low chair. He closed his eyes and let his mind wander, letting the warmth and sound of the fire wash over him. He tried to remember the faces of the other earls that he had seen in the round hall, trying to guess which ones his father would refer to as being 'Swegen's' and those who weren't. As sleep started to envelop him, he made a mental note to remember clearly those who were in the latter.

Godric, Archbishop of Westmynster, had managed to install himself in the most lavish of the main tower's rooms in Oxnaforda Castle. Richly coloured cloths were draped over padded long chairs and tapestries hung from the walls of the large room about which he now paced. Two floors below them, the evening's feast was descending into drunken raucousness, but he and Swegen had retired temporarily to his chambers before the final course.

"Please don't do that; those are important charters," Godric said in a pained voice, as a tired parent would to a child.

Swegen was sitting at a table covered in documents, pouring wax from one candle to another. "My Prince," he replied, not taking his eyes off the droplets of wax as they dripped onto from the candle onto the papers underneath.

"Pardon?"

"Please don't do that, my Prince."

Godric stopped pacing for a moment and stared at the Earl of Berrocscir. The man was only two years off his fortieth birthday, yet at times, he had a childlike manner that irritated the churchman greatly. Some called it humour, but he labelled it obtuseness.

"Who was that brute you had sat at the front today, cheering your every word?" Godric asked, changing the subject.

"I have no idea to whom you are referring, dear Archbishop," Swegen replied, wiping wax from his tunic.

"You know perfectly well; giant of a man, scarred face," Godric said testily.

"Ah, you mean my good friend and loyal thegn, Ricmund? He's an old acquaintance from Readinga, a man of great potential."

"He looks a thug."

"He has his uses; I do admit they are perhaps more of the martial kind than political though. Father always used to suggest that there was some kind of family link, due to grandfather's philandering, but I've never wanted to ask Ricmund if his father was a bastard."

Godric stopped pacing. "Is this the same man you were telling me about, who may be of some use to us?"

"Yes," Swegen replied.

"Saints preserve us," Godric crossed himself. "But he is trustworthy?"

"Like a dog to his master, fear not." Swegen turned to the archbishop. "You look pale, are you eating?"

"I'm losing my appetite I think. No doubt it's from having to stare at the smug face of the Archbishop of Cantwaraburg."

"What would you like me to do about it?"

"Nothing yet. You know what I want you to do about it though. Firstly, my cathedral, my ceremony."

"I could declare that tomorrow, if you wish," Swegen suggested.

"Too soon, too soon," Godric tutted. "Wait a while until their minds are on other things. If you impose any change now, Cantwaraburg will kick up a fuss and complain to Rome. I think we can convince him, but it will need a bit of time. Let him think that it's his idea, that he's bargained for it. He'll soon have other things to worry about. And in return..." He left the sentence hanging.

"Absolve any sin?" Swegen asked slowly.

"Any sin, my lord Prince," Godric replied, a smile slowly forming in one corner of his mouth. Talk of sin and retribution were one of the few things that would make Swegen calm down, albeit for a moment.

"Any sin," Swegen echoed wistfully. He stood up and walked over the narrow window that looked out over the city of Oxnaforda. The lights of houses and street braziers lay below them, the orange glow the only source of light on an otherwise overcast night. Somewhere below him, he could hear the clatter of horses and the gates opening. Some night patrol, no doubt. "It will be for the good of the country, Godric, you do know that. "

"I know, Swegen, for the good of its people. You can't expect them to understand, but in centuries to come, they will thank you and praise your good name for what you did."

Swegen breathed deeply, tapping his fingers lightly on the stone. A series of images, some golden and filled with glory, some red and filled with horror, flashed before his eyes. He knew that he would have to face all of them at some point in the near future.

"We shall speak no more about it tonight. Let us return to the feast and drink to the good health of Queen Adelise," Swegen said. He turned and strode over to the door, which he held open for Godric.

"To Queen Adelise," the archbishop agreed, stepping out into the corridor, letting the door shut behind him. From the window, the sound of horse hooves faded into the night and the sound of the feast grew louder.

27th April 1166
Jorvik, Northland

The western tower of Jorvik Cathedral was easily the tallest building in Northland. The cathedral had been built at the turn of the century to replace the earlier Saxon church that had fallen badly into disrepair. Built following a traditional cross pattern, its stone walls were over a hundred feet high. At the end of each arm was a wooden tower, the tallest of which was another two hundred feet in height. They had been designed mainly for decoration rather than purpose, but as a statement of majesty, they certainly worked. It was a declaration by the Norse kings of Northland that, unlike their raiding predecessors, their rule was not temporary. The message was clear; they were here to stay. A man could climb up to the very top of the spire on a clear day and see each of the three thriths of Jorvik, to the north, west and east.

It was on such a day that the men from the south rode into Jorvik. The Earl of East Anglia, Edgar, and his son, Ceolwulf, were accompanied by a dozen armed riders and had travelled from Oxnaforda, far to the south in distant Ængland. The party had entered the city via the tall southern entrance, the Mykla Gate Bar. The huge wooden gates were framed by the impressive stone walls that had originally been built nearly a thousand years before, by the long-departed Romans.

They had been greeted at the Bar by a Northlandic captain, a huskarl of the king's own royal household. The greetings had been courteous, formal, if a little stilted. Even though they had sent advanced notice of their visit, the captain had made them wait the best part of half an hour as he checked their documentation, much to Edgar's displeasure. Once they had been permitted to enter, they followed the captain through the narrow winding streets of Northland's capital, the tall western tower of the cathedral ever present over the tops of the houses and stalls.

"How many inhabitants does the town have?" Ceolwulf asked his father. It was his first time to Jorvik; in fact, his first time to anywhere in Northland other than the southern marks of Kesteven and Hoiland. His father had visited several times though, usually as an envoy and once in his youth at the request of King Erik, the current king's grandfather, to join him for a week of hunting. East Anglia had enjoyed slightly warmer relations with Northland than the rest of Ængland, possibly due to its own slightly fractious relationship with Winceaster, or possibly more as it had been itself an Anglo-Norse kingdom two centuries previously.

"Fifteen, possibly twenty thousand? It seems much busier than the last time I visited," Edgar said. He was leaning heavily on the pommel of his saddle. The long journey had not been easy, but he had taken to sipping an infusion of herbs and petals that he kept in a clay bottle in his scrip. A draught of the drink in the morning allayed the worst of the pain, although it did make him sleepy and his movements feel clumsy.

The captain, a long-bearded man with thick red hair bunched into a long single plait that ran down his back, turned to the Ænglisc envoys. "Nearly twenty-two thousand at the last count. The town is expanding rapidly on the north road to Dunholm, outside of the gates. I guess at least four thousand souls there, so we're probably around twenty-four thousand in total, although two thousand of those are the king's own household," he finished, with what seemed to be a grin of pride.

"Don't fret, we're not thinking of invading," Edgar said, returning the smile.

They rode on, the people in the streets streaming around them, weaving in and out between their horses. They maintained a respectful distance from the armed riders, but were certainly not stopping to stare at, what was for them, quite a common sight. Only once or twice did the captain have to holler at someone to move out of the way, but when he did, he was dutifully obeyed.

The riders turned north down a wider street, lined with plenty of two-floor buildings, many of them with shops or workshops on the ground floor. Ceolwulf was impressed; he had visited Lunden that was much larger and had many more impressive buildings; but he had always been led to believe that the Northlanders lived in small towns, filled with cramped, mud-caked wooden huts.

As they headed towards the cathedral, the street opened into a large open square, lined with elm trees. In the centre stood a large stone statue of King Harald Hardrada – Harald the Conqueror, holding a giant bronze sword. Around the foot of the statue, various vendors were selling hot food; meats, sweet cakes and pies. In the corner of the square an innkeeper had placed a large barrel outside his door and was serving flagons of ale directly to young men on the street. A number of these seemed to have already imbued great quantities of the inn's wares and were engaged in the activity of leapfrogging over one another, with varying degrees of success.

They rode across the square and then turned eastwards, away from the cathedral. Riding under a large stone arch, they emerged into another square, slightly smaller, but one filled almost entirely by a single building. Jorvik's Konge Hall, the king's longhall, was the largest wooden building Ceolwulf had ever seen. He had read about the mead halls of Norse kings in the old legends, those of Snorri or Hrothgar, but he had never envisaged one so big. It was as large as a cathedral from wall to wall, but was little more than a single storey high. Down each side, three large wooden columns supported the roof with curved beams, giving the building the appearance, from a distance, of a ship's hull under construction. Two giant doors adorned the front of the hall, flanked by large pillars that supported the overhanging roof. As they neared the doors,

Ceolwulf could see that the columns were ornately carved with designs of dragons and ravens intertwining with swirling patterns.

The captain dismounted and handed his horse to one of several pages standing in front of the hall. The Ænglisc envoys did likewise and then followed him up to the great doors. He beat twice with his gloved fist, the dull thud demonstrating that these were thick, solid doors. From inside Ceolwulf could hear the sound of a bolt being drawn and then a small door, hidden within the detailed panelling, swung open. A sentry waved them in and the men stepped inside. The captain turned and took off his sword, and nodded slowly towards Ceolwulf and Edgar.

"Your weapons, my lords," the captain requested. The two men and their escorts quietly removed their swords and scabbards, without complaint; it was common courtesy not to bring weapons into your host's hall. The sentry that had opened the door drew back a leather curtain that had hidden the rest of the hall from them so far and they stepped into the great room.

The Konge Hall was dark, smoky and malodorous, and seemed to be totally empty, yet it still emanated an earthy majesty. It had little in the way of natural light from windows, using instead rows of iron braziers, each of which held several tallow candles. Two rows of large wooden columns that supported the roof ran the length of the hall, this one room taking up almost all of the building's floor space. Towards the back of the hall, there were wooden partitions in the corners, marking out private chambers used by guests and hosts during festivities. A central hearth was gently smouldering, giving out more smoke than heat, it appeared.

"Welcome back, Earl Edgar!" a voice shouted from down of the bottom of the hall. It belonged to a tall, lean man dressed in fine leather armour. The Northlandic captain urged the Ænglisc envoys forward, leaving their escorts at the door. They walked briskly to the far end of the hall where the loud-voiced man waited, a broad grin on his face. He was standing at a wooden table on a raised platform, behind him just two armed guards and a serving girl. "It is good to see you again," he said, with what seemed to Ceolwulf to be sincerity. "Please, please, take a seat."

"It is good to see you again, my lord King," Edgar replied, easing himself slowly into a cushioned chair. King Hakon of Northland watched the Ænglisc earl wince with pain.

"A long journey?" he inquired with the same tone of voice that one would use to enquire about an illness.

"One of several," Edgar answered without elaborating further. The Northlandic king turned to the serving girl and took three goblets of wine from a proffered tray. "And this would be your son Ceolwulf, I think?"

"Correct, my lord King. This is my eldest and sadly my only son, Ceolwulf," Edgar replied. Ceolwulf nodded in greeting. The Northlandic king spoke in Ænglisc, even though he would have easily been able to make himself understood in Northlandic, such were the similarities between the two languages. There were few, if at all any, Northlandic nobles now who still spoke only Norse and did not at least speak a form of Ænglisc.

"Then let us drink to your health and safe arrival," Hakon proposed. "*Waes hael!*" He raised his goblet, then drained it in one gulp and smacked his lips. "Not bad stuff. I get it from Normandy, to be used on special occasions, such as these."

"Imported?" Edgar asked.

"Some of it," the king replied, with a twinkle in his eyes. "So what do you think of my hall, young Ceolwulf?"

Ceolwulf quickly swallowed the mouthful that he had been savouring; the king had not been wrong, it was an excellent wine.

"It is very impressive, my lord, very impressive indeed."

"Really?" Hakon asked with some bemusement. "I think it stinks of filth, is too smoky in winter, too hot in summer and would be better suited to stable my horses." He stared at Ceolwulf, who was not sure whether he was meant to answer the king or not. He barked a laugh and placed his goblet back on the serving girl's tray. "It is unique, I'll give it that. It exists purely for show but it does seem to impress many of my noblemen. I thought you'd quite like to see it though, Ceolwulf, but next time, I shall receive you in the castle maybe, somewhere a bit more civil."

Ceolwulf stared at the Northlandic king, unsure as to whether he was being mocked or being treated with affection. The king himself seemed to be a contradiction, in terms of what Ceolwulf had expected him to be. He was tall, well-built it would appear, but certainly not muscular in the way that Northlandic warriors were perceived to be; all barrel chest and brawn. He had a fine mane of long blond hair and a beard that reached to the middle of his chest, both of which were finely combed and well looked after. He wore a small crown; a coronet made up of intricately woven bands of silver, sparsely decorated with a few precious, colourful stones.

"I was very sorry to hear of the passing of your King Æthelgar. He was a good man, a patient and considerate king," Hakon continued.

"That he was, my lord, that he was," Edgar said, nodding slowly.

"And I'm sure in time, Prince Swegen will prove to be the same," Hakon said, picking at a cuff.

"As a wise steward to the queen," Edgar replied calmly. He did not care to correct any of Hakon's mistakes, intentional or otherwise.

"But I'm thinking that you haven't come just to tell me about this?" the king asked, glancing at father and son.

"Indeed not, lord King. Ængland requests the safe passage of Queen Adelise from Scotland, through the Northlandic shires of Westmoringaland and Suthribel to Ceaster, whence she shall ride to Winceaster." Edgar paused to cough. "We are aware of some bandit activity in the border lands and would ask that she be accompanied by your soldiers, or that you permit our riders to escort her through your lands."

The king leant back in his high-backed chair and drummed his fingers on the cushioned arm. He had known the reason for their visit from the moment they had sent their messenger ahead; he had half expected such a visit from the moment he heard of Æthelgar's death.

"Adelise does not wish to sail from the Solway to the Dee?" he enquired.

"The witan agreed that any journey by ship would be unduly upsetting for the queen, given the circumstances in which she lost her parents," Edgar answered.

"Did they now? Would you send your future queen through the barbarous lands of the Northlanders, Ceolwulf?" Hakon asked, turning to the young Ænglander. Ceolwulf knew that Hakon was playing with him, but had no intention of joining in with his game, in jest or otherwise. He was finding the Northlandic king likeable, but he was aware that he was also being probed, like an animal with a stick, to see if he would bite back.

"Of course, my lord, I have absolute faith in you," Ceolwulf replied, keeping his voice as neutral as possible.

Hakon stared at him for a second, then his eyes wrinkled and he let out a sharp, short laugh.

"Excellent, young Edgarsson. That is what I would say too." Hakon grinned like a tutor pleased with a pupil's answer. "Correct me if I am mistaken, Ceolwulf, but are you too not an heir to the Ænglisc throne, through your mother's side?"

"I am," Ceolwulf said carefully. "Although quite distantly."

"Not so distant that our dear Swegen will have forgotten though, I should imagine," Hakon mused, almost under his breath.

"We would of course require hostages, just as protocol you understand, not that we doubt Adelise's safety," Edgar said quickly, interrupting whatever new path of conversation the Northlandic king had been wanting to follow. Hakon became very still and pressed his palms together, resting his chin on the tips of his fingers. He didn't say a word for several seconds, as if he was lost in thought.

"No," he said, quite simply. "I am being asked to entrust hostages, including members of my kin I would imagine, to Swegen and the bishops, to guarantee the safety of Queen Adelise?"

Edgar nodded.

"Then my answer would be no. I can give you my word and men to ensure that your queen is escorted safely through Westmoringaland and Suthribel. I would have done it without being asked, for I have no quarrel with either you or Scotland, but I see no reason to give hostages. I will make sure that she is safe from bandits, but you do not need to protect her from me; I will not break the Morcar Oath. I apologise that you must carry this message back to your Lord Swegen, but that is my answer to him."

"I understand, my lord," Edgar said stiffly. He had hoped for a straightforward exchange of oaths and hostages, but now he was destined to be the bearer of bad news. "I imagine you will not let Ænglisc housecarls accompany her from Penrith to Ceaster?" Edgar asked wearily, for he already knew the answer.

Hakon pursed his lips and shook his head. He turned in his chair and called for more wine. From one of the rooms in the back corners a serving girl hurried forward to the table with a jug of the fine red wine. As Ceolwulf watched her shapely figure approaching the table, he became aware for the first time of a young boy sat in the shadows at the back of the room. The child was sitting in almost total darkness, visible only by virtue of his hair; it was such a light shade of blond that it was almost white.

If he had noticed Ceolwulf watching him, then he showed no sign of recognition.

Hakon refilled all three goblets himself and then sat back in his chair. He took a long sip, waited for the serving girl to disappear back into the shadows and sighed.

"Our two countries have lived side by side in peace, or a peace of sorts, if you like, for nearly one hundred years. We are, let us say, like two circling dogs, neither sure of each other's strength. Whether that's due to conflict not being in either nation's interest, or whether we really are adhering to the Morcar Oath that would forbid war between our nations, I'll let you decide. I believe that oath served its purpose at the time, that it created two smaller, stable nations, rather than letting a larger one destroy itself through civil war. I don't think it counts for much now, however; I rather think we maintain our peace through common sense and shared prosperity. So I do not think Northland will want to risk your future queen's life, nor do I think Ængland wishes to invade my country. However, I am not wont to invite Ænglisc soldiers into my country, to ride its length and breadth, whatever the reason. I understand she will have some household escort, and that is acceptable."

Edgar grunted. Ceolwulf glanced at his father, knowing the man was in pain, but was afraid that his inarticulateness would be misinterpreted as ill manners or aggression. Hakon seemed not to notice.

"Again, Earl Edgar, I am sorry that you must carry this answer back to your lord, but I can only assure you of Adelise's safety. I would happily swear on a bible, but I know many of your fellow earls still believe we worship Thor, Odin and so forth."

"I understand, my lord King." Edgar stood up slowly and pushed his chair back from the high table. "I can only thank you for your time and your promise of safe passage."

"I shall send messengers to the jarls of Westmoringaland and Suthribel immediately to ask them to prepare. I shall send notice of the day of her expected arrival in Ceasterscir, once I have corresponded with our Scottish friend, Prince Malcolm. I only hope that the next time we meet it may be under less stressful circumstances."

"Indeed, my lord King," Edgar said.

"Of course, you are welcome to stay in Jorvik as my guests this evening. I'm sure you would welcome a warm fire and good meal after your journey," Hakon said, standing up himself.

"You are kind, my lord King, but we leave immediately for East Anglia. We are already too long gone from our lands," Ceolwulf said, bowing. Beside him, Edgar nodded and winced, his hand going to his side. He bowed stiffly and the two men turned to walk back down to the front of the hall. Just before they reached where their cloaks and swords were waiting, Hakon's voiced called out loudly.

"It's a coincidence, isn't it?"

"My lord?" Edgar replied, squinting through the smoke that clouded the front of the hall.

"The Morcar Oath came about because an independent-minded Ænglisc earl trusted a Norse stranger more than a fellow Saxon, whom he certainly did not trust." Hakon was smirking again.

Edgar paused, appeared to think the statement over for a second, and then wrapped his sword belt around his waist. "I'll bear that in mind, King Hakon. Until the next time," the earl said, before bowing.

Once outside Ceolwulf did not speak until they were riding back towards the city gates. They would not stay the night in the city; they would have to head straight back to Ængland. A messenger could forward the Northlandic king's answer on to Swegen; they would not have to ride all the way back to Oxnaforda, but Theodford was still the best part of a week's ride away.

"Two things, Father," Ceolwulf said eventually.

"Go on," his father replied, staring straight ahead.

"Firstly, why? Why risk Ængland's wrath?"

"He's not. He's only risking Swegen's. He knows where the real power will lie. Hakon has nothing to lose by doing this. He wants to test Swegen. He doesn't trust him, so he won't send him hostages; by doing that he tests whether he can provoke him. He knows Swegen will not retaliate if he does not send them; at worst, he's slightly offended an earl of another country. It doesn't help our standing in Winceaster though, that's for sure."

"But you believe that Adelise will be safe."

"Hakon is no fool; it's not in his interests to risk Queen Adelise's life. What does he gain? He would far rather have a child queen and a guardian governing his neighbours, than have someone like Swegen as king. If his network of spies is as strong as we are led to believe, then he'll know full well what Swegen is like."

"That's all it is?"

"I think so. Every question he asked you he was trying to see if he could push you into saying something untoward."

Ceolwulf laughed. "It did feel like I was being tested, I do admit. Is that what he was doing with you, when he mentioned Earl Morcar and not trusting other Saxons?"

"That? Oh, he always does that," Edgar snorted. "His grandfather too, it was hardly probing. Each time I visit, they always suggest in various, unsubtle ways, that East Anglia would be better off as part of Northland than Ængland. I would have freedom to rule my own realm as a little king and in return they would get some of the finest arable land in these isles and control of almost the entire eastern seaboard from the Temese to the Tweed."

"And you are never tempted?"

"Of course I am. There are many reasons why I don't; your mother's family ties for one. But no, the main issue is even if I declare myself to be Northlandic tomorrow, I am not East Anglia.

I could go over to the other side, but I am not the shire. I do not command the loyalty and devotion that the king here rather kindly imagines me to have. He can convince one man, but East Anglia is Ænglisc, despite its history."

"But you would go?"

Edgar seemed to give this some thought. He trusted the men around him, but he knew an earl should never be too loquacious. "My first duty is to East Anglia, then God, then Ængland. I am Ænglisc though, and am proud to be so. If the young, twenty-year-old Edgar had met Swegen, perhaps things would be different, but the Edgar of today, the sick old man that your father has become? No, he is Ænglisc. What was the second thing then?"

"Who was the young boy hiding in the shadows?"

"Ha! I wondered if you'd noticed him," Edgar said. He coughed and spat into the roadside. "That, unless I am very much mistaken, was the young Prince Knut. He would have been about seven the last time I saw him, but he's not changed so much. He'll be about ten now, just a year older than Adelise. Something worth bearing in mind that; another reason why he would not want Adelise coming to harm – just think, if he can pair those two up, his grandson could rule a united Ængland and Northland."

"I thought Prince Malcolm's son was being touted as a possible husband."

"Young Kenneth? The cousin? He's only six and I doubt he'll live to seven, if what I've heard is to be believed. Every young prince in Europe has been mentioned as a possible husband to Adelise, Ceolwulf. But I am sure Hakon would dearly love for that to happen."

"Do you think he knew that Knut was there?" Ceolwulf asked.

"Oh, of course, letting him watch no doubt. Despite his attempts to appear casual and informal, very little happens in Northland without Hakon knowing about it or having organised it."

"So what happens now?" Ceolwulf asked as they turned back onto Mykla Gate.

"Now we send a messenger to Swegen, then we do absolutely nothing. We ride home, we ride slowly and we stop frequently. Then, once we're back in Theodford, I intend to sleep for a week, unless I die first, and hope to never have to travel on horseback ever again."

"So ride, sleep and then die? Try not to be so bleak, Father," Ceolwulf laughed, as they headed towards the large gatehouse.

The fates were laughing with Ceolwulf that afternoon, for within a month, that was almost exactly what would happen.

7th May 1166
The Lon Gorge, Westmoringaland, Northland

The carriage carrying Queen Adelise back home to Ængland bounced along the uneven dirt road at a steady pace, jostling its four occupants. Alongside the child-queen sat two ladies in waiting, Hild and Eadgyð, and her playmate, Tola, Eadgyð's daughter. The two elder passengers despaired at the constant movement, desperately hoping that they would soon stop for the evening. The younger two, however, were playing together, happily ignoring the uncomfortable ride.

The Ænglisc queen had successfully managed to convince Eadgyð to let her daughter travel with her. The journey from Carleol to Penrith had been uneventful and dull for Adelise. Hild was one of several women that Prince Malcolm had sent to Ængland with her, whose roles Adelise could not quite understand. She had spent the entire journey engrossed in her embroidery, without even exchanging a single word with any of the carriage's other occupants. At Penrith though, Adelise had finally got her wish and Tola had been allowed to ride with her to Lonborg. Now the two girls were playing games on the floor of the carriage, making up stories together.

"Don't get your dress dirty," said Eadgyð.

"Who?" Tola asked.

"Both of you," her mother gently chided. She winced as she watched her daughter scrabble around with the future queen on the floor of the wooden carriage. For some reason, Lord alone knew why, Adelise had decided that Tola should dress as a queen too. Eadgyð had not known until they had left the Penrith gates and crossed into Northland, when Tola had taken off her long shawl to reveal she was wearing one of Adelise's older blue dresses. Now the two girls were playing on the floor and Adelise was taking her jewellery off and giving it to Tola to wear.

If she had been told twenty years ago that her daughter would one day be exchanging jewellery with the future queen, she would have naturally considered the notion to be madness. Of course, Eadgyð thought, once Adelise was back in Ængland and at court, she would not have to resort to making friends with serving maids' daughters for friendship. For the time being though, deep down, Eadgyð quite enjoyed the idea.

"Stay still," Adelise chided Tola. She was trying to clip an earring onto the girl's left ear, but it was either tickling or hurting her; it was difficult to tell. "It will scratch if you keep moving."

"You shouldn't be wearing the queen's jewellery, Tola," Eadgyð said, but without any real passion.

"It's all right, Eadgyð, I don't mind," Adelise grinned. The girl scrabbled around on the floor for a ring she had taken off, steadying herself as the rear axle of the carriage bounced over one of the larger rocks on the dilapidated road.

Eadgyð leant back and gazed out of the back of the carriage. Rather than making the trip in an ornately decorated royal carriage, they had chosen to travel in three rather plain, cloth-topped carriages that could have quite easily been mistaken for modest merchants', were it not for the armed horseman that rode with them. The presence of the huskarl escort meant they would not encounter any trouble, but it never did to advertise any wealth when venturing through the wilds. The thick cloth that covered the curved top of the carriage kept out the worst of the cold and wind, but it was not a comfortable ride.

Eadgyð stared out at the retreating landscape, aware that the road was starting to climb. The gentle hills of the Carleol to Penrith road had given way to the deeper dales and fells of Westmoringaland. The road started to wind its way up the western side of a steep river valley that ran from north to south. The grey-green hillsides were speckled purple with heather that rippled in the rising wind. The further south they travelled, the higher and closer the hillsides grew, until the valley was less than half a mile across, the road perched above the deep gorge that contained a fast-flowing river. The tops of the fells disappeared into the low clouds that were now covering the caravan with drizzle.

Eadgyð pulled her cloak tight around her and shivered. She turned back to the two girls, the bejewelled Tola now brushing Adelise's hair.

"Wrap up now, girls," she said, wiping the rain, blowing into the back of the carriage, from her brow.

"Mother?" Tola asked. She was sitting with her legs to one side, copying Adelise's mannerisms.

"Yes, Tola, what is it?" Eadgyð replied.

"Adelise says that Northlanders eat children. Is that true?" she asked, with a grin, relishing the unpleasantness.

"They do many nasty things, Tola, but no, I don't think they do that." Eadgyð grinned back.

"Not always, and not often," Adelise said quickly, keen to save face in front of her new friend. "Just in winter time, when food is scarce and if the children are really fat."

"If food was scarce, then the children wouldn't be fat, would they?" Eadgyð answered.

Adelise put her head on one side and considered this for a moment.

"No, I suppose not," she opined. Lowering her voice, she continued, "But we better not make the horsemen angry though, Tola."

Eadgyð chuckled to herself and closed her eyes. She let her head drop onto her shoulder, hoping that the rocking of the carriage would have a soporific effect on her. The sound of the constant grinding of the wheels on the earth and broken stone was punctuated by the hooves of the accompanying huskarls, who mostly rode in silence, save for the occasional shout. Every so often, the driver of the lead cart would bellow something incomprehensible at his horses.

Eadgyð wasn't sure if she was falling asleep, but then every few minutes she would awake with a jolt that would prove that she had. Dreams of hills and rain mixed with hoofbeats until she was no longer sure what was dream and what was travel-induced stupor. On the other side of the carriage she was aware that Hild had started snoring loudly, much to the amusement of the two young girls who were unsuccessfully trying to stifle giggles. Eadgyð smiled to herself and placed one of the many cushions littered around the carriage under her head, finally letting herself drop off into a deeper sleep.

She awoke again suddenly, but this time she felt different. It had not been a jolt caused by a broken stone on the road, she was sure. She sat upright, unsure as to whether two minutes or two hours had passed since she had last been awake. Inside the carriage, Hild was still snoring, but the two girls were looking at her wide-eyed and pale-faced.

"What is it?" she asked. The caravan had stopped and from outside she could hear shouts coming from the huskarls. She crawled to the back of the carriage and pulled the cloth curtain aside. The riders were all staring up to the eastern side of the valley, where the fell tops disappeared into cloud. At first, she could not see a thing in the swirling rain, but slowly, as her eyes adjusted to the gloom, she could make out horsemen riding down the hill towards them. They were riding slowly, around twenty of them, displaying golden and red banners that flapped in the high wind.

"Who are they?" Eadgyð called to the nearest rider.

"Northymbreans, we think," he replied, nudging his horse closer to the carriage. "Stay inside the carriage though, you'll be safer. Please." His pleading tone unsettled Eadgyð. Another rider shouted a greeting to the nearing riders, but received no reply.

"Safer? Why? They are Northlanders like you, aren't they?" she asked, a growing fear making her voice rise.

One of the older riders barked at Eadgyð to be quiet, in broad Northlandic dialect, before returning to stare at the riders who were getting ever nearer. Eadgyð whimpered as the huskarls unsheathed their swords. The Northymbric riders were around five hundred paces away when they suddenly picked their speed up and started to gallop. They drew their swords, just as the escorting huskarls were starting to form a defensive line. Eadgyð crossed herself and ducked back inside the carriage's canopy and clutched the girls to her.

"What's happening?" Tola cried. Eadgyð was about to answer when from behind the carriage, coming from the opposite direction of the approaching riders, she heard an angry buzzing, like the humming of wasps. Seconds later, the sounds of arrows splintering wood and slamming into flesh filled the air. Hild's snoring suddenly changed into a gurgle; she toppled forward with an arrowhead sticking out of her throat and the girls started to scream.

Thurstan had been riding along the tops for over an hour now. As the Great South Road wound its way through the narrow river valley, Thurstan had climbed the western ridge, his pace hampered by the steep sides and lack of anything more substantial than animal tracks in the bracken and ferns. The low cloud seemed close enough to touch and the constant drizzle obscured anything but the largest shapes in the bottom of the valley. He could just make out the three carriages, and scuttling shapes he imagined were his fellow huskarls, but anything more than that was almost impossible to distinguish. Turning Svarnat to follow the curve of the hillside, he cursed his predicament.

He had set off from Kirkby two days ago, as part of a twenty-strong party of huskarls ordered by Vinder to accompany the Ænglisc queen through Westmoringaland. Thurstan had been delighted to think he was on duty for a queen, although he suspected he had only been selected as Captain Leif hadn't been happy about leaving him in Kirkby, such was the sense of animosity amongst the riders towards him. Not that he could still pinpoint as to why there was such dislike, but by now it had become a self-fuelling antipathy; if it hadn't existed for him, then it would have existed for someone else. It existed solely because men in groups, left alone for long enough, will find something or someone to dislike.

Even though he was riding escort to a queen, albeit of another country, he felt no glory, honour or pride anymore in being a huskarl. His childhood dreams had not been of riding alone, ostracised and outcast, plagued by visions of his only friend's head being cleft in two.

In his mind it had all been so easy; become a huskarl, regular pay, regular meals, learn sword-craft, ride to glory, enemies falling beneath his blade, be loved and admired, be noticed by King Hakon in some major battle or victory – he hadn't quite decided where this would have taken place – become a royal huskarl in Jorvik, be given land and titles, prosper.

It had not been a realistic plan, he had known, but it had been a dream that had given him ambition. It had a start and an end, which he quite liked; it was the work to get between the two that had presented a bit more difficulty. In his nineteen years, all he'd ever had to think about was what the next day would bring; his wealthy family had taken care of everything else.

He had not taken a wife, hardly kept any friends and had no belongings of which to speak. His family was no more than a day's ride away in Lonborg, but he could not honestly describe them as being particularly close to him. Perhaps he should return there, board a ship at the docks and never come back; seek out adventure rather than waiting for it to come to him for a few pennies a month.

Leif had more or less suggested as much the previous night, when they had camped outside the Scottish border town of Penrith. They would be riding to Lonborg – perhaps Thurstan would want to stay there when they returned, go back to his family? There were still plenty of ships operating out of the Irish city of Dyflin that were happy enough to go a-viking every year on the Frankish and Iberian coasts. Why not see if he could join one of them? Why not even go as far as the distant colonies of Vinland?

Yet there was no attraction in returning home. His father had never shown any real interest in Thurstan, at least not compared to that shown in his elder brother. He had hired a tutor to teach Thurstan his letters and numbers and some basic grounding in history, but Thurstan had proved to be a restless student. He guessed that the tutor had been hired more to keep the younger son out of the trouble than to actually instruct him.

Thurstan found himself slouching into his saddle, resting his weight on the pommel of his saddle and staring at the ground a few yards in front of his horse. The minutes passed by as he become more engrossed in his thoughts, to the point where he was no longer aware of the wind, cold or constant rain around him.

Thinking back, he had spent most of his childhood on the streets near the quays of Lonborg, playing games with other children. He thought a bit further about this and realised, no, that wasn't quite true. He had spent *some* time playing games, then the games had become a bit more boisterous, the other children had grown a bit bigger and he had spent a lot of time brawling with boys from the quayside houses, boys who were nothing short of young adults.

Thurstan lost himself in the memory of the summer he had learnt he could use his fists much better than his attackers expected. His father had chastised him the first time he had come home with a black eye and had labelled him a ruffian. Perhaps he had realised at that point though, when his shiphands had reported that Thurstan had fought off three boys, each of whom were five years his senior, that his younger son was never going to be a merchant. Lightning quick fists and a desire for glory did not make for a good trader.

Just five years later, and here he was, escorting queens; just not in the way he had imagined. He had seen Queen Adelise, briefly, when they had left Penrith. The gates had opened early, heralded by a horn blast, and three plain-looking carriages had come out of the city. A small contingent of Scottish riders had ridden to meet Leif, exchanged brief, stilted salutations that mostly seemed to consist of a large man on a fine horse instructing the Northlandic captain to remain vigilant of wolfheads.

They had then set off, the three carriages, ten riders from Prince Malcolm's household and the twenty Northlandic huskarls, along the road, south towards Lonborg. As he had ridden alongside the second carriage in the convoy he had seen two young girls stick their heads out of the back of the canopy. A voice had called one of them Adelise, the name of the Ænglisc queen, but as to which one she was, Thurstan had no idea. He assumed that the other girl was probably a relative, or one of the many minor nobles that seemed to litter Ængland. The third cousin of an uncle's stepdaughter or something, no doubt. Then Leif had suggested that Thurstan scout the western ridge of the pass – alone. Thus had ended his moment of royal glory.

He was stirred from his daydreaming by a horn blast from the bottom of the valley. Stopping his horse, he peered into the gloom and thought he could see movement among the riders. The wind swirled the rain and for an instant, he could clearly see the huskarls riding around the three carriages, stirred into action by someone or something. Thurstan felt his throat tighten and his stomach become light. He was not sure what he was looking at from this distance, but he knew something was not right.

He edged his horse to the very edge of the hillside, careful to keep Svarnat away from the treacherous patches of shale that could cause him to lose his footing. The wind gusted again and he saw many more riders, carrying shields decorated with gold and red, the colours of Northymbre, one of Westmoringaland's neighbouring shires. He could not understand what Northymbric huskarls would be doing this far west. They were riding down the other side of the valley, from the east, towards the caravan that had now stopped on the road.

He urged Svarnat forward and tentatively started descending diagonally, across the face of the hill, to prevent the horse from slipping. Closer now, he could see more clearly, despite the rain.

A dozen riders, perhaps two dozen, were charging towards the caravan. The realisation dawned on him; not towards them, but against. It made no sense, but there was no time to reason why. Thurstan kicked Svarnat into a gallop straight down the side of the valley. He could see his own huskarls, some with swords drawn, some with gungars held back, the distance between them and the now charging Northymbric riders tumbling by the second. Thurstan, riding as quickly as he dared, was still only halfway down the hillside; another five hundred, perhaps six hundred yards until he reached the valley bottom and his companions.

The Northymbric riders suddenly pulled up in the middle of their charge, turning their horses away from the awaiting Westmoringaland huskarls. Thurstan slowed his descent, straining his eyes, trying to understand what was happening. The Westmoringaland riders, lined up to protect the three carriages were hesitant to charge, unsure of their enemy and reluctant to abandon the young queen.

Without warning, off to Thurstan's left and behind the waiting huskarls, a group of thirty crossbowmen suddenly stood up in a shower of loose ferns. Thurstan shouted a warning, but his voice was instantly lost in the wind and rain. He spurred his horse downwards, angling towards the crossbowmen who were as unaware of Thurstan as his companions were of them. He watched them slowly raise their weapons and let the first, dreadful volley fly. Ten, perhaps more, of his companions died instantly, their exposed backs taking the brunt of the volleys. Other bolts pierced the wagons; one struck one of the caravan's horses in the flank, causing it to rear in pain.

The Westmoringaland huskarls were thrown into utter confusion, unsure if this was a new enemy or an attack from both sides. Thurstan could hear Leif shouting and five surviving riders turned their mounts and started to charge up the hill towards the crossbowmen. They were outnumbered, but they knew they had around thirty seconds before another volley struck. The remaining riders regrouped and faced the Northymbric riders who were now advancing again.

Thurstan was still a hundred yards from the crossbowmen, but the ground was so soft, so steep, it could have been a mile. He could see his advancing companions; he could almost see a look of recognition in the face of the nearest one as he looked past the bowmen towards Thurstan. He was almost there, he would make it, he could distract the bowmen. He was almost there.

Then a second volley of bolts was fired. The five charging Westmoringaland huskarls and their mounts crumpled. Thurstan screamed in frustration and helplessness; seconds later, he was upon the bowmen. Riding in from behind, they had been oblivious to him, the sounds of his horse lost in the wind and the sounds of battle.

Thurstan's launched gungar took down one bowman, pinning him to the heather; Svarnat rode down a second where he stood as if he were made of straw; a third's head was almost severed from his neck by Thurstan's blade. He turned his mount, ready to ride more down; he knew he had twenty to thirty seconds before they could fire again. He looked down to the valley bottom where the other horsemen were now clashing. The screams of the men, alongside whom he had once trained, eaten and lived, filled the air.

He saw Leif, his white hair recognisable from distance, go down under the blade of a giant man. The Northymbric riders now outnumbered the Westmoringaland huskarls and were pressing home their advantage, others were already slashing at the two carriages that were now motionless, their drivers slain. The third carriage, one of its four horses injured, had bolted down the road southwards towards Kirkby.

Thurstan stared at the disappearing carriage as three horsemen broke off from the other Northymbric riders and started chasing it. He glanced back at the reloading cross-bowmen, several of whom were backing away from him. He had maybe fifteen seconds. He spurred his horse forwards, then veered to the side, riding away from the bowmen's flank, trying to narrow as much as possible the angle they had to fire at. He knew there was nothing he could do for his fellow huskarls now – that battle had already been lost. He could at least help the fleeing carriage, though.

Svarnat galloped along the valley side, trying to keep level with the carriage and its pursuers on the road. Thurstan was no longer aware even of the soft ground or the rain; his focus was the only the wagon and the horsemen. From behind came the soft pounding of several crossbow bolts thumping into the damp earth, but Thurstan was already out of range.

The carriage was starting to lose pace; its wheels damaged from the rocks that littered the road. The riders were now almost upon it and Thurstan had lost ground. Although Svarnat was easily quicker than a carriage, the rough ground of the hillside was hindering him. There was no longer an advantage in hiding from the pursuers, so Thurstan turned the horse downhill towards the road.

Just before he reached the valley bottom though, the carriage swerved off to the left towards a small forest at the foot of the valley's eastern side. It charged down a small track leading into the trees and then promptly disappeared from Thurstan's view.

Seconds later the chasing horsemen charged in after it, leaving Thurstan alone in the open. He kicked at Svarnat's flanks, but stayed on the road, carrying on for a short distance before eventually turning to his left and into the trees further south. There was no path or track here and Thurstan had to swerve around trunks and leap over fallen branches in the undergrowth. From ahead he could hear shouts and a horse whinnying in pain, which was swiftly cut off. Thurstan slowed to pinpoint the direction that the noise was coming from. He knew he did not have much time if the riders were already upon the carriage.

He heard a scream from his left, possibly a woman, possibly a young girl, and he kicked his horse again and urged it forward. The soft mulch of the undergrowth muffled the sound of Svarnat's hooves, so when Thurstan burst into the clearing, he took the three riders by surprise. As he emerged into the light, Thurstan had a fleeting image of bodies and blood as he hacked down at the first rider who was slowly turning towards him, the blade sinking into his shoulder and slicing him open. Thurstan hauled on his reins to avoid the overturned carriage and leapt from his saddle. The other two Northymbric riders advanced towards him, their companion now lying on the ground, coughing and gurgling. Thurstan slapped Svarnat's flank, yelling at the horse to move out of way, giving him space. The two Northymbrians spread out, each trying to get round the back of Thurstan.

"Who the hell are you?" Thurstan shouted; not that any answer they could give would change his intentions. One of the men answered, but in an accent so thick that Thurstan struggled to understand. It was an unusual accent, certainly not a Northlandic one. Sensing Thurstan's confusion the two men leapt towards him.

The nearest man took a swing at Thurstan, who jumped back, away from the arc of the sword point. He slipped on the wet leaves and toppled backwards onto moss-covered logs. In the blink of an eye, the rider was upon him, striking down with both hands clasped on his sword. Thurstan rolled to his right, the sword missing his ear by a fraction. He swung his blade round and caught his assailant just above the ankle. The man howled and crumpled to the ground clutching what remained of the bottom of his left leg.

Thurstan was now scrabbling backwards, his sword gone, trying to stand up as the final attacker edged towards him. No wild swinging from this man; he circled Thurstan, his sword lowered, waiting for him to make a move. Thurstan pushed himself up into a crouch and the rider stabbed down. Thurstan sprang up, grabbing the his assailant's sword arm, pulling him towards him. The rider blinked in surprise as Thurstan sank the hunting knife he'd kept hidden in his boot into the man's stomach.

Thurstan stepped back and pushed the whimpering man off him. The first man was already dead, the other two were dying. In an act of mercy rather than vengeance, Thurstan finished both men with his sword to cut their suffering short – severed limbs and wounds to the stomach would have meant a slow or painful death out on the fells.

Taking a moment to get his breath back, he finally took stock of his surroundings, trying to make sense of the carnage about him. The driver lay dead, a stab wound to his chest. He had obviously survived the initial crash and had tried to defend the carriage's occupants, for there was a sword near to him, although it was unbloodied. The horses both lay dead; one had been wounded by an earlier crossbow bolt, the other with a broken leg. They had both had their necks cut, to stop them from flailing about. The carriage had overturned, possibly after striking a tree trunk that lay across the entrance to the clearing. The bottom frame was splintered, snapped like the back of an animal. The body of a woman lay on the ground, her head almost pointing backwards, her neck quite obviously broken.

Thurstan peered inside the crumpled wreckage, its cloth canopy now flapping loose. The body of another woman lay on the floor, on what had once been the roof, a crossbow bolt through her neck. She must have died sometime before, during the initial ambush, for her blood had covered almost every surface inside.

Thurstan stepped around to the front of the carriage and his heart sank. The body of a young girl lay on the leaves. She was wearing a fine blue dress and expensive jewellery, as if she had been dressed for a feast. The delicate beauty of her attire contrasted with the gore that was now where her head should have been. A sword blow had taken the poor girl's head almost completely off above the neck. The lower jaw remained intact, but the rest of the head was nowhere to be seen. Ravens were already circling above and their cries signalled that any remains would not stay untouched for long. Thurstan let out a sob and then retched; it had all been for nothing.

A shout came; again in the strange accent that Thurstan could not place. The voice was still some way off, but was possibly already in the forest. Thurstan glanced around him and called softly to Svarnat. As the horse wandered over to him nervously, Thurstan picked up the dead driver's sword and wiped it in the blood of the man with the severed foot. He placed the sword in the dead rider's hand in the vain hope that he could get away without being seen, leaving the impression that the driver had killed his attackers.

Another shout came and Thurstan leapt onto his horse. He turned Svarnat and was about to ride out of the clearing when he heard a small cry. At first, he assumed it was just a carrion bird cawing, but then it came again. It was the cry of a small girl. He stopped Svarnat and listened. The voices of the men were getting nearer; he could hear their horses braying. The cry came again. Thurstan knew he could ride away now, he could escape and no-one would suspect that he had ever been there; get back to

Kirkby and let them know that there had been nothing he could have done.

He tensed his legs, ready to ride; then the cry came again. Only this time, it was not a girl's voice. It was Sorli. His friend was calling for him, needing his help. *If you go now, if you leave us again,* the voice said, *we will haunt you for the rest of your days.*

Thurstan jumped down from the horse and ran over to the upturned carriage. The girl's cry came again, most definitely from inside. Perhaps the woman with the bolt through her neck was not dead after all, though Thurstan could not see how. He peered in and saw her still there, motionless. The cry came again and Thurstan saw movement by the dead woman's legs. He clambered inside the carriage, pushing splintered beams out of his way and turned the woman over. Underneath her body lay a blood-splattered girl, a child, shivering and crying.

"Help me," her small voice said simply. From outside Thurstan could hear another voice, this time no further than ten paces away, perhaps already in the clearing. The small girl gasped at the sight of Thurstan; a blood-splattered apparition of long hair and armour. Thurstan placed his finger on his lips and urged her to keep quiet. Gently, he picked her light body up, carried her out of the carriage and placed her across Svarnat's saddle. Hauling himself up, Thurstan kicked the horse into a gallop and charged out of the clearing.

Several seconds later a group of horsemen burst into the clearing to find four of their companions dead on the ground and the wreckage of a cart. They dismounted and the largest of them, a scar-faced man wearing thick mail, stalked over to the carriage. He looked at the bodies of the women and found the body of the girl. He knelt down and looked at her fingers, noting the rings. He prised the largest one off and pocketed it in a leather pouch, which he then stuffed inside his saddlebag. He turned to his men and nodded.

"It is done. The queen is dead. Leave the bodies here, along with those from Setburg," he announced. Another rider entered the clearing and called to him.

"My lord, there's a huskarl fleeing to the south, the only one left. Should we chase him down?"

"Leave him, let him go. Let someone go back to Kirkby and tell the sheriff how the queen was killed. It saves us the job of having to do it."

"Lord?" the horseman frowned.

"That huskarl is going to return and tell the sheriff that they were attacked by men from Northymbre and Adelise was killed. Is that not what we wanted? Better coming from him, than that witless woman we'll be leaving here. What it means, though, men, is that we leave now. Take as many horses as you can and fetch the rest from up the valley; we meet back at camp."

The men rode out of the clearing, leaving the bodies to the gathering birds. The large, scarred man mounted his horse and rode out of the small wood. The rain had finally stopped and the cloud was lifting. Up the valley came the remainder of his horsemen; apart from those in the clearing they had lost less than ten men. He patted his horse's neck and spurred it onwards; his work here was done.

8th May 1166
Kirkby Kendale, Westmoringaland

Thurstan awoke with a shout of terror, the visions of blades and broken bodies from his dreams dancing in front of him. For several seconds he lay in the small straw pallet trying to gather his senses, a weak beam of sickly light shining on his face from the room's single, small window. He was in a small stone room; somewhere near the kitchen buildings, he guessed from the smell of cooking food in the air. He stood up and stretched, causing his back to crack loudly and unpleasantly. He realised he was possibly in one of the cells used for holding prisoners on their way to Lonborg, or town drunks that needed to sober up overnight. It seemed an odd place to be, but then the memories of the previous evening started to come back to him.

He had ridden through the gates of Kirkby shortly after nightfall. The guards on the gate had recognised him instantly and had let him in without question, despite the absence of the other huskarls. Perhaps he had bellowed to be let in, perhaps he had screamed at them; he could not remember now. He had been fearful, and he had ridden his horse hard those last few miles over the hilly terrain to Kirkby, still unsure as to whether he was still being pursued or not.

At the entrance to the fort, he had been stopped and he did remember the several attempts it had taken him to explain to the men there what had happened. The others were dead, the caravan attacked, only one survivor, an injured girl. Their first question had been whether she was Adelise; their second was who had attacked them. Thurstan had not known the answer to either.

He had eventually been let in and escorted into the main courtyard, where he had practically fallen off his horse, but only once he had gently passed down the body of the young girl. It might as well have been a corpse, for her body had been cold and motionless. Only the constant flickering of her eyelids had confirmed that she was still alive.

Thurstan remembered slithering to the ground from his saddle. He had ridden Svarnat like never before from Grarigg to Kirkby and his aching body had simply started to shut down. Shouts had echoed around the torch-lit stone courtyard, mixing with the sound of the horses' skittering hooves, becoming a cacophony of hellish noise in Thurstan's exhausted mind.

Sheriff Vinder had rushed out to see him and fired a barrage of questions. *Dead,* had been the only answer he had been able to give, *everyone was dead*. At that point, the crippling wave of tiredness had finally engulfed him and Thurstan's legs had given way. His last memories had been of Vinder barking orders about where to put Thurstan and the girl for the night.

Now he tried to open the small wooden door and found, to his surprise, that he had been locked in the room. He beat on the door and called out, waiting only a few seconds before he heard the sound of bolts sliding back and the door swung open. Two guards, who had apparently been sitting outside his room all night, bid him good morning and explained that the locked room had been for his own protection.

"After all," one of them said as the other scurried off to find some food, "you are the sole survivor of an attack on the Ænglisc caravan."

"So I'm free to leave then?" Thurstan asked.

The guard shrugged. "Not really, Vinder wants you to stay here until he can speak to you. He shouldn't be long, though. Just doesn't want you to speak to anyone else before him."

The second guard returned with a bowl of weak gruel and a slice of bread, which he wolfed down ravenously. Just as Thurstan was licking his fingers clean of the last remnants of food, Vinder, Sheriff of Westmoringaland strode into the small room, accompanied by two armed men. Without exchanging pleasantries, Vinder insisted that Thurstan relate the previous day's events in as much detail as he possibly could.

Many men, the Jarl Herri of Westmoringaland for example, were oft described as harsh but fair; just men who would wield the blade or impose violent punishment when they saw fit. Vinder, the jarl's appointed second in command, however, was not one of these men. He had a reputation of being harsh but arbitrary in his judgements. On certain days he could be jovial, waft away petty crimes committed by the poor with a smile and a reprimand; other days he would order a hand cut off for the smallest theft, a home burnt down for a tax paid just a few days late; or so went the rumours that Thurstan had heard. Even those Vinder considered closest to him, and they would struggle to describe themselves friends rather than well paid retainers, would never know in which mood they would find him from day to day.

"So?" Vinder asked, once Thurstan had finished retelling everything he could remember. "Who do you think they were?" He stared straight at Thurstan, his yellowy, rheumy eyes watering. Vinder was not a healthy-looking man. His face was gaunt and his complexion pale, save for his blemished cheeks that were an unsightly shade of purple. He coughed and spluttered regularly, making distasteful, wet noises that constantly put Thurstan off his train of thought.

"I don't know, my lord," Thurstan replied, this being the truth for the time being. Vinder kept his watery gaze trained on Thurstan for several moments. Thurstan was not sure whether he was expected to say something more; had he missed something obvious to say?

"It sounds to me as if the Ænglisc queen has been a victim of wolfheads, Thurstan," Vinder mused. "Wolfheads, like those you encountered at Grarigg at Hvinfell."

"But the Northymbric shields, my lord, they were all carrying them," Thurstan replied.

"There is that, I'll grant you," Vinder conceded. "Deserters, Thurstan. The hills are rife with them, as you well know."

Thurstan did know and he was quite sure that these were not the same groups of men. They had been organised, quick, intent on killing – not desperate men forced to live as outlaws to survive.

"But they-" Thurstan started, and then stopped.

"Thurstan, I really am hoping that they are wolfheads," Vinder said, lowering his voice and stepping closer to the young huskarl, leaning down to almost whisper to him. "Because if it was our own countrymen from Northymbre who attacked and killed the Ænglisc queen, do you know what that would mean for Northland?"

Thurstan shook his head. "I don't know, my lord."

"All I ask is that we do not jump to conclusions. You say one thing to someone and then they say something to someone else, it gets distorted, becomes a lie, a wild accusation. Some might say even, for example, that you fled the scene of battle, leaving your fellow huskarls to be slaughtered. so that you could escape taking a young girl with you-"

"No!" Thurstan protested. "It wasn't like that, not like that at all."

"I know, Thurstan, I know that. You know that. It was just an example. But until we know the full facts, perhaps it's best that we do not speak to anyone else about the girl," the sheriff said, holding his hands up placatingly. "This girl may even be nothing more than a maid, a serving girl to the dead queen?"

"But she'll be safe here, surely?" Thurstan asked.

"Ah, but money makes men do odd things. A coin here, a coin there, for a quick word on the whereabouts of a young girl? A stranger in the tavern to whom you give a little bit of information in return for a month's salary? My men are good men, Thurstan," Vinder said, "but they're not that good."

"What would you like me to do then, my lord?" Thurstan

asked.

"The girl," Vinder started slowly. "She's not spoken to anyone. Not even the sisters attending her. I was thinking you ought to perhaps speak to her, perhaps she will talk to you; tell you who she is, who attacked her. I swear I will do everything in my power to keep her safe."

"I will, my lord, I will," Thurstan nodded. He wanted to see the young girl again. He had brought her this far, from almost certain death, and now, despite being safe in a stone fort, he felt more moved than ever to ascertain her well-being. Vinder stepped back and straightened up, gesturing to his men to open the door.

"One thing, though, Thurstan," Vinder said. "If she does say anything, come straight to tell me in my quarters; do not say anything to anyone else." With that, the sheriff tossed a small bag of coin to Thurstan, which he caught clumsily with both hands, and left the room.

A few minutes later, having collected his sword from the guards and extra food from an unwilling cook, Thurstan stepped out of the kitchen buildings and into the bailey courtyard. He let the cool breeze from the hills wash around him and tried to gather his thoughts. The events of the past two days had been a blur; it felt as if he had not stood still for a long time. He closed his eyes, tilted his head back and inhaled deeply. There was a faint tang in the wind of snow, unusual for May, but to the west, the highest peaks of the Lakelands did indeed have the lightest dusting of white. The small bag that Vinder had tossed him had contained the equivalent of two months' salary. This, Thurstan thought, from the man who had just lectured him about how coin made men do evil things.

He was brought back to the present by the impolite elbow of a large washerwoman barging past him, on her way to one of the smaller outbuildings in the courtyard. Thurstan quickly crossed the cobbled bailey to the door of the infirmary. It was a place that was rarely busy in the truest sense, although the sisters that ran it always appeared to be bustling about something. The recent skirmishes aside, the most serious injuries were usually those suffered by stonemasons or farmers that had been crushed by a beast or a cart. He knocked lightly on the door, waited a few seconds and then, when there was no answer, softly opened the door.

He stepped into a long, low-roofed, dim room. There were two rows of beds, each separated by a low wicker partition. As his eyes accustomed themselves to the gloom, a small pinch-faced woman wearing a wimple appeared in front of him, her scowl evident even in the darkness.

"Who are you?" she demanded.

"Forgive me, sister, my name is Thurstan," he answered. He was not wearing any armour or weapons, but his scratched face and dirty hands made him the type of person that was usually unwelcome in the infirmary. "I brought back the injured girl from the attack yesterday."

"She is doing well, but I think it best that she has no visitors," the sister replied, her manner only slightly softened by the knowledge that this was the soldier that had saved her life.

"Sheriff Vinder said that I should speak with her, and to pray for her," Thurstan said.

"Did he now?" she asked, her tone unchanged.

"Yes," Thurstan answered simply. He peered over her shoulder trying to see in which bed the girl was.

"Well, if Lord Vinder demands it, I suppose I should let you see her. But you must not trouble her or speak to her for too long," she said, relenting.

"She is speaking?" Thurstan asked, surprised.

"A little," the sister replied. "She has not spoken about herself or the attack, only to ask for water. She doesn't speak Northlandic, but she understands it well enough, and her Ænglisc is comprehensible."

"Is she badly injured?" Thurstan asked, as the sister turned to walk towards the back of the room. He quickly stepped after her, glancing at some of the other occupied beds. Most were empty, but those that were occupied seemed to be filled by pale, feverish figures that may well have been mistaken for corpses already, were it not for the unpleasant rasping and coughing noises that they emitted.

"Thankfully not, but it was not a clean cut. There is always the risk of infection over the next few days, which is why she ought to rest as much as possible," the sister replied, just as one of the infirmary's other occupants broke into a series of choking, hacking coughs.

She stopped by the very last stall in the far corner of the room.

"Here she is," the sister said. "If she is sleeping, I would ask you not to disturb her though."

Thurstan peered into the stall at the small figure lying on her side on the straw mattress. Her face was pale, her eyes closed, but her breathing was pronounced and steady. He stepped forward softly and knelt by her head. Small beads of sweat lined her brow and her lips twitched as if she were speaking in her sleep. For several moments he knelt in silence, looking at the girl that had been unknown to him before yesterday, yet for whom he now felt responsible. He turned to look at the sister who jerked her head to one side, as if to suggest he should leave. Thurstan turned back to look at the girl, whose eyes were now wide open. They were of a piercing dark blue and seemed to be so alert that Thurstan found it hard to believe that she had been asleep just moments before.

"Hello," he said softly. "My name is Thurstan Ælfsson."

"Hello," the young girl replied, in voice only slightly stronger than a whisper. Although her pronunciation was unusual, Thurstan could understand her well enough and as the sister had said, she seemed to understand him. "Thank you for saving me, Thurstan." She smiled very faintly.

"You remember me?" Thurstan asked, shocked.

"I remember your horse, I remember travelling. I remember the men," her voice trailed off. Her eyes closed and she seemed to fall back to sleep, save for the single tear that ran down her cheek.

"What's your name?" Thurstan asked. The girl's eyes flicked to the foot of the bed where the sister was still hovering in anticipation. She closed her eyes and shook her head gently.

A sudden cry of pain filled the infirmary and Thurstan's hand instinctively went to his side for a sword that was not there. The sister who had been standing at the foot of the straw pallet sighed in exasperation and hurried to the other end of the room to locate the source of the suffering. As soon as she was gone, the young girl's eyes flickered open again.

"Thurstan?" she asked quietly.

"Yes?" he replied.

"You saved me, didn't you?" she whispered. Thurstan nodded. "Am I in Northland?" she asked.

"You are, but you are among friends," Thurstan replied, for the girl seemed nervous.

"I can trust you, but others-" she paused, as she seemed to draw in a deep breath. "I must tell you something, but you must promise me one thing."

"Of course, whatever you ask," he said, fearing what he suspected was coming.

"Will you protect me? Protect me until I get home?" she asked, sniffing back more tears.

Thurstan paused, then placed his right hand on hers and bowed his head.

"I promise that I will protect you. But you are safe here, I assure you."

From the other end of the room came the sound of rushing footsteps as the patient who had called out started thrashing around his straw bed; two other sisters who had been in a side room had now come in to help the pinch-faced woman hold him down.

"I cannot stay here," the girl said.

"I know it's not pleasant, but the sisters will take good care of you," Thurstan said, despite inwardly detesting the thought of having to spend even a single night in a room such as this.

"No, you don't understand," the girl replied hurriedly. She took a deep breath and then continued. "My name is Adelise; I am to be Queen of Ængland. Those men who attacked me, they wanted to kill me. Please do not tell anyone here who I am."

Thurstan's hands suddenly felt very cold and his throat became very tight.

"We, we thought you might be. Or a maid," he said weakly.

"Are they here too?" she queried.

"Who?" Thurstan asked, unsure as to whom she was referring.

"My maids, the other people in my carriage," Adelise said, her voice becoming softer.

Thurstan took her hand again and lowered his head.

"You were the only survivor."

Adelise closed her eyes and the tears came again. Thurstan had no idea how to comfort a child, let alone a royal one. He tried to reassure her again of her safety.

"The men who attacked, I know they wore Northlandic shields, the ones from Northymbre, but I promise you that you are safe here. Vinder, the sheriff, is a bit gruff, a bit strange, but he is a good lord and will make sure you will be protected," Thurstan reassured her.

He didn't have much choice about telling the sheriff. He would have to tell Vinder and have faith that she would be taken safely to Lonborg. At worst, she would then be taken to Jorvik as a prisoner for ransom, he supposed. At best, she would be taken as a guest of honour. He felt he was betraying her trust in some way if he were to tell Vinder, but what was the alternative? Let her rot here anonymously? Claim she was just a maid, leaving her to be put to work in the kitchens once she recovered?

"I know they weren't from Northland," she said, almost in a whisper now. From the other end of the room, the cries of the scuffling patient were becoming more subdued, as the sisters managed to calm him down.

"How do you know that?" Thurstan asked, puzzled by the girl's certainty.

"One of the men, I saw him. I recognised him. His name is Ricmund; he is a friend of my uncle's, the Earl Swegen."

Thurstan felt his body go rigid at the implications.

"Are you sure?" Thurstan asked, his eyes locked onto her unwavering gaze.

"Yes. It was him. I saw his scar."

At this, she closed her eyes and fell into what seemed to be true sleep this time. Thurstan slowly stood up and dusted down the knees of his breeches from where he had been kneeling on the straw-covered floor. So the girl really was the queen; he had known it was a possibility, but to have her confirm it had left him shaken; although not quite as shaken as the knowledge that Ænglisc soldiers were running around Westmoringaland. Vinder would have to be told, and immediately.

Thurstan strode out of the partitioned recess and almost collided with the returning sister.

"Well, what did she say?" the woman barked. She asked the question not with concern, but almost as a martial interrogation.

"Nothing," Thurstan replied without breaking his step and walked out of the infirmary.

Thurstan stepped into the small antechamber that led to Vinder's quarters in Kirkby Fort. The man owned several large farmsteads throughout the area, but unless the Jarl of Westmoringaland was visiting, Vinder lived as if the fort were his own private residence. It gave the impression that he was the true ruler of Westmoringaland, or so he liked to think, and that the Jarl of Westmoringaland was just a ceremonial figurehead residing in a distant castle.

For his part, Jarl Herri was only too aware of the impression that Vinder liked to project, but was happy to let him do so. He far preferred the comforts that a large city such as Lonborg could provide and the politics of dealing with the neighbouring shires of Jorvik and Suthribel, rather than the dark, wet, inhospitable hills to the north. The sheriff was left to busy himself in the northern half of the shire, collecting taxes, enforcing the laws and, if rumours were to be believed, lining his pockets quite well at the same time. The jarl, however, kept him in his service as he was an efficient tax collector, despite having his well-justified doubts that Vinder kept a healthy cut of them for himself.

The chamber was lavishly decorated with carpets and wall hangings. There were old, locally made tapestries that depicted ancient battles and gods; others were newly bought from visiting merchants. They were all of differing styles and designs, but Vinder was fond of surrounding himself with expensive items, with little care for taste or aesthetic; he was happy enough just letting visitors know of his wealth.

A guard, armed with a short sword, stood in front of the thick wooden door that led to Vinder's room. He stared at Thurstan with a disdain that suggested he thought that the young huskarl had no good reason to be there, and made no effort to step aside to allow him to knock.

"I am here to see the sheriff," Thurstan said, staring straight back at the guard, returning the same disdain he was being shown. The man, who could only have been a few years older than Thurstan, showed no sign of having heard, but simply turned and knocked twice on the solid oak door. A moment later, the door opened slowly, revealing a second guard who quickly scanned the antechamber, before almost reluctantly waving Thurstan in.

Vinder was sitting behind a large wooden table. The crumbs of food, dried pools of wine and ale-stained scattered parchments suggested that he rarely left it. The stone-framed window behind Vinder's desk was positioned so that the low afternoon sun caused Thurstan to squint, the harsh light almost forming a halo around the sheriff's head.

"Ah, our maiden's saviour, Thurstan!" Vinder declared loudly. "I trust I find you well." He leant back in his chair and picked at a plate of cold meats, coughing wetly. His other hand casually held a wooden cup that split ale onto the dry floor as he gestured. "Can I get you something to eat, to drink perhaps? Mead, ale, wine even?"

"Some water perhaps," Thurstan replied, his throat suddenly dry. The shaft of light coming in from the window illuminated the particles of dust that were floating around the room; a musty concoction created by the carpets, tapestries and papers that filled the room. An oily candle burnt slowly on Vinder's table, used to melt the wax he used to seal messages, which only added to the unpleasant miasma that seemed to surround the man.

Vinder snapped his fingers at the guard stationed inside the room. He obediently walked over to a pewter jug on a small table and filled a small wooden cup to the brim. He clumsily handed it to Thurstan, spilling half the contents over his sleeve. Vinder remained seated, watching Thurstan impassively. The sheriff nodded at him encouragingly, urging him to drink.

"Fresh from the well this morning, boy," Vinder said encouragingly. "So then, what information have we gleaned from our mute little girl?"

"My lord," Thurstan started, and then faltered. He glanced round at the guard behind him and then, almost involuntarily, leant closer across the table to the sheriff. "My lord, she has spoken. I know who she is."

Vinder, who had been raising a cup to his lips, suddenly went very still. There was a look in the young huskarl's eyes and a tone in his voice that made him hesitate. He slowly raised a finger to his lips and for a moment, Thurstan imagined he was unsubtly trying to silence him, but he simply brushed a few crumbs from his moustaches.

"Sveyn, leave us, please and make sure no-one, and I mean no-one, enters this room," Vinder said quickly to the guard. The ever-obedient Sveyn nodded and quickly slipped out of the door, closing it with a heavy thud. Vinder leant forward in his chair and thumbed his chin thoughtfully. His stubbled jaw was crusted with flecks of dried food and flaking skin; Thurstan tried to fix his gaze on the sheriff's rheumy eyes rather than watch his unsightly rubbing.

"Now then, Thurstan, I want you to think very carefully about what you are going to tell me. Take your time and tell me the exactly what this young girl said to you," Vinder said, "I want you to be absolutely sure of what you say, for any falsehoods could have some grievous repercussions."

"The young girl, my lord," Thurstan started, "is Queen Adelise of Ængland. She told me this, and I believe her. There was only one other body of a girl, at least of what I saw, my lord, and she has no reason to lie. I think she knows that she would possibly be safer not admitting to it."

"I see," Vinder said slowly, apparently unmoved by the information. "I see." He clasped his hands together and pressed them to his forehead as if in prayer. After several seconds he suddenly pushed his chair back, stood up and walked over to Thurstan and embraced him warmly, his face now wreathed in a large smile. "Well, Thurstan, it would appear you are now a hero. You have saved the Queen Adelise from bandits. You shall be proclaimed a great huskarl both in Northland and Ængland!"

"Bandits, lord?" Thurstan stammered, not sure how to react.

"Bandits, wolfheads, of course. Slyly disguised as Northlandic huskarls from Northymbre, but thankfully you saw through the deception and rescued the young queen."

"They were not though, my lord," Thurstan countered.

"How can you be so sure, young Thurstan?" Vinder asked. His face was close to Thurstan's still, the smell of ale on his breath and sour sweat so strong that Thurstan took an involuntary step backwards.

"Queen Adelise, my lord. She recognised one of the men. A warrior of Ængland, an Ænglisc thegn known to her," Thurstan said.

Vinder froze and the blood seemed to drain out of his face. He stared for a long time at Thurstan before stepping away and returning to his table.

"You know what this means, Thurstan? Do you know what you are insinuating?" Vinder asked, his voice almost a whisper. A globule of spittle trembled from his bottom lip, his bloodshot eyes staring directly at Thurstan. He was leaning heavily on his large oak table, his fists pressed into the papers that were scattered across the tabletop. Thurstan watched as the saliva dripped slowly from Vinder's lip onto a dry paper below, leaving an unsightly wet patch.

"I believe I do, my lord," Thurstan answered.

Vinder bit on his bottom lip and turned away. His hand gripped the back of his until his knuckles turned white.

"It means that the Ænglisc are setting themselves up for a civil war, or perhaps to usurp the throne treacherously. But they are not content to fight it out among themselves, they wish to implicate Northland, to blame us. Dear God, Thurstan, I didn't know."

"Didn't know what, my lord?" Thurstan asked, suddenly puzzled.

Vinder hesitated, and then quickly answered.

"That they would be so treacherous to each other. Bandits are one thing, but this?" He spat on the floor, with no particular concern for where it landed and crossed himself. "Who else knows of this, who have you told?"

"No-one, my lord, I came straight to you," Thurstan answered.

"Good lad. We two hold the most awful information in the kingdom; we cannot afford to let this get out. It would put us in grave danger. They must have had some kind of help, someone in Northland. Thank God you came straight to me. Listen, Thurstan, you can trust no-one, absolutely no-one. Do not tell anyone else of this, for they may be a spy or be in the pay of this Ricmund. We shall ride this evening for Lonborg; we must inform the jarl of what has happened. The girl will be safe here for the time being. We'll keep up the pretence that she was a maid of the queen to protect her. Go now and prepare your horse, tell anyone who asks that you are riding an errand, that you are delivering a message for me. Do you understand?"

"I do, my lord," Thurstan replied, though somewhat hesitantly. Vinder was leading him by the shoulder, guiding him to the door. "Although I am a bit confused, though."

"What about?" Vinder asked, still pushing Thurstan gently.

"How did you know it was Ricmund?"

Vinder stopped mid-stride and cursed. His right hand dropped to his waist and Thurstan instinctively jumped backwards as the glint of a dagger's blade swept past his face. The sheriff lunged at him again, his face contorted into a red visage of rage. Thurstan sidestepped the older man who still had some speed, if not agility. Thurstan grasped Vinder's wrist and in silence, the two men wrestled with the sharp dagger between them, hovering between their faces. Then Thurstan swung his free right hand and punched Vinder square on the jaw. The sheriff's eyes rolled back and his knees gave way; Thurstan quickly grabbed him under his arms and dragged him onto a chair, the dagger dropping with a muffled clang on to the floor.

The whole thing had been over in less than five seconds and almost totally in silence. Thurstan was sure that the sound of his breathing, which was coming in rasping breaths, was deafening, but he held his breath and listened for a few seconds. No noise came from the antechamber; either the guards had gone, or they had not heard any commotion.

Thurstan straightened up and scanned the room for a way out. He could hardly open the door and walk out of the room; he would have to find another exit. There were two smaller, lead-lined windows in addition to the large one behind Vinder's table, but they looked out onto the courtyard. Thurstan certainly did not feel like jumping through a window from a second-storey building and into the bailey during the middle of the afternoon.

Vinder's breathing was getting louder, his nasal rasping becoming more like a shrill snore with every breath. His head was slumped to one side, spittle dribbling on to his shoulder. Thurstan considered trying to silence him, by perhaps shoving some cloth into his mouth, but he did not want to choke Vinder. He would swing for striking a sheriff, but he still had no desire to make himself a murderer.

Then came the sound that Thurstan had feared; there was a loud knock on the door.

Arnulfhead, Westmoringaland

The horsemen rode down the last few yards of the hillside to the water's edge. Their leader, the scarred warrior known as Ricmund of Readinga, or Eoten – the monster – dismounted and scoured the horizon for ships.

"What time is it?" he called out to the other riders. "Around noon?"

Several of the riders peered into the overcast sky, trying to locate the sun, and nodded in agreement. The morning had started out brightly, but in the space of a few hours, clouds had rushed in from the sea to the west and the breeze was distinctly chill. Ricmund tightened his cloak around him and scanned the bay.

"They should be here by now," he growled. He was waiting for the two merchant ships that had brought them from the Ceasterscir port of Eswelle to Arnulfhead. In truth, they were military transport ships, usually used by the Ænglisc to patrol the Irish seas that had been disguised as traders' vessels. To a half-attentive eye, the deception would be quite obvious, but they had sailed at night and had moored at one of the more remote inlets of the Morikambe Bay to start their foray into Northland.

The riders dismounted and tethered their mounts to the trees that ran down to the waterfront. Several of them had already started chipping away at the coarse paint they had applied a week earlier to their shields, as part of the deception that they had been from the Northymbric border lands. There was no need to disguise themselves now, for Ricmund knew he would be untroubled by any riders from Kirkby.

The remaining archers, who had travelled on foot, reached the waiting horsemen less than an hour later, with still no sign of the ships. Most were too exhausted to speak to the riders and simply lay down where they had stopped marching, the opportunity to rest or sleep taken without hesitation. The archer captain, a flat-cheeked, lank-haired man from Ceaster named Wulfram, ambled over to Ricmund, who was hunched over a small fire, warming his hands.

"No ships yet, my lord?" he asked, stating the obvious.

Ricmund turned his hands over, examining his palms and then the backs, as if he was looking at them for the first time.

"No, Wulfram, as you can see," he muttered, not deigning to look up at the archer. "At this point, if the ships do not arrive within the next ten minutes, we will not set sail again before the next high tide."

"Lord, even if the tide should turn, could we not ride out onto the sands to meet the ships?" Wulfram asked.

"We could," Ricmund said, leaning back and folding his arms behind his head. "Tell him, Swiðun." He nodded towards a small man dressed in furs who was crouched near the fire, warming himself. The man, a stranger to Wulfram, spat into the flames and wiped his nose with the back of his grubby hand.

"You could ride out there, once the tide goes out. Folk often do from the north bank over there," he said pointing off to his right, "to here, or even over to Hest on the south side of the bay. A fair eight miles that. But ride out? Aye, you could, a good few miles even; that's if you've not got stuck in one of the pools, or sunk in the mud. Or even worse, got trapped in the quicksand. But then you think you're fine, as the sea is out in the distance, at the furthest point of the horizon and you convince yourself that you have hours, for no tide can cover the ground between you and the far-off waves so quickly. And then you turn around and realise that the tide doesn't come in a nice even line, and that even though the sea is still far away, you're now stood on an island of sand, for there are now channels and rivers behind you as the water is swelling, an island that is growing ever smaller. Those streams become rivers and those rivers finally swell and merge into small lakes that finally swallow you up. And the tide never comes in, but the entire bay is now underwater." He spat again into the fire, which had started to hiss with the first few drops of rain.

"So the answer is no," Wulfram replied testily, annoyed by the tone and deprecating manner that locals often use with outsiders, when discussing subjects that only locals could possibly know about.

"Swiðun is the guide we picked up at Setburg," Ricmund explained. The day before the ambush in the Lon gorge, the Ænglisc soldiers had ridden east to Setburg, a small town that sat on the borders of Westmoringaland and the West and North Thriths of Jorvik. Camping outside on the first night, they had ambushed a small patrol of Northlandic riders whose bodies they had taken with them and then later left at the site of the attack on the royal caravan.

"We have you to thank then, for having guided us through these hills and valleys," Wulfram said. It was almost honest gratitude, for if they had not had a man who knew the area well, they would have been truly lost. He was used to the open fields and rolling hills of Ceasterscir, not the dark, wet narrow valleys and mountains of the borderlands.

"Don't thank me," Swiðun smirked. "Thank your Lord Swegen, for he is most generous with his recompense."

Wulfram chuckled. "Every man has his price, I suppose."

The elderly tracker scratched at a louse under his arm, and fixed the captain with a bloodshot stare.

"Do not get me wrong," he started. "I have my pride, I am not easily bought. But I consider myself Saxon. My mother and father are Saxon, as were their parents before them. What I do now, I do for Ængland, for I consider them my kin, not some Norse king in Jorvik and the mongrels that his fellow invaders have spawned. A weak Ængland led by a young girl and her greedy advisers is not what I wish to see; a strong Ængland, led by an Ænglisc king who can one day reunite the two kingdoms is my dream."

"Then we were lucky to have found you," Wulfram replied, the slight undertone of sarcasm not completely hidden.

"I am not alone in my sentiments, believe me. There are others like me, some in high places," Swiðun said, leaving the last sentence hanging.

"Such as our blessed Vinder," snorted Ricmund, who was now lain flat out on the beach, his eyes half closed.

The guide snorted and shook his head.

"You know as well as I do, Lord Ricmund, that his motives have little to do with ideology. Power, my lord, power and money."

Wulfram sat down and made himself more comfortable in front of the fire, its flames edged blue and green by the salt-weathered wood.

"So what did Swegen promise the sheriff?" he asked, stretching his tired feet out on the sand. Ricmund pulled a face to show he either did not know or did not care, his features contorting unusually due to the thick scar that ran down the left side of his face.

"Who knows? I'm guessing that in exchange for sending out only a handful of soldiers to protect Adelise, he would expect to become Jarl of Westmoringaland, at the very least, should Swegen ever become king."

"King of Ængland or King of Northland?" Swiðun asked, grinning.

"Here's hoping for both," Ricmund said. "As soon as the news of the terrible attack by the savage Northlanders upon our glorious little queen reaches home, than there shall be more than good reason to finally go to war." He used a tone of mock horror at the outrageous massacre.

Wulfram forced a smile too, but inwardly, he felt a pang of anguish. He had convinced himself that it was for the greater good, but he could not dismiss the previous day's actions as callously or as happily as Ricmund or Swiðun.

"When will the news reach Ængland?" Wulfram asked. Ricmund lay still and did not answer. Wulfram sat in silence, watching the low, grey waves lap at the stones on the water's edge, the sound of the gentle wind rustling the dark, damp trees that lined the inlet. Wulfram was about to repeat his question, when Ricmund appeared to stir, leaning to one side and breaking wind loudly.

"I'd imagine about a week or so. The Northlanders will hopefully have picked up that bovine, gormless creature we left there, by now. She'll tell them she was a maid in the caravan, and that Northymbric riders attacked them. If they don't kill her, that is," the Eoten chuckled. "Then the news of the tragedy will be sent to Lonborg, then to Ceaster. I'd give it a week."

"What if they don't believe her?" Wulfram pressed, his tone starting to annoy Ricmund, like that of an overly curious child.

At that moment a shout went up from one of the resting horsemen. Ricmund turned to see a rider pointing out to the bay. He followed the man's raised hand and saw what they had been waiting for – a dark red sail and the bow of a low, long ship had rounded the southern shore of the headlands and was making towards the inlet.

"About bloody time too," Ricmund said, standing up and stretching. He waved once at the approaching ship, which was now joined by a second, similarly sized vessel. The ships were coming into the inlet just as the tide was starting to turn to go back out. Any later, and they would have been stranded on the flats for hours. Ricmund strode over to where he had tethered his horse to a tree trunk, took the reins and then called to the assembled soldiers.

"We board immediately; anyone caught out dawdling will be left behind. I do not want to be stranded in this godforsaken place for another twelve hours. By this time tomorrow, we shall be in Ceaster up to our eyeballs in coin and whores!"

A cheer went up from the tired soldiers. The shore quickly

became a hive of activity, full of men preparing themselves and their horses for boarding ships that would only have a few precious minutes to get back out of the shallow channel. Wulfram, much to Ricmund's annoyance, had one more question.

"With all due respect, my Lord Ricmund. Is it wise to board in daylight and risk being seen? Should we not perhaps wait until the next high tide, this evening?"

"Stop worrying, Wulfram. Who's going to see us? A couple of fishermen? What if they do? What's going to happen? We know the sheriff is not going to send any men out to hunt for us, should he hear reports of strange men camping on the coast. We know what he has done; remember that," he said with a wry grin. "Vinder is our man now."

Kirkby Kendale

When they heard the sound of breaking glass, the two guards shoulder-barged the door open. It took three attempts before the legs of the chair jammed under the handle on the other side splintered and the door flew open. Swords drawn, they charged into the room to find Vinder slumped in his chair. A small window had been broken, leaving the wind blowing in, stirring up the smoke and scattering papers around the room. One of the guards knelt by the recumbent sheriff and patted him roughly on the cheek, urging him to wake up. The second guard, the man Vinder had referred to as Sveyn, simply picked up the pewter of water and poured it over the sheriff's head. He awoke with a jolt, snorting with indignation. He put a hand gingerly to his temple and then stared groggily into the eyes of the two guards.

"The boy," he slurred, sounding drunk. "Tried to kill me. Find him." He paused a moment and his eyes flickered. "Kill him. Then find that girl. The one found on the moors. Kill her too."

The two guards looked at each other for a moment, doubting whether their lord still had his wits about him, for there was no doubting he had suffered a vicious blow.

"Do it now!" Vinder shouted, all traces of grogginess suddenly gone. The two men ran out of the room, calling out to any other guards in the vicinity. Vinder tried to sit up straighter, but his limbs felt weak. He didn't even try to stand up, for he knew his legs would not take his weight for another few minutes. He flailed an arm behind him, trying to reach a cup of ale on the table. His head was still spinning from Thurstan's blow and he was desperate for a drink, so much so that he did not hear the noises coming from the chimneybreast in the far corner of the room.

He did not notice the scratching sounds that came, or the soot and dust that fell into the unlit hearth until two leather-booted feet extended downwards into view, followed by a grime-covered and grim-faced Thurstan.

"You! I—" the sheriff managed, before Thurstan strode across the room and struck him hard again, a fist to the temple. Vinder collapsed back into his chair. Thurstan quickly checked the sheriff's breathing, making sure he had not done more harm than intended, picked up Vinder's dropped dagger and then sprinted out of the room.

He ran through the antechamber and down the stairs that led to the ground floor rooms of the private living quarters. The building seemed abandoned, with any guards that had been inside now out in the bailey's courtyard searching for Thurstan. He paused by the door that led outside, knowing that the yard and walls would be filled with people looking for him. He slowly opened the door a couple of inches and peered out. Sure enough, the bailey was as active as an ants' nest that had been poked with a twig. Although a dozen or so guards were searching for him, the one place they did not seem to be looking at was the building from which he was supposed to have escaped. Knowing he had little time before the soldiers returned to Vinder, Thurstan closed the door and turned back to the room.

Thurstan had never cared for the tapestries with which Vinder had lined the rooms of the stone building, but he offered a quick thanks to the old fool as he tore one from the wall. He rolled it up and held it over one of the several braziers that warmed the rooms. The dry canvas quickly flared up and made a crude torch, which Thurstan gingerly held by the other end. Walking swiftly over to the door, he once again checked the activity in the bailey.

Convinced no-one was watching the door, he slipped out into the courtyard and strode purposely towards the infirmary. He had long ago learnt that if you wanted to avoid unwanted attention, just act as if you had an important purpose for going somewhere; even if you had a rolled, lit tapestry in your hand.

Following the outer wall of the fort towards the infirmary, Thurstan passed the armoury. As casually as a man spat onto the ground, he tossed the lit tapestry onto the thatched roof of the low building and carried on walking. At this point, Thurstan thought, it was irrelevant whether he was seen or not, he just had to cause as much chaos as possible.

And the torch had done just that. Within seconds, a shout had gone up from the other side of the courtyard from one of the stableboys that the armoury was alight. Those men who hadn't already been searching for Thurstan now rushed to the well, searching for buckets with which to extinguish the flames. Those who had been searching were momentarily drawn towards the burning building. Unseen or ignored by them all, Thurstan slipped into the infirmary door, hoping he was not too late.

The sister with whom Thurstan had spoken earlier in the day was standing at the foot of Adelise's pallet. An armed soldier, sword drawn was gesturing towards the sister, his intentions quite clear. Thurstan hurried, treading lightly, slowing only to pull Vinder's dagger from his belt. The sister saw Thurstan approaching over the shoulder of the guard and started to appeal to him for help. Thurstan sprang forward and before the soldier could raise his sword, he sank the blade into the man's throat. Clasping his other hand over the spluttering man's mouth, Thurstan let the man sink to the floor. Blood sprayed from the dying man's mouth, out between Thurstan's fingers and on to the reed flooring. The sister stood transfixed, staring at the blood-drenched man that was either to be her saviour or killer.

"Do not say a word," Thurstan growled. He had no intention of slaying an innocent sister, but he had no time for explanations. He lowered the twitching guard, the dagger still lodged in his throat, to the floor as gently as a mother laying her baby to bed. The poor sister gulped and mouthed a silent prayer, then her eyes rolled backwards and she collapsed onto the floor in a dead faint, landing face-first in the dead man's blood. Thurstan paused to check her pulse before quickly turning his attention to Adelise.

"We're leaving," he said. The girl opened her eyes slightly and simply nodded. He picked Adelise up and placed her over his shoulder. Her small body seemed to weigh no more than his sword belt, her body was limp; yet her grip on the back of his tunic was surprisingly strong. He walked towards the infirmary door and opened it slightly. The roof of the armoury was burning brightly and commanding the attention of most of the bailey, so Thurstan simply stepped out and headed towards the stables.

He kept his head down and walked quickly. Anyone with any semblance of their wits about them would have immediately stopped him to ask why he had a young girl over his shoulder, but the panic and confusion that he had hoped for had truly gripped the bailey. The smell of burnt thatch hung heavy in the air, burning strands of straw floating around the walls, threatening to set other buildings alight. He was almost at the stable door when a scream came from the infirmary; the sister had evidently come round to find herself with a face full of blood. Without looking behind him, Thurstan ran the remaining few yards to the stable gates and kicked the door open.

There were only two stableboys tending the horses at this hour. They were not going to challenge an armed huskarl, whether he was carrying a child over his shoulder or not. They simply gawped at Thurstan as he hurried over to Svarnat. A small, freckled boy of no more than twelve years had been combing the horse's mane as Thurstan laid the girl on the stable floor, picked up a saddle and threw it onto the mare's back.

"But lord," he started. Thurstan bent down towards the boy until their faces were just inches apart.

"Piss off," he said quietly and the expression in Thurstan's eyes convinced the boy that that really was the best thing to do.

Thurstan tightened the saddle and then placed Adelise across the pommel. The girl seemed almost asleep, yet her eyes were wide open. He patted the mare's flanks to calm her then climbed up into the saddle. At that point, the stable door burst open to reveal two armed soldiers, silhouetted by the flickering light of the burning armoury. Thurstan kicked his heels back and spurred Svarnat forward. Before the two men had chance to swing their short swords, the horse was out into the orange-bathed bailey.

"Close the gates! Stop him!" a voice shouted from somewhere behind Thurstan. The entrance to the fort was slowly being pushed shut, as too late the soldiers realised the identity of the man on horseback. Svarnat sprang through the narrowing gap between the large wooden gates and out into the town of Kirkby. The gates clattered together and immediately the same voices that had ordered them closed screamed for them to be opened again.

Thurstan guided Svarnat through the narrow streets between the low wooden buildings of Kirkby, scattering villagers as he rode. His ears were still ringing, but now the rush of adrenaline and the sound of the wind brought a new level of awareness, a heightened sense of being alive and of having a purpose. Arrows were being fired into the village from the fort's stone walls, but none of them with any accuracy. The only thing they managed to achieve was to cause more panic among the villagers, hindering the horsemen that were now streaming out of the re-opened gates.

Svarnat sprang from between the last of the houses at the edge of Kirkby, into open countryside and Thurstan gave a cry of joy and relief. He glanced behind him and saw horsemen; he was not free of pursuers yet, not by a long way. On any other day Thurstan would have expected Svarnat to easily outride them, but then he would not normally be riding with a nine-year-old girl slung across his saddle.

As Svarnat streaked away from Kirkby, Thurstan heard a muffled yelp come from the small body across his saddle. Glancing down at the young girl, Thurstan could make out, despite the jolts and the blur of the road beneath them, that she was being bounced quite severely on the front of his saddle. Every hoofbeat of Svarnat sent a shudder through her small frame, lying as she was front down across the pommel.

Slowing slightly, Thurstan took the reins with one hand and pressed his other across her forehead. She was drenched with sweat, yet felt cold, much as she had when they had rested in Grarigg. She was wearing just the simple tunic that the sisters had dressed her in and a cloak he had found in the stables. He reached down to check Adelise's breathing, laying his hand on her shoulder. Despite the horse's motion, Thurstan could sense that she was shivering. He could also feel a sticky wetness on his fingers. With a sinking heart, he held his hand up to his eyes; hoping it was nothing more than sweat.

It was blood and lots of it.

He slowed Svarnat down to a slow canter, not even daring to glance behind him to see how close the other horsemen now were. Pushing Adelise's long, dank hair and cloak aside, he could see a large, fresh patch of crimson on her shoulder. The ride had caused the wound to reopen and she was losing blood. Thurstan swore aloud and slapped his saddle in frustration.

If he slowed now he would never make it to Lonborg before his pursuers ran him down, yet if he pushed on, then he would surely kill the girl. The only alternative would be to leave the road and take a slower, less direct route to Lonborg.

Thurstan pulled Svarnat up to a complete halt and took stock of his surroundings. The road here kinked around a small hill with thick woods on either side. For the time being, he was out of view of his pursuers.

Whichever choice I make, Thurstan thought, *I am sure that with hindsight it will be the wrong one.* He offered up a silent prayer to whichever gods were playing with him on this day, before kicking his heels back. Without looking behind him, he led Svarnat off the road and into the woods.

"What do you mean, they have gone?" Vinder demanded. He was slumped in a chair from which he had yet to rise, such was his dizziness. Sluta was kneeling before him, nervously delivering the news he had feared to hear. Vinder vaguely recognised the gormless features of the oaf before him. The young idiot had been one of the patrol huskarls until recently, but had volunteered to become a sentry – a great step down for most soldiers. Lazy as well as useless then, Vinder thought. Sluta swallowed nervously and glanced down at his feet.

"The huskarl, Thurstan," he stammered, knowing that each mention of the name caused the sheriff to flinch. "He escaped us, my lord, and he has taken the girl with him. Sister Magdalene was cruelly struck down; she could not stop him."

"You expected a sister to do your job for you?" Vinder scowled and then winced in pain. Two elderly women were trying to bind the wound on his forehead with a poultice and linen. Vinder waved them away angrily and gingerly touched his bandage.

"Leave us," he ordered the women, slapping a hand away when one of them tried to tighten the bandages before leaving the room. He waited for the door to close behind them before beckoning the young sentry over.

"They are a thousand places to hide between here and Lonborg. They could be anywhere by now."

"You think they are going to Lonborg, my lord?" Sluta asked.

"It would make sense, I imagine."

"Why?" the young soldier asked. "Why not flee into the hills or to the coast?"

Vinder opened his mouth to speak, but then stopped. He shifted uneasily in his chair and rubbed his forehead. His thoughts were confused; he was forgetting what he had told to whom and what each person ought to know.

"What state was the girl in?" he asked, changing tack.

"Sister Magdalene said that she was in a very deep sleep, very weak," the man replied.

"I can't imagine them galloping straight to Lonborg in that state, do you? No, no, we can cut them off before there. Get a rider to Lonborg immediately. Get a message to the jarl that a traitor to the kingdom has stolen from me, attempted to kill me and kidnapped a young girl. They must reach there before the huskarl. Then take some of the remaining huskarls and find him."

"I understand, my lord," the sentry replied after the briefest of pauses. "Though, actually, I don't understand, my lord."

"What?" Vinder snapped. "What is there not to understand?"

"Why would Thur... the huskarl take the girl with him?" Sluta ventured. The sheriff sank bank into his chair.

"Who knows?" he snorted dismissively, with a wave of a hand. "Who knows what lies in the minds of the perverse and sick in mind?"

"Then she is to be rescued?" the sentry asked.

Vinder stared at him and let the sound of the crackling braziers fill the room. "If they should be found, you will obviously kill the man who tried to slay me. The girl," he sighed. "The girl I fear has been, shall we say, polluted by him. Kill her too."

"Kill her, my lord?" Sluta, the sentry, looked up.

"Yes. Kill her and discard of the body. I do not want their corpses back here. Do I make myself clear?" Vinder asked, before adding in a quieter voice, "Captain?"

Sluta grinned.

"Perfectly, my lord."

Svarnat slowed to a halt as Thurstan scanned the unfamiliar hills around him. The sun was setting in the west now, bathing the sky in a pink haze and casting long shadows across the small valley in which he now found himself. The sound of rushing wind and clattering hoofbeats was replaced by a soft breeze in the long grass, the dusk chorus of birds and the quick, rasping breaths that he realised were coming from himself. Thurstan breathed deeply and the smells of the damp countryside filled his nostrils for the first time, for it seemed to him that loud noises could drown out the other senses.

Thurstan swore to himself; he had hoped that they were east of the River Ken, but looking around him, he realised that he was now well west of the Great South Road and the Ken estuary was between him and Lonborg.

He also became aware of Adelise's breathing, or rather, the worrying lack of it. He reached down and gently turned the young girl face up. She was still breathing, still bleeding too, but now seemed unresponsive to his touch. He spoke her name softly, and placed a hand to her forehead, to which there was the briefest flicker of recognition, but nothing more.

At that moment, Thurstan heard a distant shout and turned to see two horsemen, around a mile behind him in the bottom of the valley. The horsemen were hailing an elderly crofter that Thurstan has passed several minutes before, outside his stone cottage. Thurstan could see even from this distance that they were armed and impatient. He made out the crofter pointing towards him on the hilltop and the two riders immediately kicked back and spurred their horses in his direction.

Thurstan carefully made sure Adelise was safely secured over the saddle and then slapped Svarnat's neck and urged the horse into a gallop. If he could keep out of his pursuers' clutches until nightfall then the myriad of small valleys and inlets would surely afford him somewhere to keep hidden until the following morning.

Thurstan spurred Svarnat down the other side of the hilltop, temporarily out of view of the pursuing horsemen, and caught a glimpse of the Morikambe Bay. The setting sun reflected in golden flashes from the shallow waters and sands as they descended into the final small valley that led to the coast. From above, Thurstan had seen a village, smoke rising from fires marking the settlements. He was not entirely sure which village, unfamiliar as he was with this part of Westmoringaland, but he guessed he must have been in the area of Eilifthwaite. The village nestled on the water's edge, where the sharply sloping land made all but a thin strip of coastline suitable for habitation. Thurstan aimed towards the village, slowing Svarnat, not wanting to attract undue attention. He glanced behind him, but there was thankfully no sign of his pursuers having crested the top of the valley yet.

Svarnat was keeping a steady pace on the open land, but Thurstan knew that he would not be able to keep it up for much longer. The horse was tiring and would have to be led across the sands by hand, if they could cross tonight at all. The safest option, he decided, would be to find a barn or a small wood, to hide in overnight. Hell, he could even face down two horsemen if he had to, he thought optimistically, just as Adelise gave another small groan. Tomorrow, they could maybe find another horse, swap clothes with some villagers, or steal if he must, and slowly make their way along the coast, around the edge of the bay towards Lonborg. A longer ride, but a safer one. Once there, he could find rest at his family's home and a well-placed bribe to a guard or sentry would maybe discover whether he was a wanted man outside of Kirkby.

He relaxed slightly at this thought; a warm bed and familiar faces, when he heard a shout from his right and a horseman burst from a copse at the western end of the hillside. With a cry, Thurstan slapped Svarnat's flank and pushed her forward, urging her to use all her remaining strength to lose this new pursuer. Angling the horse now away from Eilifthwaite and to the east, he desperately tried put as much distance between himself and the horseman as possible, heading towards the rocky coastline that ran between the hillside and the sands of the Morikambe.

"Stop, in the name of the sheriff!" came a wind-muffled shout. Thurstan did not even look back, but leant lower in his saddle, urging the mare onwards, one hand gripping the back of Adelise's sweat-sodden tunic.

The road from Eilifthwaite led on to open, marshy fields and Thurstan saw with dismay, around a mile ahead, three, maybe four, more riders, heading towards him. They must have followed the Great South Road and come westwards to cut him off, while he had been floundering in woods and crossing streams. Glancing up to his left, he could see the two horsemen who had followed him from the previous valley now riding down the hillside towards him.

"Hell's fires!" Thurstan shouted and hauled hard on his reins to the right. The sands of the Morikambe Bay, which for the moment seemed so flat and inviting, were his only choice now. The tide was out, leaving an open stretch of sand that disappeared into the horizon to the south; a stretch of sand that could be under feet of water within a matter of minutes – and no man could cross the bay to the other side of the Ken estuary in less than an hour.

Thurstan turned in his saddle to see that his nearest pursuer was no more than a couple of hundred yards behind. He turned back just as Svarnat leapt across a ditch between the road and the narrow strip of scrub grass and reeds that lined the pebbled beach.

"Stop there!" the rider's voice came again and again, each time closer than before. Thurstan pushed Svarnat on, crossing the seaweed-strewn line that separated the pebbles from the sands.

Just as they reached the open sands, Svarnat skidded violently, pitching Thurstan to one side. He pulled hard on the reins, but the sound of a loud snap rang out like a whip crack. The mare reared up and screamed in pain and with gut-wrenching despair, Thurstan instantly knew what had happened. He glanced down at her flailing legs and could clearly see a compound break of her left foreleg.

Thurstan gripped the reins with one hand and clung on to Adelise with the other, struggling to get the mare under control. He leant forward with all his weight, trying to calm the horse by calling her name. Svarnat reared again and swirled on her hind legs in fear and distress, then for just a second she put her right foreleg down on the sand, giving Thurstan a moment to dismount.

Thurstan leapt on to the sand, Svarnat's reins still in his blistered hands. At first, his knees almost gave way upon landing on the soft ground, his legs numb from the ride. He pulled the reins towards him, trying to stop Svarnat from rearing up as Adelise was still laid across his saddle, all the while attempting to avoid the grotesquely flapping broken limb. The pursuing rider was now less than a hundred yards away, about to cross the dirt road. Aware that there was no time to soothe the animal, Thurstan pulled the mare's head towards him. Her eyes were red, wild and filled with pained madness; the horse that he had loved and cared for was no longer there. He held her gaze for a moment and then, seizing the small girl's body, he let the reins go and left Svarnat to thrash around in agony on the sands.

Thurstan turned and ran a few paces, putting some distance between himself and the stricken mare, then set Adelise down on the wet sand and drew his sword. The pursuing rider had ridden around Svarnat and already had his blade drawn. Thurstan had just seconds to position himself as his pursuer was almost upon him. There was no cold calculation, no slowing of time where he could sidestep to the rider's left side and strike out; the exhausted Thurstan simply screamed and held his sword up, leaping, almost stumbling back at the last minute as the rider hacked down. He closed his eyes, expecting a killing blow and felt a crunch of steel against bone, before opening his eyes.

Glancing down he saw that his body was intact and that the hunched-up shape of Adelise a few paces behind him was unharmed. Then a shriek of pain caused him to look up; the rider was clasping the stump of what had been his right arm. His sword, gloved hand still gripping it, lay a few feet away, leaving a spray of fine, dark blood on the sand. The horse wheeled off back towards the pebbled shore, depositing its mewing and bleeding rider on the sand.

Thurstan attempted to run over to Adelise, but the best he could manage was a lurching hobble. He picked up her feather-light body, pausing only to check he could sense the faintest of breaths, and placed her over his shoulder.

Thurstan turned back towards the shore, the sword still in his hand, and saw that the remaining pursuers had now converged on the road in a group, but were not immediately riding out to strike him down. He waved the bloodied blade in a futile gesture of defiance, then turned and started walking across the Morikambe, waiting for the sound of the hooves in the soft sand to signal his impending death. It was around a three-mile walk from here to Seolferdale, the nearest village on the other side of the Ken estuary, a walk that would take at least an hour and a half, perhaps two.

"Thurstan Ælfsson, you miserable son of a whore, come back here!" shouted a voice that made Thurstan stop. He turned and recognised the lead rider as Sluta, the treacherous bastard who'd attacked him in the stables. He stared at his erstwhile companion for the briefest of moments, then turned back and continued walking to the far shore. The sand, although wet, felt hard underfoot, and Thurstan could keep a good pace on this surface, despite carrying the girl over his shoulder. Sadly, he thought, so could horses.

"Thurstan! Come back! I promise you no harm!" Sluta shouted across the sands. There was no response from the fleeing huskarl. The group of horsemen now numbered six and they sat impatiently, waiting for orders from Sluta; the once-huskarl, now-sentry who appeared to be in a position of authority again.

The agonised whinnying from Svarnat was making their mounts nervous and a few shifted uneasily in their saddles. Sluta spat onto the grass. He rubbed his elbow, which was still sore from when Thurstan had nearly broken his arm. It still clicked noisily whenever he tried to hold anything heavier than a dagger or shortsword. "Will someone go put that fucking horse out of its misery?" he snapped angrily.

Thurstan paused only briefly as the sound of Svarnat's pained cries stopped suddenly. He turned to see a dismounted rider wiping his blade down with a handful of sand and his once-sleek mount lying still on the sand. He turned back and pressed on towards Seolferdale, crossing the first of many small streams of saltwater, some running seawards, some running upriver.

Knowing that Sluta was in the pursuing pack had oddly given him some hope. Sluta, he thought, was more likely to make a decision based on hatred and a vindictive desire to wreak revenge than on common sense or guile.

"Thurstan!" the voice came again. "Thurstan! It's for your own good. The tide is coming in."

Thurstan glanced up and shifted the weight of Adelise's slight body to one side to afford him a better view of the horizon. There was no telling from this point where the wet sands ended and the sea started, but it was just possibly nearer than it had been when Thurstan had first ridden down the hillside. He pressed on and for the first time, his foot sank a few inches into the sand of the bay. The surface here was pitted in a shell-shaped pattern, each depression filled with a tiny puddle of water; it was no longer the hard sand nearer the coast.

"Thurstan! Come back!" There was no request this time in the voice; it was a command, almost a shriek. With a wave of his hand, Sluta sent two riders out on to the sands to ride Thurstan and Adelise down. The remaining four horsemen edged their horses out to the edge of the pebble beach and watched the two mounted huskarls gallop out towards the fleeing figures. Wet sand sprayed up from the hooves of their mounts as they covered the first hundred yards across the hard sand towards Thurstan in no time. Sluta clapped his hands in anticipation, shouting encouragement at the other three horsemen.

Turning to see the approaching riders, Thurstan hobbled forward quickly and leapt over another of the myriad of small streams, all of which now appeared to be flowing back in towards the coast. His boots sank in the soft sand and he stopped to catch his breath. His mouth felt dry and salty, his nostrils filled with the smell of rotting seaweed and sand. He set Adelise gently down on her back, hoping the salt water from the damp sand would not seep through her cloak and tunic to her wound. Turning, he watched the two horsemen getting ever nearer. They had covered over half the distance between the shoreline and Thurstan in less than a minute. Thurstan drew his sword, the blade still encrusted with sand and blood from the previous rider, and held it aloft in defiance.

The two riders were only fifty yards from Thurstan as they approached another stream between sandbanks. The lead rider leapt and his horse's hooves disappeared into the soft sand as it landed. He was thrown heavily from the mount as it crashed to the ground, both its forelegs broken from the momentum of its heavy body. The second rider swiftly wheeled his horse round to stop it from jumping the small stream. Thurstan watched with trepidation, slowly stepping backwards towards Adelise.

The fallen rider clumsily got to his feet, drew out his sword and put his wounded animal out of its misery. Without a glance towards Thurstan, he turned and staggered back towards the shore. The remaining rider watched his departing companion and then kicked his heels back, urging his horse forward. Instead of jumping the small stream, he trod lightly through it, hoping to avoid the same fate of his companion. His mount, though, smelt the blood of the slain horse lying no more than ten yards away, its nostrils flaring in fear at the scent and at the water. The rider shouted at the horse to push on, but the first hoof placed forwards sank deeply into the sand, forcing him to retreat onto firmer ground.

Thurstan turned and picked Adelise back up and started to walk backwards, away from the frustrated horseman, but keeping him in view. Looking further back, beyond the rider, he could see that the first stream he had crossed from the shore had now tripled in width, if not more, becoming a small, shallow river.

The rider was now standing in his stirrups, gauging the distance between himself and Thurstan. Without a word, he unslung the gungar from his back, hefted it once in his gloved hand and then launched it towards the fugitives. Thurstan watched the flight of the spear as it flew quickly and quivering towards them, sidestepping at the last moment, leaving it to slam into the sand, a good eight inches of the blade and shaft forced into the surface. Thurstan placed Adelise down gently and then, gripping the shuddering spear, returned the compliment of attacking silently.

He threw the gungar towards the mounted rider who, struggling with the low sun in his eyes, saw the spear at the last second. He kicked his horse forward, but too late to avoid the gungar completely, which caught the horse's hind leg. The wound, although nothing more than superficial, caused the horse to panic and bolt towards the widening streams and the shore, leaving the rider nothing more than a cursing passenger.

Back on the shore, Sluta cried out in anger and frustration, seeing Thurstan and the girl hobbling further and further away across the sands. The huskarl whose forearm had been sliced off was lying moitionless on the sands; his blood was streaking the sand red with each lap of the incoming tide.

"Dismount!" Sluta shouted at the remaining three huskarls. "We'll have to do it ourselves, on foot."

"But, Captain," one of the huskarls protested, hesitating.

"What?" Sluta replied, dismounting and drawing his sword.

"Should one of us not ride to Seolferdale or Arnulfhead to meet them on the other side, to track them?" he suggested, looking down at the angry, bearded face of Sluta.

"No," Sluta said, shaking his head wildly. "We kill them now, we kill them quickly. I'll not have you slunking off for another ride through the countryside. Get off that horse and go kill them."

The remaining riders stepped out onto the sand and pressed on. To their left, the rider with the bolting horse had either managed to dismount or been thrown off and was now limping towards Sluta.

"Not to me, to him!" Sluta shouted, pointing towards Thurstan. Sluta spat again, his mouth full of the salty taste of the sand that was already encrusted in the fur collar of his cloak.

"I'm coming for you, Thurstan! I'm coming for you!" Sluta screamed, his voice become hoarse with the shouting.

Thurstan had seen the other riders dismount but paid no heed to Sluta's shrieking. He pushed on, the once light weight of Adelise's body starting to feel ever heavier. His breath was coming in short bursts, each step taking twice the effort of a normal step on dry land. The back of his throat felt as if it was burning, his mouth and lips covered with an unpleasant salty film.

Each step became more laboured, each small stream wider and each footprint he left deeper. The minutes passed as hours and all the time his pursuers were gaining. Not as quickly as they could have, for they too were slowed by the sand, but surely and steadily they were gaining. Thurstan looked to his right, into the distance. The sea did not seem that much nearer, but the first small stream he had crossed had developed into what now appeared to be a main channel into the river estuary.

The rider of the slain horse had now staggered back to meet Sluta's advancing group. The huskarl's face was a glistening white colour, save for an ugly purple bruise on his left temple where his helmeted head had slammed into the sand

"Get my horse," Sluta said, gripping him by the shoulder, "And ride to Seolferdale; alert any men there, wait for them on the shore, then kill them." The injured rider winced and squinted at Sluta in confusion. The man was not even sure he could stagger to the coast, let alone mount a horse and ride around the estuary. Before he could reply, Sluta was gone, pressing ahead with his three remaining men.

Thurstan glanced back across the sands, trying to judge how quickly he was being caught or whether it was possible to put any distance between himself and his pursuers. Each time he tried to run or at least walk more quickly, the force of his footsteps drove his boots down into the wet sand. The promontory of Seolferdale now seemed as close in front of him as Eilifthwaite did behind him, but with no visible buildings on the coastline and the setting sun casting everything into a murky shadow, he was struggling to judge distances. It seemed impossible to tell whether he was looking at shrubs on the shoreline or more distant trees. There was one recognisable shape though; a ship, he could see now, facing seawards, but with no sail unfurled. From here, it seemed like a small trading vessel, perhaps anchored up on the beach waiting for the tide to come in. From behind him, Thurstan heard another insult and shout; he lowered his head and pressed on, thinking no more about the ship.

Sand was now filling Thurstan's boots, wet sand that was acting like a scourer on his skin, each footstep scraping his feet raw. He could not go on like this, he thought, he would not outrun his pursuers, and were his pace to drop any more, he might not even outrun the tide.

A distant scream caused him to turn, as it did to Sluta and his men too. The sound had come from the thrashing black shape of the injured huskarl trying to make his way back to the shore. He had tried to cross the first channel that was now as wide and fast-flowing as many inland rivers. He had either been too heavy, in full leather armour, or the blow he had taken had rendered him unable to swim. He waved his arms frantically for a few seconds before sinking, his head resurfacing momentarily before permanently disappearing from view.

Thurstan saw Sluta gesticulate before urging his men forward. Putting Adelise down on the sand, Thurstan quickly pulled his boots off. Standing on leg at a time, he tugged at the leather straps around the tops of the boots, which clung damply to his feet. Tossing them aside onto the sand, he picked up Adelise again, placing her as gently as he possibly could over his shoulder and set off with renewed vigour over the sands.

The initial sensation of the cold wet sand on his bare feet was now refreshing, instead of painful and his pace increased to a slow run. He had let Sluta and his men catch him further; the nearest was only a hundred yards away now.

The low sun was glaring off the wet sand, making it ever more difficult to see where water or sand started or finished. Thurstan kept his head low and his legs moving. There was a burning in his calves and his shins felt as if nails had been driven into them. He dared to glance at the coastline in front of him and his heart skipped a beat as he realised he was nearing the far shore. The nearest pursuing huskarl, however, was also much nearer. Although booted and well-armed, he had made ground on Thurstan.

Approaching the ship that he had thought to be moored on the far shore, Thurstan could see that it was actually stuck on a sandbank. Evidently, it had tried to leave on the last tide, but had been caught out by the ever-changing channels and was now waiting for the next opportunity to get afloat. There was a slight flicker of movement on the deck, but Thurstan could not make out any figures. Heading straight for it, he imagined he could at least use to it to give him cover from Sluta's sight.

Thurstan could hear the splashing feet of his nearest pursuer, even his panting. He was not going to make it to shore before being hacked down, as there was at least another quarter of a mile yet. He placed Adelise down on the sand once again; each time it felt a great weight had been unburdened; each time he picked her back up, she felt as if she weighed nothing. The nearest huskarl was only twenty yards behind him, Sluta a further fifty. The huskarl didn't say anything, he merely grunted as he raised his sword, his breath coming in ragged gasps. Thurstan pulled his sword out and planted his feet wide apart, almost squatting, waiting for the first blow.

Sluta shouted something inaudible to Thurstan; his ears were filled with the sounds of his own lung-bursting breathing and the rush of adrenaline. Just before the huskarl reached him, Thurstan sensed movement behind him. The huskarl's eyes flicked upwards then widened in surprise, but Thurstan did not dare risk a glance behind. A brief look of confusion crossed the pursuing huskarl's face, before a black-fleeted arrow buried itself in his forehead and Thurstan threw himself to the sand.

Ricmund the Eoten was in a foul mood. One of the two ships his men had boarded that morning to sail back to Ængland had only gone and grounded on a sandbank at the next village down the river channel. As his accursed luck would have it, it was the one he had chosen to travel on. The tide had gone out quicker than they could sail and they had been stuck like some beached whale on the bay for nearly half a day now. The ship's captain, it seemed, had not factored in the extra weight of horses and men compared to his usual commercial cargo, when estimating how much time he would have to get in and out of the channel.

After the initial cursing, shouting and beating of the captain, Ricmund had resigned himself to waiting for the next high tide. He had stationed himself in the one half-decent wooden chair on board the vessel, drinking the captain's personal bottle, which might have been wine, possibly something else; Ricmund was past the point of caring and just happy to drink. The captain was currently somewhere below in the bilges, with the promise that should they not make Eswelle by noon the following day, he would be thrown overboard with the anchor firmly shoved up somewhere painful.

The sound of clattering feet came from the deck above, which much to Ricmund's disappointment, led to a knock on the door.

"What is it?" Ricmund barked. The door open slightly and the beardless face of one of the feckless younger archers peered into the room.

"Sorry, my lord, but some men have been sighted on the sands," he whispered.

Ricmund leant back in the creaking chair, his feet up against the table. He rubbed his face with his palms, to highlight how pained he was with yet another waste of his time.

"So?" he asked.

"Well, my lord. They are armed. They appear to be chasing a boy we think, we can't rightly see from the deck in the dark and everything. We think he has stolen something, but he's running away, and we reckon he's a thief or he's poor 'cos he's got no shoes or nothing, and these men, these men have swords and are shouting at him and everything..."

The boy's voice trailed off as his eyes became accustomed to the gloom of the dank quarters and he could see the expression on Ricmund's face. The buffoon had evidently drawn the short straw of interrupting the Eoten's rest.

"Soldiers, you say?" Ricmund asked.

"Yes, my lord," the boy replied.

"How many?" There was an exchange of muffled whispers from the boy back to the deck.

"Five, my lord. We think," he said, with a touch of panic in his voice.

"Does this thief carry a sword?" Ricmund asked.

Another brief babble of voices seeped down into the cabin from above.

"Yes, my lord, but he isn't holding it."

Ricmund stroked his chin. Even if Vinder had betrayed him, he thought, he couldn't have known that they'd get stuck on a sandbank, unless that was the captain's purpose all along. But no, surely Vinder wouldn't have sent only five men, unless there were other men on the nearby shore just waiting for him. It seemed unrealistic, but he had no time for this nonsense. Ricmund came to a decision.

"Kill them," he said. The captain would be tossed overboard as soon as they set sail, just for good measure. Another flurry of muffled whispers came from the door and the boy, only daring to show half his face now, started stammering.

"Speak up, boy!" Ricmund snapped.

"Captain Wulfram asks are you sure?" the boy replied, then fled as Ricmund swore loudly and stood up angrily from his chair, cracking his head on one of the low wooden beams. He stomped up the stairs onto the deck where Wulfram was being his usual, difficult self. Looking out he could see four dark figures struggling in the sand, chasing, or possibly following another man, who in turn was challenging a bootless man, who had laid something on the sand.

"Kill them," he said simply. He had no desire to waste time dealing with armed men near their ship. He did not even bother to address Captain Wulfram, but ordered his archers directly. Fifteen archers who had restrung their bows now stood up and aimed towards the men. The main group of pursuing men stopped in their tracks and their apparent leader shouted something towards them.

"What did he say?" Ricmund asked, unaccustomed to the Northlandic dialect.

"Something about being Sheriff Vinder's men I think, my lord," Wulfram replied. Ricmund paused for a moment.

"Kill them," he repeated, without any trace of emotion. Fifteen archers fired down into the sands, fifteen arrows fell. The pursuer nearest to the fleeing thief dropped dead, an arrow protruding from his forehead. One of the four other men in pursuit also died in that first volley, three arrows piercing his breast. The man who had shouted up had used him as a shield to protect himself. The suspected thief had dived to the ground and was now crawling over to the loot he had laid on the sand. Ricmund was about to turn away, leaving the archers to finish their task, when he something occurred to him. That thief's loot looked awfully like a body; possibly even that of a young girl.

"Hold your fire!" he shouted, just as the archers were about to unleash a second volley. They paused, arrows held taut against quivering bowstrings. "Bring that to me," he said pointing towards the bundle on the sand. "Kill the others."

The archers lowered their bows and stepped aside for a dozen soldiers that had been summoned by a wave of Ricmund's hand. They had been enjoying the evening's proceedings, but were now scrambling to follow Ricmund's orders. Checking weapons and buckling belts, they stepped over to the side of the ship and started lowering ropes. There was sport to be had tonight: to kill on the sands.

Thurstan had peered up from the sand in amazement to see the body of his erstwhile attacker crumple to his knees and then topple forward with a splash. He quickly scrabbled over to Adelise, checking briefly to hear a soft wheeze, picked her up and ran as hard as he could before a second volley could be fired. There was no running to the shore now; running around the ship and to the other side would leave his back open to archers. Instead, he ran southwards, the direction the ship was pointing, to give the archers the smallest angle possible from which to aim. By doing so though, he was running parallel to the coast, and more importantly, alongside a deepening channel that would become ever more difficult to cross.

Looking over his shoulder, he could see men climbing down from the ship, waving their swords. He stopped, wondering if the men on the ship were in fact in his saviours; it was possible these men were enemies of the sheriff, for he had made many amongst traders. He watched from a distance as at least ten men hacked Sluta's two companions down. These men would have been his fellow huskarls at Kirkby at one time, though not ones he had ever been acquainted with; yet the impassionate detachment with which he had watched their deaths did not strike him as strange. The men were part of a past life, a life that had betrayed him.

Sluta himself was fleeing away from the ship, westwards towards the incoming tide, pursued by the soldiers. A group of four swordsmen had detached themselves and were running towards Thurstan. For a moment, he thought perhaps they were coming to help him, but there was nothing friendly about the manner in which their swords were drawn.

Thurstan turned and ran; ran as if the pursuit across the sands was starting afresh. He had a good distance between himself and the men behind him, but they had the advantage of not having already crossed three miles of the bay. Behind him, he could hear Sluta shouting his name, but this time the shouts were begging for his help, not threatening him with death. He did not turn to look at him; he did not turn around even when the shouts became blood-curdling screams, screams that became inter-mittent as they might if someone's head was being repeatedly forced underwater or into sand. The screams abruptly fell silent and Thurstan pressed on. A hollow sense of detachment had overcome him again. Had the roles been reversed, Sluta would not have spared a moment to save Thurstan's life. His responsi-bility was the girl he carried over his shoulder, not to the man that would have slit his throat for the price of an ale.

It was almost dark now and Thurstan's field of vision

extended to a stretch of ground a few feet in front of him, an ever-repeating view of wet, rippled sand accompanied by the rhythmic pounding of his bare feet. He was aware of the soldiers behind him, but with no idea how far or near they were; at times he felt he was no longer moving, but just running on the same spot as the sands shifted beneath him. The sound of the tide, of the incoming sea seemed much closer now, somewhere off to his right, but the gloom made it impossible to see. He was aware that the channel he had been running alongside was now turning westwards, out towards the open sea. He would have to cross it soon or risk not being able to cross at all.

Without breaking step, Thurstan lurched to his left and plunged into the river of seawater. The water came up to above his knees and it was all he could do not to lose his footing in the soft riverbed and topple over. If he dropped the near-comatose Adelise into these waters, he knew he would never find her again, should she disappear under the surface. Doubling his grip on her small body, he steadied himself against the flow of the water, tensing his leg muscles. He took one step forward, pushing against the sucking force of the current and planted his leg in front of him, hoping to God that the water did not get any deeper. Step by agonising step, inches at a time, he was crossing the channel.

Halfway across, Thurstan heard a shout of triumph behind him as the swordsmen spied him in the water. Sensing they were only yards away from their quarry, three of the men leapt hurriedly into the channel, towards Thurstan. All three plunged for a moment under the water, totally submerged, caught out in their haste by the soft bed. Only two surfaced; coughing and retching from the saltwater they had ingested. The third never came up; an arm flicked out of the water and waved manically for a few seconds, before sinking beneath the waves forever.

Thurstan saw a fourth man stood hesitating on the on the far bank of the channel. This man had no sword, but had a bow strapped on his back, although he did not seem overly eager to use it. Instead, he stood against the setting sun, gazing into the churning water, clenching his fists open and closed repeatedly, watching Thurstan. Not caring for who he was, nor the reason for his uncertainty, Thurstan turned his back and pressed on.

Wulfram had stopped running just before the channel, and watched the three swordsmen foolishly throw themselves into the water. The two surviving men called him to join them, but Wulfram could not swim; in fact it was more than an inability, there was a fear: there was not a chance in hell he would launch himself into any water that went even an inch above his boots.

He watched as the fugitive slowly hauled himself and the human parcel that he carried over his shoulder out of the water and onto the sand on the far side. The unknown man stopped to look directly at Wulfram for a second and then loped off into the shadows.

Wulfram could have unslung his bow and tried a shot in the dark, but he had no interest in wasting his arrows to appease Ricmund in this folly. He had only joined the pursuit as Ricmund had ordered him directly, even though he knew about his fear of the sea. He cursed himself for having come onto the sands, for having meekly obeyed Ricmund, but most of all, he cursed the Eoten himself.

In the time that it had taken the thief to cross the channel, the intensity of the water rushing in from the sea appeared to have doubled. His two companions were struggling frantically; the water was now past their midriffs, but slowly, and in much more time than it had taken their quarry, they had made it to the other side. With no further sign of the man he presumed to have drowned, he turned to start the long walk back across the sands towards the beached ship.

Only there was no longer an expanse of sand. He was now standing on an island. In the few minutes he had been watching, a second channel had formed fifty feet behind him. Where there had previously been flat sand with no indication of anything untoward, there was now a rushing river of foaming brown water. A river, he noted with despair, which was widening and rising, as was the channel behind him, leaving him standing on an ever-shrinking circle of sand. He recalled the self-satisfied and smug words of Swiðun, and looked towards the sea. Sure enough, the tide was still far out, but the sand between the sea and the shore was now a labyrinth of deep, fast-flowing channels. He ran, backwards and forwards, looking for a place to cross, watching the water getting nearer and nearer. As the murky water washed over his feet and the froth started to lap at his ankles, he began to weep.

Thurstan was no longer aiming for the shore near Seolferdale; the unexpected beached ship had blocked his path. He was now faced with taking a more southerly route across the sands, a further three miles past the promontory on which Seolferdale and Arnulfhead lay and towards the fishing village of Hest. Thurstan was familiar with the place; the Great South Road passed through the village on its way to Lonborg and it offered a sheltered beach for the smaller boats his father sometimes employed. Hest could be used to carry goods to the north of the bay, being a short cart ride north from Lonborg, cutting out the great loop larger ships would have to make around the large headland of the Lon estuary.

In the near darkness in which he now found himself, Thurstan could see a handful of lit fires, marking the houses and cottages of Hest. The going was increasingly slower, despite his pursuers. The crossing had taken only a couple of hours, three at most perhaps, but Thurstan could no longer remember what it was like to walk on solid ground. After having crossed the main channel that had run south from the stranded ship, Thurstan had shed his remaining leather armour. If the pursuing swordsmen caught him, then no amount of armour was going to save him, for he had no energy left to defend himself. The only concession he had made was to keep his sword and belt. The latter was his only leather item remaining; he was down to his woollen undershirt and trews, and even these, when wet, felt as heavy as any armour.

Thurstan thought there could be no more than half a mile to the shore. Yet only five minutes before, he had been convinced the lights were no more than a few paces away, such was his disorientation due to the dark and exhaustion. From somewhere at the back of his mind came a flicker of caution that it would be prudent not to stagger straight into the village, should the sheriff have already sent someone ahead to wait for him. He altered his course to keep Hest slightly to his left and prayed he would soon feel soft grass under his feet.

The ground started to slope downwards, as if they were about to encounter another, final channel. Thurstan braced himself for the water, slowing his pace; but the expected splash into cold water never came. Instead, the soft patter of his bare feet on wet sand told him he could cross easily. Behind him, a shouted warning of caution told him that his pursuers had reached the same point in the dark too. Thurstan hurried his pace, pushing forward with heavy strides and then, without warning, his right foot disappeared into nothing.

One minute he was running on wet sand, the next he had disappeared up to his waist, the wet sound of the ground swallowing him like that of a rock being thrown in to a pool of mud. His first reaction was instinctively to hold Adelise up higher, above his head. His second reaction was to want to thrash about, to kick his legs to escape, but this one he resisted; he had heard the tales of quicksand victims.

Gently he lowered Adelise's now shivering body and with the gentlest of pushes, rolled her onto the sand as far in front of him as he could. Although she was still close, Thurstan knew that it was motion and weight that would suck a body down; the prostrate body of a young girl ought not to break the surface, or at least he hoped.

"Quicksand!" Thurstan called out. "Don't come any closer." He took a few breaths and tried to still his body. He hoped that his pursuers would realise that he was not worth risking their lives for, after all, who were they except opportunistic pirates from a stranded ship? He paused and gave this more thought; what type of pursuers were these that would chase him over three miles against the incoming tide? "Go back, leave me and tell your master I drowned. Save yourselves."

The two swordsmen stopped at his calling. The first man, a narrow-faced, red-haired Ænglander who understood more Northlandic than his companion, held his arm out in warning.

"Quicksand," he said to the other swordsman, whose long black braids of hair were caked with wet sand. He pointed towards the faint outline of Thurstan, his pale face just visible against the dark sand.

"He's lying. The girl is there," the dark-haired man said, shrugging off his companion's warning. The red-haired man stepped back and watched as the second swordsman stepped down the slight slope towards Thurstan, drawing his sword. He had only gone a short distance when his footsteps started to sink into the sand. He glanced around him and tried to step out of the glutinous mire, but each step he took simply took him further down.

Thurstan watched as the man neared him, preparing to defend himself with half his body trapped in the slime, but the dark-haired swordsman never made it that far. Once the sand was up to his ribcage, he started to panic. He twisted his body back and forth, trying to push himself out, but each successive effort forced him further down under the sand. He started screaming for help, imploring for Thurstan or his companion to help him. The man was not speaking Northlandic, but Thurstan understood the meaning. He understood also that it was the same odd dialect used by the Adelise's assailants.

The sand was up to the man's armpits now and his screams had become whimpers, his face a mask of pure terror. Thurstan shouted at him to stop moving, but the man either did not understand, or simply did not hear him. He continued to push down, trying to drag himself out and the sand continued to suck him down. When the sludge passed his chin, he gave one final scream before being choked off. His eyes were bulging and panic-filled as the sand passed and closed over his head. All that remained were the last few trails of filthy, long black hair on the surface, before finally they too disappeared, accompanied by a slow stream of large bubbles.

Thurstan slowly reached down to his waist and tugged at the pommel of his sword. At first, it would not move out of its scabbard, the wet sand filling the space between steel and leather, but inch by inch, he carefully pulled it free. As he brought it to the surface, he could feel the sand and mud trying to suck the weapon out of his fingers. He pulled the sword clear of the surface with a damp squelch and felt the sands shift, rushing in to occupy the empty space where his arm had been.

He checked to make sure the sands had not moved around Adelise's body, then softly leant forward and planted the sword blade down in front of him. Using the blade as a grappling hook, he dragged himself forward a few inches. Pulling the sword free from the sand, he repeated the procedure, shifting a small distance each time. He did not try to pull himself out, but waited for the ground to become just that bit firmer to allow him to free himself of the sands.

After what seemed like an eternity, when he was almost level with Adelise, Thurstan found he could place his elbows on the surface of the sand without breaking the crust. He gently pushed his knees up and found the slightest amount of resistance, using it to lever his body just a few inches further forward. He paused, waiting for the sand to settle, before trying again, this time pushing the sword as far possible into the sand and pulling himself forward. With a wet clapping noise, he was free and on the surface of the sand. He crawled over to Adelise and, as he had seemed to do so many times over the last two days, checked for that weakest of breaths, before dragging her body on to his.

Thurstan hauled himself towards the shore, crawling along the surface of the sand as a climber might scale a rock face. He stared past his feet to see the red-haired man still standing on the sandbank. The man seemed to give the gentlest of nods before turning and disappearing into the dark. Thurstan sighed and let his body go limp. He propped himself up on one elbow just in time to see his sword's hilt disappear below the surface of the sand. The sword, like his horse, had been a parting gift from his father, but he was beyond caring for sentimental possessions now; he was free.

The sound of the incoming tide reminded him that that thought was not entirely true and he resumed crawling. The crawling became a slow walk as soon as the sand underfoot felt hard enough; the walk became a light run the minute he felt pebbles start to replace the sand. All of a sudden, his almost numb feet detected grass and Thurstan knew he was ashore. Hest was to his left, Lonborg to his right and even in this moment of absolute exhaustion and near delirium, he knew he could not find shelter in either; for no place of the jarl or sheriff's would be safe for him now.

He picked up Adelise for what he hoped would be a final time and walked up the gently sloping, open fields away from the sea, the noise of the tide growing weaker with each tired step. The exhilaration of survival had numbed the pain though and the fading sound of the sea filled him only with joy. Walking across open ground seemed so easy now by comparison, his feet felt so light and agile. He crossed the Great South Road, deserted at this hour and started climbing the first small hill that formed the northern side of the Lon valley. Even the incline of this slope seemed leisurely compared to the wet sand.

After what he judged to be a mile or so from the coast and the road, Thurstan found a small copse of birch trees. He carried Adelise's damp body into the centre, where there were several old trunks offering some protection from the growing wind. He placed the young girl down and tried to make her as comfortable as possible, making sure her wound was not bleeding still. Then he lay himself down on a bed of yellowing leaves, curled into a ball and let the darkness take him.

9th May 1166
Theodford, East Anglia, Ængland

Ceolwulf closed the door to his father's sick room and quietly descended the wooden stairs to the courtyard of Theodford's longhall. Visitors had arrived, one of the servants had informed him, and were waiting for him in the main hall. It pained Ceolwulf to leave his father, but since returning from their journey north the previous week, the earl had taken to his bed and not risen again. The visit to Jorvik had, as Ceolwulf had feared, sapped what little strength his father had left, leaving him seemingly unable to fight whatever accursed disease was afflicting him.

Ceolwulf crossed the cobbled courtyard, nodding in acknowledgement at bowing stable boys. For a brief moment, he caught a glance of the new serving girl walking across to the kitchens. She had arrived at the hall only a couple of weeks previously. A freed slave from Flanders, he had been told, who had preferred to remain in service in Ængland than return home. He slowed his pace for a moment, and then she was lost from view.

From within the longhall's walled enclosure he could hear the morning activity of the town's traders and merchants, the bustle of carts and animals. When the longhall had been built, it had been on the outskirts of East Anglia's capital; it was now almost at the centre of an ever-expanding city.

Nearing the door that led to his family's private chambers, Ceolwulf paused to regain his composure and to his collect his thoughts. It was not behaviour becoming of an Ænglisc earl to display his emotions, but the sight of his once proud, warrior-like father reduced to a shallow-breathing husk of a man made Ceolwulf's throat tighten each time he saw him.

A man could be considered hotheaded, impetuous or rash; he might be unable to control his expressions of raw emotion that lead him to anger or combat and yet he could still be considered a true man. Yet should a similar lack of self-control betray sentimentality, he might well be thought of as a lesser man.

He pushed the oak door open and stepped into the stone-flagged reception room. In one corner sat a man with his back to Ceolwulf, warming his hands in front of a small brazier, a half-finished chicken leg and pot of ale on a table next to him. At the sound of the door swinging open on ageing hinges, the visitor stood up, pulled back the hood of his cloak and turned to Ceolwulf.

"Uncle Ælfric?" Ceolwulf said in surprise. "You are most welcome; but why did you not send word of your coming? Where is your party?" The only other occupant in the room was a lone wolfhound, stretched across the floor, chasing rabbits in its sleep.

"Nephew," his uncle replied, as way of a greeting. "I have Lyfing and two men with me; they are already ensconced at some whorehouse, no doubt. I do not need them or a grand retinue to see my kin." They briefly embraced in the sincere, if somewhat cold manner that Ceolwulf had become accustomed to from members of his mother's family. "I have not come as the Thegn of Byrig though, but as a visitor to my family."

"Does my mother know you are here?" Ceolwulf asked.

"We have already spoken. She is at prayers now, but I was hoping to speak to you about important matters," Ælfric replied.

"Me? Surely, you ought to speak to father? He is sleeping for the moment, but I have no doubt he will wake soon. Would you care for some wine?" Ceolwulf looked over his uncle's shoulder for signs of servants.

"No, no, let us not disturb him," his uncle replied. "It was with you I did really wish to speak. Come; let us take a walk together." With that, he strode out of the hall, leaving Ceolwulf to run after him.

They walked through the gates that surrounded the longhall

and into the streets that were a mix of mud-splattered cobbles and manure. Theodford was a small town by Ænglisc standards; a longhall and tower built on a hill on the northern banks of the river Thet, the surrounding houses encircled by a wooden palisade that had been reinforced with stone over the past two centuries. Away from the centre of the town, one could walk along the bluebell-lined banks of the river and escape from the cursing oxcart drivers and bustle of the market. The tree-lined banks provided a secluded place for those who wished for a few moments of peace and tranquillity. Crossing one of the town's two narrow stone bridges that spanned the river, the two noblemen wound their way towards this quieter area, their hooded cloaks affording them a level of anonymity.

Ælfric and Ceolwulf sat down on the southern bank, in the shade of a broad-branched lime, and stared across the river, back towards the longhall. Ceolwulf idly tossed small stones into the slow-flowing river, waiting for his uncle to speak. Between the hall and the riverbank, they had walked in silence. Ceolwulf was beginning to wonder whether his uncle would ever start speaking at all, or if there had been any purpose whatsoever to this walk.

"I remember coming here as a child," Ælfric finally started, causing Ceolwulf to pause mid-throw. "This was a few years before your father met your mother, but I knew him at that point. My father would visit your grandfather and bring me with him. We would often come fishing down here, or so we called it, as we rarely caught anything. I soon learnt that a few quiet words in the trees by the river could achieve more than hours of procrastinating discussion in smoky halls."

Ceolwulf smiled and launched the stone in his hand to skim across the water. The two men watched it bounce twice off the surface before it sank with a satisfyingly loud plunk.

"Did I tell you about the troubling affairs we've had in Byrig recently, Ceolwulf? All manner of crimes, debauchery and violence; mostly from pilgrims, mind, if I'm honest. I seem to spend more time in the courts than I do with my own family. Lord alone knows what we would do in a time of war; most thegns are too busy with juries and checking land ownership deeds to find time to raise a fyrd. Did you hear about the merchant on trial for having sold dog meat as pork? Turned out that the jury of eight consisted of six men of sound mind and reason and then two others. One was one of his bitterest business rivals and the other, so they say, was his lover. Whole thing descended into farce; we'll have to do it all again next month, bring some jurors in from Stow, though no doubt they'll be bought off before they even make it to the court. Perhaps we would still be best off to make him stick his hand into boiling water or some other such nonsense," Ælfric snorted. Ceolwulf sat in silence for a moment, staring across at the wooden hall and the two-storey building behind it that housed his father.

"I am thinking, Uncle, that you did not ride to Theodford to discuss your sodomite jurors?" Ceolwulf ventured, picking at a patch of wild primrose beside him.

"And you would be right," Ælfric replied. He inhaled deeply and turned to look at his nephew. "Your father is sick, Ceolwulf, very sick. He may not ever recover but should he do so, and God willing he will, he may never be in a position to govern again. Perhaps it is time for you to declare yourself earl. The longer you wait for your father to recover, the weaker East Anglia becomes."

Ceolwulf did not reply immediately. He continued picking at the ground, pulling the petals off the small flowers.

"I sometimes say the wrong thing at the wrong time, Uncle, I know this. I sometimes speak without thinking, it is a weakness, and I admit it. But I will not leap into my father's boots and claim his place whilst he still breathes," Ceolwulf said calmly.

"No-one is suggesting you usurp your father, but East Anglia needs a leader."

"Is it not for the witenagemot to decide whether I should

succeed my father?"

"And I have no doubt that the current witan would. It is for that reason that you should declare yourself now, whilst we await a new monarch; before malign influences take hold at court," Ælfric replied.

"You mean Swegen?"

"I mean," Ælfric sighed, "I mean, do what is best for East Anglia now; do not wait for someone else to decide for you."

"And if I don't? Will you look to become earl?" Ceolwulf's voice started to rise.

"No, no, no," his uncle replied, slowly shaking his head. "It is not and has never been a position I seek. No, no, I will remain a loyal thegn and caring uncle."

"And what would my mother say to me taking my father's place whilst he lies dying? What kind of a son would that make me?" Ceolwulf snapped.

"It was your mother that suggested the idea. She thought it best you hear it from my mouth though," Ælfric replied calmly.

Ceolwulf fell silent and picked at clothes that had become greasy from days of not leaving the smoky confines of his father's quarters, trying to make sense of the confused thoughts pummelling the inside of his head.

"You don't trust yourself, do you, Ceolwulf?" his uncle continued, his voice gentle and low. "You know that it's for the best. Deep down, even though it makes you feel guilty, you know it really would be. Yet you are so convinced that you are impulsive, so obsessed with the sense of responsibility to your father, that you see any move to replace your father as sinful, that it will be interpreted as a sign of your own impatience. Listen to me; this is not ambition, this is your duty to your land, to your people. And no man, no man at all, will say you have betrayed your father."

"Not to my face at least," Ceolwulf replied quietly.

Ælfric nodded. "There'll always be those happy to spread

rumour and ill will, but there are times when you have to make a sacrifice. The fact that you resist doing what a hundred other earls' sons are desperate to do already shows that it is not ambition that guides your actions. Think about it at least." Ælfric slowly got to his feet, stretched his arms back and let out a yawn. "Let us head back, before your mother sends soldiers out to search for us, or some opportunistic thief unwittingly decides to slip a dagger into East Anglia's finest noblemen. No doubt that damned steward of mine, Lyfing, has already drunk the taverns of Theodford dry."

A flicker of a smile appeared on Ceolwulf's face.

"I fear..." he hesitated. "I fear...that if I declare myself earl, or even if I just take on my father's duties, then I am declaring him dead; that he is already gone. That by doing so, I am condemning him to a death that we can still not be entirely sure about, for nothing is ever certain, whatever old spinsters say about fate"

"Put it this way," Ælfric said, putting an arm around his nephew's shoulders. "If a witenagemot were called tomorrow, would you expect your father to attend, or would you go in his place?"

"You know I wouldn't drag him from his sickbed," Ceolwulf answered.

"Then the responsibility already lies on your shoulders. You are already earl in all but name. Let your people know, let East Anglia know, let Winceaster know that your lands are not lamed, that they are not there for someone else to take for themselves," Ælfric said, helping his nephew to his feet.

"I feel as if I have spent my entire adult life biting back my tongue, Uncle; it seems odd that you now urge me to shout from the rooftops that I am the Earl of East Anglia while my father still draws breath," Ceolwulf said, as they retraced their steps along the riverbank. "Give me until the feast of Saint Dunstan to decide. If my father is no better in ten days' time, then I shall consider assuming the earldom."

"I shall ask no more of you, Ceolwulf. I sincerely hope for your sake that the Gods permit us time for such a deliberation," his uncle replied.

The two men continued their walk through the graveyard of the small church dedicated to Saint Edmund the Martyr. From the church tower came the mocking caw of a jackdaw, as it flapped its wings and launched itself into the greying skies. For the moment, just for a few days, the future was uncertain. Sometimes though, the spinsters were right.

10th May 1166
Catune, Westmoringaland

Thurstan's eyes snapped open with an immediate realisation that he did not know where he was. His body still felt asleep, numb from exhaustion, but his mind was awake and whirling. He was lying on a mattress of straw that had been beyond its best many months ago, staring straight up at a thatched roof. The rotting beams and sparse thatch was letting in bright sunlight, a shaft of which was shining straight into his eyes. He levered himself up and swung his blistered feet onto a damp earthen floor and looked around him. In front of him, on a small pallet, lay the pale, injured child that was apparently the Queen of Ængland. She was sleeping, her steady breathing a comfort to Thurstan, given that her pallid face was ashen and feverish.

The events of the previous day were still a blur in his mind. They had slept in the copse until at least early afternoon, such was his exhaustion and Adelise's poor health. Once he had awoken he had still not dared move on until sundown that evening. For several hours he had sat in the shade between the trees, listening out for hoofbeats or the sound of men close by. Only when the sun had fully set, had he picked up Adelise and slowly started weaving his way through the small hills around Lonborg to reach the Lon valley.

He had intended to get as far away as possible from the city, but his body and Adelise's ever-shallower breathing had soon convinced him that they would not get far that night. They had covered less than four miles, but Thurstan knew he would have to find shelter or risk losing the girl altogether. Crossing the Lon river and heading south, Thurstan skirted around the small village of Catune, and started climbing the southern side of the valley.

As the crescent moon had disappeared behind a blanket of

cloud and the first few drops of rain had started to fall, Thurstan had stumbled upon a stone hut that appeared to be abandoned. It was a battered, crumbling building from which there emitted neither light nor smoke. He had gently pushed the wooden door open, bracing himself for any sudden cry of surprise, but had found naught but the remains of the straw beds. He had set himself and Adelise down, falling to sleep immediately, as he had done in the copse the previous night.

Now the sun of the following morning had awoken him, he stood up and slowly opened the weather-battered wooden door. His priority today was to find some food and clean water. He had a handful of silver coin in his scrip, enough to buy provisions for a few days, though how he would do that without arousing suspicion, he was not sure.

Peering around the door, he could make out the huddled houses of Catune, the occasional stone building standing out from the huddled wooden huts that made up most of the village. A small church tower's bell rang out, leaving Thurstan worrying for a moment whether it was being sounded in alarm, but it stopped after only a few peals. Relaxing, Thurstan stepped out into the sun.

"Good morning," came a deep voice. Thurstan leapt backwards, grasping for a sword that was no longer at his waist. He span round to see an elderly man, dressed in a woollen tunic and hose, leaning on a crook.

"Calm yourself, calm yourself, young man. I don't mean to frighten or harm you, and I hope you mean neither to me," the stranger said calmly. Thurstan looked at the man and quickly scanned the surrounding fields. It was apparent that this was not a soldier in disguise, even though the man's weather-worn skin and clothes marked him as someone who lived most of his life outdoors. His genial manner seemed genuine, although Thurstan still regretted not having a weapon at his side.

"Who are you?" Thurstan asked.

"My name is Egbrand; I watch the village's sheep here, on the hillside. I live with my wife down in the village," he said, pointing towards one of the small groups of houses in the valley floor. "The interesting question is, who are you, young man?"

"Why is it so interesting?" Thurstan asked, feeling his agitation growing.

"Well," Egbrand started, leaning his chin on his crook, "There's not many folks from around these parts that would take shelter in the old leper house."

Thurstan turned in horror to look at the hut, noticing for the first time the crudely painted red mark on the battered wooden door that had been invisible to him the previous night.

"Now I know that you cannot catch leprosy from a hut months after a victim last lived there. Either you know that too, or you didn't know it was a leper house. I'm guessing the latter," Egbrand continued, in the same mild manner. Thurstan knew he didn't have to answer that question; his surprise was obvious enough.

"How did you know I was here?" Thurstan asked, the fear of being caught by the sheriff's men still with him.

"I was out here last night, tending the sheep. You won't have seen me, but my eyes have grown accustomed to the dark over the years. Saw you carrying something in here late on. Now there's a desperate man, I thought to myself, a man in need of shelter. As a good Christian, I thought I ought to see if I could help."

Thurstan stared at the old man for a few seconds, wondering just how much of the truth he should tell. A sick, possibly dying girl in the hut and the lack of a plan left few options open to him; the need for assistance outweighed the risk of telling a shepherd some of the story.

"My name is Thurstan, I am, or was, from these parts. My sister is here with me, she is sick. She lies wounded in the hut and needs medicine. I—" Thurstan paused, searching for the right words. "I am being searched for, although I swear my innocence. I have been accused of a crime I did not commit, north of here, in Kirkby Kendale. I would have stayed to fight my case at trial, but the girl, my sister, I dare not risk her life."

"Your sister?" the shepherd asked. "How was she wounded?"

"An arrow. A stray one. It was meant for me," Thurstan replied, looking the old man straight in the eyes. The shepherd held his gaze a long time then gave a slight shrug.

"Perhaps I best have a look at this girl then," he said and stepped towards the hut's door. Thurstan instinctively stepped back, barring the old man's way, holding an arm out.

"I don't think she ought to be disturbed, but I can offer you coin if you could perhaps fetch some bandages or linen," he said. The old man shook his head genially.

"Young man, I don't know what type of trouble you're really in, but I don't mark you down as a murderer. I care little for what the sheriff or jarl say; I pay my taxes to them every year, but I've no great love for them. I'm thinking you could really do with my help at the moment." Egbrand tilted his head to one side. Thurstan paused for a moment, and then lowered his arm, allowing the old man to step inside the hut.

Adelise was sleeping, her countenance as pale as it had ever been. The shepherd bent down and gently stroked her forehead, lifting an eyelid to stare into her unseeing eyes. He softly pulled her tunic back to look at her wounded shoulder and tutted to himself. He prodded the wound lightly with a gnarled finger, causing a drop of pus to escape from the ragged cut. Adelise moaned and mumbled a few quiet words of protest. The worlds were muffled, but the language was clear enough; Ænglisc. The shepherd turned and looked at Thurstan.

"What's her name?" Egbrand asked.

"Adelise," Thurstan replied quietly, after a moment's hesitation.

"Adelise, Adelise," the shepherd echoed. "Like the Queen of

Ængland, so I'm told. Adelise, sister of Thurstan."

Egbrand stood and turned to Thurstan, placing a hand on the young man's shoulder. Thurstan flinched but then felt embarrassed at reacting so cautiously to the friendly gesture.

"The wound is infected, but I've seen worse," the old man said. "My wife can make poultices which can help, or at least they do on lambs. I can fetch linen and bedding. She doesn't seem very responsive, but I've seen this before; a young lad in the village some years back, whose parents and siblings were killed one night in a fire. Physically fine, but the shock of it made him act asleep for months, if you follow."

"She has been through a great deal recently," Thurstan admitted, without elaborating. "So you will help us?"

"I shall, though I must tend to the sheep first. I shall come back tomorrow. For the time being, take these," Egbrand said, proffering a pouch of water and some dried bread from an old leather scrip tied to a piece of string around his waist. Thurstan rummaged in his own pouch to find some silver coins to offer the shepherd, but the old man waved him away.

"Keep your silver, keep it. I have offered to help you, young man, you have not hired my services. I don't know who you really are, or your sister, but I will help you. And do not fret; I shall tell no-one of your presence, save my wife. If you are discovered before I return, I give you my word that it shall not be due to me. Now keep out of sight, if you can. The house is hidden from most parts of the village, but you never know who may be in the hills. There's a small brook of clean water about four hundred paces further up the hill from here, but I would wait until nightfall. Light a fire only after dark, but I think the weather will be kind to us tonight. Until tomorrow."

With that, he patted Thurstan on the shoulder and stooped to exit the hut. Outside he gave a shrill whistle and a small dog, which Thurstan had not realised had even been there, sprang out of the long grass to join him. The shepherd walked off down the hill without looking back, leaving Thurstan to return to Adelise.

He poured as much water as he could between her lips, not wanting to choke her, drank a little for himself and then used the rest to clean her wound as best he could. He chewed on a bit of the bread and tried to feed Adelise some, cursing himself for not having saved more water with which to soften it. She ate a little, without waking up it seemed, but enough to ease his fear that she might starve to death. Then, lying back down on the straw-filled pallet, his head swirling with fears and hopes about the shepherd, Thurstan started the long wait until nightfall.

13th May 1166
Winceaster, Ængland

Swegen, Earl of Berrocscir, Steward to the Queen and self-declared Prince of Ængland, was dreaming of murder. Pleasant dreams, for although he did not particularly enjoy the act of killing, they were dreams that spoke to him of glory, power and success.

He had draped himself across one of the low, long chairs in the 'Roman Room' in Winceaster Castle. His grandfather, Tostig II, had developed a great love of all things antique or Mediterranean and had built a room to resemble his idea of a classical emperor's suite. He had never visited Rome, or any of the faraway countries around it. His notions of this classical ideal had been forged from books read ravenously in the Great Library of Oxnaforda. He had made a great many aesthetic changes to the castle at that time; to the deficit, his critics said, of its military defences.

Swegen had little love for the place, but the Roman Room often afforded him the peace and quiet he required to think clearly. Few visitors would disturb him, as the room had fallen out of fashion with the castle's occupants, associated as it was with decoration over utility. He had heard of Roman parties, 'symposia' was possibly the name, which had sounded quite interesting. Perhaps they should be reinstated once he was king, the merest thought of which brought a broad smile to his face.

He swung his legs off the low loungers and sauntered over to the leaded window, which looked out onto one of Winceaster's newest tree-lined avenues. The occasional cart and horse meandered its way down, but this was a sleepy town, he felt. It did not have the bustle of Lunden, and it served as a capital in name only. It made no sense to Swegen why the capital would not be the richest city, the city with the most powerful merchants, the largest city.

Instead, he was stuck here, faced with the tedious duties of a judge and steward. His past week had been nothing more than a siege by whining market traders and petitioners complaining to him directly over the most trivial of matters. A monarch ought not to be troubled with such insignificant issues, he thought. He would let these matters be decided by courts, by hired, no, come to think of it, by licensed judges, who would pay for the privilege. The people would love him for it, for he would be seen as being keen on bringing justice to the masses.

Just as his mind started to explore the possibilities of percentages that could be paid between the judge and crown, he heard the sound of heavy footsteps coming from the stone-floored corridor leading to his room. There was a brief inter-change of mumbled conversation outside the door where two sentries had been posted, and then a knock came.

"Yes?" Swegen called, cautious not to sound too expectant.

"My lord, Thegn Ricmund of Readinga, is here to speak to you," one of the sentries called.

"Enter," Swegen replied neutrally.

The door opened and Ricmund stalked into the room, wearing heavy furs despite the mild weather, bringing with him a stench of ale and sweat. His face wore an expression of thunder, as if he had just been gravely insulted outside the door, but then again, Swegen mused, he more or less wore that expression perma-nently. He waited until the door closed behind the brutish figure of Ricmund, then spoke hurriedly and quietly.

"Well then?" he asked, his voice almost quivering with excitement.

"It is done, my lord Prince," Ricmund replied flatly, a grimace that could also pass as a grin flashing across his face. He held out a gloved hand that contained a small ring, which still bore the bloodstains that showed that its previous owner had met with a violent end. Swegen smiled briefly and exhaled happily.

"Excellent work, Ricmund, excellent. Were there—," Swegen started to ask, glancing towards the door. "Were there any problems?"

Ricmund looked around behind him.

"Are we safe to talk?" he asked quietly. Swegen shook his head.

"Not my men, although I don't think they're the sort to make trouble. Come to the window."

They crossed the intricately mosaicked floor to a shuttered window on the far side of the room. Swegen opened it and let the noise of the street below into the room.

"I will have more men arriving next week from Berrocscir, as they would expect a steward to bring. Until then we should act with some degree of caution, although I think most of the men know who their true lord is already," Swegen said with a smirk. "You were saying you had some issues?"

"No, my lord, none really," Ricmund replied. "The plan went as you foresaw. We left the woman to act as a survivor, as you instructed. She should be back within a few days, although I expect news will be here soon. There was one huskarl who we let escape, in the old Norse fashion; one survivor to tell of the massacre. All he will have seen are Northymbric shields."

"You permitted to him to escape then? The woman was not enough?" Swegen's brow furrowed in disapproval.

"It was not planned, but it's not a problem, my lord, I'm certain. In the long term it may benefit having had a witness, maybe?"

Swegen rubbed at one of the large rings adorning his clammy fingers.

"Did you leave any injured?" he asked.

"We suffered some losses, but we left no injured behind. We killed those who could not make the ship where they lay in the field." The Eoten spoke without regret.

"Slit their throats?"

"No, my lord, that would have looked too intentional. Stabbed them through with spears and swords."

"Good, good," Swegen said distractedly, staring back at the door. "It would be unfortunate to have any loose ends, you understand."

"There are none, my lord," Ricmund said with an emphatic nod of his large, scarred head. "We killed the guide before leaving and the archer captain died in battle."

"And your men?" Swegen asked.

"Garrisoned back in Ceaster, where they are already pickling themselves with alcohol. They won't be leaving for Readinga until this has blown over, by which point loose tongues will no longer matter," Ricmund answered. The man may have been short on wit and cunning, Swegen thought, but he did command loyalty in his men.

"It wouldn't be easier to maybe..." Swegen left the unfinished question hanging in the air.

"My men? They are good men, not the kind you can replace. I doubt your house guards would even last two minutes against them even if they outnumbered them two to one. No, my lord, they will not be an issue," Ricmund bristled.

Swegen flashed a quick grin at the large man and placed a friendly hand on one of his broadly muscled shoulders. Ricmund stared at the hand as if a bird had just fouled on him, but said nothing. Crass, crude, but respectful, Swegen thought to himself approvingly.

"Of course, soon you will have many more men, as many as you could wish for. I will, of course, have to hold someone responsible for our poor little queen's death. I was thinking, the men who were sent to guarantee her safety and so utterly failed. Then the earldom of East Anglia would then be without a lord. Earl Ricmund perhaps?"

Ricmund smiled slowly and nodded his scarred head.

"First your earldom, then who knows? Once Northland's

treachery is revealed, we can repeal this Morcar Oath nonsense. Rome would surely forgive us a war to defend our kingdom against the Northmen. Then Ængland can see about reclaiming what is rightfully hers. Hoiland, Kesteven, Snotenga, they could all do with a strong leader," Swegen said wistfully.

The Eoten's smile broadened and he slapped a hand onto the earl's shoulder, causing him to wince slightly.

"My lord, your rewards are most welcome," he grinned.

"Speaking of which," Swegen said, as the sound of muffled sobbing grew in the corridor outside. "I believe you share my taste in the finer, tender meats. I have already seen to your first reward straight away. Come in!"

The door was opened and two weeping slave girls, dressed in Roman-style togas, were dumped unceremoniously onto the floor. They had been bought just the previous day from the Flemish slave traders in Winceaster market, picked especially for their beauty and youth. If they were of marriageable age, then it was only by a matter of months, Swegen noted with approval.

Outside, the grim-faced guards shut the door behind them and exchanged baleful glances as the room that had been built to contain beauty started to fill with terrified screams.

14th May 1166
Catune, Westmoringaland

"You carried me across the bay?" Adelise asked, her tone almost one of wonderment.

Thurstan meekly nodded. The girl had woken early that morning and for the first time since the infirmary in Kirkby, they had held a conversation. Her appetite and colour had been improving over the last three days, thanks in no small part to the supplies that the shepherd Egbrand had continued to bring. That they had not been dragged from the hut in the middle of the night had finally reassured Thurstan that Egbrand's intentions were genuine and he was to be trusted.

"I did, but I was worried that I had hurt you. We had to escape from arrows, horses, men, even pirates, I think," Thurstan replied. He was sitting on the floor cross-legged next to her pallet and had been since first light when she had first stirred. It was as if she had awoken from a deep sleep and despite plainly still being weak, her wound was looking much less angry today.

"So my uncle's men tried to kill me and then your lord tried to kill you?" the girl asked. She had shed no tears, nor shown any self-pity, but asked simple questions. Perhaps she did this just to make herself understood to the Northlander, but Thurstan guessed that it was simply her nature.

"We don't have many friends at the moment, I fear," Thurstan answered truthfully. He dipped some rags of linen into a bowl of water and dabbed at the girl's forehead. Her temperature was still high, but it seemed a minor complaint compared to the fever she had fallen under during the second night of their stay in the hut.

How long the nights had seemed since they had arrived. Thurstan had slept fitfully, waking every hour to check the girl's breathing, leaning over until he could hear her breath or see her move. The previous night he had been awoken by the snuffling of an animal, possibly a dog, a fox, Thurstan was not sure. He had not slept after that though, overcome with the sense of isolation and imprisonment, but most of all, of helplessness.

"But you are from Lonborg, though, Thurstan?" she asked, her pronunciation of the city's name causing him to smile.

"I am, or rather, I was. My family are still there, but I have not seen them for nearly a year. I have already thought about going to them, believe me, but I think I am dead to them," he replied, instantly cursing himself as he remembered that the girl was an orphan. She frowned, trying to make sense of his words.

"That is bad. My parents are dead, but they loved me, I think. My aunt told me they did. I have another family, but I think they are dead too now. They were in the wagon with me. Did you see them when you rescued me?" she asked, showing for the first time the slightest hint of a tear in her eye.

"I didn't, sorry," Thurstan lied. "I didn't see anyone else, perhaps they escaped. There are a lot of hills around that part of Kirkby."

"It's as if everyone who has ever cared for me dies," she said, her voice becoming very quiet.

"I care, and I'm still very alive," Thurstan said. "Alive, but very hungry. Hopefully Egbrand, the shepherd I told you about, will be here soon with some pottage or broth." He rummaged around behind him, looking for any remaining bread from the previous day, but found naught but a few nuts and wrinkled berries.

"You are very kind, Thurstan. Thank you," Adelise said, closing her eyes. Her breathing became deep and rhythmic, leading Thurstan to assume that she had fallen asleep. "Where are you going to take me?" She had not opened her eyes, but her voice was clear.

Thurstan did not reply. He had been wrestling with the same question for the last three nights. There was no going back north.

Scotland offered sanctuary with Adelise's family, but he could not risk passing anywhere near Kirkby. To the west lay only Lonborg and the sea. By now, Vinder would have undoubtedly sent men to the city to look specifically for Thurstan; he would never get the chance to speak to the jarl or his family, he was sure. Southwards? To carry on along the Great South Road to the Ænglisc border, to Ceaster? Given his last encounter with the Ænglisc and what they were trying to do to Adelise, he could not see any benefit from turning up in a provincial Ænglisc city carrying what he proclaimed to be their monarch.

East would mean crossing the Pennine hills into the Thriths of Jorvik. East would mean towards the capital. East would mean towards the king. And what then? If they survived the crossing, and it would be on foot, then how would he present Adelise in the Northlandic capital? Would they be her saviour or would they relish the chance of holding their neighbour's monarch hostage? Would they even recognise her as the Queen of Ængland? Each path seemed to offer little hope, but the great possibility of a swift death.

"I have not decided yet," Thurstan answered truthfully. "My first concern is your health, and then we can think about your kingdom."

The sound of soft footsteps on the grass outside was followed by a knock on the door and the voice of Egbrand greeting them. The old man limped inside the hut and set down a small sack containing a loaf of bread, a few withered vegetables and a finger of dry cheese.

"You have hurt your leg?" Thurstan asked, making room for the shepherd to squat by Adelise's pallet.

"Bah, it's nowt but a twinge I get in wet weather," he replied. "I get it now and again, which is a bugger for a shepherd, but I'll live." He turned his attention to girl who was now almost certainly asleep, Thurstan thought.

"My wife made a bit more of this poultice. Smells foul, but it seems to have done the trick," the shepherd continued. "Has she woken at all?"

"This morning, early. She was speaking until a few minutes ago," Thurstan replied. Adelise opened one eye and beamed.

"Hello. You're Egbrand, aren't you? Thank you for helping me," she said, again surprising Thurstan at how she could appear asleep one minute and be wide awake the next. Egbrand seemed to not be surprised at all, or at least acted as such. Nor did he seem to take issue with Adelise's obvious Ænglisc accent. He simply acted as if he had expected this reaction all along.

"Good morning, young lady," he said conversationally. "I see your brother here has been taking good care of you." Adelise's eyes flickered to Thurstan for an instant and he replied with wink. She nodded weakly.

"Now this stuff," Egbrand said, scooping out a yellow, glutinous paste from a small clay pot with a wrinkled, brown finger. "It smells awful, but my wife assures me it's the best in the valley for cuts and bruises like yours. Nailwort, burdock, honey, butter and fish oil, so I believe. Don't eat it for heaven's sake, but it seems to be doing its job." He spread a film of the green-flecked paste onto Adelise's shoulder, and then took out two cabbage leaves from his scrip, which he pressed onto the wound, before carefully wrapping a freshly washed bandage around her.

"Why are you helping us?" Adelise asked. Thurstan chuckled again at her direct manner, which he had already found quite disconcerting.

"Why not?" the shepherd answered genially.

"Everyone has been trying to attack us for the last week. I thought everyone in this land was violent and hated my people," she blurted out, before glancing at Thurstan in horror at her admission.

"We're not all savages in the countryside, little *gefæmne*," Egbrand chuckled, using the Ænglisc word. He finished tying the last strip of linen in silence. He then sat back and fished out of his sack a small pouch of oats and grains, which he gave to Thurstan. "To make more pottage at night," he said, by way of an explanation.

Egbrand had returned on the second day with a small clay pot that Thurstan had used for cooking food after nightfall, when any smoke would be almost invisible against the normally cloudy night sky. Thurstan had been most grateful, for there were few villagers that owned one decent cooking pot, let alone a second that they could give away. He had not asked, but suspected that Egbrand and his wife were perhaps doing without at the moment.

"My wife and I, we never had children. We wanted them, but the Lord never saw fit to bless us with them. The Lord or nature, I suppose, I'm not sure which. The one regret we have always had. I'll see my kin's children from time to time, they live further down the valley, but it's not the same, is it? We've been left with a soft spot for younger folk such as yourselves. You seem in trouble and I am not too interested in the hows and whys, but you seem too young, young lady, to have ever done anyone any real harm, so I see no reason not to help you." Egbrand smiled at Adelise and nodded to Thurstan.

"What is your wife's name?" Adelise asked.

"Bathylle."

"Then thank Bathylle for her kindness," Adelise replied. Thurstan inwardly chastised himself that in four days it had not occurred to him once to ask the man's wife's name, given that she was currently keeping them both alive.

"I shall do that, Adelise," the shepherd said.

Ten minutes later, once Egbrand had bid them farewell for the day and had departed to tend to his flock, Thurstan was wetting some bread to give to Adelise.

"I am lucky, I think," she announced, rolling onto her side, trying to lie on any other part of her body than her sore back. "I know lots of bad things have happened, but I think I am lucky to have met people like you and Egbrand."

Thurstan paused for a moment to consider her optimistic statement. Given the circumstances, given the infinite number of violent alternatives, then yes, he was forced to agree that she had been lucky. He nodded at her and continued to soften the bread.

"I think this afternoon, I might like to sit up," she continued. "But I am worried though. What if the person who lives here comes back. I don't want them to think I have taken their home for myself."

"They won't be back, don't worry about that," Thurstan replied, offering Adelise a mouthful of bread. "Egbrand assured me about that."

"Good," Adelise said, taking the bread and enjoying the simple pleasure of being able to feed herself again. "I'm glad we can trust Egbrand. We can, can't we?" she asked, a hint of doubt trembling on the edge of her voice.

"We can," Thurstan said and his thoughts turned to the old man's final gift before departing that morning. An old, well-used knife, the type used for slaughtering pigs which Egbrand insisted Thurstan keep. He could feel it at his side now, keeping it hidden from Adelise's view. It was no sword, but there was a sense of relief, of security at having a weapon at his waist.

The old man had said that he should use it if it ever became necessary, to not let themselves be captured. He wasn't quite sure what the shepherd had meant by those words, but he understood that Egbrand had realised that they were still in danger. They were still well within reach of Lonborg and Kirkby, should Vinder convince Jarl Herri to search for them. For all Thurstan knew, the jarl may well have been part of the plot all along.

"Do you have a blade, Thurstan?" Adelise asked suddenly, staring at him. Thurstan was startled; could she even read his thoughts now?

"Why do you ask?" he replied cautiously.

"You need a shave. Your lip looks funny," she said simply, before taking another bite of bread. Thurstan raised his hand to his top lip and felt a week's growth of hair, more than he had ever grown in a week before. He started to laugh and he kept on laughing; laughing at Adelise's comment, laughing because she was recovering, laughing because for the time being, they were still alive. He continued until Adelise joined in, chortling at each other until they didn't know why they had started laughing to begin with.

Further up the hill, sat on a rock, staring out across the green valley, Egbrand smiled to himself at the sound of happiness.

Twifyrd, nr Winceaster, Ængland

The squeal of the rabbit as Swegen's goshawk swooped down and seized it by the neck could be heard from on top of the hill. From where the hunting party watched, the land rolled away in a series of meadows and small hills, striped in different shades of green and gold from the cloud-veiled sun.

Swegen congratulated himself as one of the dogs was sent to retrieve the catch. He did not care for the meat, but neither did any of the other noblemen on the hunt with him today. It was the thrill of the chase, the rush of excitement as the prey was hunted down and killed. The earls of Wiltescir and Suthseaxe were riding a few yards behind him, each with their own goshawk. They were pleasant, if somewhat dull company; men who had once been warriors, men who had fought on the continent on behalf of one small kingdom against another, but who had grown fat and comfortable in their old age.

"Well done, my lord Prince," the Earl of Suthseaxe, a red-haired and equally red-faced man called Leofwin, congratulated him. Swegen acknowledged the compliment with a nod of his head. The hunting was becoming a bit too easy now and his patience, which was never great at the best of times, was starting to wear thin. They had ridden out from Winceaster castle early that morning, towards the village of Twifyrd and in the space of three hours had already killed more quarry than would normally be expected in an entire day of hunting.

Swegen watched with amusement as the Earl of Wiltescir's goshawk attacked, then lost its intended rabbit. It was left hopping among the undergrowth, searching for the fleeing animal which was now long gone.

During the last week Winceaster castle had started to fill with Ænglisc noblemen, ahead of the expected arrival of the new queen. Of course, there had been no sign of her, but thankfully,

Swegen's barely concealed excitement at his impending promotion had been easily disguised amongst his fellow earls' anticipation of their young monarch.

Yet while they had been impatiently waiting for news of her return to the nation's capital, Swegen was growing troubled at the lack of news of her death. Ricmund had assured him that everyone travelling in the caravan was dead, and he had her bloodied ring, that had once belonged to her mother. Swegen kept it in a pouch around his neck, the feel of the small leather drawstring bag against his chest a reassuring confirmation of the power he now held in the country.

"My lord?" Leofwin asked.

Swegen snapped out of his reverie and turned to look at the earl's round face. "I beg your pardon, Suthseaxe, you were saying?" he blustered. He had recently adopted his late uncle's habit of addressing his earls and thegns by the lands they held, hoping it would lend him a king-like manner.

"I was asking, my lord, whether you had received notice at all of Queen Adelise's progress? Surely Ceaster or Lichfeld would have sent word by now?" he said, scanning the sky for his goshawk, which had decided to disappear for the time being.

"I'm sure everything is in order, as planned. Sending us messages will not spirit her to us any quicker, will it?" Swegen replied mildly. He watched on as the Earl of Wiltescir's accompanying falconer went in search of the hopping bird that had disappeared into a patch of ferns and refused to come back out. The earl was berating the falconer, having decided that it was somehow the poor man's fault, much to Swegen's continued amusement. His own goshawk chose that moment to gently glide back down and land on his outstretched gauntlet, which only seemed to further annoy the Earl of Wiltescir.

"Bad luck, Wiltescir, they will do that at times," Swegen commiserated, with a minimal amount of sincerity.

The sound of approaching hoofbeats caused them all to turn

in their saddles. Swegen's heart skipped a beat to see a poorly dressed rider that he surmised could only be a messenger, approaching at a gallop.

"Earl Swegen!" the rider called, whilst still some distance away. *Prince*, Swegen thought to himself, *you little scrote*, but this was one time he was happy to let it pass.

"Good news? The queen has arrived?" Earl Leofwin asked, as the panting messenger hauled his foaming mouthed mount to a halt. The boy had evidently ridden from further away than Winceaster and it was all Swegen could do not to squeal in excitement.

"Well, boy?" Swegen asked. The boy simply reached inside his tunic and brought out a wax-sealed letter, which he passed to the nobleman. Fingers trembling, Swegen opened the letter and quickly scanned its contents, biting down on his bottom lip to suppress any inappropriate emotion. The words confirmed what he had hoped to hear for so long now. In a calculated move, Swegen bit down hard on the tip of his tongue inside his mouth. The stinging pain brought tears to his eyes and he turned to his fellow earls.

"Woe, my lords, woe and tragedy. Adelise, she—," and he let his voice falter, as the pain from his tongue started to subside. "She has been slain. So cruelly slain. Ceaster writes that she was attacked and killed by bandits in Northland seven days ago."

"God save us and rest her soul," Leofwin said, crossing himself. He removed his falconry glove and threw it to the floor in grief.

"Yet this is not the worst. This message from Ceaster says that on the very same day that Lonborg sent word of a bandit ambush, a survivor arrived in the city swearing that Northymbric horsemen had attacked the caravan. Treachery, my lords, treachery. After a hundred years of the Morcar Oath, this is how the Northlanders see fit to break it; the murder of our child queen." Swegen bit down again on his tongue and fresh tears rolled down his cheeks.

"You, boy," he said to the messenger. "Take this message on to Lunden. Let the Archbishop of Westmynster know. Rome must hear of this immediately, for with this act, the Northlanders have gone against the Pope-sworn Morcar Oath and committed the foulest of sins." He tossed a small purse of coins to the flush-faced youth who seemed to have little enough energy to ride to the end of the field, let alone Lunden; yet on receiving the coins, he kicked his heels back and spurred his horse into a gallop.

"Today is the saddest day of our nation's history, my lords, sadder possibly than the loss of the northern shires, for never has Ængland's future been so embodied in so small a rose, only for it to be plucked and destroyed so cruelly. Come, let us ride back to the castle, united in our grief," Swegen announced morosely, nudging his stallion forward.

"Are we to summon the witan, Lord Prince?" the Earl of Wiltescir enquired, his ability to state the obvious never ceasing to surprise Swegen.

"Yes, Wiltescir, yes we are," the queen's guardian and next in line to the throne declared. He turned to face the collected group of stewards, falconers and two earls and raised his voice to a defiant shout. "And for the first time in a hundred years, it will be a witenagemot of war!"

16th May 1166
Catune, Westmoringaland, Northland

The clear night sky was a panorama of a thousand points of light, giving the reclining figures on the hillside a rare opportunity to see into the heavens. Thurstan and Adelise were lying on the ground, gazing up at the stars, safe in the knowledge that they would be unseen from the village below. Only the occasional owl or fox disturbed the silence and those who did seemed uninterested in the two human figures.

At nightfall, Adelise had ventured outside for the first time, taking her first steps for more than a week. They had walked around the hut several times, until the stiff muscles of her legs began to ache in objection to their sudden revival. It was progress, Thurstan thought, but given the walk that would no doubt face them in the near future, it was but a small first step.

"That one is Ursa Major," Adelise said, pointing up to the sky.

"Which one?" Thurstan asked, trying to see where her finger was pointing in the darkness.

"From the bright one there, below that," she replied, waving her hand in its direction.

"They're all bright, Adelise. Which bright one?" he asked, following the line of her finger. "That one? I call that one the Wagon."

"Then what do you call the one to its left, Ursa Minor?" she asked.

"That one is the Little Cart or the Little Bear, I sometimes heard it called," he said.

"Well yes, that is what it means in Latin. I learnt their names from my tutors in Winceaster and Carleol," she said with a tinge of sadness, remembering happier times.

"I learnt the names from my father, the names the sailors use to navigate by," Thurstan replied, the memories of his family less infused with melancholy nostalgia. "How do your legs feel now?"

"Sore. But happy," she replied.

"Your legs feel happy?" Thurstan laughed. "Well that's no bad thing, I suppose."

They lay in the silence on the cool turf for some moments, the sensation of the soft grass a welcome change from the brittle straw of the hut's pallets. Thurstan turned to look at Adelise and he wondered how a small child, a girl that looked no different from thousands of others, was so important to two countries. It was almost impossible to comprehend; so much so that he found it easier just to treat her as he would any another little girl. She spoke like one, generally acted like one and, to Thurstan, only her strange way of speaking marked her as being different from any of the female cousins with whom he had grown up.

"Thurstan," she asked, her high-pitched voice seeming so loud in the night air. "Can I ask you a question?"

"Of course," he replied, wondering what overly direct question she would pose now.

"Have you killed many men?" she asked, as casually as if she was enquiring about his favourite food.

Thurstan gave the question some thought for a moment.

"None until last month," he replied. "Since then, quite a few I think. I don't know really. When I get attacked, I don't really think about it, I just try to defend myself and stop the other person from attacking me."

"I thought that you had maybe killed many men. That you were the best soldier in your castle and that's how you saved me. I thought the Northlandic men liked killing each other."

Thurstan laughed in the dark at her simplistic view. Then again, he thought, the Northlandic dynastic wars of the previous decades would appear a bit like that to a child from another country.

"No, no, no. I was new in Kirkby. To be honest, I wasn't so

popular. I wouldn't say I was the best, not by a long way," he replied.

"Why were you not popular?" she asked, never missing the opportunity to ask personal questions.

"Because my father was rich, because he had provided me with expensive equipment," he replied honestly. He found the girl's manner of asking questions refreshing, and it enabled him to speak more candidly than he had done in many a month.

"So people dislike you if you are rich?" There was a slight tone of worry in her voice.

"I don't think they automatically do. Let's say that many rich people are rich because they've done bad things to become rich. Or once they become rich, they think they can do bad things. It makes people without as much money angry," he answered, trying to simplify his answer for the young girl, though he suspected she probably could have put it better.

"So corruption can earn wealth and wealth corrupts," she asked sweetly, proving him right.

"I suppose, but I don't think the other soldiers saw it like that. They just disliked me because I was new and had a horse." Thurstan sighed. It all seemed so long ago now, as if he were relating the story of someone else that he had once known.

"Why did you save me?" she asked suddenly.

"Because I was guarding your caravan. It was my duty."

"But only at first. You are a very good man, Thurstan. You've saved me since, you carried me here. Why?" she pressed.

Thurstan sat up and gave this some thought, chewing on a long strand of grass.

"I think at first it was just instinct. To save another person in peril is a natural thing to do, isn't it? To save someone your age, well, who wouldn't? Since then? Because I didn't want to leave you, I suppose. I once left someone in a moment of need and he died. He had been my good friend, and I let him die. So perhaps I am doing it for myself, not for you, I don't know. I used to want to be a huskarl so much, to cover myself in glory and riches. Now, I just want to do the right thing. But perhaps that is still a selfish thing?"

"Everyone does something for a reason. Even the man who gives his money away to the poor does it a little bit because it makes him feel good inside. Not totally, but a little bit, I think," she said. Thurstan smiled. She was either very simplistic or very deep. He was aware they were having to converse in dialects not wholly familiar to each other, but at nine years of age, the little girl already seemed to think more about life than most of his friends had ever done in theirs. He was about to suggest he go check the coney traps he had set the previous night in the nearby trees, when he heard the dull sound of approaching footsteps from somewhere further down the hill.

"Get in the hut," he whispered urgently. Adelise half ran, half scrambled on noncompliant legs through the door, closing it behind her. Thurstan squatted low in the grass, trying to make out any shapes in the dark, gripping the hilt of the knife at his waist. The footsteps continued to come nearer and Thurstan tensed, waiting for the walker to appear out of the dark. Suddenly the voice of a man started to sing an old drinking song in a low voice; Thurstan recognised it as that of Egbrand. With his heart still pounding, he stood up and called out a greeting in the loudest whisper he could muster. Egbrand's white-haired face loomed out the dark with a finger pressed to his lips.

"Hush, young master Thurstan, the night carries sound. Let us talk inside the hut," he said striding past Thurstan and into the hut. *"Waes hael, gefæmne!"* Adelise returned the Ænglisc greeting. It had become customary over the last couple of days, though no-one had ever brought up the significance of her curious accent or dialect. Even when Egbrand had told them about the death of the Ænglisc queen just a few miles north, he had not pointed out the coincidence.

Thurstan followed him inside, to see him setting down a

small lamb that could not been more than four weeks old. It bleated pitifully and tottered weakly around the rush lined floor in the flickering gloom.

Egbrand had brought them a single, tallow candle the previous night. The country shepherd would be unlikely to have owned many and Thurstan was grateful again for the man's generosity. They had covered the hut's windows with draped rags on the inside, enabling Thurstan and Adelise to use the candle for some light during the night.

"Found this little chap down by the ford, looks like he's got separated from his mother. Going to take him back up the hill tonight, so I cannot stay long. How is your wound then?" Egbrand asked her. She pulled the shoulder of her woollen dress down to show him. It was pink, but the pus had gone and the edges were now neatly scabbing. "Lovely," the shepherd remarked with a quick grin. He stared at Thurstan and Adelise for a moment, mixed emotions passing across his weathered face, the briefest flicker of sadness showing in his eyes before he started speaking.

"I heard—," he started. "I heard some disturbing news from the village's priest today. A message arrived from Lonborg, a message to all the villages in the valley. Jarl Herri's men are searching for a criminal, they say, a criminal who has kidnapped a young girl. They say the criminal was a soldier who attacked the sheriff in Kirkby Kendale and that the girl is some distant relation of the jarl. There is a reward out for information that leads to their capture."

Thurstan started suddenly, looking around the hut as if he expected the windows and doors to burst in under the weight of soldiers at that very instant.

"Calm down, Thurstan Ælfsson, calm yourself. You have nothing to fear tonight and I will not say a word, nor will Bathylle. Folk know I roam these hills and if I say there's nowt untoward, they'll believe me. But I cannot say for how long they won't ask questions, or rather, how long before they come to investigate. Should Lonborg hear of your presence, horsemen from the castle could be here in less than an hour. I hate to say it, but I believe this place is no longer safe for you."

"You know my surname," Thurstan said quietly.

"It was in the message given to the priest," Egbrand replied.

Thurstan let his head sink into his hands, the full implication striking home. He had hoped that the sheriff would not have wanted to draw attention to the one man who could expose his treachery. Perhaps his parents would have been told he had died gloriously in battle, so that for once, they could have been proud of him. Instead, their unwanted son would now be known as a fugitive, an outlaw and a kidnapper.

"I'm sorry, Thurstan," the shepherd said, laying a hand on his shoulder. "I don't want to know your story, though I fear I can guess at much. If what I think is true, you really need to leave tomorrow. Will the young lady be able to walk?"

"No, no, she's still too weak," Thurstan replied, looking up. He shouldn't have been surprised, he knew it made very little difference; but to have his name proclaimed as outlaw, he had never thought that that would have been the consequence of becoming a huskarl. "We would need at least another three or four days and even then, we will not be able to walk far."

"Where are you going to go?" Egbrand asked, the one question Thurstan had still not managed to answer himself.

"Well, we can hardly go to Lonborg now. I was thinking of travelling to Ceaster, maybe taking a ship there from Skippool. Or to Jorvik, across the hills; if we can't escape the jarl, we could maybe appeal to the king, plead our case." Thurstan realised that he was no longer trying to conceal the importance of Adelise's identity. She was sitting cross-legged on the floor, playing with the lamb, feeding it imaginary grass from her fingers.

"If you do go that way," the shepherd replied, showing no surprise at mention of the king, "then I'd take the tops, away from the roads. The fewer people who see you, the better."

"Is Jorvik safe?" Adelise asked. Her eyes looked red-rimmed, as if she were about to burst into tears.

"I think, Adelise," Thurstan replied. "At the moment, if we were to go anywhere else, we would never totally be safe. But if we go to Jorvik, if we can speak to the king or someone close to him, then it ends. What I don't know is if it ends well or ends badly. But there is a chance; a chance that the king will help you, to get you back home to..." he voice trailed off and he glanced at Egbrand. The old man nodded.

"To become queen," the shepherd finished the sentence.

The young girl sniffed and wiped her eyes.

"I don't want to be queen at the moment. I want to be happy again, I want to be safe. Can I not stay here?"

"I don't think people will let us, Adelise," Thurstan replied. "For the time being it doesn't matter. You cannot go anywhere until you can walk again."

From outside the window, the call of an owl on its nightly hunt rang out. The hut's three occupants sat in silence, listening to the sound of the soft wind that was gently building, ruffling the long grass. The lamb, which Adelise had picked up to cradle, bleated mournfully.

"I ought to leave," Egbrand announced, standing up and taking the lamb from Adelise, which only seemed to compound her sadness. "Give it some thought, Thurstan, but not too much. Time is the one thing I fear you do not have. Tomorrow you shall not see me; I must work on my lord's land. The sheep will have to look after themselves." He tickled the lamb under its chin.

"Your lord, is he the Thane of Catune? He won't be looking for us?" Thurstan asked.

"I shouldn't worry too much. He lives back towards Haltune way. Being so close to Lonborg and the jarl, the thane here is not such a powerful man. There are those out in the wilds that believe themselves little jarls, but my lord is just happy to see us tend his crops and give him the occasional lamb."

"Will your wife come see us before we leave?" Adelise asked.

"I don't think so," Egbrand replied. "She isn't one for walking great distances, especially not up hills. The last thing she ought to be doing at the moment is to suddenly start strolling up fells, if we wish to avoid unwanted attention."

Adelise sagged with disappointment at his answer.

"It's enough for her to know that she can help," the shepherd continued. "I tell you what, though. Each morning she walks down to the river to wash clothes and gather water. I don't want you making yourself seen, but if you were look out of that far window, towards the river, you will probably see her. I'll ask her to take the longer path, so that you'll see her better."

Adelise beamed at his suggestion.

"How will I know if it's her? Can I wave?" she asked.

"Absolutely not." Egbrand stopped to think. "I'll tell her to put her wash basket down, as if she needs to adjust her dress or something. Just for a second, mind, but in view of the hillside. You keep yourselves out of sight."

Adelise grinned excitedly at his suggestion and gave the startled Egbrand a hug. He finally made his excuses and left, taking the increasingly loud lamb with him. Thurstan extinguished the candle with spit-dampened fingers, leaving the hut in total darkness. Adelise lay silently in the pitch black, her sadness a novel and unpleasant experience for Thurstan, who had grown used to the smiling, cheery little girl.

"Thurstan?" came Adelise's small voice, just as he was dropping off to sleep.

"Yes?" he replied.

"I know I am not your queen, because you come from Northland, but can I ask you something?" she asked, sounding unusually serious.

"Of course," Thurstan replied, unsure of what was coming next.

"In the infirmary, you promised to protect me. Do you still mean that? Will you promise not to leave me?" Her voice was trembling as if it were about to break into sobs at any minute. Thurstan swung himself out of the pallet, stood up and relit the candle with a small piece of flint. In the candlelight, he took out his knife and holding as if it were a sword, knelt in front of Adelise.

"I swear on my life, that you have my undying fealty and I promise I will protect you until you reach Ængland or I die in the attempt," he said. The words came naturally and he knew they were not empty promises; they were not a hollow attempt to please the girl. They contained real meaning, the only one he had left in his life now.

"Good," Adelise replied simply, and turned over to go to sleep.

Thurstan smiled, blew out the candle and climbed back onto the pallet. From somewhere outside, he could still here the lost lamb's distant bleating. Thurstan fell off to sleep, into dreams of children being lost, children being reunited and the fearful inevitability of the butcher's blade.

19th May 1166
Theodford, East Anglia, Ængland

Ceolwulf looked up from the parchment in his trembling hand as his mother quietly entered the dining hall. The Lady Cinedred spent a lot of her time nowadays wandering from room to room, or so it seemed to her son. She spoke little and divided the majority of her waking hours between tending to his sick father and visiting the Abbess of nearby St Wihtburh's. Ceolwulf was becoming convinced she would retire to the abbey the moment his father eventually died. She had lost none of her intuition, however, and her ability to gauge the mood of an individual at a quick glance; particularly that of her son or husband.

"What's wrong?" she asked. Ceolwulf was pale, the message in his hand held limply and his gaze focused on an empty space in mid air, some distance in front of him.

"Adelise," he said, his voice hoarse. "She's dead. Killed in Northland."

His mother blanched and steadied herself by gripping a chair. She had suspected that a message of some import had arrived, given all the shouting and clattering hoofbeats in the courtyard, but never something like this.

"How?"

"It doesn't say. It just says that the queen is dead." Ceolwulf passed the parchment to his mother.

"Saints preserve us," she said to herself, rereading the message. Ceolwulf rubbed his eyes with his palms and sighed.

"There was also a summons to a witenagemot of war from Earl Swegen. It doesn't say against whom, but surely a gemot of war can only mean one thing? Can they do that?" he asked. The Lady Cinedred laid a hand on her son's shoulder and peered at the second message, scanning it quickly.

"He's signing himself as Prince Swegen nowadays, is he? It's also signed by the Archbishop of Westmynster, I see," she said, with evident distaste.

"Is that significant?" Ceolwulf asked.

"Possibly. Probably not. I don't know what goes on in Winceaster anymore. Or Lunden, which is perhaps more important." She sat down next to her son and called for a serving girl to bring them some wine. "Yet you say Hakon seemed amicable when you met?"

"As someone plotting murder doubtlessly would," Ceolwulf mused. "It makes no sense, unless Swegen knows something we don't. There must be more to it."

"There are many things Swegen does that we know nothing about; most of which I wouldn't like to know about. I agree that a gemot of war seems hasty, but he must have some reason. It is no secret, Ceolwulf, that he is an expansionist. He has long wanted Ængland to reclaim the six shires south of the Hymbre, and it would be more than convenient for him to have a war," his mother observed, accepting a goblet of wine from the serving girl who had just scurried back into the room.

Ceolwulf leant back in his chair and took a second goblet from the young girl, the Flemish maid he had noticed more and more over the last couple of weeks. She was outstandingly beautiful, Ceolwulf thought, as his gaze locked on to hers for a second, just long enough to make him feel uncomfortable. He turned quickly back to his mother, hastily sipping at the wine.

"Convenience, coincidence; the fact remains that I must ride to Lunden within the week. I only hope that I will not be gone too long," Ceolwulf said. "I really ought to be here, when or if anything should happen to father. I mean, when he recovers." He smiled weakly at his mother. She returned the smile and gripped his hand.

"It would be best maybe if Ælfric were to accompany you on the trip?" she asked softly, tilting her head to one side. Ceolwulf placed the goblet down on the table, careful to avoid the eyes of the serving girl now standing in the corner of the room, behind his mother's shoulder.

"A week ago," he replied, his fingers drawing patterns in the spilt drops of wine. "You were chastising me for not assuming the responsibility of being earl. Now you wish me to be accompanied by my uncle, like a child visiting a relative."

"Don't be angry, Ceolwulf, Ælfric would be there just to help. You ask too much of yourself sometimes," his mother said.

"I'm not angry; but either I am assuming the role of earl or I am not. What kind of earl turns up to a witenagemot holding his uncle's hand?"

"You'd be surprised. No earl travels alone. No earl is without a retinue. Even kings have advisers, family members to guide them; you may not see it, but they are there."

Ceolwulf pinched the bridge of his nose between his fingers and yawned. He was getting testy and he cursed himself for being overly proud simply because of the presence of an attractive serving girl.

It was time, his mother had repeatedly insisted, that he married. His failing, according to the Lady Cinedred, was that he was looking for perfection, as he did with many things. A titled wife for children, a whore for the bedroom and a friend to talk to, as his father would have said. It was not clear if he had meant three separate women, or whether these were virtues to be found in one woman; he had certainly never divulged to Ceolwulf how many he had considered his mother to be.

"You're right, you're right," he said wearily. "I shall send word to Ælfric right away."

"It wouldn't surprise me if my brother already knew. Take him as an adviser, son. I fear things will be difficult enough at Lunden; you will need all the help you can get. Do not assume that when your father passes on, you will be automatically chosen as the next earl; these are strange times and nothing is to be taken for granted."

"What of father?" Ceolwulf asked.

"Speak to him before you go, take his advice. His mind is still sound, even if his body is failing him. But once you leave the walls of Theodford, put his illness far from your mind. You will be the Earl of East Anglia, and only you, whilst you attend the witenagemot. When this is all over, then you can think about father again."

"So we go to war because father and I did not secure safe passage?" Ceolwulf asked wearily.

"You know it will not be as simple as that. Even the mightiest of kings cannot have full control over the wilds in his country. The witan should never have let her travel by caravan through the mountains; she should have sailed," his mother said bitterly.

"I have nought but fond memories of her. Notwithstanding she was a queen, she was a most pleasant, good-natured child," Ceolwulf said, leaning back. The Flemish maid glanced sadly at him; he pretended not to have seen her.

"She would have grown up to be a well-balanced young queen, I like to think; thanks in no small part to us," the Lady Cinedred said with a trace of pride. "To think that she has met a violent end so far from home, it breaks my heart."

"I would swear an oath to seek revenge on the man who dared raise a hand against her, but I fear we may never know," Ceolwulf said, straightening in his chair.

"And it is this that worries," his mother chided him. "Your desire, your fondness for impetuous, righteous heroics. You will hear some fine examples of blustering rhetoric, of well fed and well wined old men, telling a full hall of how their mighty fist of vengeance shall punish the perpetrators of such a crime. You will hear many exaggerations, many outlandish claims and some outright lies. There are times to hold your tongue, to use it another day; there are times to take a stand. Learning the difference between the two is more difficult than spotting a lie or knowing right or wrong. Knowing which way the witan are swimming in the political river is no easy thing."

The Lady Cinedred finished her goblet of wine and stared at her son. "I have been the wife of a nobleman for over thirty years, attended justice courts, lived around royalty, watched so many important men act like fools and it never ceases to amaze me the ease with which otherwise intelligent men can say the most stupid of things when they let themselves get caught up in the fires of passion. Watch what you say, to whom and think about why you would say it."

She stood up, pushed her chair back and leant over her son, placing a hand on his head.

"The same goes for women too," she said quietly, a gentle smile playing across her lips. She stepped away and walked towards the door, which the Flemish maid opened for her. She paused in the open doorway and turned to Ceolwulf. "I shall write to my brother immediately, telling him to be here within three days. If we send it now, it will be with him by tonight."

With that, she left the room, leaving Ceolwulf, his cheeks tinged with the faintest of blushes, to mumble a few words of thanks to the attractive young girl. He clumsily stood up and placed the chair back at the table. On his way out, he paused to speak to the girl, instantly regretting the decision the second he opened his mouth and found that he had no words to say to her.

"You," he started. He felt his mouth go dry, his tongue felt enormous and heavy; his throat felt as if an apple were lodged in his windpipe. The girl's golden tresses swayed gently down the front of her red woollen dress, bouncing gently against the curves of her chest that the shapeless garment did little to mask. Ceolwulf realised that she was smiling at him; her teeth were an almost pearlescent white; unusual for a slave he had thought, but then again, those with the best teeth fetched the best prices.

"You," he tried again. "You are from Flanders?"

"Yes, my lord," she replied. Her head was bowed, but her eyes were gazing upwards, politely meeting his. Ceolwulf had no idea how to reply to that. He had heard of Flanders, he had met merchants and minor noblemen from there, but he had never visited.

"Good," he heard himself reply, before his brain could stop his mouth. He turned and walked out of the room, not pausing until he had left the hall, crossed the courtyard and submerged his head in a butt of rainwater. After several seconds, he pulled his face out, wiped his eyes dry with his sleeve and tried to gather his thoughts.

Adelise was dead, his father was dying, he was to act as the Earl of East Anglia at the witenagemot and he might yet be held responsible in some part for the queen's death. And he was also worrying about what a freed slave girl thought of him; a girl whose name he did not even know.

Once this was over, Ceolwulf thought to himself, he really ought to visit the Thegn of Castra. The thegn owned large swathes of land around Dunwic, and as far as Ceolwulf could remember, had five unmarried daughters.

He would spend the rest of the day practicing his swordwork at the town's garrison, he decided. Physical exercise could clear the mind of all kinds of vexation and worry, and he greatly felt the need for that at the moment.

Ceolwulf stared up into the sky and watched a marsh harrier hovering over the fields outside the town walls. Calm, still, patient, just waiting for the right moment to dive down and take its prey in one swift, killing stroke. It would be no bad thing to emulate should war come to East Anglia, Ceolwulf thought. The question was, against whom would he be forced to strike?

24th May 1166
Catune, Westmoringaland, Northland

The tears streamed down Adelise's face as she watched clumps of her hair fall past her shoulders to the floor. She had tried to suppress her sobs, but her eyes had welled up the moment Egbrand had cut the first tress with shears normally used for his sheep. Thurstan was standing in front of her, showing encouragement, but she felt utterly miserable. She thought back to the last time her hair had been brushed, laughing with Eadgyð, talking to her aunt; now she was stood wearing naught but a woollen shift and having her hair cropped short like a boy's.

"You do understand why we must do this, don't you?" Thurstan asked her.

She nodded sullenly, watching the final strands fall away. She flinched as the old scissors pulled at her scalp, struggling to cut through her thick hair.

"The clothes I brought, there," Egbrand said, nodding towards a bundle of rags in the corner of the hut. "They belonged to a little boy in the village about your age. He slipped on the ice last winter and cracked his head. He died of a brain fever two weeks later, sadly. He was my wife's cousin's boy; she gave Bathylle the clothes to make into cloths or a blanket, I'm not quite sure. But you can use them, they're clean and warm. There are a couple of bits of leather that might have once been shoes for you too, Thurstan."

Adelise thanked Egbrand, but her voice and face betrayed her misery.

"If I am disguised as a boy, can we still not enter Lonborg?" she asked.

"I would not do so. There may be some of Vinder's men who know my face and I cannot be certain that the jarl was not part of the betrayal," Thurstan answered.

Part of her wanted to suggest that they return to Scotland, to Carleol, to her family, but she knew they could not risk travelling through the valleys and hills near to the Great South Road again. She knew that at the moment, that which she wanted and that which was best for her future were not the same thing. Egbrand moved in front of her, squinting through his wrinkled eyes, trying to trim a straight line into her new fringe. Gingerly she reached a hand up to the back of her head and gasped.

"It's like I've got a bowl on my head. A bowl of hair. My neck feels cold," she complained. "I almost feel like a Norman."

Thurstan laughed and reassured her that it would pass. He stepped around to admire Egbrand's inelegant handiwork from all angles.

"Have you hurt your neck?" he asked, looking at an angry patch of raised skin on the back of her neck.

"No, I was born with that. It doesn't hurt," she replied. She sniffed noisily, the last of her tears starting to dry.

"We'll probably have to cover that up, just in case," Thurstan commented, half to himself. Egbrand stepped back and looked down at Adelise, his face a contrast of pride at a job well done and sadness at what he had just inflicted on the girl's beautiful long hair.

"There, you look just like a good little Northlandic boy now," he remarked jovially, causing a fresh flood of tears and Adelise to fling herself onto her straw pallet in the corner of the hut. Thurstan gave the old shepherd a shrug and beckoned him to step outside. It was raining heavily, but the hut's overhanging thatch roof offered some protection. They would be unseen from the village in this weather, but they still walked to the back of the hut to be certain.

"How long has it been since the priest received that message about fugitives being sought?" Thurstan asked, squatting against the wall.

"Nearly a week," Egbrand replied, kneeling beside him.

"And yet still no sign of any soldiers or huskarls. No-one has come asking questions?"

"Not a soul."

For a week, they had awoken each morning expecting to hear the sound of boots outside, of the door being kicked down. But each day had passed and there had been no search parties, no soldiers hunting them. With each day that passed, Adelise's strength grew, to the point now that they felt ready to leave. If the weather abated, they would set off tomorrow, Thurstan thought, if not that very evening.

"The rumour goes," Egbrand continued. "That the order did not come from the jarl, but from Sheriff Vinder. Jarl Herri did not take kindly to that; he doesn't like what Vinder gets up to in Kirkby and the Cumbric wapentakes, but he can normally turn a blind eye to it. Coming down here like that, so soon after the ambush; well let's say the story going around is that Vinder and Herri are not the best of friends."

"Has no-one made the connection between us and the attack?"

"I don't think so, no. The story was that all the huskarls had been slain and that the only Ænglisc survivor had identified the queen's body. Nobody has any reason to think that it's you, although folk in these parts are always suspicious of stories from outside of the valley. They even say that the fugitives had been found at Glæssen a few days ago."

"So we may yet be safe from search parties?" Thurstan asked. Egbrand shrugged.

"Who knows? Is anyone ever safe when there is a reward at stake? For Vinder to be searching down here is strange, but I believe the sheriff is a strange man."

"That he definitely is, I can assure you," Thurstan replied.

"So you will walk to Jorvik from here then?" Egbrand asked.

"That's the plan, if you can call it a plan." Thurstan said wearily. "There do not appear to be many alternatives; but then last night Adelise herself declared that we would go to Jorvik.

She would parley with King Hakon, as Queen of Ængland."

"She looks like a stable boy," Egbrand noted. "My advice would be to make sure she speaks to no-one, and don't let anyone have a good look at her, particularly her birthmark."

"I agree," Thurstan said. He gazed into the gloom, where a huddled mass of sheep could just be made out. The water was cascading off the thatched roof, forming tiny rivers in the mud around the hut. The thought of walking to the next field or valley seemed unpleasant enough in this weather, let alone to Jorvik.

"Just follow the east road, into the hills and keep going to Scipton. From there the road to Jorvik is fairly well trodden, I believe, but you will have to pass over the peaks. They're no mountains, but if you get caught out in the open in bad weather, they can be as treacherous," Egbrand said. "More than that, I cannot say. I have never travelled the road myself, but we see plenty of travellers pass through here to and from Jorvik."

"I think we will not take the road, but follow it at a distance, keeping it in view. We don't want to have to encounter more people than absolutely necessary."

"I understand," Egbrand replied, shivering in the damp. The rain started to come down even heavier, which Thurstan had not thought possible. Visibility was such that even the hedgerows at the bottom of the field could not be seen.

"How do we ever thank you, for what you have done? Without you the Queen of Ængland may well have died in those first few days," Thurstan said. Egbrand snorted and wafted his hands in the air, as if he were waving away such a suggestion.

"I would have helped her even if she had been the poorest farmer's daughter. I've spent my whole life tending to the lost or weak; I see no reason to change now. I want nothing from it; your salvation is reward enough. Although you could ask King Hakon to exempt me from my taxes," Egbrand laughed. He stood up and looked around for his crook. "I think in this weather, you are probably safe to light a fire. I would burn the girl's hair; leave nothing behind if you can. There should be enough food for you for a few days, as long as you don't eat too much. I shall try to come by tomorrow, but if you can leave earlier, then do so; do not wait for my visit."

Egbrand wrapped his cloak around him, leaving only his beaked nose sticking out from his hood. Heavy raindrops ran down his forehead and converged to form a constant trickle from the tip of his protruding nose. The cold and wet didn't appear to bother him though; the years of herding sheep on the fells had rendered the old man impervious to all but the foulest of weather.

"Fare thee well, my Lord Thurstan," the old man said, gripping the huskarl's shoulder.

"Thank you," came the reply, heartfelt and sincere.

With that, Egbrand set out in to the dark, without as much as a glance behind him. Thurstan watched until his grey cloak had disappeared into the gloom and then returned inside the hut. This night, hopefully their last, he would follow Egbrand's advice and light a small fire. He stepped through the door and found the small shape of Adelise lying in the corner asleep. Instinctively he checked she was breathing, then relaxed as he realised she was no longer in danger of not waking each time she slept. He watched her blanket rise and fall softly in the gloom, as he tried lighting some dried grass with flint. As the fire took hold, the first high flames cast long shadows around the hut, making Adelise seem even smaller than she was.

Thurstan settled back and reflected that for the first time in his life, he had something tangible, something worthy to fight for and defend. Something other than himself, something more than ego. Was it happiness? No, he could not be happy that he was being hunted, nor did the thought of having the life of a child in his hands make him joyous. Responsible, he thought; he had been given a duty, a purpose. He had little more than a couple of leather scraps and twine for boots, few rations, a natural gift for self-preservation, a general sense that Jorvik lay to the east and a nine-year-old girl recovering from an infected wound.

He closed his eyes and let the warmth seep into his legs. There was though, Thurstan mused, the slightest scintilla of excitement that only the thrill of facing a challenge can bring. As his chin dropped and his eyes started to close, Thurstan recalled a saying his tutor used to quote about over-confidence, by one of the old writers from a faraway country. It was a sobering flicker of caution at the back of his mind just as sleep overcame him.

There is nowhere I can safely put my trust.

25th May 1166
Lunden, Ængland

The red kite soared over Lunden, its arched wings twisting as it curved through the air, searching for the carrion and waste that lined the streets of the city below. The city that was the largest in Ængland, the largest of the British islands and, if the recent emissary to Rome's claims were to be believed, now the largest city in Christendom. The kite glided over the eastern walls at Aldgate, originally built by the Romans, strengthened and restored by Tostig II's father, and passed over the dilapidated Tower of Lunden. It swept down towards the markets around Walbrook, tempted by the food and rats, but the bustle of bodies kept it away.

Over thirty thousand humans lived in this nest of streets and alleys, all packed into an area that had not expanded for nearly a thousand years. To the west, the towers of St Paul's cathedral came into view, its roof recently repaired after a fire had damaged it in the 1080s. The kite swept north, over the packed houses of Cheapside, towards the King's Hall, nestling in the north-west corner of the city by Cripplegate. The bird flew around the longhall, over its stone walls and courtyard, circling the only building that was even higher than the kite.

The Ivory Tower of Lunden emerged out of the fortifications of the King's Hall and loomed over four hundred feet above the streets below. Construction had been started during the reign of Tostig II and was completed nearly forty years later by his son, Æthelgar. As with many things commissioned by Tostig, it had been built purely for the sake of existing. It had but one purpose —simply to be the tallest building in the world, to show other nations the ability of Ænglisc stonesmiths and architects. Yet unlike many of the late king's buildings, it did at least possess some practical function.

From its top a man could see to the horizon in all directions; it was said that during the summer, the setting sun would cast its shadow across the entire city to the eastern walls and Bishopsgate. Built in stone but painted with limewash, the tower stood like a shining pillar, radiating across the city, visible for miles around. Such was its scale, it was reckoned, that once painting had been finished at its top, the team of men perpetually employed to keep it white would have to start again at its base. It had been lauded as a symbol of peace, a symbol of God, a symbol of power; most people just thought of it as 'The Tower'.

Swegen observed the kite gliding around the tower from the viewing chamber on the top floor. Every year, when visiting Lunden, he would challenge himself to scale the maze of staircases that led to the very top. It would leave him breathless and aching each time, but the view was most certainly worth the exertion.

Swegen watched the bird swoop down and disappear between the roofs of the huddled houses by Aldersgate. He shivered as his cloak flapped around him; what was a gentle breeze at ground level howled through the open stone windows of the viewing chamber, hundreds of feet higher. A gust of wind caused the iron crucifix fixed on top of the church-like spire above him to whistle.

A loud knock came from the wooden trapdoor that led to the staircase below. Swegen shouted a reply and the trapdoor opened to reveal a guard whose face was bright red from the climb up the tower. He was followed by Ricmund, the Eoten, who appeared to have not even broken a sweat. The man truly was a beast, Swegen thought. He was wearing new leather armour, he noted; finest black leather trimmed with crimson felt. Since his return from Northland, Ricmund had been spending money freely in Lunden. At least that was what Swegen's normally reliable sources had told him. Though many would question the man's newfound wealth, most would hopefully just assume it had come from some ill-gotten gains in Readinga; bribery by local officials or fleecing a local priory. Ricmund already had a reputation for raising personal funds in a less than legal manner, but Swegen wished the man would show more sense and spend subtlely.

"Leave us," Swegen said brusquely to the guards that had joined them on the top floor. He waited until the trapdoor shut before turning back to look out across the city from the window, his hands clasped behind his back. Ricmund walked slowly across the large circular room to join him, the wind causing his clothes to flap violently around him.

"Look out there, Ricmund," Swegen said.

Ricmund looked out across the roofs, churches and the snaking form of the river Temese, across to the rapidly growing town of Suthwerc, and feigned interest.

"Impressive, isn't it?" Swegen asked. He started walking clockwise around the large room, pausing to look out of each window. "It's the biggest city, the richest city, the most populated city and yet it is not the capital. Does that make sense to you?"

"No, my lord."

"Likewise if a lord, an earl say, is widely considered to be the most powerful, the most capable, able to raise the largest army or command the most loyalty, then it would make sense for him to be king, would it not?" Swegen asked. He paused to look out of the western-facing windows, towards the small town of Ealdwic. Further west, around a southern bend in the river, the imposing cathedral of Westmynster sat on Thorn Island, dwarfing the single-storey buildings huddled around it. Ricmund remained silent; sensing an answer either way was not needed.

"I, as king, would make this city my capital. I would have the largest cathedral here, the most prosperous court. You, my dear Ricmund, would become the most powerful earl, lord of our largest shire. Yet the whole thing might not happen, which troubles me greatly." Swegen turned to Ricmund. Swegen's narrow face looked pained, the Eoten thought, his thin lips clasped together tightly.

"My lord?" Ricmund asked. Swegen walked on, seemingly ignoring Ricmund.

"You understand that the house of cards, upon which we are gently building my kingship, could be knocked down with the slightest clumsy mistake. All it takes is one oversight, the wrong word said in the wrong ear. If Rome were not to support my bid for the throne, should the earls not believe for one minute that my ascension is anything other than legitimate and that Adelise's death was anything other than an accident, or the responsibility of Northland, then the future may well turn out very differently. Badly. Especially for me. But most of all, for you."

Swegen snapped the last few words out in short bursts, as if they were swift dagger blows. He looked at the Eoten, trying not to stare at the thick, smooth scar that ran down the left-hand side of his otherwise craggy and pock-marked face; in the morning light the taut skin was almost shiny, as though it had been polished. Ricmund stared back, his expression blank and motionless except for when he blinked, which he did slowly and infrequently.

"Why do you think it is," Swegen asked, leaning in towards the taller man, "that I am hearing from my sources in Northland, and more specifically, in Lonborg, that the Sheriff of Westmoringaland is searching for a missing girl? A missing girl kidnapped, I am told, or possibly rescued, by a soldier, a huskarl?"

Ricmund replied with a simple shrug, displaying he had little interest in such matters, now he was back in Ængland.

"That this girl has been sought since the time of our attack? Does that not worry you? Does that not make you wonder just what girl the sheriff would be so interested in, that he would get half a shire looking for her?" Swegen pressed.

"Girls go missing all the time, kidnapped, sold into slavery, forced into marriage; I don't see this being so unusual, my lord," Ricmund replied. "We found Adelise's ring on her corpse, my lord. Surely this more proof than some random missing girl in Northland over a week later?"

"It is somewhat coincidental, don't you think?" Swegen continued, though the mention of the queen's ring that he was now wearing on a chain under his tunic had given him a warm and calming feeling of pleasure.

"Has their King Hakon issued any edict? Has the Jarl of Westmoringaland involved himself in any of this?" Ricmund asked.

"No," Swegen replied, with a shake of his head. "It's apparently just Vinder. He's sent men riding into the valleys around Lonborg, though apparently the descriptions of the fugitives are rather vague, save for the fact they're looking for a girl of around nine years of age. No explanation, apart from that. It's all rather pathetically discreet by all accounts."

"Then I wouldn't worry," Ricmund said calmly. He stared out across the city, the breeze ruffling his thick, matted hair.

"You wouldn't, would you not?" Swegen sneered.

"If Adelise was still alive, which I know she isn't, my lord, as I saw her headless body, then wouldn't we have heard by now? Even if she is, then she'll probably never be found. Vinder can hardly explain himself to the jarl or the king, can he?" Ricmund asked. He was convincing himself as much as he was trying to convince Swegen. "If she is found, then Vinder would have to kill her; he'd end up doing the very thing we set out to do in the first place. In some ways, that would be better – Northlanders would have killed her after all."

Swegen mulled this over for several seconds before clasping his hands in front of his lips and shaking his head slowly.

"No, Ricmund. I would suggest that under whatever circumstances, if Adelise is still alive, then that is a bad thing. A very bad thing. A catastrophe, to be precise. Should I discover that the task you had promised me complete was in fact, not complete, then I am sure you can appreciate that I would be most grievously upset."

"I saw her dead on the floor, I don't know what more I could have done, my lord," Ricmund retorted, keen to end this conversation and to find himself an alehouse.

"But not her head, I understand?" Swegen asked.

"No. Not her head. We assumed the Northlanders would find it, we didn't have time to start searching in the undergrowth for all missing body parts," Ricmund replied tersely.

"Unfortunately for us, by the time the girl's head was found, it had already been severely disfigured by blade and by animals; by all accounts it will be impossible to recognise her by the time she reaches us," Swegen said.

"Unfortunately, my lord?" Ricmund asked.

"There will always be a doubt that perhaps it was not Adelise, that perhaps it is the body of some other girl, a serving girl, a maid. Sadly, it is from stories such as these that myths are made." Swegen sighed.

"The body I saw wore the royal ring, my lord, it belonged to a young girl; too young for a maid. Besides, my lord," Ricmund said, changing tack, "what matters most is that the earls recognise you as the heir. If this body convinces them to do that, then surely whether it is her is irrelevant. It's not what is that counts, it's what the witan believe. Who's going to challenge you, once you become king? If a small girl from Northland turns up in years to come and announces that she's Adelise, who's going to believe her?"

Swegen exhaled loudly and started pacing around the room again. Ricmund followed him, keeping a few paces behind him, despite Swegen continuing the conversation.

"Ricmund, I know you are trying to reassure me, but let us not delude ourselves. I do not like uncertainty; I do not wish to depend on the fact that there are no other reasonable alterna-

tives. I want it to be understood clearly that Adelise is dead."
Swegen turned and flashed a grin; a narrow sliver of white teeth
showing between thin lips. He placed a slender hand on
Ricmund's massive shoulder. "My friend, if the queen really is
dead, then this country will owe you a great debt of gratitude.
When the Norse invaders are finally driven back into the sea,
when our land is reunited, then your name shall be hailed as one
of our saviours. They will not ask the means of how or why, only
of the great service you performed."

"I would rather they didn't mention my name at all,"
Ricmund interrupted. Swegen gave another quick smile.

"Let me ask you frankly then. Do I have any reason to be
concerned?" Swegen asked.

Again, the images of the fleeing shapes across the sands
returned to Ricmund's mind, the fleeing huskarl from the copse.

"No, my lord," Ricmund replied, holding Swegen's gaze.
Swegen stared back for several more seconds, and then took his
hand away from the Eoten's shoulder.

"In which case we shall speak no more about it," he said. The
grin flickered once more, then Swegen span away and strode to
the centre of the room, leaving Ricmund to gather his thoughts.
He gave three sharp tugs on a small length of rope that ran up
from the trapdoor. Somewhere below, a shrill bell rang out,
followed a few moments later by the sound of boots on stairs. The
trapdoor flew open, and the two guards that had accompanied
Ricmund up the stairs appeared. The Eoten tensed for a moment,
fearing they were being summoned to seize him, having been put
ill at ease by Swegen's dismissive manner.

"I trust I shall see you at supper this evening?" Swegen asked
cordially.

Ricmund nodded, mumbled a farewell and let himself be
escorted back down the series of staircases to the bottom of the
tower. Several minutes later, his feet aching, and cursing Swegen
for insisting on meeting on top of that damned building,

Ricmund stepped out onto the narrow cobbled streets that surrounded the King's Hall.

He stood for a few minutes on the street, letting the bustling crowds wash around him. He toyed with the idea of riding back to Readinga that evening and sending men to Northland, to hunt down whomever it was that Vinder was seeking. How would they find her though, without drawing attention to themselves? They could not use the same deception twice.

Ricmund shook his head and cursed himself; he was becoming soft. Adelise's corpse was arriving tonight; there was no time to start chasing another girl hundreds of miles away. Trying to cleanse the nonsense from his mind, Ricmund snorted and spat into the road, then strode off for a much-deserved drink at the nearest alehouse.

Candlelight flickered off the stone walls of St Edward's Chapel, where Queen Adelise's small, linen-wrapped body had been lain out on a wooden table. It had arrived at St Paul's Cathedral that evening, on a black painted carriage, accompanied by twelve armed riders; much as she had meant to arrive for her coronation, but fate had cruelly twisted the circumstances. Now, as the time for compline neared, the monks from the nearby monastery of St Albinus were already working on the unenviable task of preparing her body both spiritually and physically.

In the shadows of the nave, Ceolwulf watched as the robed figures murmured their prayers. He knew that the words were attempting to ensure that her spirit passed safely into the realm of God, for many believed that it was at risk. Even though the Norse invaders had converted to Christianity over two hundred years ago, many Ænglisc still believed that their northern neighbours retained their erstwhile Pagan ways. There were people who believed that by dying in the ungodly far north, Adelise's soul might well have been lost. Ceolwulf had not seen anything during his trip to Jorvik to suggest that Northland was any less

Christian than Ængland. Many of their churches appeared to reflect the nation's Norse origins, but then again, did not many Ænglisc buildings show traces of Roman influence?

Ceolwulf and his uncle, Ælfric, had made the two-day ride to Lunden with twenty men, leaving his sick father lying on what would no doubt become his deathbed. They had arrived the previous evening, housing themselves in one of the many buildings surrounding the King's Hall. As two of the few remaining kin of the late queen, albeit distant, Ceolwulf and Ælfric had seen fit to accompany Adelise's body from Bishopsgate to St Paul's. Not even Swegen had visited his cousin's body, but no doubt, he had more pressing matters to attend to before the gemot. Ælfric was now deep in prayer by the altar, but Ceolwulf had stayed with the body to watch the sad ceremony.

He winced as one of the monks who was not occupying himself with the Latin rites unwrapped the swaddling from around the corpse's head and neck. The discoloured skin looked black in this light, but even from where Ceolwulf stood, he could see that the girl's features were no longer there. A horrendous wound had destroyed any semblance of a face, which the intervening week had decayed into a twisted mass of bone and dead flesh. He looked on, viewing the sight not as one of a human body, of a girl that was distantly his own kin, but of a thing, an unseeing, unfeeling object. To think for more than a moment that the abomination on the table had once been the cheerful, sweet girl that his family had hosted for a summer, would have caused the nausea swelling in his stomach to overcome him.

The monk leant forward and seemed to sprinkle water around the wounds, not to clean them, but to purify from sin, Ceolwulf imagined. He wafted a hand in an attempt to disperse some of the thick incense smoke coming from the chapel. It was used to allay the stench of decay, but he was finding it as putrid a miasma as that which it was meant to cover.

Although Ceolwulf had heard of the poor girl's decapitation, it still came as a shock when the monk gently lifted her head away from the remains of the neck and jaw. He turned away, not wanting to stare at the gore unnecessarily, and waited for the bile in his throat to subside. The monk had laid the head reverently onto a cushion, the hair plaited into a single coiled braid. He slowly bent down and removed from a small chest a small white plaster mask, which Ceolwulf understood was to be used for the funeral. Placed on to the remains of the head, it gave the face a strange, statue-like appearance. Ceolwulf thought it possibly unnecessary, but it did at least restore a much-needed degree of humanity to the poor girl.

The monk turned the body over and started to clean from the back of the head downwards. He unwrapped some of the dirty swaddling covering the neck and shoulders to be able to cleanse properly around the blackening wound. Ceolwulf gasped loudly, causing the monk to turn. Stepping into the chapel, Ceolwulf walked between the line of chanting monks to stand beside the body. The elderly monk tending to the body frowned at the nobleman, but nodded sadly when Ceolwulf gave his name and explained that he was a distant cousin of the late queen.

Ceolwulf peered down at the bottom of the corpse's neck. The skin was mottled, darkening, but he was quite sure his eyes were not deceiving him. Even in this light, Ceolwulf could clearly see no sign of the birthmark that he knew Adelise possessed. He had noticed it during her stay in Theodford; he had even queried it with the family's priest as such marks were often interpreted as signs of witchery. Despite the damage to the head, despite the decaying skin, it was clear that there was no such mark on this body, nor was there a wound to suggest there had ever been. He glanced around to see whether any of the other monks had noticed, but he realised that very few people would be aware of such a birthmark; certainly not those present.

"Is something troubling you, my lord?" the monk asked,

seeing the torment on Ceolwulf's face.

This is not the queen, he thought, *this is not Adelise.* Ceolwulf looked at the body for several seconds then shook his head.

"Just the tragedy and deep sadness I feel at seeing such a terrible thing done to one of my own kin, one so young too," he said, crossing himself. "Take good care of her, won't you, brother?"

The monk nodded. Ceolwulf stepped away from the table and walked, almost blindly to where Ælfric was praying. He knelt down beside him, bowing his head as if he were saying a prayer for the soul of the late queen. His uncle was talking quietly in Latin, his eyes closed, reciting a passage from memory.

"That's not Adelise," Ceolwulf said in a whisper.

"*...libera nos a malo...*" his uncle's voice tailed off. He remained silent, not moving a muscle.

"I said..." Ceolwulf started to whisper.

"I heard," Ælfric replied. He raised his head and looked towards the large wooden crucifix behind the high altar. "Are you sure?"

"Absolutely," Ceolwulf replied. Ælfric stood and wiped the dust from his knees.

"*Libera nos a malo* indeed, then," the elder man said weakly. "Let us go."

The two men walked quickly down the nave, passing the chapel that contained the monks tending to the girl's body, their boots echoing loudly on the stone flags. St Paul's appeared to be almost empty, save for the monks, but to the sides, hidden in the shadows behind the columns that ran for the length of the nave, Ceolwulf could see pikemen standing guard. He was not sure exactly against whom they had been deployed, or whether they were there ceremonially, but he knew it would be best not to discuss the queen in their presence. Pausing only to collect their swords from a sallow youth at the main door, the two men stepped out into the night air.

Ceolwulf let the cool breeze and noise of the city wash over him, letting it clear his head and refresh him. The darkness and incense of the cathedral had made him feel light-headed, but out here in the fresh air, the implications of what he had seen still seemed nightmarish.

They crossed the small Roman-style square in front of St Paul's, collecting Lyfing, Ælfric's steward and the five armed escorts who had been waiting for them outside. Without exchanging a single word, they walked the half mile through the narrow streets, back towards their lodgings. The walk only took a manner of minutes; the combination of the late hour and travelling in a party of armed men ensured they were not hindered in their progress. Only when they were back in their lodgings, behind several closed doors and alone together in Ælfric's chambers did either man dare to speak.

"Who else knows of this birthmark?" Ælfric asked, once Ceolwulf had recounted everything he had seen and knew.

"I do not know for certain; I imagine many of them to be dead. My parents and their servants, obviously. Her family in Scotland, but they will never see the corpse," Ceolwulf replied. He shuddered as he imagined he could still smell the stench from the cathedral, as if it had become trapped in the folds of his clothes, unleashing itself each time he moved.

"Does Swegen know about it?" Ælfric asked. He was pacing around his chamber, hands clasped behind his back, speaking but never looking at the seated Ceolwulf.

"Good question. Again, I would say I do not know. He is family, but I doubt he has ever shared sleeping quarters with her. I suppose it would be more common knowledge amongst servants than earls and noblemen," Ceolwulf replied.

"Priests would know," Ælfric said, still pacing.

"Her priest would, possibly, or those of whomever were in close contact with her," Ceolwulf said, recalling his own conversation with a priest about her birthmark. "Who baptised her?"

"It was here in Lunden, if I recall correctly. There was a big thing about it, a big ceremony, that I didn't go to, but your father did." Ælfric closed his eyes in recollection.

"Westmynster, wasn't it? The archbishop is the same one now, isn't he?" Ceolwulf said. Ælfric nodded with an expression that seemed to suggest that that fact was not the best news.

"So what do we do? Surely we must tell the witan?" Ceolwulf asked. "The earls must know."

Ælfric stopped pacing and took a chair next to Ceolwulf. He sat down and spoke quietly and quickly to his nephew.

"Ask yourself this: why did you not tell me in the cathedral? Why did you wait until we returned? Why did you not cry out immediately?"

"Because," Ceolwulf started, trying to find the right words. "Because it seems such an impossible thing, such a momentous thing to happen, that it must be said with certainty and to the right people."

"And?" his uncle pressed. Ceolwulf exhaled and lightly punched the table.

"And because I would not trust Swegen to not to have resorted to foul deeds to ensure his path to the throne is clear. If I shout out that Adelise is alive tonight, I might not see the morning," he replied, frustrated by both his cynicism and the realisation that he was probably right. "I'm not suggesting that Swegen had any hand in her death, but he certainly stands to gain the most by it."

"But you think that tomorrow, you can stand up in front of the witan and announce this. That you will be safe from Swegen, protected by the numbers present?" Ælfric asked.

"You obviously believe I won't be," Ceolwulf replied.

"You obviously underestimate how much support he has," Ælfric retorted.

"You don't think more earls would want irrefutable proof that Adelise is dead."

"I think it doesn't matter whether they believe she is dead or not. What matters more are the promises of wealth and land to be gained should Swegen ascend to the throne."

"So you are suggesting I say nothing, that I keep it to myself?" Ceolwulf snapped.

"That is precisely what I am suggesting. All you can say is that you believe that that poor thing lying in St Paul's is not Adelise. Unless you can produce the actual queen, alive and well, it all means nothing. No, it's not Adelise, Swegen will tell his earls, but the actual one was hacked to bits, so we used some peasant girl's corpse as we needed something to entomb."

"You think that is what he has done?"

"I have no idea. What I do think though, is that if you stand in front of the witenagemot and announce that Adelise is not dead, then you risk much, much more than being wrong."

Ceolwulf stood up and walked to a window that looked out into the courtyard of the King's Hall. Even here, on the eve of a witenagemot, whores were permitted to freely wander the arcades and squares around Ængland's largest longhall.

"What would my father do? What would he say if he knew the body was Adelise?" Ceolwulf asked. Ælfric sighed and ran a finger across his brow, trying to rub away the strains of the day.

"Your father would not say a word. He would not stand up in front of a witan led by the earl who stands to inherit the throne, who is supported by the archbishops and counter him by saying that the queen is not dead, but yet be unable to produce the evidence."

"I cannot stand by and watch Swegen take the throne and plan Lord alone knows what, if Adelise is not dead. You've heard the rumours, I take it. That he plans to discuss military matters, that the death negates the peace treaty of the Morcar Oath?" Ceolwulf asked, his hands outstretched in exasperation.

"I have heard them and I believe them. I don't think for a minute that Swegen's expansionist or warlike ambitions are going to help your cause if you accuse him."

"But I won't be accusing him. I'm just saying that that...that thing in St Paul's is not Adelise."

"I'd be very surprised if he doesn't see it as an accusation. Swegen has spent the last ten years surrounding himself with his favourites and not being told 'no'. Take my advice, Ceolwulf; do not say a word tomorrow."

The door rattled on its hinges as it slammed behind Ceolwulf on his way out. Ælfric sighed and shook his head. As if matters were not complicated enough, he thought to himself. He took out the message that had arrived that afternoon from Theodford and reread it. Tomorrow, he mused, was going to be a very eventful day indeed.

26th May 1166
Catune, Westmoringaland, Northland

The early morning sun dried the rain-drenched fields, the patchwork of vivid greens bright against the pale blue sky. The rolling dark forests, the mirrored ribbon of the River Lon and the sheep-dotted pastures; all of them seemed as if they had been created as a living tapestry just for Adelise's pleasure. Cabbage whites fluttered past her head as she sat outside the door, letting the sun warm her feet. The fragrance of drying grass and wild flowers hung in the air, a welcome contrast to the smell of damp straw that lingered in the hut.

Thurstan emerged from around the back of the hut, having returned from the small woods where they performed their ablutions and collected water. He was drinking from a small leather pouch and for the first time in many a day, felt refreshed and ready for the trip ahead. He studied the reclining Adelise and noted with approval that she really did look like a young peasant boy. Only by looking closely would one note the girlish features, and even then, a spot of dirt or mud on the cheeks could easily persuade the casual observer that this was a typical, albeit not particularly talkative, Northlandic boy.

He ducked inside the door and checked their provisions. They had two small bags of dry food and a couple of water pouches. They would not be short of fresh water, Thurstan imagined, for they would be following the river, then crossing the stream-laced hills to the east. His main fear was that of exposure, being caught in bad weather, but they had precious little choice in the matter. Adelise had wanted to wait until they had bid Egbrand farewell another time before leaving. Thurstan had doubted the wisdom of such sentimentalities, but waiting for dusk before setting out did not seem such a bad idea. Travelling during the day, particularly on one as clear as this, only put them at risk of being seen.

Thurstan stepped outside and his heart skipped a beat as he realised Adelise was nowhere to be seen. He glanced around, fearful that she had been snatched by an unheard assailant. A movement further down the field, towards the valley floor caught his eye. He relaxed as he saw the figure of Adelise, only for fear to retake him as he saw that she was waving. The old leper house was mostly unsighted from the village, due to the surrounding trees, but by walking downhill, when the valley was free of fog, one could easily see the winding river and houses of Catune. And be seen.

Thurstan sprinted towards Adelise, not daring to call out and attract any more attention than she already was. Even from the valley side, Thurstan could see that she was trying to attract the attention of a figure carrying a clothesbasket between the houses and the river. Bathylle, he thought, the shepherd's wife she had promised to greet. He called Adelise's name as loudly as he dared, but she was jumping and laughing with delight, oblivious to the approaching Thurstan, as Bathylle waved back. Thurstan reached Adelise at a sprint and flung her to the ground, both of them rolling into the long grass. She gasped in surprise and slapped at his face in fear and, once she realised who it was, in annoyance.

"What are you doing?" she asked angrily.

"What are *you* doing?" Thurstan snapped back, his fear matching her anger. "Are you trying to get us killed?"

"I said to Egbrand that I would wave to Bathylle, and so I am," Adelise replied, trying to get free of Thurstan's arms, which were pinning her down.

"Keep still," he whispered brusquely.

Thurstan gently released her arms then raised his head, to peer over the long grass, towards the valley floor. He sighed with relief as he saw the distant woman pick up her washing basket and start to walk back to the village. He was about to haul

Adelise up and return to the hut when he saw the distant figure of another woman stop Bathylle to speak to her. He held his breath as he watched the two women, then ducked his head down as the stranger pointed up the hillside towards them.

"We've been seen," he said to Adelise, but without any trace of anger. She stopped fidgeting and clasped Thurstan's arm in fear.

The conversation seemed to be growing more animated, the woman gesticulating up the valley and Bathylle, for Thurstan assumed it was the shepherd's wife, shaking her head in apparent denial at whatever accusation had been made. A third woman joined the discussion, arriving on the road that lead off to the right, where Thurstan's view of the village was obscured by trees further down the hill. The newly arrived woman turned her head towards their position on the hillside and Thurstan ducked down again, lying almost flat in the grass.

"What's happening?" Adelise asked.

"I don't know. Trouble I think. When I say go, I want you to run back to the cottage, do you understand?" Thurstan replied. Adelise nodded, her eyes welling with tears.

"I'm sorry," she said, so quietly that Thurstan almost did not hear her.

"It doesn't matter now. We have to go anyway. Get ready," he replied. He risked another glance to see the conversation was getting ever more animated. Bathylle was trying to walk back to the village, encouraging the other women to go back with her. This appeared only to infuriate the first woman, who slapped the clothes basket out of Bathylle's hands. At this point a fourth woman appeared, leading a small child by the hand. Seconds later, she too turned her head to stare up towards the leper cottage. Thurstan's heart sank as the group turned and a male figure stepped into view.

Thurstan pressed himself flat into the grass, hoping that his dark-coloured clothes did not stand out too clearly against the green field. A ewe that had been grazing nearby ambled slowly over to where he and Adelise were lying in the grass. As it neared, it spotted their recumbent bodies and ran off up the hill, bleating in fear, causing Thurstan to curse. He tried to calm his breathing, hoping that if he kept as still as possible, then maybe the growing crowd would just go away. He knew it was folly to think that the difference between exhaling deeply and shallow panting would determine whether they escaped unseen or not. Nevertheless, he dared not move a muscle.

Even from their position on the valley side, almost half a mile away from the village, he could hear the sound of raised voices carried on the wind. He lifted his head so that the path to the river appeared just over the heads of the grass and cowslips, to see that a group of around a dozen people had now surrounded Bathylle. One of the group, possibly a blacksmith, seemed to be carrying a tool of some kind, a chisel or possibly a hammer, which he was waving in the air and pointing towards the hillside. A woman, possibly the first to challenge Bathylle, Thurstan could not tell, started to walk towards the hill. Bathylle grabbed her arm, pulling her back, visibly pleading with her. The woman lashed out, sending the shepherd's wife tumbling to the ground. The crowd surged towards the foot of the hill, headed for the hiding Thurstan and Adelise.

Thurstan dejectedly recalled that a reward had been offered for information leading to their capture. It seemed that greatest act of kindness could so easily be cancelled out by the merest suggestion of financial gain. He drew his knees up to his chest, ready to spring into a run. What had been a near-empty footpath just three or four minutes ago, now appeared to be swarming with half the village; an angry mob making their way towards them.

"Go!" he shouted, not caring how loud or conspicuous they were now. Adelise remained transfixed and wide-eyed for a moment before turning and scrabbling up the grassy hillside, back towards the cottage. Thurstan made to follow her, but as he stood up, he saw another figure hurry from the trees, trying to cut off the mob as they made their way up from the path towards the open ground. Thurstan recognised the limping figure as Egbrand, waving his hands desperately, trying to convince his fellow villagers that there was nothing of interest in the old leper house.

Thurstan glanced behind him; Adelise was almost halfway to the cottage now. He was slowly walking backwards; he needed to run, he knew that, but he could not take his eyes from the crowd and the shepherd. People who had probably lived alongside Egbrand for many a year tried to brush him aside, the prospect of a reward or the fear of the jarl's men proving stronger than neighbourly friendship.

Thurstan watched in horror and despair as Egbrand held his crook out, trying to block the crowd's progress. The shepherd appeared to stumble, then the arm of the blacksmith rose, a reflected glint of sunlight on sharpened metal and the weapon fell once, twice until a third time it rose and Thurstan could see blood. Blood on the blade of the tool, blood on the blacksmith's clothes and blood on the body of Egbrand as it crumpled to the floor. Thurstan heard Bathylle's shriek from far up the hillside and watched as she collapsed to her knees by the dying shepherd. Then, the crowd swarmed past her, leaving her prostrate with grief, kneeling in the mud next to the body of her husband.

Thurstan did not wait to see anymore. He sprinted back up the hill towards Adelise who was now inside the leper house. He ran through the long grass as if he were running through water, each step lasting an eternity yet seeming to take him no nearer the cottage. He looked up to see Adelise coming back out of the cottage with the two small sacks that contained their rations. She stared down the hillside, towards where Egbrand had fallen and a cloud of comprehension passed over her face.

"Don't look!" Thurstan shouted, as he reached the stone building. They had the benefit of having a few moments of being unsighted from the approaching mob. "Run to the trees!" he barked to Adelise. Without stopping, he pushed the girl away from the door and ran in to find the leather pouches that contained their drinking water. He cursed as he picked them up, for one had not been stoppered and spilt its contents over the rush flooring. He ran back out, saw that the mob were still not yet in view, although their shouts could be heard and fled towards the small forest behind the cottage.

Thurstan patted his side to check that the blunt knife Egbrand had given him was still tucked into his belt; it was not a decent weapon by any means, but he might yet be forced to use it. Catching Adelise up in a few strides, he took the food off her then grabbed her hand, dragging her towards the comparative safety of the woods. She cried out in protest, for she was already running as fast as she could on legs that had hardly been used over the last two weeks. As long as they entered the cover of the trees before the villagers came into view, they had some advantage. Thurstan glanced behind him a final time, seeing only open fields, before they entered the shade and cover of the trees. From what he could remember of the valley, the woods covered most of this side of the valley, stretching off to the east as far as the eye could see.

Five minutes of running, stumbling and sliding their way through the dense woods later, Thurstan and Adelise collapsed in a hollow made by the roots of a large, dead oak. They did not exchange a word, the girl's wheezing lungs devoting all their energy to getting her breath back. Thurstan strained his ears for any sound of the mob, but the only noise was that of the wind through the high branches above them and the calls of the forest birds. There had been no discernable path to follow. Thurstan had weaved his way through the trees, hoping to take the least obvious route. They had scrambled up loose earth banks at points, crossed streams at a jump, slid down loose rock faces, all the time heading eastwards.

Thurstan sat back down next to the panting Adelise. They were not safe, but they could afford a few minutes to recuperate, he decided. He doubted unarmed villagers would split up to track them in a forest and the few foolhardy enough to follow them, would hopefully not cross their path. Now the hue and cry had been raised, though, Thurstan knew it would only be a matter of time before word was sent to Haltune, or Lonborg even, and armed horsemen would no doubt be sent to scour the valley sides for them. The lure of coin would be too much for the villagers, the prospect of recapturing the queen too great for Vinder. Thurstan cursed himself for not killing the sheriff when he'd had the chance. He took a swig of water from a pouch, and then passed it to Adelise.

"If we walk, I can continue," she said after draining nearly half the pouch. She wiped her mouth on the back of her sleeve, and then set off again, leaving Thurstan to stopper the pouch and follow her.

"Don't worry; we have a long walk ahead of us, and we cannot run all the way there," Thurstan reassured her. "As long as we don't have a militia at our heels, we can just keep a brisk walk up, if you can manage that."

The girl nodded and pressed on, pushing fronds out of her face. Thurstan stepped in front of her to lead the way, clearing a path for her. As long as he kept the sun to his right and behind him, then they should be heading in the right direction. The next stream they crossed though, he would have to refill their pouches. He did not want to have to head to the valley floor to the river if possible. Eyes wary of any sudden movements in the foliage, ears listening out for the sound of footsteps, Thurstan and Adelise pushed on deeper into the woods, towards the hills, towards Jorvik, towards the unknown.

The hunt was back on.

Lunden, Ængland

Swegen held the crown tenderly over his head, letting it hang just above him, savouring the moment. He watched the light reflect off the fine gold thread, weaved into swirling patterns and adorned with precious stones. He held it until his fingers started to tremble, then, with his eyes clenched shut, he slowly lowered it onto his head.

King Swegen the First, King of Ængland and Kernow, saviour of the Ænglisc nation, deliverer of the lost Northern shires. Murderer.

He flinched at the last thought. Why did his own mind continue to torture him with the accusation? Why could he not get the image of his cousin's face out of his mind? He had not dared view the corpse when it had arrived in Lunden. Not because he was made squeamish by the horrendous descriptions he had heard; it was the sense of fear, or responsibility for the child's death. He was terrified the body would reanimate itself, would sit up and accuse him, point a greying finger at him. Nonsense, he knew, but the nonsense with which his dreams were currently filled.

Nevertheless, he had sent enough men to visit the body, men who had reported that Ceolwulf, the trouble-making son of the Earl of East Anglia, and his uncle had visited the cathedral. No Edgar then; a shame really, he would have like to have had the bothersome earl here, where he could deal with him. Swegen opened his eyes and held a hand mirror up to admire his reflection. Perhaps he should shave his beard off, go clean-shaven, as was the fashion on the continent, he mused, model himself more on the classical emperors of long ago and less like his crude northern neighbours.

A knock on the door disturbed his reverie. He hastily took the crown off and placed it in a small chest by his bed. He had commanded the largest rooms in the King's Hall, by virtue of, well, for various reasons, he thought. He was royalty, he was the most powerful earl and of course, God willing, he would be the next king. It made sense that he should have the finest rooms. He quickly walked over to the thick oak door as a second knock sounded and the squeaking voice of an adolescent page called him.

"Yes?" Swegen asked amiably, whipping the door open.

"My lord Earl, the witan have been gathered for more than an hour now. The archbishop, the one from Cantwaraburg, has already started the proceedings. My lord Archbishop of Westmynster sent me to fetch you," the young servant gabbled, his sweaty face flushed red with nerves and the exertion of having run up two flights of stairs. Swegen glanced up and down the corridor outside his chambers, as if surprised, then glanced behind him, out of one of his quarters' windows to check the sun.

"Is it that time already? I had no idea," he lied. He had had no intention of sitting around, waiting for the witenagemot to start as various bishops and earls from the smaller shires filed into the Great Hall below. He had planned all along to arrive at least an hour after it started, to make his entrance as the king-in-waiting, to great acclaim, he imagined.

"Thank you, boy. I shall be there presently," Swegen said. He shut the door in the adolescent's face and waited, counting to fifty before striding out, down the corridor and towards the stairs. His feet echoed on the stone flags as he passed the portraits and tapestries of monarchs past; Edward I, The Confessor; Tostig I, The Righteous; Edgar II, the king that had reunited the Ænglisc nobility, all framed ornately or weaved from the richest, most expensive thread.

He took the spiral staircase down two floors to the corridor leading to the Great Hall. Here he paused and patted down his tunic; a blue velvet garment tied with an elaborate belt that had cost him much more coin than he could really afford. He knew, however, that his entrance to the gemot and the impression he would make as a warrior prince and the future of the nation was of paramount importance. Behind the curtained doorway, he could hear the low voices, the monotone of Eadric, the Archbishop of Cantwaraburg, rambling through a series of obligatory notices and declarations. He waited for a break in the archbishop's discourse, and then strode forward, sweeping the curtain aside.

Swegen's entrance prompted a sudden clamour of raised voices. Noblemen stood and applauded, cheering and calling his name; the same noblemen and minor thegns he had made sure would occupy the front rows of the Great Hall. The Archbishop of Cantwaraburg took a few seconds to realise that the cheers were not for his proclamations and turned to watch Swegen wave and take a small bow to the assembled witan, like a travelling player to a crowd.

Swegen took his seat at the table at the head of the hall, next to the more powerful earls, minor royalty and bishops. Edgar, Earl of East Anglia was absent as predicted, he noted. That scrote of his son, Ceolwulf, had not had the sense to take his place at the top table and was sitting among the lesser members of the witan. Raising his hands in mock supplication to the cheering men in the hall to quieten down, he apologised for his late arrival and begged the archbishop to continue.

Eadric had been informing the witan that King Æthelgar's funeral would still take place, the following week, as planned. With all the events of the past week, the king's funeral had almost been forgotten about. The archbishop went on to say that the king would be interred in Westmynster Cathedral alongside his wife, Queen Helgete, who had predeceased him by ten years. All of this could have been explained much quicker, Swegen mused, if Eadric had let Godric explain the details. Finally, much to Swegen's relief the old fool began speaking about Adelise's murder.

Eadric droned on for another twenty minutes at least, alternating between Ænglisc and Latin, describing the natural progression between life and death, how God's will had been done, even though his motives could seem unfathomable. He then described the need for peace and how their Northlandic cousins would also grieve for the loss of the queen, as the good Christians that they were.

Swegen raised an eyebrow and rolled his eyes, much to the amusement of his friends sitting in the front rows of the hall. The Great Hall was as long as a large cathedral's nave, its walls clad in plaster and oak beams, which served for nothing except decoration. The witan were seated on wooden pews, each of which was uniquely decorated with ornate carvings of beasts and birds. Those at the front sat on benches that displayed carvings of dragons, falcons and lions; those towards the back had more humble creatures: coneys, badgers and kingfishers.

Swegen's eye caught sight of the flowing blond mane of Ceolwulf. The young idiot seemed to be visibly ill at ease, fidgeting, as if he were about to leap out of his seat at any moment. Good. Let the cretin make a fool of himself in front of the witan by blurting out some nonsense; he was soon to get his just rewards. Swegen observed with some amusement that Ceolwulf had seated himself someway towards the back, on a pew decorated with a dove, of all things. He also noted that Thegn Ælfric, Ceolwulf's uncle, did not appear to be in the hall at all – one less hindrance.

With something not even nearing a flourish, Eadric, Archbishop of Cantwaraburg, finally finished his speech. Or sermon. Swegen could not be sure what it was meant to have been. He stared up at the dusty rafters and the embossed wooden shields that decorated the ceiling, as a murmur of halfhearted agreement spread through the hall. To his great relief the next man to stand and address the witan was Godric,

Archbishop of Westmynster. Swegen picked up a goblet of wine and casually took a long sip, letting the drink mask his obvious contentment at the clergyman's confidence and the knowledge of the foundations that were about to be laid. Putting the wine down, Swegen reassumed the role of a concerned nobleman and leant forward, as if to listen intently to Godric's words.

"Fellow members of the witan, friends, a great tragedy has befallen our nation," the archbishop started, his arms spread out wide, supplicating the assembled noblemen. "Our young queen, Adelise, daughter of Edmund, the Flower of Ængland, was slain cruelly in Northland during the return to her homeland. She will remain forever young in our hearts, taken so early into our Lord's embrace. Queen Adelise, the Queen Who Shall Never Be, the bright flame that represented our nation's future, snuffed out brutally in Northlandic wilds."

He paused and appeared to offer a silent prayer. Several members of the witan bowed their heads to join in, glancing up occasionally to see if the archbishop had finished. A half-voiced 'Amen' brought their heads back up and Godric pressed on.

"Our Northlandic cousins have assured us that she was the victim of banditry, of lawless men in the hills. If this is so, then let us find it in our hearts to forgive. Forgive Northland for not having provided adequate protection for our future monarch. Forgive the Earl of East Anglia for not having ascertained that Northland would not provide the necessary escort. No blame should be attached to them; for they only did what they thought was right in their hearts. May the Lord forgive them for their failings. Let us even forgive those who slew her, for they were no doubt little better than savages; wild, lawless beasts for whom the sanctity of life holds no import."

Godric paused and leant on his crosier, gripping it with both hands. He sagged as if the weight of responsibility and the gravity of the situation were forcing him to hold on to the staff for support. He lowered his head for a moment, causing the witan to prepare for another prayer, then his head rose and he fixed the assembled noblemen with a hawk-like glare.

"There are also those who say that our queen was murdered by soldiers from Northymbre. The sole survivor of the vile ambush attested to as much, although the witnessing of such evil deeds sadly caused the poor woman to lose her mind. I heard only this morning that she has since tragically passed away. Now I know of course, that such a deed, were it to be true, would violate the Morcar Oath, sworn a hundred years ago; sworn to His Holiness that neither Northland nor Ængland should ever attack each other. I have already written to Rome and obtained a confirmation that should this vile rumour be true, then the oath would be considered forfeit and that Northland would risk excommunication.

"Now I know, there are men who would wish to see us at war, who say that we should reclaim the Six Shires, if not the whole of Northland as Ænglisc again, and I have been left in little doubt that His Holiness would send men, soldiers from the Papal States, should such an unfortunate turn of events befall us, but I beg you to think of peace. Do not seek war, but resort to arms only when all other options have failed. There is no glory in killing for revenge; but should you be forced to abandon peace, then know that God is on your side. I state again, however, that as far as we know, Queen Adelise fell victim to bandits. I for one have no reason to doubt the veracity of this."

Godric's words hung in the air and on cue, just as Swegen had hoped, the Earl of Ceasterscir stood up and coughed loudly, gaining the attention of the entire hall.

"My lord Archbishop," he started, slowly. "Forgive me, but I must speak. We in Ceaster have received nothing but reports confirming that the men who attacked the queen's convoy bore the colours of Northymbre. That the Westmoringa escort was woefully under-prepared and stood no chance. This is what we hear from across the border, from messengers coming in from

Suthribel. I'm not saying Northland or its king wished her dead, but it's not beyond the realms of possibility that some rogue group brigade attacked her, or that she was the victim of a dispute between jarls."

The Archbishop of Westmynster appeared to consider this and nodded. "They have been known to fight amongst themselves in the past; let us not forget that their own king seized his throne having killed several members of his own family!" There were more growls of agreement through the hall.

"What is more," the Earl of Ceasterscir continued, "I have heard reports, of Northlandic troops massing near the border in Suthribel."

The last few words were stammered, then rushed and to Swegen's horror, the earl appeared to look towards him for reassurance of a job well done. The fool had been easily bought, with a promise that Suthribel would be merged into Ceasterscir. As with the most of his pawns, earl and serving boy alike, he had bribed them to support him in war; he had not told them about how he had directly brought about the queen's death. Only the Archbishop of Westmynster, Ricmund and his men knew about that 'unfortunate necessity', as he preferred to think of it. Of the latter, only a handful remained, following that tragic fire at the Ceaster garrison, and they could easily disappear, Swegen mused. He glanced around the hall; no-one had appeared to notice the Earl of Ceasterscir's gormless staring, thankfully.

The roars of discontent, anger at Northland's aggression, grew ever louder. Men were banging their fists on benches, their boots on the floor; no-one appeared to be taking any notice of where the earl's nervous glance flickered. Swegen took advantage of the raucous crescendo of noise and stood up, his arms spread out placatingly.

"Brothers," he called out. "Brothers, calm, please. I call for calm." He let the noise subside before pressing on; a great many of the witan were very interested in hearing what the ambitious nobleman, the most direct male descendent of the late king, had to say.

"This talk of war, this talk of defending our nation against a Northern aggressor, is surely premature. How can we presume to define our future whilst our nation has no monarch? Might I humbly suggest that we occupy ourselves with the nominations for the throne before any discussion of retaliation? How can we plan our next move if our next king, or queen, were to desire to act differently? Of course, many a hot-headed lord, such as myself, would demand instant punishment and retribution for the vile act inflicted upon our nation, should such accusations prove to be true..."

This brought a round of cheers and more foot stamping in the dusty hall. Swegen waved the vociferous support away.

"Yet, the witenagemot's laws and customs must be observed. With the high table's approval, I suggest we halt proceedings to take our evening meal, with perhaps some liquid refreshment, as I fear our talks may last long into the evening, and I, for one, function so much better on a satisfied stomach." He beamed at the assembly and was greeted with laughter and shouts of agreement.

The archbishops and earls sitting at the high table, Wiltescir and Suthseaxe, nodded in agreement and almost immediately the large doors that lead from the Great Hall to the dining area swung open. The witan slowly filed out, led by the attractive odours of roast meats and ale. Swegen watched them as they shuffled through the doors, keeping an eye in particular on Ceolwulf, the son of the Earl of East Anglia. He was the impending successor to the largest earldom in Ængland, and yet he sat towards the back of the hall amongst the three-pig, one-acre holding thegns.

Swegen waited in his chair until the hall was almost empty, and he and Godric, the Archbishop of Westmynster, were alone at the high table. He snapped his fingers at the nearest serving girl to bring them something to drink, and then leant over to speak to Godric, once she had disappeared.

"Are we ready for the next step?" Swegen asked.

"I think the whole witan are," Godric said enthusiastically.

"And there is plenty of liquid encouragement in the dining hall?"

"The wine is strong and the ale plentiful, dear Swegen."

"And Cantwaraburg is obliging us?"

"Eadric, for all his theological acumen, is blissfully gullible once his head is out of a book. The fool has convinced himself that the whole thing was his idea," Godric chuckled.

"And thus we discredit two irritants in one go. Let us hope this works, or your head is on the line," Swegen replied, his voice souring. Godric did not blink an eyelid at the threat, but simply smiled back.

"Mine? Really? I shouldn't think so."

Swegen glared at the archbishop, snorted indignantly and stood up. He stalked out of the hall and into the dining chamber, passing the confused serving girl that he had sent to fetch him wine only a few moments before.

"Youth ages," Godric mused, drumming his fingers on the oak tabletop, "but stupid lasts forever."

Less than an hour later, the witan were reassembled in the Great Hall, many of them holding the horns of ale or goblets of wine that had been foisted upon them during their meal. No longer was the hall silent in reverence at the solemnity of the occasion or in respect of witan; feasted men now talked loudly to each other, agreeing and disagreeing in equal measure about how to respond to Northland and who to elect to the throne.

The rap of Godric's crosier on the high table brought a silence of sorts in the hall. Ceolwulf returned to the seat he had occupied all day, next to the empty place where his uncle should have been. He had sat alone all day, wondering where Ælfric had disappeared to. His uncle had said that morning that he had had a task to see to before coming to the witan, but he had not specified what, or how long it would take him. Ceolwulf had tried to find out where Ælfric had gone during the meal, but the men he had left stationed outside the hall had either wandered off during the day, mingling and gambling with other earls' retainers or had not seen his uncle or his steward, Lyfing, since morning. He settled back, trying to concentrate on the Archbishop of Cantwaraburg, who had launched into another one of his long, rambling speeches about the succession and the customs of the witan.

Ceolwulf was struggling to concentrate though, his mind filled only with the recurring thought; *the body in the chapel is not Adelise's.* Whether that meant she was alive or not still was a different matter, but surely, the witan had to know? Perhaps some knew already, perhaps they would not care. Would he cause the hall to burst into cries of outrage, if he stood up and proclaimed the deception, or would he be met by steely glares of suspicion and disbelief? Even though his head was spinning, Ceolwulf still knew that the best course of action would not be to stand up and declare it out loud. A word in this ear, in that corner, a surreptitious enquiry there; his father would have known how to handle the knowledge.

"And I nominate, Ceolwulf, son of Edgar, Earl of East Anglia, to be our next king," the Archbishop of Cantwaraburg's voice rang out. Ceolwulf was jolted from his conflicted thoughts into a sober, silent hall. Had he just imagined the words he thought he had heard? The turn of heads, many bearing surprised expressions, towards him convinced him otherwise.

"I..." Ceolwulf stammered, for he was the most surprised of any the assembled witan at this proclamation. "Surely, you are mistaken, Archbishop." The heads turned back to the high table.

The elderly man shook his head amiably. "You are of noble birth, are you not? Descended from Tostig the Righteous?"

"But I..." Ceolwulf said, standing up, his knees trembling. He had never spoken to the Archbishop of Cantwaraburg, let alone discussed the royal succession with him. He didn't even want to assume the earldom of East Anglia. "I've not even put myself forward."

"The lack of political ambition and greed serves only to do you credit, my lord Earl. Ængland needs a steady hand, not a power hungry nobleman, in these dark times."

The Archbishop of Cantwaraburg must have seen Ceolwulf's eyes flicker to Swegen, for he continued, with his head tilted to one side as if he were explaining to a child.

"My lord Earl of Berrocscir, Swegen, has already stated, both today and before the witenagemot, that he does not wish to be considered, for he believes himself too martial and warlike." This prompted a mix of cheers and groans of disappointment from the front rows of the Great Hall. Swegen looked benevolently at his supporters and gave a slight shrug, as if the matters were out of his hands.

"Do you accept the nomination?" Godric, the Archbishop of Westmynster asked. Throughout the discourse, he had remained impassive, following the proceedings with an air of detachment.

Ceolwulf's mind span at the implications of saying yes. He could become king, King of Ængland. He did not know of any other noblemen with royal ties, at least none present or not in exile. He had assumed Swegen would be selected without challenge or dispute. He was about to answer when Leofwin, the Earl of Suthseaxe, stood up and planted a heavy fist down on the high table, causing several cups to spill ale.

"Lords of the witan!" he called, trying to make himself heard over the growing rumble of confused and disgruntled voices. "My lords, with all due respect to the Earl of East Anglia, is he truly the best nominee that we see here today? Although our thoughts are with his father, let us not forget that Ceolwulf is not yet quite earl. He has not had direct experience of leading men, of commanding a shire, never mind a nation."

Leofwin's words were predictable and few doubted his allegiance, but the ale-and-wine-fuelled younger members of the witan cheered and shouted in agreement.

"We need a man of experience, a man who leads, a man of decision. I mean no offence to my Lord Ceolwulf, but he cannot even decide if he wants to be nominated." The cheers grew louder. "I heard that his uncle had to convince him to attend here today in place of his father, such are his misgivings about assuming power and responsibility. Is this the man we wish to lead us when the Northlanders are on our borders like wolves at the door?"

Ceolwulf felt the back of his tunic suddenly get wet, as a shouting thegn stood up and swung his ale-filled flagon into the air, liberally spraying the row in front of him with beer. He was not alone, for the hall was becoming ever more filled with hollering men, men wanting war, men wanting Swegen; men not wanting Ceolwulf.

Five minutes ago, he had never wanted the throne. Now men, resenting him for even being associated with the kingship, were uncomfortably surrounding him. Ceolwulf tried to placate the men around him by holding his hands up in a gesture of bewilderment; he scanned to the room to see if any of his retainers were in the hall, but he appeared to be alone. The two archbishops had not moved; Godric in his chair, looking amused by the whole thing and the Archbishop of Cantwaraburg beaming like a proud father, oblivious to the rising hostility and aggression festering in the hall.

"Was it this same indecision and lack of ambition that let our queen be so woefully unprotected in Northland?" Leofwin asked, letting this words hang in the air.

The hall quietened for a moment, letting the occupants consider the question. Ceolwulf felt a wave of nausea wash over him. So this is what was happening; a character assassination. To be accused of not being ready to be a king was one thing, but the

earl was effectively accusing him of treason. None of this had
made sense, but it was starting to become clear that Swegen's
cronies were simply seeking a scapegoat and a reason to beat
their own drum.

Ceolwulf stared at the Earl of Suthseaxe, all indecision and
timidity suddenly gone. Leofwin, possibly out of shame, possibly
embarrassed by how obviously scripted his words were, turned
away. The quick glance he gave to the pinch-faced Swegen told
Ceolwulf all he needed to know.

"Surely the only man suitable for the throne, the only man
who is of noble blood, the only man who has the courage to
punish Northland for what they have done is Lord Swegen, Earl
of Berrocscir?" Leofwin called out, having to almost shout to
make himself heard. He sat back down to the cheers of the
increasingly intoxicated witan.

Swegen, Swegen, Swegen the chant went around the room,
growing in volume, feet stamping in time to the name. *Swegen,
Swegen, Swegen.*

Ceolwulf knew that he had never been a valid nominee for the
throne, but he was fearful now of the vitriol against him; that
accusations of indecision would soon turn to those of incompetence or treachery. He felt a shiver go down his spine, keeping his
eyes fixed on Swegen as the Earl of Berrocscir stood and walked
towards the centre of the raised dais on which the high table
stood. He kept staring even as he heard the large doors behind
him open and close, ignoring the cheering and chanting around
him. His mouth had gone dry, but he knew that his name and that
of his family could not be besmirched by malicious and mendacious accusations.

"My lords of the witan," Swegen called out, waiting for the
chorus of cheering voices to subside. "My lords, please. Let us
not speak ill of my lord Earl and friend, Ceolwulf. It is not upon
him that the blame for our queen's death should be placed,
though I fear there are already those who see it that way. Her

killers are surely to be found in Northland and as such, we should concentrate our anger towards them, her murderers. The invaders."

The last word brought a fresh round of angry cheers. Swegen flashed a quick smile, one of those that came so easily to him and lowered his voice. "I do not seek command of the realm, I do not seek power or ambition; but I cannot stand by and let us be consumed by the aggressors from the North, to watch them finish what they started one hundred years ago. I appreciate there are those who would see me nominated as king, and if they did so wish to nominate me, then I can only promise that I will fight to protect our lands, fight to protect our people and to revenge ourselves upon her murderers. That is, if someone is willing to nominate me formally?"

The assenting shouts were deafening, the wooden beams that vaulted the ceiling shook to the sound of boots being stamped, of fists hammering benches and tables.

"That is of course, if my cousin, the Lord Ceolwulf, the future Earl of East Anglia, wishes to withdraw his candidature?" Swegen asked mellifluously.

It was Swegen's patronising tone that drove Ceolwulf to fury. Cousin? Yes, but distantly. Earl of East Anglia? Not yet and he strongly resented the insinuation that his father was already dead, or that by supporting Swegen, he would be considered earl. To hell with them; if the other earls were happy to use him as a pawn, then he would not sit here in silence; he knew the one thing that would hopefully throw Swegen's manipulative slithering into turmoil.

"My lords," Ceolwulf said, still standing. "My lords, we cannot speak of war, or revenge, or of duties not done." The hall quietened, but only just; the shouts of support for Swegen quickly turned into shouts of disapproval of Ceolwulf. "For one, we still do not know who was responsible for the death of our queen. We do not know if it was bandits, if it was a Northlandic jarl, perhaps plotting treachery against his own king. But most of all," he paused. His mouth had gone dry, his mind blank as how to phrase the possibility that Adelise might not be dead. He was surrounded by shouting men, men accusing him of cowardice, of betraying Ængland, of being in league with Northland. "But most of all.." His throat tightened, and he could feel his vision become enshrouded in darkness, his ears began ringing. "Not dead." His voice was little more than a whisper, but it did not matter, for the hall had suddenly gone very quiet.

"What?" Swegen asked, a look of mild confusion on his face, before his eyes rose to the back of the room to stare at what had rendered the Great Hall quiet.

"What my son is saying, is that I am not dead," came a strong, if somewhat gravelly voice.

Ceolwulf spun round to see his father walking slowly down the central aisle between the benches of the hall. His face was ghostly pale, his skin seemed almost translucent and he was being supported by Ælfric. His voice, though, was loud and strong; he was dressed in his finest leather armour and robes and he had brought instant respect and quiet to a hall that had believed him already dead.

Ceolwulf did not know whether to run to his aid, to run to embrace him or to simply stand there and marvel at the man that he had left bedridden a week before. A glance passed between his father and him, a glance that contained the briefest of nods.

"I am still alive, my lord Earl of Berrocscir and I would nominate my son for the kingship. I believe him to be a wise, noble man, capable of reason and not wont to lead to his nation to war over lies and falsehoods," Edgar said, spitting the last few words out.

"Lies, Edgar?" Swegen asked, abandoning his usual formality. His face was no longer amiable or smiling. A look of pure hatred was directed towards Edgar, Ceolwulf and Ælfric. Edgar stopped beside his son and simply placed a hand on his shoulder. He looked into his son's eyes for a moment, and then turned to the dais.

"The body that lies in the chapel at Westmynster is not that of our queen. I should know, having housed her for many months. That is not Adelise. If our queen is not dead then I see no reason to elect a warmonger to the Ænglisc throne."

The hall erupted into pandemonium, leaving Godric and Swegen to remain staring blankly at Edgar.

"Sit down, son," Edgar said quietly to Ceolwulf. "You will need to fight other battles, on other days. Your uncle has told me everything." Ceolwulf nodded and without saying another word, sat back into his chair.

"You know this *how*?" Godric asked, having to almost shout to make himself heard.

Edgar waited for the noise in the hall to subside before continuing.

"I went to see the body for myself, when I arrived here this morning. I apologise for my late arrival, but as you well know, I have suffered from a bout of ill health recently. Nevertheless, I have still ridden here, having been kept informed of proceedings by my brother-in-law, Thegn Ælfric. If any of you had bothered to visit the chapel to examine the body or to just pay your respects, you may well have noticed that the corpse in there is missing Adelise's distinctive birthmark."

"And this birthmark is?" asked Godric.

"A strawberry-coloured growth at the base of her neck," Edgar replied, using a trembling hand to show the location on his own neck.

"Nonsense!" a voice screamed. All eyes in the hall turned back to Swegen whose skin was now like marble, glistening and pale. He had lost all semblance of self-assurance and confidence; he was trembling, gripping the hilt of the eating knife at his belt so tightly that his knuckles were flushed white. "Nonsense! The queen is dead; everyone knows it!" His voice was shrill, sounding like a petulant adolescent. Edgar let the younger man's words hang in the smoky hall air for a few seconds before replying slowly, but deliberately.

"The body in the chapel is not that of Adelise."

Swegen burst into laughter; not a natural or amused laugh, but a nervous, almost hysterical giggle.

"Why? Because of a birthmark on her neck. The girl has no head! You worry about a blemish, when the entire neck has been cut in two!" Swegen shouted, anger now replacing the panic. There were some shouts of agreement to this, but far less enthusiastically than those of a few minutes previously. Ceolwulf noticed that sentries were moving from the back of the hall towards the front of the room, Swegen's hired men, no doubt. His father would no doubt have a contingent of men stationed outside the hall. At least Ceolwulf hoped he did; this might turn ugly very quickly.

"Nevertheless, the blemish is conspicuous by its absence," Edgar replied calmly. He seemed to sigh deeply, then placed a hand on Ceolwulf's arm, gripping it tightly. Ceolwulf quickly helped his father to sit down on to the bench. The old man said nothing, but visibly winced as he lowered himself. A faint trace of smirk returned to Swegen's face; Ceolwulf knew that whatever facts or opinions were shouted out, the sight of his father sitting down would lose him authority and credibility.

"Perhaps it was cut off, East Anglia," Swegen said, tilting his head to one side, looking down on Edgar as if he were to be pitied. This roused some muted laughter in the front rows of the hall. "Fine! The body is the chapel is not Adelise. It happens to be some other girl the same age, dressed in the queen's clothes and wearing jewellery belonging to the royal family. My question to you then, East Anglia, is this: where is the queen?" The last four words were shot out with venom, spittle visibly flying from Swegen's mouth. Edgar sighed and seemed to shrink ever smaller. He was losing momentum in the argument, Ceolwulf feared, but then his father seemed to rally, mustering strength from his reserves and stood back up, using the bench in front as support.

"That I cannot say, Swegen. Possibly dead in Northland, possibly still alive. Perhaps she is here in Lunden; I cannot answer that, but until we can answer that with any certainty, we should not be electing a new king."

"So what you are saying," Swegen snarled in response, "is that the queen is either dead or being held captive in Northland? Northland is still our aggressor, we are still without a leader. How very convenient for you to fantasise of a world where Adelise is not dead, where you cannot be held responsible for her death through your incompetence in Jorvik. Or did they promise you help in your quest to put your son on the throne?" The raucous cheers in support of Swegen came flooding back.

"I do not care for fantasy, supposition or mindless, rabble-rousing rhetoric, Swegen. I resent your suggestion of betrayal on my part; I think we all know in the Great Hall here which of the witan harbours the most ruthless ambition," Edgar replied. Ceolwulf noted that despite the cries of outrage from the usual Swegen supporters, some of the more powerful, longer-established members of the witan; the earls of Grantbrygscir and Wærwicscir, the Bishop of Oxnaforda, seemed to have taken great interest in his father's words. The Earl of Wærwicscir had even nodded slightly to his father's last statement.

"You are accusing me, Edgar?" Swegen asked, his eyes narrowing.

"I am not accusing you of anything, Swegen. I would simply ask that the witan suspends its decision on the succession until we establish the fate of Queen Adelise," his father said, keeping the same, calm, measured tone. Swegen stood for several moments, not speaking, not blinking, just staring at Edgar.

"Very well. We shall suspend our legitimate discussions until tomorrow afternoon. Tomorrow morning, you, I and any members of the witan who wish to join us, will convene in the chapel of St Edward to re-examine the body," Swegen said. "However, it is doing nothing more than wasting time that we do not have as a nation. The body has already been examined by many men and confirmed to be that of Adelise; is that not correct, my lord Archbishop of Westmynster?"

Godric, who had up until that point returned to surveying the proceedings with his customary detachment and bemusement, suddenly went very still.

"Correct, my lord Earl?" he asked.

"You examined the body and can confirm that it is that of Adelise, our late, much-beloved queen?" Swegen asked, not even turning to look at the archbishop. Godric spent several seconds starting at the earl's back, his face not flickering even the briefest registration of emotion.

"That is correct," he finally said. "I suggest we meet tomorrow morning, perhaps just after matins, to avoid us losing the best part of the day. The witan shall reconvene later in the afternoon, would that be agreeable, Swegen?"

The Earl of Berrocscir nodded and almost immediately the large doors at the end of the hall swung open and those seated towards the back were ushered towards the entrance. Ceolwulf stood and took his father's arm, his head spinning, struggling to comprehend precisely what had happened. A declaration of war between his family and Swegen, it felt like, yet the assembled members appeared to have enjoyed the discussion as if it were friendly banter. As he and his uncle led the ailing Edgar away between the lines of benches towards the exit, he did not see Swegen nod towards a corner of the hall, where a man detached himself from the shadows.

A tall, scar-faced man.

The Lon Valley, Northland

Thurstan and Adelise emerged from dark woods into open fields as the light started to fade into a murky dusk. The setting sun behind them cast long shadows as they trampled through the rough grass and heather, wafting away the first midges of the year from their faces.

"Where are we heading?" Adelise asked. Thurstan paused and pointed towards a small, flat-topped mountain that stood out from the other peaks on the horizon, its sides dark grey and grassless.

"We're walking up that?" she asked, her voice betraying the trepidation at the thought of climbing. It was certainly not the tallest of mountains, it was really only a large hill, a fell, but its scree-covered, cliff-like sides looked formidable. Thurstan shook his head.

"Don't worry, we're not walking up it. That is our marker to head for, though. That fell is Ingleberg; that marks our entrance to the West Thrith of Jorvik. From there we turn south and follow the road, or at least shadow it towards Scipton. After that, my knowledge of the land is patchy at best. I think there's a road to Jorvik itself, possibly two, over the tops of the Pennines." He paused to look down at Adelise and winked. "We'll figure that out when we get to them. "What can you hear?" Thurstan asked suddenly, scanning the hills around them for any sign of pursuers.

She tilted her head to one side and squinted, her eyes screwed up in concentration. A sheep bleated loudly nearby.

"A sheep," she announced, proud of herself.

"Good," Thurstan replied and nodded emphatically. They set off across the field again, keeping Ingleberg ahead of them. There was a road to Scipton, but he had kept to the fields and woods, not daring to risk encountering any horsemen, even if their pace would have been much quicker. There were too many small watchtowers along the valley floor, one for each village it seemed.

Then the sound came. Thurstan suddenly stopped and gripped Adelise's hand tightly. She looked up at him in surprise and he responded by waving her into silence. He turned and stared at the trees behind them, listening again for a noise he thought he might have just heard. A flock of birds erupted from the treetops from within the woods and Thurstan, without waiting for another sign, picked Adelise up, placed her over his shoulder and ran.

A stone wall, a hundred yards in front of them, offered the nearest protection. On the far side of the wall was a small wood, not as dense as the one they had just left, but out of the open nonetheless. Thurstan's poorly clad feet pounded heavily in the soft grass, the added weight of Adelise causing him to slip and slide where the ground was wet. He did not dare risk a glance behind him; he was running as fast as he could already; seeing the horse he feared he'd heard would not make him go any faster.

Thurstan hardly slowed at all when he reached the wall. He flung Adelise into the soft bracken and ferns on the other side of the damp, moss covered stone wall, then scrambled over and threw himself flat onto the ground. Adelise crawled over to him and they huddled together, trying to occupy as small a space possible. Thurstan pulled his cloak over them and they waited, listening out for hoofbeats.

Thurstan caught the faintest sound of a horse just on the edge of his hearing; faint but unmistakable. He held his breath, for it seemed so loud that Thurstan worried the sound of it would carry across the field. Mouth trembling, Thurstan tried to gauge the distance of the approaching rider, before exhaling slowly and deeply. He quickly peered out from under his cloak, but his view was one of just damp stones, rotting branches and woodlice.

The hoofbeats were louder now, distinguishable as just a

single rider, which offered some hope to Thurstan. There could have been an innocent reason for a rider in the hills, but someone riding at such a pace, following that morning's events, left Thurstan in no doubt that he and Adelise were the horseman's quarry.

"Is he there?" Adelise whispered.

Thurstan placed his finger on his lips and shook his head. He pulled the cloak back over their heads and let his world become dark and filled with the sound of their breathing. The sound of the approaching horse suddenly became much clearer and defined and Thurstan guessed the rider was now out of the woods and into the open field.

Thurstan pressed himself up against the stone wall as much as possible, letting a sharp edge press into the small of his back, but he just bit his lip and tried to curl himself into an even smaller ball. He gripped Adelise's tiny frame closely to himself; he could feel her trembling with fear, her breathing coming quickly, in short rasping breaths.

In less than half of the time it had taken them to cross the field, the rider was almost at the wall. Each hoofbeat was distinct now, growing ever louder, ever closer. Thurstan was sure that the horse was upon them, yet the noise kept getting louder and louder until the ground was shaking and it seemed impossible that the rider could be so close and yet not be upon them.

Just when Thurstan thought the horseman must have been about to inexplicably ride the wall down, he heard a male voice cry and the world fell oddly silent. He braced himself, squeezing Adelise even more closely to him. From under the cloak, he sensed a dark shape pass over them, then an explosion of leaves and earth and a giant shudder told him that the rider had leapt the wall. For a split-second, the horrendous thought that the horse's rear legs might slam down on top of them filled him with terror, but then, almost as quickly as the horse had arrived, the thunder of hooves assailed his ears again and their presumed pursuer was riding away.

Thurstan did not move, save to release his grip on Adelise slightly. She did not seem to be breathing, frightening him into thinking that perhaps he had clasped her too tightly, but then she let out a long breath, a sigh mixed with a whimper. Only then did he too permit himself to breathe out.

The sound of the horse had almost disappeared by the time he dared to peek from under the cloak. Nudging the edge of the garment aside with a trembling finger, he peered out. The ground sloped away from the wall, a gentle hillside covered with trees that blocked Thurstan's view of anything except the ground nearest to him. There was neither sign nor sound of the rider now, save for a few patches of churned-up earth, imprints of the horse's shoes left in the damp soil.

"I think we are safe to continue," Thurstan said finally, pulling back the cloak that covered Adelise. She blinked as she emerged back into daylight, gently rubbing her elbow.

"Did you hurt yourself?" Thurstan asked.

"It stings. I fell on a nettle, I think," she replied, gazing down at the spiny green leaves of the offending plant on which she had landed. "What do you call it in Northlandic?"

"A nettle," Thurstan said, smiling. He helped her to her feet, brushing off the leaves and soil from her tunic. He kicked at the plant until its stem broke. "There, you have been avenged, my lady."

Adelise laughed at him, then gripped his hand and started down the slope, between the trees. Thurstan laughed at the thought of the young girl leading him through the wilderness. He took her hand gently from his, and pushing her behind him, peered around the wide trunk of an elderly oak, trying to scan the woods for any sign of the rider.

They made good progress for the next quarter of an hour. There was no further sign of the mysterious horseman and on any other evening, the walk would have been a pleasant one.

Aside from the midges, the weather was fine, the terrain gentle and the woodland scenery pleasant; yet Thurstan was only too aware of the ever-present threat of violence that would surely follow them now until they reached Jorvik.

Thurstan gripped the blunt knife hanging at his side that Egbrand had given him. It gave him some measure of reassurance, not nearly as much as his hunting knife had, and certainly not the confidence a half-decent sword would have, but it was at least something. The memory of Egbrand brought a brief pang of pain, of guilt. Thurstan did not doubt that the old man was dead; he had sacrificed his life to let them escape. How many more lives would he and Adelise cost; how many were theirs worth? He was mulling over how many people had already died when he stepped, almost blindly, into the clearing.

The rider was sitting on his horse, his back to them, taking a long swig of water from a large pouch. Thurstan froze instantly, but Adelise walked into him, loudly stumbling and treading on a dry branch as she did so. The noise snapped the rider's head around instantly; a helmeted, leather-clad and most importantly, armed rider. The expression on his face showed he was as surprised as Adelise and Thurstan were to see them. Thurstan's hand gripped the knife hilt at his waist, waiting for the horseman to respond. The rider was young, possibly no older than Thurstan. His face was flushed and beaded with sweat, his eyes narrowed to see more clearly in the gloom of the trees.

"Good afternoon," Thurstan offered. "We were just collecting mushrooms." The explanation was weak, but he said it with a forced joviality.

The rider slowly turned his horse around to face them, allowing himself a proper view of the two mushroom collectors. He noted the hand on the knife hilt, and the fear in the eyes of the child who was gripping the young man's arm. He urged his horse forward, leaving about twenty yards between himself and the edge of the clearing where the couple stood frozen.

"I don't think so, Thurstan Ælfsson," the rider spat, and kicked his heels back, drawing a sword. Thurstan swore, pushed Adelise to one side and drew the knife. For the briefest moment he judged its weight, the speed of the oncoming horse, then hurled it towards the rider, and with it his fate. He had one chance, for he had now left himself unarmed against a sword-wielding horseman.

The knife flew true. It glanced off the nosepiece of the rider's metal helm with a spark and embedded itself in his eye. The horseman emitted a high-pitched scream for a second before toppling from his slowing horse, which cantered past the statue-like Thurstan. The rider was dead by the time he hit the ground next to where Adelise lay. His head hit a rock with a metallic clang, a spurt of blood spilling from the gruesome wound. Adelise screamed and stumbled away from the one-eyed corpse, turning her head away from the twitching body.

Thurstan remained frozen where he stood, until the sense of relief washed over him. Quickly gathering his wits, he turned and walked swiftly, but softly towards the riderless horse. Talking to it in a low voice, he took its reins and led it back to the clearing, gently stroking its mane. He found Adelise staring at the corpse, midges already swarming around the knife hilt protruding from the eye socket. Tying the horse's reins to a tree, he walked over to Adelise and took her hand.

"Are you hurt?" he asked, for he had thrown her to the ground with some force when the rider had charged. She shook her head and he picked out several leaves from her short hair.

"I had to kill him, Adelise, otherwise he would have killed us," Thurstan said. Adelise nodded slowly, her eyes still on the corpse, unable to turn her gaze away.

"What would you have done if your knife had missed?" she asked, turning to look at Thurstan. He shrugged a reply.

"I don't know, I hadn't thought beyond that point. Died, I think," Thurstan said. He stepped over to the body and, keeping his back between the corpse and Adelise, pulled his knife out of the rider's head with a sickening, wet pop.

The rider was of a similar age to him, and he could have quite easily been him just a few weeks ago. *It could have been me,* Thurstan thought; *it could have been me who died for no other reason than I simply followed orders.* He turned to see Adelise, tears streaming down her cheeks, sit down on the soft ground and bury her head in her hands. He paused and thought again.

No, he thought. *No, it wouldn't have been me. The fact I am here now, walking across Northland with a nine-year-old girl as a fugitive, no, I am not the man who would ride down a young child simply because he is told to.*

He sheathed the knife, and then set about unstrapping the man's boots. He was not given to looting corpses, but a good pair of boots could mean the difference between life and death if they were going to have to cross the dales and fells of the Pennines.

A horse, a sword, leather gloves and a pair of boots; perhaps they were lucky to have been discovered after all. Perhaps the rider had been another unwitting sacrifice to allow Adelise to survive and return home. As he pulled on the boots, leaving Adelise to gather herself, he wondered if he too would end up being a pawn, rather than a protagonist in the quest to restore another nation's monarch.

Ten minutes later, they were riding through the low valleys of Jorvik's West Thrith. Adelise was still quiet, but it was a novelty to ride with her being conscious for once. Thurstan jokingly pointed this out to Adelise, but a muted grunt of a reply implied that it was not to her great amusement.

The sun was setting behind them, lighting the flat-topped fell of Ingleberg in swathes of pink and grey. Their journey would be quicker now, but the horse would also make them more conspicuous, cause more questions to be asked. They would ride as much as possible at night, Thurstan had decided, and rest during the day, meaning two, more likely, three days to ride to

235

Jorvik. Three days that might become four, might become a week, for keeping off the ancient roads and crossing the hills to Jorvik would slow them considerably.

Thurstan knew, though, that they needed every advantage they could take, for they were without food, without friends and without any certainty of what lay ahead across the tops. He kicked his heels back and pushed the horse towards the Pennine hills; an enemy and fugitive in his own country.

Lunden, Ængland

Edgar held the parchment nearer the candle and squinted at the scrawl. He knew that he ought to read it, it was one of a bundle brought with him, but neither his mind, nor his eyes, could focus. Something to do with land, held by a church, that was to be donated to a widow, or was it a widow who had left land to the Church?

Fingers trembling, he placed the parchment down on the oak table in his room and drew his cloak tighter around him. The day had been warm, or so he had been told, but he was constantly shivering. He struggled out of his seat and walked over to the fireplace. The crackle of the logs was the only noise in his room, housed as they were, far away from the main hall. His son, Ceolwulf, was hopefully asleep in the next room, although Edgar imagined that he was no doubt keeping himself awake, worrying about the day's events.

Things had not gone as he would have liked; things never did. Of course it had been foolish, unwise, and perhaps even dangerous to challenge Swegen. Yet he had not been prepared to see Ceolwulf accuse the earl in front of the witan. Edgar was dying, he knew that, and he could possibly afford to accuse Swegen more than his son could; the more extreme accusations could be explained away as the product of a wandering, failing mind.

Yet there came a point where Swegen had to be challenged. Irrelevant of his power, of where his tendrils extended to in court, someone had to challenge his seemingly unhindered and corrupt path to the throne. If they could prove in the morn that the body was not that of Adelise, then at least that bought some time. Precious time that perhaps the witan would use to consider the true merit of electing Swegen as king; not to let the drink-fuelled moment take them, as they had most certainly done the previous night.

The fire in the hearth flickered for a moment, orange tongues snapping at each preceding flame before disappearing into oblivion. Edgar pulled the collar of the cloak tightly around his throat, careful to avoid the angry lesions that now covered most of his body. He raised a thin hand and gingerly touched his neck, where his collar had rubbed the sores raw during the horse ride to Lunden.

He thought of Ceolwulf and of the burden he would be leaving him. Even if he had stopped his son from accusing Swegen in front of the witan, he could not protect him forever, not once he was gone. Should the Earl of Berrocscir be elected king, then there was no reason to suppose that he wouldn't exact his revenge on Ceolwulf. Edgar could use his last days to hinder Swegen, but would that save his son from a life of persecution afterwards?

He dearly hoped the boy was sleeping now. Ceolwulf tortured himself too much, guilt about his impetuousness, fears about assuming responsibility. The boy needed to learn to distinguish between personal and duty, between ambition and necessity. What he really needed was a wife, someone to relax with, to provide him a family, to divide his attentions. Hell, even if he just got a mistress to rut with, that would at least be a start.

Ceolwulf would all too often say the first thing that came to his mind, and then spend the next week regretting it, berating himself for not being wiser. Edgar had never felt that same sense of regret; perhaps it had come from his mother. Say something, for right or for wrong, but say it with conviction and stand by it. If someone did not like it, so be it. There was always time to learn the right thing to say – the way you said it counted for more.

Edgar felt a draught of air across the back of his neck and cursed that there must be an open shutter somewhere in the room. Then the sound of a floorboard creaking caused him to freeze. He was alone in the room; he had asked the two guards outside not to let him be disturbed. The sound of shutter swinging on a hinge made him smile ruefully. He turned to confront the intruder.

"I've been expect..." he started, but got no further as the glinting blade sank into his throat.

Ceolwulf rolled off the whore, his face flushed red and dripping with sweat. Almost immediately, he was consumed with shame. Shame at his nakedness, shame at his congress with a prostitute, shame that he had visited a brothel on tonight of all nights.

Like a misbehaving youth, he had let himself be talked into going to a nearby tavern by his uncle Ælfric's steward, Lyfing, and had crept out of his lodgings, hoping not to disturb his father. What had initially been a drink to unwind had become several drinks and when Lyfing had suggested visiting some of the young ladies in the rooms upstairs, it had seemed a good idea. Only once the act had been committed had the sobering realisation of his deeds hit home.

Ceolwulf grabbed his clothes from the dirty wooden floor and rummaged for his purse. He tossed a number of coins, which he hoped were enough, to the young girl on the bed. She seemed more than pleased with the sum and thanked him, a broad grin showing from under her long red hair that was now clinging to her perspiring face.

She had remained lying on the small bed, unashamedly naked, making no effort to cover herself or to leave. She was undoubtedly beautiful, Ceolwulf thought, and he could not deny he had enjoyed himself, but were these the actions of a future earl? Well, according to Lyfing, yes, they were. In fact, most earls enjoyed themselves in a much more depraved manner on quite a frequent basis, if his stories were to be believed.

Ceolwulf clumsily got dressed, stumbling as he hurriedly tried to step into his hose, causing the girl to laugh. If truth be told, although Ceolwulf knew that the girl was attractive, he would have been hard pushed to describe her looks. Throughout their intimacy, Ceolwulf had envisioned the face of the Flemish maid from back home in Theodford on the whore's body.

Alice! That was the maid's name, he thought, though he chided himself for not being certain. He might have even said her name aloud, but he dared not ask the girl on the bed. Grabbing his boots, he mumbled a few words of thanks and backed out of the room. The dark passageway led down to the tavern via a rickety, wooden staircase. As Ceolwulf stepped back into the smoky room he was greeted with a roar of approval from his now deeply inebriated companion.

"And about time, you randy sod!" Lyfing shouted. "Had your balls in such a twist, your brain wasn't working!" He embraced Ceolwulf playfully, ignoring his obvious discomfort. He glanced around him, worried the entire tavern's occupants would be staring in disgust at an earl's son visiting whores. Yet no-one appeared to be paying him any attention, and any that did appeared to be only out of interest as to whether the red-haired girl was now available. Ceolwulf leant to whisper into Lyfing's ear that he wished to leave.

"What?" Lyfing shouted, above the noise of the singing, cursing and dancing occupants of the tavern. "But we've only just got here!"

"No, Lyfing," Ceolwulf replied, "We've been here two hours already."

"Have we?" the steward replied, suddenly appearing to sober up. "Oh well, you've done what we came here for." He tipped the remnants of his flagon down his throat, and slapped the vessel down onto the table, wiping his mouth with the back of his sleeve, and emitted a satisfied belch. Lyfing tossed a small pouch of coin towards the barman, who replied with a courteous nod and they shuffled out into the night. Two of Ælfric's swordsmen, who had spent the entire evening stationed by the door, sipping water and weak ale, followed them out of the tavern.

The fresh air must have helped Lyfing to sober up, for the next time he spoke, he appeared far less drunk than he had seemed in the tavern.

"I know what you're thinking, lad. I know you think this was wrong, that it was inappropriate. But you need to let go at times, to relax," he said as they made their way along the narrow, house-lined, cobbled streets near Aldersgate.

"But what if my father or uncle were to find out?" Ceolwulf asked.

"They wouldn't mind. In fact, they'd probably approve," Lyfing replied. He gave this some thought, then added, "Actually, no. Approve is probably too strong a word. But they'd be relieved if you could unwind some more."

They continued back towards the King's Hall, where the glow of lights illuminated the Ivory Tower. Their pace had increased as Lyfing's drunkenness rapidly disappeared. A dog barked somewhere in the distance, but the streets were otherwise quiet at this hour of the night, or rather, early morning.

"What will happen tomorrow, do you think?" Ceolwulf asked.

"Well," Lyfing started, sniffing loudly and spitting onto the cobbles. "You'll say the corpse isn't Adelise's, Swegen and his cronies will insist it is. Even if neither side can convince the other, which is highly unlikely, some bishop or half-sensible member of the witan will hopefully move to suspend the proceedings until we can establish what has exactly happened. At that point, both sides will withdraw and hiss at each other like two cats across an alleyway. That's when Swegen will be at his most dangerous, when he is not being closely watched or is under the other earls' noses."

"And if we cannot get the proceedings suspended?" Ceolwulf asked, the nearing glow of the King's Hall starting to cast shadows on the street.

"Then Swegen will no doubt become king and you'll be in

trouble," Lyfing replied, sniffing again. He stopped and looked at the orange glow of light coming from the hall. "Can you smell burning?"

Ceolwulf barged his way though the crowd that had gathered to watch the blaze. They stood transfixed, staring at the building that had been his father's lodgings alight, the orange flames hypnotic and brilliant against the pitch black night around it. Floating sparks drifted in the air like flakes of fire.

Ceolwulf screamed at them to move out of the way, but his voice was lost in the noise of the roaring flames and crackling beams. Residents of the surrounding houses were coming out of their homes to join the spectators, causing the streets around the King's Hall to become ever more congested with bodies moving towards the blaze.

All except one. One man that Ceolwulf knocked into, sending him spinning to the floor. A hooded man, walking briskly away from the fire, whom Ceolwulf had been unable to avoid. Falling onto the cobbles, Ceolwulf saw the man turn briefly to stare down at him, long enough for the large scar that ran down the edge of his face to reflect the orange glow of the flames. Then he was gone, and Ceolwulf was helped to his feet by Lyfing and his men. Ceolwulf thought for a second about following the hooded man, then turned and continued trying to make his way to the hall.

The sentries on the gate of the King's Hall complex made little effort to stop the desperate Ceolwulf as he rushed towards the collapsing building, screaming his father's name. He would have rushed into the building to save him, but there was no doorway left to rush into, no semblance of walls or rooves; just a skeleton of timbers and beams now engulfed in thick flame and smoke. Ælfric rushed from the crowd and held his nephew back, shouting at him that it was too late, much too late to save his father.

Ceolwulf screamed curses at those stood around watching, for there appeared to be no chain of men trying to put the fire out, no volunteers trying to extinguish the flames. There had been no warning, Ælfric explained; one moment there had been peace and quiet, the next both storeys had erupted into billowing flame. The roof had collapsed in a matter of minutes.

Ceolwulf asked desperately about the men that had been posted in the building, his father's guards. Perhaps they had saved his father; perhaps they were safely taking refuge somewhere and had not been discovered. No, he was told, no-one had made it out alive.

Ceolwulf let a cry of rage, of pain and anguish out; half sob, half scream. His father had been dying, but God would have taken him in his own time, not like this. His father had not deserved to burn. He struggled free from his uncle's grip and rushed towards the building, hoping desperately to see some trace of his father; perhaps there was a cellar in the lodgings that had offered refuge. Ælfric screamed at his nephew to come back, for he seemed about to leap into the flames.

But Ceolwulf was not listening. He had been overcome by grief and anger. He did not hear the crack as one of the remaining roof beams sagged, then dropped in a shower of sparks and flame towards the very spot where Ceolwulf was standing.

Ceolwulf was lost in a world of helplessness and despair, staring at the blackened shapes in front of him when the sudden blow of pain and heat rendered him senseless and he willingly welcomed the beckoning darkness of unconsciousness.

From the top floor of the King's Hall, Godric, Archbishop of Westmynster turned away from the window and shook his head at Eadric, Archbishop of Cantwaraburg.

"What a terrible tragedy," Eadric said.

"Indeed it is, my friend," Godric replied, his voice richly

laced with sadness.

"The messenger said it was East Anglia in there?"

"It would appear so."

"And with no survivors. A tragedy indeed," Eadric said, sitting down and wiping away a tear, only partially caused by the noxious smoke of the fire.

Godric offered him a small glass of wine and sat beside him. The two archbishops, by virtue of being the two most powerful churchmen in the country, had been given rooms within the top floors of the building of the Great Hall itself. Godric's room had offered a clear view of the vicious blaze and Eadric had joined him the minute the messenger had brought the terrible news. Godric cleared his throat lightly and set his glass down.

"Under the circumstances, perhaps we ought not to disturb the late queen's body tomorrow after all? It no longer seems appropriate, does it?" the Archbishop of Westmynster asked.

The elder of the two bishops appeared lost in thought, then stirred, shaking his head.

"What's that? Umm, yes, possibly. You're probably right, Godric," he said distractedly. "Such a terrible waste of life. Good family that; they had always shown such strong support. So sad."

"Quite," Godric replied, before standing up and walking back over to the window. He held up his half-empty, or rather, he thought, half-full glass, to watch how the flames reflected in its thickly cut sides. He downed the remaining wine and smiled to himself. No survivors. Tomorrow had just become a whole lot easier.

27th May 1166
Lunden, Ængland

The doors of the Great Hall burst open, hinges screaming loudly before the solid oak panels bounced off the wall behind in a cloud of dust. The hall's occupants turned in their seats to see who had so rudely interrupted the proceedings. The newly confirmed king-elect, Swegen, Earl of Berrocscir peered over the witan's heads to see Ceolwulf, his head bandaged, limp into the hall.

"My dear Lord Ceolwulf, I am relieved to see you are still alive," Swegen called out, his voice silencing the exclamations of surprise and outrage at the unruly entrance. "I am so sorry to hear about your father, let me extend—"

"You!" Ceolwulf shouted, cutting Swegen off mid-sentence. "You are not sorry at all. You are responsible!" He strode down the central aisle of the hall, his arm held aloft, a finger extended and pointing directly at Swegen. From the back of the hall an ashen-faced Ælfric scuttled into the room, desperately trying to stop his nephew before he said something he would regret.

Swegen flashed his usual smile at the witan and raised his hands in supplication. These were the men that barely an hour before had agreed that he would become the next King of Ængland. No Edgar had meant no morning inspection of the corpse in St Paul's. No Edgar or Ceolwulf, who had initially been believed dead, meant no challenge to his ascension. All there remained to finalise were the details of his coronation. The ramblings of a grief-stricken fool were not going to change their minds now.

"Ceolwulf, my cousin, you have suffered a cruel blow, both physically and mentally. Please let us not say such untruths," Swegen called to the ever-nearing Ceolwulf. His mouth spoke of friendship, but his eyes shimmered with hatred.

"You know that girl is not Adelise. You killed my father last night; I saw your man in the crowd, hurrying away. Too long have you tried to take East Anglia for yourself, you couldn't even wait for my father to die of his illness. You had to silence him, lest this farce of an election be exposed for the corrupt sham it is!" Ceolwulf shouted. A trickled of blood flowed out from underneath the linen bandages around his forehead and dripped into his eye. Ceolwulf did not even blink or attempt to wipe it away.

"You!" Swegen shouted, and then paused, trying to calm himself. "You are not in possession of your senses, brother." The last word was virtually spat out. "I suggest you go for a long, quiet lie down somewhere." He snapped his fingers and Ceolwulf was immediately surrounded by several armed men, just as Ælfric reached his nephew and seized his arm.

"My lord Earl, forgive my nephew, for he knows not what he says," Ælfric called quickly to the dais.

"I know exactly what I am saying," Ceolwulf shouted, trying to brush his uncle away. "I am stating the truth, as you all know, yet no-one else dares say it out loud. Shame on you all, shame on you for electing such a man as your king. You are a murderer, Swegen, I declare you responsible for my father's death and I swear that I shall avenge him by taking your head!"

The hall erupted in consternation at Ceolwulf's declarations. On the dais, Godric, Archbishop of Westmynster sat with the usual smirk on his face, seemingly enjoying the proceedings. The Archbishop of Cantwaraburg was close to tears, appalled by the confrontation. Swegen appeared to possess the indifference and confidence that only a man very recently elected to become king could enjoy.

"Bloodfeuds are all so very old-fashioned, don't you think, Ceolwulf?" he asked amiably. He nodded at the armed men who seized Ceolwulf, one placing a sword blade at his throat. "So that's your evidence then. You saw a man in the crowd who knows me? I believe everyone here in this hall saw your lodgings

246

burn last night, Ceolwulf. Are they all guilty?"

"Everyone in this hall knows that Ricmund, the Eoten of Readinga, is your attack dog. Why was he trying so desperately not to be recognised as he ran away; away, note you, from the hall?" Ceolwulf said clearly, making sure everyone in the hall could hear him. Swegen's cheek twitched and his hand instinctively went to his side. Ceolwulf had stopped struggling against the men holding him now, his uncle whispering quickly in his ear. The members of the witan appeared to be glancing around the room for the man accused of being Edgar's killer, but there was no sign of Ricmund, save for an empty space on the front row where he normally sat.

Swegen appeared to gather himself and called for order in the hall. Instructing his armed men to let go of Ceolwulf he stepped down from the dais and addressed his distant cousin face to face, his voice calm and low.

"I am going to give you a choice now, Ceolwulf. I am going to let you make a sensible decision. If you continue with your mendacious, vile claims against my person, against your future monarch, against the man the witan have elected to be their leader, I shall be forced to take your head." He raised one finger to show the first choice, then flicked up a second finger. "Or, you can retract your claims, go into exile and never return to Ængland again. Though I recommend the latter, I would suggest you don't go to Northland, lest people think that you were complicit with them in the murder of our late queen. Which will it be?"

Ceolwulf opened his mouth to speak, his face contorting into a snarl, but his uncle squeezed his arm tightly and whispered fervently into his nephew's ear. Ceolwulf blinked, and then took a very deep breath.

"I recant, my lord Earl," he said finally, a single tear of frustration rolling down his cheek.

"*Prince*, Ceolwulf, my lord *Prince* now," Swegen said. "You have until sunset tomorrow to leave the country, after which your life will be forfeit. I trust the witan supports me in dealing with such treachery and accusations?"

He was answered by shouts of agreement and nods from the high table.

"I like to think of myself as a good man, a reasonable man. I would have hated for my first act as king to have been one of violence," Swegen said, walking away from Ceolwulf, returning to the high table.

"My lord Prince Swegen," came the voice of Godric. "As you are a just man and wish to have no stain on your good character, might it not be wise nonetheless to investigate claims of Ricmund's involvement in the tragic fire?"

Swegen appeared to be surprised by Godric's question initially, but then gave the proposition some thought. After a few seconds of deliberation he slowly nodded his head.

"Yes, yes, of course. In this court, in this land, the law applies equally to everyone. No-one is exempt from it. I shall of course investigate any wrongdoing by Ricmund; but let me assure you now, I knew nothing of his activities, and they were certainly not on my instruction." He bowed to Godric, who nodded benignly back at him. The hall appeared to approve the fair and just hand that Swegen had shown. "Of course, should your accusation prove false, Ceolwulf, I see no reason why my trusted friend should not become Earl of East Anglia, now the title is vacant. Is that not justice, my lords?"

Ceolwulf stepped forward again, but Ælfric pulled him back, quickly away from the sword blade that flicked up to block his path.

"Leave it be, Ceolwulf, leave it now," he said quietly. "Keep yourself alive; you will avenge no-one if you are dead."

Ceolwulf stared at the high table for one moment, spat on the ground, then turned and walked out of the room. He clicked his fingers at the armed men surrounding him, ordering them to follow him as if he were their leader, rather than their prisoner. He left the hall without looking back, his uncle following several paces behind him.

"My Lord Ælfric!" Swegen called just as the thegn was about to leave the room.

"Yes, my lord Prince?"

"I trust I will see you at tonight's feast? I assume you have no wish to forfeit your lands and family too?"

Ælfric stood and stared right back at Swegen for just a second longer than was comfortable for those watching.

"No, my lord Prince."

With that, he turned and strode out, the doors gently closed behind him by two serving boys. A rumble of raised voices quickly consumed the hall, leaving Swegen to recline in his high-backed chair and exchange glances with Godric. He waved at a boy, who quickly brought him a goblet of wine.

"Take this message to the captain of the household guards. Have Ricmund come see me tonight, after vespers, in the Ivory Tower. The captain will know where to find him," Swegen whispered into the boy's ear. Godric, having overhead the message, nodded approvingly at Swegen once the boy had gone.

"This whole affair was been somewhat, untidy, shall we say?"

"Do not worry, Godric. Tonight, we shall make things a little..." Swegen paused for a moment, mimicking the archbishop's manner of speaking. "Tidier."

The two men toasted each other and emptied their cups. Things were finally going to plan.

The corpse of Ricmund of Readinga, the Eoten, was found early next morning at the foot of the Ivory Tower. A servant, on his way from the kitchens to fetch water from a well, had spotted what he had at first assumed to be a bundle of damp clothes left on the cobbles. On closer inspection, prompting much screaming and panic, it turned out to be what had once been a man.

The body had been cruelly disfigured and misshapen after what must have been a fall from near the top of the tower. Only the man's jewellery and a closer examination of what remained of his face had indicated that the bloodied mass had formerly been Swegen's trusted thegn.

Later that same day, a proclamation was issued by Swegen and approved by the witan that Ricmund the Monster had been found guilty, posthumously, of the murder of Edgar, Earl of East Anglia. The lands would now pass under direct control of the Crown and the new earl would not be nominated until the next witenagemot.

Ricmund's vile actions had been brought about through greed, the proclamation read, for various witnesses had come forward to say that he had been seen fleeing carrying a fistful of jewellery and with a pouch full of coin. The future king, of course, had had no knowledge of Ricmund's intentions. He was said to be aghast at such treachery and naturally could not be held responsible in any way.

Which, for the time being, tidied all Swegen's loose ends up, which was good, for Swegen disliked loose ends very much.

28th May 1166
The Pennine Hills, Northland

The rain was no longer falling from the sky, but blowing horizontally straight into Thurstan's face; a constant torrent that felt like a bucket of water being perpetually flung at him. It had started during the night as they had tried to sleep. Thurstan's intention had initially been to travel by night to avoid unwanted attention, but the tops were so deserted and potentially treacherous that he had decided it would be safer to stop. The land was mostly mile after mile of rolling fells, an undulating sea of purple heather and golden ferns, laced with treacherously narrow, steep valleys and quick-flowing streams. The darkness could conceal any number of unseen crags, cliffs and crevices that could easily break a limb or kill if they were not wary.

They had taken shelter in a small copse that had offered somewhere to tether the horse's reins and gave some small protection from the wind, if not the persistant midges. The horse's name, Adelise had decided, was to be Bucephalus, after that of Alexander of Macedon. She was surprised that Thurstan knew of the name, but he had been tutored and a huskarl, as he pointed out, should know the horse of the greatest military leader of all time.

The rain had come whilst they had slept on makeshift beds of fern and grass. It had turned their few remaining rations, a lump of hard bread and dried fish, to sludge and had soaked their clothes. By sunrise, the weather had shown no sign of letting up and Thurstan decided it was best to press on towards Jorvik. Adelise had been reluctant, but the trees were offering precious little protection from the elements, so she had relented.

Noon had come and gone but the rain had not yet eased. At least, Thurstan thought noon had gone, though he could not be sure. The sun was an almost distant memory, for the sky was a solid, impenetrable wall of grey. Now it was early afternoon and the streams and brooks that they had initially trotted through or quickly jumped over were fast-flowing torrents that were washing the earth away with them. Thurstan had tried to cover Adelise as best he could with his cloak, but there seemed to be nowhere into which the rain could not find its way.

In every direction, as far as the eye could see, Thurstan could make out nought but valleys and hilltops. Not that he could see very far in this weather, but he feared that they were simply walking in circles, with no sun to guide their direction. A series of miserable sneezes from under Thurstan's cloak broke the monotonous drone of the rain as Bucephalus made his way down yet another valley side.

"Are you feeling all right?" Thurstan asked, slowing the horse to a standstill.

"No," came a miserable voice, followed by a loud sniff.

"Are you unwell?" Thurstan twitched his cloak aside, worried for Adelise's health. She had by no means recovered from her wound yet; even the mildest of ailments or colds could have serious consequences for her.

"I'm hungry. I'm cold. I want to stop," she replied.

"We can't, I'm sorry," Thurstan said. He knew they would have to stop soon, at a farm or a village. They would have to risk being seen to spend their last few remaining coins to purchase supplies. For the time being, Thurstan wouldn't know where to find the nearest village even if he wanted to. He had imagined that he would have seen a plume of chimney smoke to conveniently mark out a friendly hamlet of some sort, but that had been before they had been forced to cross the tops, before the rain had set in.

Bucephalus reached the foot of a small hill and immediately started to climb another of the seemingly never-ending fells. His hooves squelched noisily in the soft turf, the ground churning instantly into mud under his weight. As he made his way upwards, he stumbled and lurched to one side. Thurstan grabbed the reins and steadied himself, but Adelise almost fell out of the saddle, only keeping on the horse because she was wrapped so tightly in his cloak.

"Hold on to the saddle," Thurstan chided her.

"I can't," she complained.

"Why not?" Thurstan asked, turning Bucephalus to climb the hill at an angle.

"I can't feel my hands anymore," Adelise shouted, almost crying.

Thurstan looked down and saw that she had clamped her hands under her arms, trying to keep warm. Her teeth were chattering and his cloak was no longer offering any real protection from the rain, but was just clinging wetly to her.

A moment later, Bucephalus stumbled again, this time his hooves slipping a few inches in the soft turf. Thurstan pulled him up to a halt and cursed loudly. He could not risk their horse breaking a leg, not out here in the open.

Thurstan sat for a minute, letting the rainwater cascade down his face and drip off the end of his nose. He felt Adelise shudder and draw herself tighter into a huddle whilst Bucephalus tossed his head uneasily. Thurstan swore again then gingerly dismounted from the horse, taking great care not to lose his footing on the wet grass. He lifted Adelise down and placed her on the ground before taking his cloak off and wrapping it around her; it went around her small frame almost three times. He stepped back, took Bucephalus's reins, and looked up to the sky.

"Fine! Have it your way!" he shouted to the god or gods he thought responsible for the rain. He picked Adelise's now wool-cocooned body up and placed it over his shoulder, then turned Bucephalus around and slowly led him down the hillside. He would follow this hill down until he reached the valley floor, and then follow whatever stream or brook ran along the bottom. At some point, he imagined, it would become a river, and then at some point that river would have a village or town on it. The need outweighed the risk.

By the bottom of the first hill his calves were already burning, the soft ground making each step laborious, the weight of his wet clothes and Adelise feeling impossibly heavy. The sound of thunder rumbled somewhere in the west and although Thurstan had believed it to be impossible, it started raining even harder.

There was no alternative though, he had no choice; there was no time to sit down and bemoan his fate. Bucephalus on the other hand, seemed much happier. Shorn of the extra weight of his passengers, he seemed quite content to follow his new master.

"I bet Alexander of Macedon never got rained on like this," Thurstan muttered to himself, cursing as he slipped and stumbled through the gorse and heather.

"There is one good thing," came a muffled voice, followed by a loud sneeze. "At least the midges have gone."

Blackwater Estuary, Eastseaxe, Ængland

The *Angelfire*'s prow plunged down into the white crested waves, buffeting those standing on its deck, forcing them to hold on to anything solid to keep their footing. The weather had been poor ever since leaving the port of Mældune, the estuary's choppy waters even worse now they were almost out into the open sea. To the ship's right the Kentish coastline faded into the distance; unseen to the North, beyond Eastseaxe, lay East Anglia.

Ceolwulf stood on deck gazing towards where his homeland had faded into the blue grey of the sky and waves. As the ship lurched to one side, slamming into another surge, the *Angelfire*'s captain once again asked Ceolwulf if he wouldn't be more comfortable below deck. And once again, the young nobleman refused, preferring to remain on deck, staring into the distance.

He had hardly said a word since boarding, but that was to be expected, the captain supposed. He was aware that Ceolwulf had been sent into exile, but felt no particular animosity towards him. The captain, a stoic, red-cheeked East Anglian man from Gipeswic, possessed no great love for Swegen and reckoned a man who had crossed the Earl of Berrocscir doubtlessly had no shortage of reasons for doing so.

"My lord!" the captain shouted. "My lord!"

There was the merest hint of acknowledgment from Ceolwulf. "If you wish to stay on deck, then at least keep away from the side. Come stand with me at the wheel. Please, my lord."

Ceolwulf grunted what appeared to be an assent, and then struggled lopsidedly over to the captain. He should be grateful, Ceolwulf thought, that at least he hadn't been thrown overboard, which if Swegen had had his way, would have most likely been his fate. As it was, his uncle had been able to organise his passage to Flanders, using a ship and captain of his choice. Ælfric had convinced him that if he had tarried one night more, or allowed

Swegen any more time to determine his fate, then he would never have left Ængland alive.

There had been no time to return to East Anglia, to see his mother one final time. He had hardly slept that night, but had spent the time writing letters, discussing with his uncle plans for the future, all the while under armed guard. At around four in the morning, when the two sentries watching him had finally fallen asleep, he and his uncle had finally been able to properly discuss his exile, planning for what ought to happen, what could happen and all eventualities in between.

For now, he was on his way to Flanders, to a new life with distant cousins, where he would no doubt be kept, well fed and comfortable, out of harm's way. He would spend the rest of his life hoping that Swegen would contract some fatal disease and die without issue, in the hope that he would one day be welcomed back to his homeland. He would spend his time in alehouses, telling anyone who would listen about the injustices he had suffered and how someday he would wreak his revenge. Even a pardon would not be enough, for no pardon from Swegen's lips could ever be fully trusted. He would welcome him back with one open arm, and then slide a blade into his back with the other.

The Angelfire's sails snapped in the wind, sounding like tiny claps of thunder and the captain grunted with the effort of keeping the wheel straight. Ceolwulf knew he ought to make more effort to be cordial with the captain, for he appeared to be a good man; a good man who could have quite easily taken advantage of Ceolwulf's miserable circumstances.

"Thank you," Ceolwulf finally mustered.

"For what, my lord?" the captain replied, cheerfully.

"For taking me," Ceolwulf replied. "For not tipping me overboard, I suppose."

"No need to thank me, my lord. I am only sorry that you find yourself the victim of such an injustice," the captain said. He scanned the deck to see if any of his crewmembers were listening. "If I were you, I would have stuck my dagger right up that snake's arse, hilt first, if you'll pardon my language, my lord."

Ceolwulf laughed at the man's honesty.

"Do you trust your crew?" he asked, having noticed the captain's caution before speaking. The rosy-faced man gave this some thought before replying.

"I trust them with my life, yes. But the thought of having a man such as Swegen as king will make every man think twice before speaking aloud from now on. Where there's no trust, there can be no honesty, sad to say."

Ceolwulf nodded and returned his eyes to the horizon. The waves seemed to be coming faster now and Ceolwulf felt his stomach was about to leave him every time the ship crested a wave. The sound of the sea and wind was broken only by the discordant choir of gulls that had been following them since they had upped anchor.

"How long will it take us to reach the Flemish coast?" Ceolwulf asked.

"Depends on the weather, my lord. Three, maybe four days if the weather is this bad and the wind blows against us. Can sail to Frankia in an afternoon if the wind blows right on certain days," the captain replied. Ceolwulf did not respond for several minutes before he suddenly spoke again, his voice oddly high pitched and emotionless.

"How long would it take us to sail to Northland?"

The captain didn't respond immediately. He span the wheel, straightening the ship as it slammed into another high wave, then whistled out through his teeth.

"Up the river Hymbre?" he asked.

"Yes."

"Two days, maybe? Again, with this weather, could be longer, could be less. You have thoughts of going there? To Jorvik, my lord?" the captain asked. He had heard the rumours, the accusations that Edgar, Earl of East Anglia and his son had colluded with the Northlandic king in the assassination of their queen. Not that he had believed them, but now the earl's son was asking to be taken to a land that Ængland was soon to be at war with, if stories were to be believed.

"I know what you're thinking," Ceolwulf replied, as if he could read the captain's mind. "Let me assure you though. I am no traitor. I am Ænglisc and always will be. But I am an enemy of Swegen. An enemy of the king is not an enemy of the country, Captain."

"In his case," the captain said eventually, quietly, almost in a whisper. "The opposite could be said to be true. Whoever gets rid of him would be doing the country a favour."

"Then turn us north. Turn us north and let me right the wrongs that have been done," Ceolwulf. "That is, if you think your men will not object."

"My men will do as they are told. Most of them won't even notice the difference between Flanders and Northland anyway; they get confused speaking to anyone from outside Eastseaxe."

"Then you'll do it?" Ceolwulf asked.

The captain did not reply, but simply hauled on the wheel and shouted instructions to his men on deck.

"Already done, my lord. Now get down below deck and get some sleep. Sounds like you're going to need it."

Ceolwulf nodded and clasped the captain's shoulder.

"I shall forever be in your debt," he said.

"No you won't," the captain replied cheerfully. "'Cos if anyone asks, you held a blade to my neck and made me do this. Understood? Now let me sail."

The *Angelfire* turned northwards, the waves pounding her side now, lurching across the sea towards Northland. Ceolwulf settled into an uneasy sleep, unsure of what awaited him. Was his new plan folly? Would he be welcomed with open arms as the Ænglisc earl who could exonerate their country of regicide, or would he be discarded, as a political liability? As his thoughts descended into dreams of murder and betrayal, the ship rode on, into the storm.

Nidderdale, West Thrith of Jorvik, Northland

Dark had already fallen by the time Thurstan and Adelise reached the village. Just as they had given up hope of finding shelter, they had made out the lights that signalled human habitation.

The rain had finally eased, but the ground had been rendered treacherous by the inundation. Thurstan's boots were caked with mud up beyond his calves and the damp leather had rubbed his feet raw. Each painful step through the final field was agony, his shoulder screaming at the now impossibly heavy Adelise.

As they neared the lights, Thurstan could make out a handful of low, wooden buildings, no more than a hamlet. They were loosely arranged around a central area, which didn't quite qualify as a town square, but appeared to represent the focal point of the village.

Thurstan stopped and scanned the buildings for any sign of movement. A dog barked somewhere in the distance and a pony was tethered behind one of the larger buildings. Seeing nothing that troubled him too much, Thurstan decided to head towards the nearest building to them, and significantly, the furthest from the village's centre. If they had to leave in a hurry, Thurstan did not want to be confronted by too many pitchfork-wielding villagers.

The building was attached to a small plot of land that ran from the back of the house down to the river. Various crops and vegetables were planted in neat rows, doing their best to not be swept away by the streams of water that cascaded through the village. Thurstan tethered Bucephalus to the fence that marked out the small field, where the horse would be unseen from the rest of the village. Unwanted questions about the appearance of a fine horse would certainly not be welcome.

Adelise had fallen off to sleep on Thurstan's shoulder, but

now he had stopped she had stirred to enquire what was happening. He gently lowered her to the ground, and then spent some time rotating his shoulder, massaging the joint.

"We're going to try to find somewhere to sleep and buy food," Thurstan explained. "Try to look like a boy, if you can. And try not to speak."

Adelise scowled at him, but nodded, placing a finger on her lips to show that she understood an Ænglisc girl's voice would not help with her portrayal of a Northlandic boy.

Wiping away the rain from his eyes, Thurstan walked to the wooden door of the house and knocked firmly. He was answered by the sound of shuffling feet, and then the door swung open revealing the round, friendly face of a white-haired man.

"Who are you and what can I do for you?" he asked, his amiable voice laced with an element of mistrust. Thurstan quickly explained that they had been travelling across the fell tops but had become lost in the rain and were now seeking food and shelter for the night. He patted his coin pouch to show that they could pay their way, doing his best impersonation of the accent of this part of Northland. The old man's bright eyes narrowed.

"Where are you from and why are you out on the tops on a day like today?" he asked.

"Gikelswic," Thurstan lied quickly. "Our village was attacked by soldiers from Lonborg, I do not know why, but we ran. I was hoping we could call on your Christian charity, for we are quite desperate. My younger brother here was that frightened that he has not spoken for over a day now."

"Soldiers, eh?" the old man asked. He looked Adelise up and down, then at Thurstan's clothing. He had strapped the sword and gloves underneath Bucephalus's saddle, but the quality of his leather boots denoted him as no ordinary peasant. "Very well." He nodded and waved the rain sodden strangers into his house, giving a quick glance around the deserted village before shutting his door.

Thurstan and Adelise stepped into the dimly lit room that constituted the man's home. A cooking pot, a bed and various animals occupied the one living space. They sat themselves down in front of the fire without prompting, instantly warming themselves and stripping any unnecessary outer layers of clothing. The old man introduced himself as Biarni, a widower who lived alone in the village, which went by the name of Midelesby. He joined them by the fireside, where he and Thurstan exchanged pleasantries. Adelise, keeping her under-tunic tightly wrapped around her, sat to one side, not uttering a word.

"You have a horse I think, tied up out in the field?" the old man said, cocking an ear to one side.

Thurstan nodded. "We appreciate your help, Biarni, and I will gladly pay you for your hospitality."

"Can't say I'm too rich or proud to refuse your coin, young man," he said with a wink. "So Gikelswic's been swarming with soldiers? Can't say that surprises me too much, there have been a fair few about over the last week or so."

Thurstan stiffened, fearing that the search for them had already extended to outside of Westmoringaland's borders.

"They say, or the cart drivers that come up the valley say, that there's a war brewing. War with Ængland, if you can imagine such a thing. Soldiers, riders, been around the valleys, recruiting volunteers," the old man explained.

"But why?" Thurstan asked. "Why would Northland attack Ængland?"

"Not attack they say, but prepare to defend. The folks say that the Ænglisc will attack us in revenge for killing their queen. I thought they had a king myself, but then I hear otherwise. We don't get news that often in these parts, save for the carters that come up. Still, better to attack before you get attacked, eh?"

Thurstan nodded out of politeness, and then turned the topic of conversation back to the rations they hoped to purchase. The old man disappeared into a dark corner of his small house and came back with small bags filled with an assortment of beans, vegetables and flat bread. Thurstan thanked him for his kindness and asked him the best road to take to Horgagate.

He had invented a cousin who lived in the market town, which lay on the road to Jorvik, hoping to avoid any questions about their real destination. Biarni was explaining how the valley road led directly to the Horgagate road when Adelise sneezed.

The rain had eased off and the sneeze sounded very loud in the small house. Very loud and very feminine.

"Bless me," Adelise said, instinctively.

Biarni stopped and turned to stare at Adelise.

"Bless you."

The Ænglisc and Northlandic blessings were almost identical and a half-attentive listener could have easily confused the two, but Biarni's gaze lingered just slightly too long for Thurstan's liking.

"And that road leads to Horgagate directly, then?" Thurstan asked, as if Adelise had not spoken. Biarni turned back and nodded.

"It does, it does. Now then, the hour is getting late and I like to rise early, with the sun. You boys," he replied, pausing slightly to wipe his chin with a grubby hand. "You may sleep in here; the horse should be safe outside. No-one will be passing by I should think; at least no-one to worry about." He rose from beside the fire and shuffled towards a pallet of straw in the corner of the house, shooing a thin, angry looking cat out of the way.

Adelise glanced at Thurstan, who nodded, then walked over to sit beside her.

"Try to get some sleep," he whispered. "We will leave at sunrise, not a minute later."

She nodded, but her face betrayed her unease at sleeping in the hut.

"Think of him as another Egbrand," Thurstan said, glancing over his shoulder. Her distrust of strangers was understandable, but a night of sleep under a roof, warm, would be invaluable. "Besides, I'll be here just next to you," Thurstan said, laying his now dry cloak on the ground so that his head would be just a few inches from her feet.

Adelise sighed, and then lay down on a small woollen blanket. She screwed her eyes up as tightly as she could, wishing that sleep would take her as soon as possible. After several moments, flashes of purple and white made her open her eyes again; she felt even more awake now, if anything.

"Good night, sleep well," Biarni said jovially, clambering noisily into his bed. Thurstan wished him good night then fell silent, leaving Adelise to stare at the roof beams.

The thatched roof had long been in need of repair and Adelise spent what she reckoned to be hours gazing at the stars through the gaping holes. Finally, the fire went out, the final embers lingering for many minutes, before their glow faded into nothingness. With that, a still wide-awake Adelise and the room were plunged into darkness.

Lunden, Ængland

The Archbishop of Cantwaraburg, Swegen had decided, might give the impression of being a bumbling old fool, a country priest elevated beyond merit, but he could also be a wily and stubborn irritant.

"The Church answers first to God, my lord Earl," Eadric droned on. "Then to the king. As such, a man of the cloth should be tried by his bishop, not by some common sheriff. He should sit in the court of God, not that of the common layman."

"But surely, my lord Archbishop, as you have told me many times, we are all judged by God when we die, so what difference does it make?" Swegen replied, goading him.

"You know full well that it is different, my lord Earl." Cantwaraburg insisted on referring to him as an earl still, even though he was now the king-elect. He was doing it on purpose, Swegen was sure.

"Rome agrees with me. The Pope himself has written to me and your predecessor stating as such on several occasions. Surely you would not wish to counter His Holiness?" the archbishop asked.

Eadric had waged the argument for many years, from even before Swegen had been born. Ænglisc clergy accused of a crime currently faced trial by bishops who sat alongside sheriffs or earls in the regular shire courts. The Archbishop of Cantwaraburg, like his predecessor, proposed that these ecclesiastical trials be separate from the common, lay ones. Swegen knew the result would be murdering priests and corrupt church officials being punished less severely, if at all. A few years in some monastery abroad instead of swinging on a rope, as they really ought to, he thought. He did not embrace the idea of the Crown relinquishing any power to the Church; he knew that the bishops were already too lenient on their own. If Cantwaraburg wanted this so badly though, then perhaps he could use it to his advantage.

"You're no fool, Eadric," Swegen said, contradicting what he normally thought about him. "You do not simply expect the Crown to hand over responsibility of trying clergy to you without, let us say, something in return?"

The old man cackled and rocked in his chair. The two men were alone in Swegen's private quarters in the King's Hall. Now that the witenagemot had officially ended, most members of the witan had dispersed back to their shires and dioceses, but Cantwaraburg had remained in Lunden. Eadric had stationed himself in Swegen's own chair, behind his table, leaving the future king to sit as if he were a guest in his own quarters.

"So are you willing at least to compromise?" Eadric asked.

Swegen cracked his knuckles and leant forward.

"Why do you care so much? What do you really want?" he asked. Eadric feigned shock and surprise.

"My lord Earl, I am offended that you doubt my motives are anything other than those I have stated. For the greater glory of God and the Church," he said, before leaning in closer to Swegen. "Although of course, we both know the ability to absolve the sins of one's peers, subjects and, dare I say, friends, gives one not a small amount of influence."

So the doddering old dog did have a sharper side, after all, Swegen thought, leaning back. The fading light cast long shadows in the room, the low sun shining straight into Swegen's squinting eyes, as normally he intended his visitors to endure.

"What could I possibly offer you?" Eadric asked. "Me, a man of such little material wealth and humble power, when compared to yourself or some other powerful nobleman."

Swegen translated this as 'name your price'. He pretended to think for a minute, then hesitantly replied.

"I owe Godric, Archbishop of Westmynster a favour, though I know not how to repay it. Perhaps if he were in someway shown some favour by you, then you would repay my debt to him?"

The Archbishop of Cantwaraburg raised his eyebrows and grinned broadly, revealing a mouth half filled with yellowing teeth.

"What kind of favour?"

"A not inconsiderable one."

"Some kind of financial agreement for his diocese perhaps, the loan of a relic?"

"I think he was thinking along the lines of official recognition, a more prominent role," Swegen said, hopefully nudging Eadric into the right area.

"Ah, I see. He wishes to take part in the coronation, rather than just hosting it in that gaudy church of his?" the old man asked. Swegen smiled at the pious, Latin-mumbling bore of the witenagemots labelling Westmynster Cathedral gaudy.

"Now there's an idea. Well suggested, my lord. It was rather a large favour I owe him though," Swegen said slowly.

"He wishes to conduct the entire ceremony himself?" the Archbishop of Cantwaraburg probed. Swegen nodded. The old man chewed on his lips, giving this some thought.

"So I shall stand behind him, like some watchful matriarch at a wedding, and let him be seen as the foremost churchman in the land? Is that it?" he asked.

"I wouldn't say that, my lord. The power still lies in Cantwaraburg; it would just be this ceremony," Swegen replied.

"And so it shall stay. I would not like to think that this is just the first step in a transfer of power from Kent to Lunden. The Church does well to stay away from merchants. And kings," Eadric retorted bitterly.

Swegen shook his head reassuringly. "It's just one ceremony, it means nothing," he said.

"It obviously means something to Godric," the old man snapped.

"The Archbishop of Westmynster is a less spiritual man than

you. He takes more pleasure in the show of things, how they appear to the masses," Swegen said. The Archbishop of Cantwaraburg fell silent and closed his eyes, retreating into thought.

"So, one coronation ceremony in exchange for my ecclesiastical courts and the benefit of the clergy?" he said finally, without opening his eyes.

"Yes, my lord," Swegen replied.

"It all rather seems very much to my advantage. It must be a very large favour you owe. Some kind of forgiveness, a blessing perhaps?" Eadric asked, his eyes twinkling. Swegen shifted uneasily in his seat. The sunlight into his eyes was starting to give him a headache now.

"A rather unfortunate indiscretion I committed, which needed absolving," Swegen said.

"Ah, a young lady? Or a boy perhaps?" Eadric almost appeared to be enjoying himself.

"Something along those lines," Swegen said quietly. "An ill-advised tryst with a lady I ought not to have had. There were some complications." He added the lie in the hope of making his excuse sound realistic. The Archbishop of Cantwaraburg crossed himself, then looked to the ceiling.

"Agreed, then. I expect you to pass some kind of edict within six months," he said finally, his tongue clicking in triumph.

"Surely, my lord, it would be prudent to delay the announcement until well after the coronation. We would not want people thinking we had struck some sort of vulgar deal," Swegen said. "And of course, the coronation is impending, so that must take precedence."

"So you wish to announce that the Archbishop of Westmynster will perform the coronation and I must wait for you to fulfil your promise?"

"Before Christmas, I swear on the Holy Bible. So that by January next year the new ecclesiastical courts will be taking place."

Eadric fell silent again. Then, using the table to steady himself, he stood up and walked around to the table to where Swegen remained seated. The old man was unsteady on his feet, but there was a steely glare in his eyes.

"Don't think I don't know what you and Godric are up to, Swegen," he said, bending down so that his face was level with Swegen's. "I know all about your little plans and what you've done in the north."

Swegen flinched as the old man spoke, spittle flying from his peg-toothed mouth. Eadric kept his head level with Swegen's for just a moment too long for comfort, then straightened up and stepped towards the door.

"Very well. I will have my courts and you can have your theatre. But do not think for one moment about trying to supplant me further. Rome will not have it. I will not have it. Understood?" Eadric asked. Swegen nodded. His mouth had run dry and his fingers were tingling.

"It is for the good of the country, my lord Archbishop," he stuttered. "You understand that. One day, people will see that, should they ever find out, that is."

The Archbishop of Cantwaraburg paused at the door and turned, snorting back a chuckle.

"It doesn't matter what people think; you're both going to Hell. Announce your ceremony and be damned. Those courts by December, at the latest."

Without saying another word he left the room and slammed the door behind him. Swegen took several deep breaths, then reached across the table for a quill and some scrolls of parchment. There were several edicts, orders and important messages to write and he had just been forced to add one more to the list.

29th May 1166
Midelesby, West Thrith of Jorvik, Northland

Adelise woke to find the house still in total darkness. Something had disturbed her sleep, perhaps a sound from outside or something moving in the room. She lay with her eyes wide open for a several minutes, trying to adjust her vision to the dark. Had she imagined the shuffling sound in her dreams, possibly a cat or fox outside? She waited, and then it came again, a quiet shuffling noise. She realised fearfully that the sound was coming from within the house. She wanted to check that she was near Thurstan, that she could see him, but she dared not turn her head to scan what little she could see of the room.

The noise grew louder; it was getting closer and she realised with a certain element of relief that it was just Biarni, their host for the night. The relief was short-lived as it became clear that the old man was shuffling over to where Adelise was lying, causing another wave of fear to wash over her. She turned her head slightly to see the grinning face of the old man just inches from hers. She made to speak, but he placed a finger on her lips, shaking his head, urging her to remain silent.

Adelise stiffened and although she could not be sure why, she suddenly felt very frightened and vulnerable. From behind Biarni came the sound of Thurstan snoring and she wished desperately that her guardian would wake up.

"You're a pretty boy, aren't you?" the grinning man asked, his breath stinking and warm on her cheek. "Almost like a little girl?" The man's round face and ever-present smile, which had seemed so friendly was now only serving to unsettle Adelise more and more. His fingers clasped the neck of her tunic, which he did not pull open, but gripped firmly whilst starting at her straight in the eye.

"I wager you're Saxon too. A Saxon girl, here in Midelesby,"

Biarni said, his grin spreading even wider, almost laughing. "Now what is a Saxon girl doing here in old Biarni's home?"

Adelise twisted to one side and tried to call out to Thurstan, but a grimy, calloused hand roughly covered her mouth and forced her down in to the straw. Adelise could hear Thurstan mumble quietly and turn over his sleep, but he refused to wake up. She twisted frantically, but Biarni pressed his hand hard over her face until the pain forced her to lie still.

"And to think that only two days ago soldiers came by, asking old Biarni to look out for a huskarl and a Saxon lass. A reward for their capture or information. Now let's find out what you really are," he said. A strand of spittle fell from his chin onto her shoulder and then the hand at her neck moved down towards her legs.

It was at that point that Adelise's hand flew up and stabbed the farmer. Egbrand's knife glinted, the briefest of shimmers in the dark, and plunged straight into the old man's neck. He staggered back away from the bed, the knife still protruding from the side of his throat, making a terrible bubbling noise.

Adelise cried out in fear and distress as Biarni sank to his knees, his gurgling becoming a low scream. The man's choking was growing louder in the quiet night, when up from behind him loomed Thurstan who simply gripped his head and twisted, silencing him with a sickening crack. Adelise sprang from the bed and clutched at Thurstan, hugging him tightly. Tears streaming down her face, she could not take her eyes off the body of the now-dead man at her feet.

"I'm sorry," she repeatedly apologised between muffled sobs as she buried her face into Thurstan's shoulder.

"No, I'm sorry," Thurstan replied. "I'm sorry, not you, I am. It was my fault, I shouldn't have fallen asleep. I'm sorry. So sorry."

He repeated the mantra through guilt and fear, for he felt that for the first time, just for a few minutes, he had abandoned her.

Adelise tried to stifle her tears, but they kept coming.

Thurstan did nothing to stop them, but held her tightly, mindful that any noise could easily carry to neighbouring houses at this time of night. He listened out for any indication that they had disturbed someone, but the only noise to be heard was that of the river nearby.

Several minutes later, once Adelise had regained some composure, she sat down on the floor and told Thurstan everything that had happened

"I don't think he wanted to hurt me," Adelise said. "He just wanted to find out if I was a Saxon girl."

"Money," Thurstan said slowly, "Or rather, the promise of it, makes people do funny things. You're probably right." He said nothing more, preferring not to discuss the matter further with Adelise.

"But how did you get Egbrand's knife?" he asked. "I'd hidden it in my boot."

"I know," Adelise replied. She explained how once the fire had gone out, she had lain in the darkness for over an hour, feeling ill at ease. She had crawled quietly towards Thurstan, finding his boots in the dark and taken it before going back to bed.

"I don't know why I did that," she said. "It just made me feel safer in the dark."

"Well it's a good job you did," Thurstan remarked. Fresh tears came again and Thurstan hugged her. "It's going to be all right."

"But I killed him, I killed him, Thurstan," Adelise cried. "I'll go to Hell."

"No, Adelise, you defended yourself. You did what you had to do," Thurstan said, patting her shoulder softly. "Anyway, you scratched him, I killed him." Before Adelise could reply, the noise of a cockerel crowing broke the silence of night and heralded the onset of dawn.

"Come on," Thurstan said, standing up. "We haven't got time to talk now. We must leave and not be seen." He filled their bags with what little food he could find in the old man's house, enough to last them until the reached Jorvik, he hoped.

"What do we do with him?" Adelise said, pointing, but not looking directly at the corpse.

Thurstan paused and looked at the body. The flow of blood from the neck had stopped quickly, but there would be no disguising how the man had died. He walked over to the old man's body and hauled it onto the pile of rags and grass that he had used for a bed.

"There's nothing we can do apart from leave the village as quickly as we can," Thurstan said, taking Adelise by the wrist. She flinched at first and Thurstan let go, apologising.

"You lead the way, my lady," he said, offering what he hoped was a gentle smile. Adelise smiled weakly back, then slowly opened the rickety wooden door to the house, peering out into the gloomy village. What little light there was showed the area around the house to be deserted, save for a pair of prowling cats.

They crept out, closing the door behind them, wincing as the hinge gave the briefest of squeals. Bucephalus was thankfully still tied up where they had left him. The horse seemed unsurprised and uninterested by their sudden appearance. He tossed his head gently as Thurstan first lifted Adelise delicately into the saddle, then hoisted himself up as quietly as he could.

Ever so slowly to begin with, they rode through the village, Bucephalus's hooves making the softest of thuds in the still-drying mud. They did not encounter another soul; stopping only once to let the cockerel stride across the road in front of them. Once they were at least fifty yards past the last building, Thurstan kicked his heels back and urged Bucephalus into a gallop.

Adelise turned in the saddle to watch the village disappear into the distance behind them. As hard as it would be, she decided then and there that she would never think about this place again. This night had not happened; the old man had not attempted to betray them. People, like Egbrand, were intrinsically good, not like the man here.

Fingers clasped together, she prayed that whatever images she tried to eliminate from her waking thoughts would not come back to haunt her in her sleep. The gloom and mists of the morning combined with Adelise's tears to blur and obscure her final glimpse of the village of Midelesby. And then, as Adelise finished her silent prayer, it disappeared into the darkness forever.

30th May 1166
Jorvik, Northland

Thurstan and Adelise arrived at Jorvik's western gate behind a long queue of traders' carts. The morning's journey across the final miles of the flat Vale of Jorvik had been an easy ride, pleasant almost. They had been able to see the cathedral's large spires since sunrise that morning, thanks to the clear skies and the towering height of the building. Since leaving the unhappy, rain-sodden Nidd valley the previous day, they had made good progress. They had followed the main road to Jorvik ever closer, risking being seen by fellow travellers until they had become convinced they were not being hunted in this part of Northland.

That morning, passing through one of the small villages dotted around the city, they had encountered armed men on horseback. The horsemen had thundered into view from behind some farm buildings, leaving Thurstan no time to get off the road. Yet the men had passed, not even giving them a second glance, paying them no more attention than they would a farmer or trader. Bucephalus's bedraggled appearance, his matted unbrushed coat and mud-splattered legs, was clearly working in their favour.

By the time they had ambled along the loose stone road to the Mykla Gate Bar, the southwestern entrance to Jorvik, the memories of trekking through the wilderness had faded like a bad dream. Their fears now were much more tangible; armed men guarding the entrance to Northland's capital city. The traders' carts were lined up in front of them, each man having to pay a toll to enter, depending on his goods. The queue was being held up by one particularly vociferous merchant who was arguing that he should pay less for his glassware for he had so little. The guards were insisting that he paid more for they were considered a luxury item.

After several minutes and impatient shouts from further down the line, with the end of the dispute seemingly no closer, the city guards started to wave through the queuing traders. They tutted and cursed as they passed the incensed merchant, filing around him to enter the city. People on foot appeared to be let in without charge, Thurstan noted. Most of them appeared to know the guards, or at least the guards knew them by name. Nodded greetings were exchanged and the air, as they neared the front of this new second queue, seemed very amiable.

The guards' captain had now been called to deal with the argumentative trader. Thurstan thought that arguing with bored, armed men was folly, but he could also remember his father arguing with fellow merchants until he was purple in the face, if he thought he could save one piece of silver in the hundred.

The captain, a large, red-bearded man, appeared to have no time for such nonsense, as a pat on his sword hilt indicated. If the merchant did not like the price, then the captain could happily double it. Alternatively, and here the captain used an extravagant gesture, the merchant could head off home.

Thurstan's overriding concern had been the same since leaving the Nidd valley, since leaving Catune even – how to gain an audience with the king; how to even broach the subject; how to explain what a young man with a horse and a child wanted with the monarch. He was neither peasant nor trader, yet here he was, on horseback, wishing to enter the city. He had considered abandoning Bucephalus in the fields outside the city, but the use of a horse was too valuable, particularly if they needed to leave Jorvik in a hurry.

Thurstan and Adelise had discussed the dilemma over the last two days, partially to avoid talking about what had happened in Midelesby. Should they try to sneak in, pretend to be traders, possibly lay low for several days? No, they had decided, this was their last chance. If the king would not see them now, then they were doomed. Honesty and an admittance of Adelise's true identity would be the best way to approach the king. Approaching a city guard, however, was a different matter.

"And what are you here for then?" the guard asked, as Thurstan came to the head of the queue. He had dismounted and was leading Bucephalus by hand, Adelise propped up in the saddle, making her already diminutive frame seem ever smaller. Thurstan drew a deep breath.

"We're here to see the king," he said. He bit his lip and braced himself for the response. The guard simply snorted.

"You and a thousand others. Come to petition him, have you?" he asked, passing a curious eye over Bucephalus, noting that the beast underneath the mud was no farmer's workhorse.

"No. It is a matter of urgency," Thurstan said, turning to gesture at Adelise. "The boy here is the son of a Scottish thane and his life is in danger." A half-truth, he considered, would hopefully work as well as the actual facts, without endangering them. The surrounding crowd went quiet, and the red-haired captain suddenly lost interest in the haggling carter and turned to Thurstan. He raised an eyebrow and coughed politely.

"Thurstan Ælfsson?" he asked, with an innocuous air.

Thurstan turned in surprise and immediately regretted his reaction. The captain took a step towards them, but Thurstan was already pulling on Bucephalus's reins. He leapt into the saddle and pushed past the guards that were rushing to surround the horse. The captain shouted orders to hold them, but Thurstan was away and into the stone-cobbled streets of Jorvik.

"Thurstan!" Adelise cried in shock and fear. "What's happening?"

But Thurstan did not reply. He raked his heels back against Bucephalus's flanks and urged him forward, narrowly avoiding complaining street vendors and pedestrians. The advantage of being on horseback was all but lost on Mykla Gate, such was the crowd. Thurstan screamed at people to move out of the way, echoed seconds later by the city guard who were now following him in pursuit on foot.

Baskets of produce scattered across the cobbles, with people diving for cover cursing his ill manners as Thurstan guided Bucephalus down the street and on to the bridge across the River Use.

"Where are we going?" Adelise shouted.

"The castle," Thurstan said in between grunts as he struggled to steer Bucephalus.

"Don't!" Adelise shouted, gripping the saddle, desperately trying to keep on the horse.

"Don't be afraid, we can make it!"

"Go to the cathedral instead! We can claim sanctuary." Adelise's voice was shrill with fear.

Thurstan momentarily slowed Bucephalus's pace to give this some thought.

"Or at least I hope we can," Adelise's muffled voice said quietly.

Thurstan glanced behind him to see an ever-growing number of soldiers running towards them. He kicked his heels back against Bucephalus's flanks and spurred the horse forward, clattering onto a cobbled bridge that crossed the river. He screamed at pedestrians to clear a path, giving them just enough warning to move out of their way, before they stepped back into the street to watch him disappear and into the path of their pursuers.

Thurstan reached the other side of the bridge and hauled hard on his reins, turning Bucephalus to turn down one of the narrower, darker side streets. He was now heading for the cathedral's towers that loomed over the Jorvik skyline, the one point he could aim for in a city completely new to him.

The streets were less crowded here and Thurstan tried to let Bucephalus build up some speed in order to put some distance between them and their pursuers. Yet as the streets became narrower and darker, so the cobbles became damper and more slippery. More than once, Bucephalus's hooves skitted across the stones as Thurstan desperately tried to avoid colliding with an unaware townsperson.

The cathedral's towers were getting ever nearer, though Thurstan had no clear idea of how to get there. Each street corner turned seemed to turn him back on himself, every huddled-house-lined alleyway appearing the same as the last. Just as he started to fear that they were utterly lost, they rounded a corner and Bucephalus burst out into bright sunlight and the open square in front of the cathedral.

They were only a matter of yards away, but away to their right, Thurstan could see a group of several city guards hurrying towards the cathedral's doors, trying to block their path. The labyrinth of back streets had been a longer, slower route. The city guards on foot were almost already at the door; they had understood what Thurstan had been trying to do.

"Go, go, go!" Thurstan cried, slapping Bucephalus's rear. Adelise gave a small cry, partly through terror, partly though excitement as the horse found yet another burst of acceleration. His hooves hammered the square's cobbled flags, racing the men to the cathedral. Just as five or six guards tried to form a line across the front of the building, he pulled hard on Bucephalus's reins, swerving left and around the men, and straight up the small flight of stairs that led to the main doors.

Thurstan praised Jehovah, Odin and whomever else was listening, for the doors had been left open that morning. Thurstan had no hesitation in riding straight into the church and up the nave, much to the shock of the cathedral's occupants. Outraged priests and worshippers screamed and leapt out of the way, as Bucephalus skidded and slid to a halt on the marble floor. Thurstan leapt down, grasping Adelise by the wrist as the church filled with the noise of the city guards hurriedly entering.

Thurstan picked Adelise up bodily, and then ran as fast as his tired, bruised legs would carry him. A cursing priest who attempted to block their passage was shoved unceremoniously to one side as Thurstan ran through the transept towards the altar.

The distance from one end of the cathedral to the other seemed enormous; surely no building could be this big. Sensing the guards almost at his heels, the weight of Adelise slowing him, Thurstan flung himself towards the altar. His hand reached out to touch the cloth and he screamed in relief and delight.

"Sanctuary!" he called. He turned to see the red, angry face of the guard captain raise the butt of his sword. He called out for sanctuary again in fear and confusion as the hilt was slammed down on his forehead, knocking him to the floor.

"This isn't Ængland, you fool," the captain muttered.

As Thurstan lost consciousness, he was aware of people screaming, Adelise crying, Bucephalus whinnying loudly and a metallic clang as he dragged the altar cloth and candles on to the floor with him. Despair at having failed Adelise was his last thought before the blackness consumed him and then he knew no more.

31st May 1166
Jorvik Castle, Northland

Thurstan awoke with a jolt and sat bolt upright. He immediately regretted it as stars flashed in front of his eyes and a dull, throbbing pain pounded his head. He groaned loudly and raised a hand to a tender spot on his brow. He thought back, trying to remember how he had come by the injury. Brief images of churches and swords, cobbles and shouting men flashed before his eyes, before a large, red-bearded man stepped in to his squint-blurred vision.

"Decided to join us then, have you?" the large man asked, patting the pommel of the sword at his side. The memories flooded back and Thurstan gave another groan as he realised where he was. He sank back down onto the floor of the stone cell in which he now found himself. Between him and the speaker were thick iron bars, which left Thurstan in no doubt as to what kind of situation he now found himself in. He closed his eyes, desperately trying to remember what had become of Adelise before he had lost consciousness.

"The girl?" Thurstan asked, his voice sounding groggy and strange, as if it were not his own.

"Is fine. She's being taken care of," the bearded man replied. "Now then, son, what's your name?"

Thurstan thought for a moment, as the answer did not come immediately. His eyes were aching and he pinched his nose, trying to gather his thoughts.

"What's yours? Tell me yours and I'll tell you mine," Thurstan replied, trying to buy some time.

"Don't mess me about, son, I may be the only friend you've got at the moment," the large man replied, though not unkindly. The memories were coming back now, about why he was here and what the future potentially held. He took a deep breath and shook his head, hoping to dislodge some of the cobwebs that seemed to be filling his mind.

"Thurstan," he replied finally. "Thurstan Ælfsson of Lonborg, huskarl of Westmoringaland, until recently in the service of Vinder, the Sheriff of Westmoringaland. Now, I imagine, to be considered a fugitive. Where is the girl?"

The captain of the city's guard nodded to someone else in the room, whom Thurstan could not see. He heard the sound of a door opening and closing again, before the captain handed Thurstan a wooden cup of water through the bars.

"The girl is fine, I promise you. You'll see her soon enough," the captain said, stepping away from the cell and taking a wooden stool to sit on. "My name is Hrafn; I'm the captain of the city guards and sometime chaser of fugitives through streets."

Thurstan thirstily drained the cup in one go, and thanked the captain as it was refilled through the bars. "What time is it?" he asked, gingerly touching his forehead.

"Late morning," Hrafn said, sitting back down.

"Is that all?" The memories of the chase through the city seemed much longer ago.

"Late morning, Wednesday that is," the captain said. "I'm afraid I gave you rather a hard blow, harder than I had intended."

"What did you hit me for then?" Thurstan asked, checking his fingertips for signs of blood.

"Well, I'd had orders to stop you, should I come across the pair of you, but then you tore off through the city, armed and on horseback. Couldn't have you doing that, could I?"

Thurstan finished the second cup of water and gingerly tried to stand, using the bars for support.

"Oh, and that sanctuary thing. That's an Ænglisc thing, doesn't work here. Just a word of advice," the captain added jovially.

"Thank you," Thurstan replied, unenthusiastically, gripping the bars to keep upright. "I'll try to remember that for next time

I get chased through the streets of Jorvik."

There was a knock at the door and the captain stepped out of Thurstan's view again. He heard a muffled conversation, before Hrafn came back and unlocked the cell.

"Come on then," the head of the city guard said. "King Hakon wants to see you."

Rubbing his forehead and slowly taking a few steps at a time, Thurstan went to meet his king.

Thurstan was not sure what he had expected; ornate curtains, golden candlesticks, bejewelled ornamental weaponry on the walls perhaps. Instead, he was shown into a square room that spoke of comfort and simplicity, the only item of furniture being the single large table around which were sitting several sombre-looking men. Thurstan did not recognise any of them immediately, but he sensed that they were men of importance. They each wore heavy, expensive furs and jewellery, their wrists weighed down with richly decorated bracers. One of the men caught Thurstan's eye and gave a slight nod; his face seemed slightly familiar.

"Ah, welcome to the moot, Thurstan Ælfsson!" hailed the man sat at the head of the table. He stood up and walked to the open door where Thurstan was standing, flanked by two guards.

"My lord King?" It was asked more as a question by Thurstan, rather than a greeting, for he had never seen his monarch before. King Hakon's appearance surprised many people, as it did Thurstan. He was tall, slim and finely featured, finely tailored in blue cloth and marten furs. He did not look like a Northlandic warrior, although Thurstan knew from the stories that the man had waded through rivers of blood to claim his throne; most of it his own kin's.

"Thurstan Ælfsson, who has walked, ridden and sneaked his way across my kingdom with the sole survivor of the Grarigg massacre, if I am not mistaken?" The question was asked genially, yet Thurstan was aware of the dozen or so pairs of eyes in the room fixed on him. Many of them belonged to men who seemed much less genial than their king. "You eluded the Sheriff of Westmoringaland's men, and you've eluded and I suspect killed the men of the Jarl of Westmoringaland, have you not?"

"I," Thurstan stuttered, not knowing how to reply. "I was simply trying to survive, my lord. That and to save Adelise. I mean, the queen."

Over the past weeks, Thurstan had thought of her as the Saxon girl, not the future queen of a neighbouring country. Now, in the company of these men and his king, he found it difficult not to speak about her as just a young girl he knew.

Staring at their faces, Thurstan realised that the man who had seemed familiar was Jarl Herri, his own jarl, the man who had been in power in Lonborg for most of his life. The man who had been hunting him down for the last few weeks of his life. He instinctively took a step backwards and put a hand to his belt. King Hakon laughed and patted Thurstan lightly on the shoulder.

"Do not worry about Jarl Herri, he means you no harm. He was searching for you, acting in Northland's best interests, based on information received from Kirkby," Hakon said. The jarl nodded, and raised a hand as if to proclaim that there was no animosity on his part towards Thurstan.

Thurstan realised that in this room sat the entire Northlandic council; all the jarls of Northland and members of the clergy, for there were three men wearing religious robes. There was Svarðkell, Jarl of Suthribel, a short red-haired man with a finely embroidered eye-patch; Sigtrygg, the elderly Archbishop of Jorvik; Galinn, Jarl of Northymbre; the jarls of the six southern shires that were the source of so much friction with Ængland and the jarls of the Thriths of Jorvik.

Attendants were stood around the edges of the room, ready to serve the food and drink laid out on a side counter at the request of any of the moot's participants. In one corner, away from the rest of the participants, sat a man who did not appear to be taking any part in the proceedings. He wore his long blond hair loose, dressed in just a simple woollen jerkin, but the thing that Thurstan noted the most was the melancholic expression his face bore.

"Now then, Thurstan, please take a seat at the table, have a drink, if your head feels able to cope with it, and tell me everything that has happened over the last four weeks. Everything." Hakon said the last word with feeling and Thurstan knew that he could do nothing but obey him.

For the next twenty minutes, Thurstan retold as truthfully as he could the events that had engulfed him, from the day he had ridden out from Kirkby to Penrith, until his arrival the previous day in Jorvik. He hesitated when he came to Vinder's betrayal, but his description of the sheriff's attack did not seem to cause any consternation between the assembled men.

Only when he reached the conversation he'd had with Adelise in the infirmary did one of the men react. He described the man that Adelise had recognised, the Ænglisc warrior in the service of her uncle, who had a distinctive scar running down his face. Thurstan gestured with a finger, from his eye down to his mouth. At this, the silent man in the corner, who appeared to be straining to follow the conversation, started suddenly and uttered just one, single word.

"Ricmund."

"Yes," Thurstan replied, turning to look at him. "Yes, Ricmund, I think she said his name was."

The blond-haired stranger spat on the floor and said no more, sinking back down into his chair. The other jarls sat and listened attentively to the rest of Thurstan's tale. They would interrupt occasionally, to question the location or date of events and Thurstan tried hard to remember when and where things had taken place. They would discuss then between themselves, agreeing or disagreeing in which wapentake something had happened or what they had been doing on a given date.

"So, my lords, there we have it," Hakon announced loudly, once Thurstan had finished his tale. He stood up and started pacing around the room, his hands waving animatedly as he spoke. "Let us assume for a moment that the young man here speaks the truth, that the girl is indeed Queen Adelise of Ængland. What situation does that put us in?"

"One of war," the Jarl of Northymbre muttered, amidst grumbling from those seated at the table.

"So it would seem at the moment, so it would seem. To the world it appears that we have killed the Ænglisc queen, broken the Morcar oath and that Ængland has every right to attack us. And who would blame them? The Church will support them and no doubt so will Scotland, possibly Frankia or Normandy if they thought they could get something out of it.

"So their forces are massing at the border, the reports say. We have started gathering ours in response, to defend our lands, but to outsiders, to those who gain their information by word of mouth, we are the aggressors. They'll say we murdered their queen and raised our armies first, for ours is a permanent one anyway. And who will challenge it, who will challenge the falsehood?"

He stopped pacing for a moment and gripped the back of the Jarl of Suthribel's chair, Svarðkell raising his one remaining eye in expectation.

"So she is alive. What do we do? Do we announce through proclamation and messages that she is alive and that we have her in our safekeeping? As our envoy has already said, Swegen would simply claim that we have kidnapped her, holding her hostage. Do we invite an Ænglisc party to come claim her and carry her home? What hope would we have of her surviving that journey?" Hakon paused and took a sip from a goblet of wine proffered to him by one of the servants.

"So we put her back on the throne?" the Jarl of Suthribel offered.

"So we do. I do not want Swegen on the Ænglisc throne if this is just a taste of what is to come. Although the Morcar Oath is nothing more than a tale, an oath in name only nowadays, I do not wish for Northland to be seen as an aggressor. The smallest lie here would echo around the continent, growing, becoming even more outrageous, until it reaches the point where everyone believes it and no one thinks to seek the truth. I have fought too many wars for legitimate reasons than to go to war against the Ænglisc because of that scrote Swegen," Hakon said, the last sentence fired out with a viciousness that he rarely, but effectively, used.

He sat back down in his seat and pressed his hands together, letting his body sag. His voice became calm and measured again, his stare sure, steady and direct into the eyes of his jarls. "So what do we do? We can hardly use military force to restore her, can we?"

"We would surely win though," the Jarl Herri said, stroking his chin. The Jarl of Snotenga, who lands were on the Ænglisc border, bridled at the suggestion.

"Easy for you to say, Jarl Herri. It's not your shire that would be used as the battleground," he snapped.

"The question is not of whether we could win," Hakon interrupted, cutting the men off. "It's possible that we could, but not without great losses. Expensive losses. Unnecessary losses. Bravado tells you that we would crush a raised fyrd with seasoned huskarls, history tells us there is no such thing as a sure victory.

"Besides, we would be attempting to prove that we are not military aggressors by invading another country with our army. Dear Pope, we promise we did not attack Ængland, let us prove it by attacking Ængland.

"We cannot be seen to be forcibly restoring her. She would

never be trusted; she would always be suspected of being an impostor or a puppet queen. There would be no guarantee of success or peace afterwards and I do not care to plunge Northland into years of war." He sat back and sighed, taking a deep sip from his goblet, letting the jarls mull the options over.

"If we do nothing?" the Jarl of Kesteven asked. Like Snotenga, his lands were on the Ænglisc border and he risked losing the lot in the event of an Ænglisc invasion.

"If we do nothing, then we are as we are now. With the threat of war, suspected of regicide, seen as treacherous. We remain with our little girl hidden away, until one day the truth comes out and we are seen as kidnappers." Hakon shook his head.

"And if we, ahem, if we…" the Jarl of Kesteven said quietly.

"Yes?" Hakon asked, raising an eyebrow.

"If she, erm, disappeared?" he said, scanning the room for any support.

"Kill her?" Hakon asked loudly. Both Thurstan and the silent man in the corner shot a look of disgust at the Jarl of Kesteven who shrugged apologetically in return.

Hakon laughed out loud and waved the man back down into their seats. "No, no, no. For then we will have done the very thing of which we have been accused and Ængland would have every right to attack us."

"My lords?" Thurstan's voice was so quiet that he almost went unheard. All eyes turned to him and Hakon prompted him to speak. "Might I ask something?"

Hakon nodded, before beckoning a serving girl over to fill Thurstan's cup. Thurstan spoke nervously, his hand playing distractedly with the hair on his chin.

"When the Ænglisc queen's caravan was ambushed, I noticed, as I said before, that the shields bore the markings of Northymbre. It has always troubled me, but are we absolutely sure that the men were not from our own lands? I mean, not sent by my lord Jarl, but perhaps traitors or renegades?" Thurstan kept his gaze fixed at the table, not wanting to meet the stare of the Jarl of Northymbre.

"My men are loyal," Jarl Galinn started before Hakon waved him into silence.

"Now, Galinn, it is a valid question. Thurstan, I asked myself the same question as soon as I heard the stories. Even in the strongest of armies there maybe men whose hearts are swayed by promises of coin. But no, those men were not treacherous, but also victims. They weren't from Northymbre for a start."

"They weren't?" Thurstan asked.

"No. They were from the North Thrith of Jorvik. Or rather, the corpses were. The Northymbric shields were Ricmund's though."

Thurstan bristled at the revelation, more confused than ever.

"This here," Hakon said, pointing towards a round-faced man sat towards the other end of the table, "is Abbot Arnewulf. Father, if you will, please tell Thurstan, what you told the table before his arrival."

Arnewulf cleared his throat and turned in his chair to address Thurstan.

"I encountered the scene of the ambush the morning of the following day, the eighth of May. I had been riding towards Tibeg from Setburg, on my way to visiting my brethren in the Scottish borderlands. And yes, before you ask, I am Ænglisc," Arnewulf said, noting Thurstan's look of curiosity at his pronunciation.

"Abbot Arnewulf has lived and worked for many years in Jorvik, under Archbishop Sigtrygg," Hakon explained, indicating the elderly, richly robed man sat next to Arnewulf. "If you ignore his strange accent and odd Saxon mannerisms, he is a decent fellow. His roots may be Ænglisc, but his branches spread far and wide. His aristocratic siblings are spawning half of Europe's future nobility."

"I came across the bodies of the Kirkby huskarls and those of the queen's entourage. Their wounds were evident, some still fresh, suggesting that maybe some had not died immediately, but had lingered through the night." Arnewulf's words had a disquieting effect on Thurstan, with the thought that his companions had suffered for hours. "Among those with Northymbric shields and colours were men who by my reckoning had been dead for at least two days. Of this I have no doubt.

"Strangely, a great many had wounds inflicted by a blade, a sword or a dagger post mortem – after they had died. What had actually killed them were arrow shots. As if someone wanted them to look like they'd died under a sword blade, as might be made by a huskarl."

"You can tell the difference between a wound made before and after death?" Thurstan asked, intrigued.

"Oh yes," Arnewulf replied simply.

"A patrol of my men had disappeared the previous day, near Setburg," the Jarl of the North Thrith of Jorvik said. "We imagine their corpses were planted in the ambush. Vinder burnt all the bodies, ambushers and caravan alike before we could request their return."

"The pertinent thing though," Arnewulf added. "Is that I counted far more corpses than men who went missing. So either new men joined, unbeknownst to the jarl here, or someone else perpetrated the massacre."

King Hakon waited several moments before speaking, leaning back in his chair and playing with a large ring on his hand.

"My lords, it seems clear what has happened, all accounts appear to concur. The attack was an Ænglisc one, no doubt orchestrated by that turd, Swegen, to make it seem that Northland had killed their queen. He expected and has received, by all accounts, enthusiastic support with his martial rhetoric and promises of vengeance. He has now been elected to the throne on the crest of an unthinking wave of ignorance."

He stopped and rose from his chair, pausing to squint at the sunlight coming in through the windows. Suddenly he slammed his fist down on the table. "This is Northland and we will not be bullied or cajoled into being an Ænglisc earl's puppet. He can have his war if he wants and we will face him, head on. We Northlanders are descended from warriors and he shall rue the day he sends his farmers and boys against our soldiers."

He glanced momentarily at the silent man in the corner, who appeared to be nodding in agreement, before continuing.

"However, I would rather not be manipulated into a war we did not seek. I say we put Adelise back on the throne, if not because it is the right thing to do in God's eyes, then just to consign that weasel Swegen to the cesspit he belongs in."

There were shouts of agreement from around the large table, although Thurstan remained silent, unsure of how to react in front of the land's most powerful men. Hakon waited before gesturing towards the silent man.

"Our friend here assures us that there remain loyal Ænglanders who do not wish to see Swegen on the throne, that he has a network of contacts and allies that could smuggle her to Lunden. However, if what he says is true, then Swegen has surrounded himself with such a collection of ubiquitous toads who are so desperate to please him, that if Adelise presented herself at court she would more likely disappear again sooner than be recognised as the queen."

Hakon started pacing around the room again, seemingly speaking more to himself than the assembled jarls. "Now his coronation is in two weeks, as we are told; I would suggest that no better occasion will present itself for Adelise to be seen by those who will recognise and name her as their true monarch. Clergy, loyal thegns and earls; not the illegitimate sons of whores Swegen has pandering to his every whim in his court. This does not leave us much time at all."

Hakon had circled the room and was now standing by the silent stranger who Thurstan had judged to be unknown to the rest of the room too.

"We cannot stand by and do nothing, and we cannot keep her here. We cannot invade, nor can we force our will on the south. I do believe our hopes of resolving this dilemma remain with this man and his plan to smuggle her into Lunden. As has often been said, where a thousand men may fail, a handful might succeed."

The jarls shifted uncomfortably, not happy with the thought of letting this Saxon take away such a powerful political hostage.

"Surely that would be suicide, my lord King," the Jarl of Lindsey said. "Could she not remain here and this Saxon recruit the necessary support, with the knowledge that she lives?"

"I would like to think so, but the longer we keep her here, the more a stranglehold Swegen of Berrocscir will have on the Ænglisc throne, until the only people willing to listen will no longer be in any position of power."

"But, my lord," Ivar, the Jarl of the East Thrith of Jorvik, interjected. "Can we be absolutely sure he is who he says he is?"

Hakon patted the shoulder of the longhaired stranger. The friendly pat turned into a firm grip, prompting the man to look confusedly at the Northlandic king.

"Of course the thought did occur to me. Open the west door!" The last order was barked by Hakon, the sudden shouting causing Thurstan to jump in his seat. A smaller side door in the room swung open to reveal two richly dressed ladies standing behind a child. A child that Thurstan did not recognise immediately, for Adelise had once again been dressed in the fine clothes and jewellery that her rank normally required. Her short cropped, boyish hair had been disguised by a richly decorated coif, giving her the true look of a queen that Thurstan had never seen.

"Thurstan!" she cried, a look of joy erupting across her face.

"My lady," the longhaired stranger said in a strong Ænglisc accent, kneeling, leaving Hakon to look on bemusedly.

"Ceolwulf!" Adelise exclaimed, sounding even more

surprised than she had been to see Thurstan. She ran across the room and the two embraced. Tears ran down the girl's cheek as Ceolwulf stroked the back of hair, surreptitiously checking the back of her neck for the reassuring birthmark.

"What are you doing here? Why are you in Northland? What has happened? Why was Ricmund in Westmoringaland?" Adelise asked, once she had pulled herself away from Ceolwulf's shoulder. She spoke so quickly that the Northlandic jarls struggled to comprehend her questions, but it was obvious that the two Ænglanders knew each other very well.

"Terrible things, but things I can talk to you of another time. I am just happy to see you alive," Ceolwulf replied, smiling for the first time since Thurstan had entered the room.

"I think," King Hakon said, returning to his seat, "That our question has been answered." He clicked his fingers to a boy stood by the doorway, beckoned him over and whispered something in his ear. The boy scuttled out of the room without another word, leaving the occupants to return their attention to the garbled conversation in Ænglisc that they were struggling to follow.

"Ceolwulf, I want you to meet Thurstan Ælfsson. This is the man who carried me across Northland when I was ill, who has saved my life ten times or more. He is my hero," Adelise announced, dragging the Ænglisc nobleman across the room by the hand to meet the slightly embarrassed Northlandic huskarl. The two men nodded at each other in greeting.

"Ceolwulf is a distant cousin of mine. His father is the Earl of East Anglia, the most important man in Ængland, after my family of course. And the Archbishop of Cantwaraburg. He looked after me when my parents died. I am sure you two will be best of friends, in fact, I know it," Adelise announced with a broad grin.

Thurstan managed an uncomfortable smile, which was mirrored by the Saxon.

"But where is your father? Why isn't he here too?" Adelise asked.

A shadow passed across Ceolwulf's face, before he shook his head.

"As I said, my lady. There are many things to tell you, many stories and tales."

"But first of all," Hakon said in perfect Ænglisc, before continuing in Northlandic, "we must plan a way of taking you back home, my lady."

She nodded, before squeezing Ceolwulf's hand and smiling up at him. In her other hand she had gripped Thurstan's arm and for the time being, she looked the happiest that Thurstan could imagine a girl being. She appeared to be about to make another uncomfortable declaration when there was a knock at the door.

"Would you mind just standing to one side, please?" King Hakon asked the trio, pointing towards a small recess by the door that was hidden from view by a decorated screen. Waiting until they would not be seen by anyone entering the room, Hakon ordered the door to be opened and went to stand by the Jarl Herri. Thurstan, peering through a gap between the screen's tapestry covered panels, saw the door swing open to reveal a dreadfully familiar face. The Sheriff of Westmoringaland, Vinder of Kirkby, shuffled into the room, limping, looking for all the world like an infirm and sick old man.

"My lord King!" he exclaimed, not waiting to be addressed by Hakon. "There has been a terrible misunderstanding. My lord Jarl mistook my message, I promise you."

Thurstan moved so that he could see the shoulders of the Jarl of Westmoringaland slowly turn around to face his underling. Vinder gave a small shriek of fear and quickly tried to backtrack.

"Not that you were mistaken, my lord, but more in the sense that you received the wrong message about what I was looking for. There was no girl really, it was a boy. A man who killed a boy, nothing to do with the Ænglisc queen," Vinder stammered, slowly stepping backwards as the large frame of Herri unfurled itself to tower over his one-time chief tax collector and law enforcer. "Nothing at all, I promise, she was killed by wolfheads, you know the problems we have had with them."

King Hakon held an arm out to hold the jarl back, before putting an arm around the flinching Vinder and leading him over to the screen, behind which Adelise and Thurstan stood.

"Vinder, Vinder, Vinder. I want to believe you, I really do. But searching for a missing girl a week after the queen's ambush? Tearing up Lonborg and Westmoringaland, right under the nose of your jarl? For a girl? What kind of girl was it you were looking for?"

"It wasn't really, my lord King, I don't know..." Vinder stuttered, before the king interrupted him.

"It wasn't a man and a girl like this, was it?" Hakon asked, before pulling the screen out of the way to reveal Ceolwulf, Adelise and Thurstan, each wearing an expression of hatred and disgust.

Vinder's shriek condemned him. Two faces he had not expected to see again, or at least, not alive, here, in the king's rooms at Jorvik Castle.

"You!" he said, pointing a trembling finger at Thurstan, slightly regaining his wits and voice. "This man, this man, this man. He kidnapped this poor girl. She was a maid to the dead Ænglisc queen and he kidnapped her, my lord King. This man needs arresting before he spreads his lies." Vinder's voice tailed off as he realised no-one appeared to be reacting to his protestations.

"No, no and no on all accounts, Vinder," King Hakon said, nodding towards armed guards at the door who seized the struggling Vinder under the arms. "Now the only question remaining is what do we do with you?"

The Jarl Herri opened his mouth to speak, then glancing at Adelise, leant over to whisper in Hakon's ear. The king appeared to consider his words for a few seconds before nodding.

"So be it. I shall let you take care of it, if you so wish," Hakon replied.

"Thank you, my lord," Jarl Herri said, before casting a look of pure venom towards the whimpering Vinder who had now let his body fall limp in despair.

"What is a 'spread eagle'?" Adelise asked, turning to Thurstan, struggling with the unfamiliar Northlandic phrase.

"It doesn't matter, just some Northlandic legal term," Ceolwulf said quickly, his eyes pleading Thurstan to agree with him.

"Yes, what Ceolwulf said. Just some old phrase," Thurstan said.

"Thank you," Ceolwulf replied, much to Adelise's delight.

"See? I told you, you'd both get on." Her joy was cut short by Vinder's screams as he was dragged away, imploring for mercy. King Hakon shut the door himself after Vinder's heels had finally scraped out of the room, before turning to the moot and clapping his hands.

"So then. We have five days to plan, by my reckoning. Five days for Northland to restore the Ænglisc throne and thus avoid a war. And it all depends on this exiled unfortunate," Hakon said, turning to Ceolwulf and regaling him a look of unbridled optimism. "Nothing could be simpler. The tricky part now is how."

6th June 1166

From the walls that surrounded the north bailey of Jorvik Castle, one could see the whole of the city and the plain beyond. The snaking rivers of the Ouse and Foss converged to the south leaving the castle at the head of a triangular peninsula, below which nestled the capital city of Northland.

King Hakon and his son, Knut, were standing on the battlements, looking across the sprawling mass of cluttered houses and shops, a sea of small wooden buildings broken only by the enormous structures of the cathedral and the Konge Hall.

"Is it difficult to look after, Father?" the small boy asked.

"Is what difficult?" Hakon replied.

"The city? The country?" Knut asked.

Hakon chuckled and ruffled his son's hair. "I don't have to look after it, Knut. It looks after itself. If I died tomorrow and nobody in Jorvik knew, I'm quite sure the city would go on just as happily as it did before."

"But surely, you do something?" the boy asked, almost protesting. His father did everything, could do everything; surely everything depended on him?

"Let's say I sometimes have to guide things along. Perhaps I tidy up, you could call it, when things go awry. I don't have to look after anyone, but I have to appoint the right people to look after certain things." He gestured at Ivar, the Jarl of the East Thrith of Jorvik, who was walking with them around the castle walls. The jarl had remained behind in Jorvik after the moot had ended at Hakon's request, for his ports would be invaluable to them.

Within a day of the moot, a plan had been formulated to return Adelise back to Ængland. The term 'plan', however, Hakon thought, was to be used loosely. More of a case of hoping for a miracle, but there was such little time to get the girl to

Lunden before Swegen's impending coronation that every day of inactivity was a day lost.

Besides, Hakon did not want the girl in Jorvik; her presence created more problems than any advantage to be gained. He could have ransomed her, he supposed, but he very much doubted there was anyone currently in Ængland willing to either believe she was alive or pay such a fee.

It was Sigtrygg, the Archbishop of Jorvik, who had first suggested the plan. That morning after the moot, Abbot Arnewulf had come to see Hakon to inform him that a surprise invite had arrived. A surprise, for it had come from Ængland. It was a formal invite from the Archbishop of Cantwaraburg to his Northlandic brothers to attend the new Ænglisc king's coronation. Sigtrygg was alone in being the only member of the Northlandic council to receive such an invitation, such was the hostility and tension between the two nations.

The Archbishop of Jorvik had no intention of trekking to Lunden. He was well past his seventieth year and had never had any great love of travel. However, he was willing to send an emissary in his place, to maintain relations between the churches of the two nations. The Northlandic representative would be expected to travel with a small group of monks and servants – why not conceal Adelise and possibly Ceolwulf in that group? There would be no better opportunity to gain access to the coronation ceremony itself. A haircut here, a shave there, and who would know that the monks and servants were not quite who they said they were? Very few people had seen Adelise in the flesh during the last few years, Sigtrygg had argued.

Or rather he hadn't, for Hakon strongly suspected that Arnewulf was both the messenger and originator of the plan. He was ambitious and bright, which Hakon admired, but he was also Ænglisc by birth. It would certainly give them an advantage travelling, but as trustworthy as the priest appeared, there would always linger a doubt about the priest's intentions. If truth be told, Hakon thought, in times like these, nationality would count for little. Loyalty to the Church, political allegiance and personal interests usually took precedence over romantic ideals of patriotism.

Ceolwulf had been keen on the plan and had enthusiastically set about writing messages to contacts he believed still to be loyal to himself and against Swegen. Hakon had not stopped him, even though he had his reservations about the plan, for the sooner they were gone the better.

"What I don't understand," Ivar asked, as they circled the northern courtyard, "is why Ængland would invite our archbishop, when we are about to go to war."

"They didn't," Hakon replied. Knut was trying to feign an interest in his father's discussions, but was more engrossed in throwing small stones from the battlements. "The Archbishop of Cantwaraburg did. Not out of any great love for Sigtrygg, but more as a mischievous reminder to Swegen that he considers the Church above and more important than the state, that Church matters transcend petty political squabbling. He seems quite keen on these kinds of notions."

"Can he do that? Could any Northlandic contingent not simply be turned away at the city gates?" Ivar asked.

"They could, they could do that. Odd thing too, it appears that Cantwaraburg is not even going to lead the ceremony. That snake, the Archbishop of Westmynster is. His cathedral I suppose. I imagine Cantwaraburg has got something in return. But the invite is here and we may as well take advantage of it," Hakon replied.

Ivar shook his head. "I have to say, my lord. I am not convinced by this plan of theirs; it seems hopeful adventurism and more than likely destined to fail."

"I can't say I totally disagree, Ivar" Hakon replied. "But what is the worst outcome? I do not want the girl here. If we do nothing we are probably at war. If she succeeds, then all the better. But if they go and fail, then nothing changes, and at least they die in Ængland, not here."

He said the final part quietly, hopefully out of earshot of Knut who had run on ahead. Ivar gave this some thought and nodded in agreement. The plan would involve letting Ænglisc ships, requested by Ceolwulf from his uncle, to sail from the port of Burgh in the East Thrith Hymbre estuary.

"So we let them go and just pray?" Ivar asked.

"So we do," Hakon replied. "Let us say I expect war, but hope for a miracle. What I do not like though, are loose ends. I like things to be tidy. Don't I?" The final sentence was aimed at Knut who had run back to them holding a sheet of crumpled paper.

"A message for you, Father, from the captain of the city guard," he said, panting from the short run. Hakon looked up to see Hrafn stood in the doorway that led on to the battlements.

"A message from Ængland, my lord," Hrafn shouted. "Came just ten minutes ago, with the utmost priority."

Hakon broke the wax seal on the back – the Archbishop of Cantwaraburg's he noted – and read. Then cursed.

Adelise laughed at Ceolwulf's glum face as the last of his beard was shaved off, the hairs drifting down onto the stone floor.

"Don't worry, Ceolwulf, I had to do the same thing with my hair," she reassured him cheerfully.

He winced as another clump of blond hair fell past his knees and onto his feet, the young boy shaving him apologising for having nicked his chin. His face was now red and dotted with specks of blood. His skin felt cold and exposed, this being the first time in ten years he had not worn a beard. The floor was a carpet of what had once been his long hair, mixed with his moustaches and whiskers, leaving the raw-faced Ceolwulf looking much younger, markedly different and definitely unhappy.

Thurstan was standing by the door of Adelise's rooms,

watching the poor nobleman's misery with bemused sympathy. Adelise had insisted that she watched Ceolwulf's transformation into a priest and, being aware of all she had suffered during the last month, the nobleman had felt unable to refuse the queen. Taking delight in other people's misery was not the best trait for a monarch, Thurstan had joked, but not an uncommon one either.

Adelise had been installed in the largest, warmest and most lavish of the available chambers in Jorvik castle. She had been looked after well, although she was not permitted to be seen nor spoken to by anyone, save for a select few serving staff or members of the Northlandic council.

Hakon had kept his distance, Thurstan had noted, although he was always courteous and amicable in Adelise's presence. To his surprise, Hakon had offered him a position in the royal huskarls here, in Jorvik. Possibly as a way of rewarding him, or maybe it was to keep him under the king's watchful eye. It had been Thurstan's long-held ambition and naturally, he had accepted the offer, yet there was not the sense of satisfaction that the offer surely warranted.

"Thurstan?" Adelise asked, once she was content with the new-look Ceolwulf.

"Yes, my lady?" he replied. She found his new tendency to address her formally amusing.

"Is King Hakon a good king?" she asked. Thurstan shrugged.

"I don't really know, to be honest. He doesn't seem to be a bad one. I don't remember any other king."

"Define 'good'," Ceolwulf said, wincing at his reflection in a hand mirror.

"What do you mean?" Adelise asked.

"What do you mean by a good king – a good man or a good leader? There are plenty of nice men who are not good leaders and there are plenty of good kings who are not particularly nice men," Ceolwulf said.

Thurstan nodded in agreement.

"I suppose you could say that our King Harald the Conqueror wasn't a particularly nice man. He was a warrior, a killer. But when he died, he left a kingdom that was much stronger than it had been before his reign. Well, he created it really. We think of him as a good king, but perhaps not in the way that stories talk about good kings."

Adelise gave this some thought.

"So would Swegen be a bad king?" she asked.

"Yes," Ceolwulf said emphatically. "But not because he kills people, although of course murder is a mortal sin. He'll be a bad king because he kills people for enjoyment; he lets personal interests come before the country. He is petty and he is self-serving. People will forgive many things as long as you are good for the country."

"So you can be nice but a bad king? Or queen?" Adelise asked.

"Well," Ceolwulf started slowly, not wishing to add to the already extraordinarily long list of things that Adelise seemed to worry about. "I suppose so. Your great-grandfather, if you'll forgive me, my lady, Tostig II, was a genial, peaceful man who did no harm to anybody. However, he spent a great deal of money on beautiful buildings, decorations and personal fancies that did no benefit to the nation. I suppose some may say he was a bad king, but not an evil one."

"We say he was a bad king," Thurstan said, matter-of-factly.

"Thank you, Thurstan," Ceolwulf said sarcastically.

"I think that King Hakon has had to do a great many unpleasant things in the past. I imagine he does unpleasant things now, which perhaps we do not know about, but funda-mentally, yes, he is a good king. He looks after his country. Whether he is a nice man or not does not come into it."

Adelise chewed on her bottom lip and stared up at the ceiling for several seconds.

"So," she said slowly. "To be a good queen, I shouldn't be too nice to people?"

"I don't think you have to go as far as that, my lady," Ceolwulf said. He stood up and took the girl's hands in his. "You are a good person, my lady. You will know what to do. Follow your own heart as to what is right or wrong, listen to others and do not willingly make decisions that harm your land. At least, that is what I learnt from my father."

Adelise squeezed Ceolwulf's hands.

"Thank you, Ceolwulf. I think that if I were not to be queen, I would like you to be king."

Ceolwulf laughed at the suggestion.

"Thank you, but I'm not sure it would be for us to decide."

Thurstan smiled at the scene and at the notion of elected kings. That was one Saxon tradition that Harald the Conqueror had replaced immediately with the more conventional custom of the throne passing from father to son. Not that it had necessarily been of benefit to Northland, for a great many wars had been fought between various offspring of Harald in the past hundred years. Surely, he mused, an elected ruler and no standing army was not the way to build a stable kingdom.

A knock came at the door and before any permission to enter was given, King Hakon strode into the room, closely followed by Abbot Arnewulf. He nodded briefly at the room's occupants and took a seat.

"I have received some disturbing news from Ængland," he said solemnly, not bothering with the pleasantries of exchanging greetings. "Eadric, the Archbishop of Cantwaraburg, is dead."

Adelise, unsure of the significance of this announcement, glanced round at Thurstan and Ceolwulf, who seemed shocked by the news.

"How?" Ceolwulf asked.

"All official reports say of natural causes, although I'm sure they would do even if the causes were anything but natural," Hakon replied. "It would appear to have happened just a day, maybe two after he sent the invitation to the coronation."

"So the invite was genuine then?" Ceolwulf asked.

"I believe it was," Arnewulf answered. "The archbishops of Cantwaraburg and Jorvik often corresponded with each other. Eadric used certain phrases in Latin and a style of prose that has convinced the Archbishop Sigtrygg that the letter is genuine."

"So the invite still stands?" Ceolwulf pressed.

"So it would seem," Hakon said. "I'm sure the invite was not a popular thing to have done in the first place, but we have not heard or received any message to the contrary, so as far as I am concerned, the Archbishop of Jorvik is still invited.

"It does, however, raise questions about your safety. Attempting to murder you in the distant hills of another country is one thing, but, if we are to believe the suspicions that I'm sure we all share, when Swegen is prepared to kill his own archbishops in his own land, then an already dangerous mission becomes even more perilous."

"Nothing changes then," Ceolwulf said. "We will still be in mortal danger from the moment we step ashore in Ængland."

"As guests of someone who is now dead," Hakon reminded him. The king pinched the bridge of his nose and yawned. "I don't know, it may even have some advantages. You won't have to find excuses to avoid attending official Church functions."

"Who is the new archbishop then?" Ceolwulf asked.

"Ah," Hakon said wearily. "Tell them, Arnewulf."

The abbot nodded at Hakon, stepped forward, and spoke in Ænglisc.

"Swegen, in his infinite wisdom, has declared Cantwaraburg Cathedral to now be a royal peculiar."

"What does that mean?" Adelise asked.

"Essentially, that the cathedral no longer belongs to the Church, but becomes under direct jurisdiction of the Crown. What it also now means is that Westmynster is definitely the most important and powerful see in the Ænglisc Church,"

Arnewulf replied.

"Can he do that?" Ceolwulf asked, incredulously.

"It's not unheard of, but to do it to Cantwaraburg and so quickly, no, not really. Rome will not be pleased one bit, nor will the other archbishops, I imagine. What it does show is that Swegen already believes he can do as he pleases, an indication of the autocratic rule Ængland can come to expect from him," Arnewulf replied.

"So we will be unwanted guests of a dead man whose church no longer exists, in a land that thinks we are dead or in exile and we're going to march straight into the coronation of a man who will stop at nothing to get his own way?" Ceolwulf asked in a tone that bordered on cheerful.

Arnewulf gave this some consideration and nodded.

"Yes, you could say that. But what is there to lose?"

"Our heads, hands, tongues," Ceolwulf started, then noticed the look of horror on Adelise's face and quickly corrected himself. "Only jesting, my lady."

She laughed weakly back at Ceolwulf, then turned to Hakon and addressed him formally.

"My lord King, might I request a favour from you?" she asked. Hakon smiled and nodded. "Might I request that Thurstan accompany us to Burgh, as an escort for my final trip through Northland? Not to Lunden, of course, but at least as far as the boat."

Hakon looked surprised, but not as much as Thurstan, for this was the first time he had heard of such a suggestion.

"Well, I suppose so, if Thurstan would agree to it," Hakon replied, pretending to give the proposition some deep thought. "Although given he is now a member of my personal huskarls, shouldn't he be busy in training?"

"He is?" Adelise asked in delight. She clapped her hands together, ran over to Thurstan, and embraced him, causing no little embarrassment. "Oh, Thurstan, I am so happy for you, I know this is what you've always wanted. Why didn't you tell me?"

Thurstan mumbled a few words but Adelise started chattering excitedly over him.

"But you could still come to the boat couldn't you? Couldn't he?" she asked, supplicating King Hakon.

"I see no harm in letting Thurstan accompany you, provided he returns straight back to Jorvik. Is the idea agreeable to you, Thurstan?" Hakon asked.

"I started this journey with Adelise, I suppose I should finish it with her," he said.

Adelise clapped her hands with delight again. Thurstan thought she was treating the expedition to Ængland as a pleasurable trip abroad rather than the dangerous mission it really was, but he did not say as much. The young girl and Ceolwulf were likely to end up imprisoned or dead, but whether she realised this or not, he would not begrudge her a final few days of enjoyment.

"We leave tomorrow then?" he asked.

"Tomorrow," Hakon replied. "Lord Ceolwulf, you have sent ahead the messages to your contacts?"

"I have," Ceolwulf replied.

"Let us hope then that they reach the right hands and are read by the intended eyes. We will send out two or three false convoys tomorrow before you leave for Burgh. In a city as large as Jorvik, I am sure there will be many a man paid to report the activity in and out of the city. We cannot afford to let this one chance pass us by."

"Thank you, my lord King. Thank you for everything," Ceolwulf said.

"Think nothing of it, my lord Earl," Hakon replied. "Should things not work out as planned, then my offer of coming to reside in Northland still stands."

"Should things not work out in Ængland, then I don't think

you, or anyone else, will ever see me again," Ceolwulf said sadly.

"Then let me bid you a safe journey," Hakon said, standing to leave. "May God be with you," He walked towards the wooden door, and then paused before opening it. "But most of all, good luck."

As the door shut, Ceolwulf crossed himself.

"We're going to need it."

7th June 1166
Lunden, Ængland

"The trick, Suthseaxe," Swegen called over the sound of the waves slapping against the barge's hull, "is to focus on a point in the distance and keep staring at that."

Leofwin, Earl of Suthseaxe, had gone a most peculiar shade of white, his normally plum-coloured cheeks almost a mottled blue. Swegen laughed and strode down the length of the royal barge towards him. He was about to slap the earl on the back in an attempt to cajole some enthusiasm into him when Leofwin staggered to the side of the boat and vomited noisily into the snapping waves. Swegen took a few steps back, careful to keep upwind from the retching nobleman. He retreated and walked over to Godric, the Archbishop of Westmynster, who had joined them on the outing.

Swegen had started taking weekly trips, sailing up and down the River Temese from the most western point of Westmynster, to the most eastern point of the city of Lunden. Only from the river, Swegen had repeatedly declared, could one appreciate the majesty and beauty of Ængland's capital. When it had been pointed out that Winceaster, not Lunden, was Ængland's capital, Swegen had waved a hand dismissively.

"The capital, Archbishop, is wherever the king is at. And the king ought to be in the largest and richest city."

Godric tolerated Swegen's little declarations such as these, for although he considered the future king a fool, he had benefited greatly from him over the last several months. There were limits though, boundaries of behaviour that could not be exceeded and simply explained away as idiosyncratic quirks or eccentricity. Swegen's taste in bed partners, for one, caused him great concern, though he imagined it was no worse than some of his predecessors. His willingness to do away with those who caused him the even the mildest inconvenience was an increasingly worrying trait. His latest request was also causing Godric some concern.

"So, Godric," Swegen called out, striding back down the length of the barge towards him. "What do you think?"

Godric waited until Swegen was close enough that he did not have to raise his voice before answering.

"I think, my lord, that raising the fyrd now would not be a good idea."

"Why not? Get the churls armed and ready to fight now, before harvest time. If we wait any longer we may not get them at all this year," Swegen said, grabbing a chicken leg from a plate proffered by a serving girl, before sitting down heavily next to Godric at the barge's prow.

"My lord," Godric said, lowering his voice. "By raising the fyrd you are actively showing that you expect and are planning for war. Surely your actions ought to be those of a victim nation, forced to defend itself, not one seen to be preparing for battle?"

"Nonsense," Swegen replied, through a mouthful of chicken. "Everyone knows we have been wronged by Northlandic aggressors. I see no reason to be so cautious, Godric."

"Would the fyrd come, though?"

"The fyrd will do as it is told. Earl, thegn and freeman. Farmer, farrier, cooper and carter and alike. They will do as their king tells them to."

Swegen spat the words out before standing and waving the half-eaten chicken leg at Suthseaxe, who had recovered somewhat and was now walking down the barge towards them.

"Get some chicken down you, Suthseaxe! Lovely and succulent it is!" Swegen shouted. The earl rushed to the side of the boat and heaved violently as his empty stomach tried to expel what little was left inside of him.

"Odd man," Swegen noted, sitting down again. "Useful though, for gauging the other earls' moods and thoughts."

"And what do the earls think about the notion raising an army before you are even crowned? Raising the fyrd is never a popular move, unless the country itself is being attacked or subjected to foreign invasion," Godric reminded him.

"The earls know that we are being attacked by a hostile Northland. The people will do their duty as instructed."

"But only because we have told them so," Godric replied.

"Precisely because we have told them so. They will do as we say," Swegen said forcefully, his voice tinged with frustration. Godric did not reply, but chose instead to watch the northern bank of the river and the hive-like activity of the Lunden docks. Leofwin finally managed to stumble down the length of the barge to join them, where he made his apologies for having been sick.

"It is true, is it not, Suthseaxe," Swegen asked loudly, once the earl had recovered enough to take a seat. "That Northlandic forces are amassing on our northern border? Ceasterscir and Northamtunscir have all reported as such."

"It is, my lord," Leofwin replied. "Reports have stated sightings of large numbers of cavalry moving into the six lost shires over the last week."

"There," Swegen announced proudly, turning to Godric. "I told you that Northland is preparing to attack."

The archbishop acknowledged the statement with a dismissive shrug and returned his attention to the northern riverbank.

"Do you not agree then, Suthseaxe," Swegen continued, "that a prudent king would raise the fyrd now, in anticipation of any Northlandic aggression?"

"My lord?" Suthseaxe asked, taking a sip from a beaker of water, most of which dribbled down his beard as the barge bounced across the waves. "The fyrd? Now?"

"The best form of defence is to attack, is it not?" Swegen said cheerfully.

"Well, I, I wouldn't say that, my lord," Suthseaxe replied. "I cannot think that it would be a popular move."

"What? To defend one's nation will not be popular? Nonsense!"

"It may not be the best thing to do, as your first act as king," Godric intervened. "Perhaps waiting just a few weeks would be best. My lord." The final two words were added emphatically and slowly, in the absence of a reply from Swegen.

"The best thing for the nation," Swegen said finally, standing up and throwing the chicken leg he had been gnawing on over the barge's bows, "is whatever the king orders."

Godric and Suthseaxe shared a brief exchange of raised eyebrows, before Swegen turned on them.

"I am king because I am right and I am right because I am king!" he snapped.

Leofwin recoiled at Swegen's outburst, but Godric simply snorted in amusement.

"Somewhat like His Holiness then, my lord?"

"The difference being, Archbishop," Swegen said with a snarl, "is that the Pope is sat far, far away in Rome and I am here. This is my country now."

Godric let the sound of the waves slapping against the barge's hull fill the silence that fell upon the three men. Swegen stared at him intently for several seconds before the anger that had so suddenly descended on him visibly melted away. His shoulders sagged and he let out a brief bark of laughter.

"Come, my friends. Let us not bicker about these finer details. Once I am king, everything will resolve itself. If I ask for something to be done, it will be done. Quite simple."

Leofwin coughed and spoke quietly.

"What was that?" Swegen asked, straining to hear the earl's voice.

"I said that the witan may not approve."

"The witan can disapprove all it wants. Its days are numbered in our new Ængland, I feel." Godric and the earl shared another glance and this time it was not missed by Swegen.

"My lords," he said, leaning in towards them. "God has given me this chance to be king. I do not intend to waste it. Ængland will be mine and it will be led with fortitude and courage. I will have no time for dissenters. Is that clear?"

Godric shifted in his seat and took a sip from his goblet.

"My lord," he said calmly, "it is becoming perfectly clear."

"The future of Ængland is too important," Swegen said, sitting down again, "to let interfering old men stand in my way."

Godric sat back and closed his eyes, letting the screeching of the circling gulls wash over him. Perhaps, he thought, just perhaps, he had made a very, very serious mistake.

Burgh, East Thrith of Jorvik, Northland

Orange-bathed shadows flickered off the canvas sides of the carts parked around the campfire. The caravan containing the missing, presumed dead, Ænglisc queen had left Jorvik at first light and had reached Burgh, on the bank of the river Hymbre, late that afternoon. They had set camp in a meadow next to a church half a mile outside of the main town. The carts had been positioned to encircle the campfire, offering some semblance of a private space. They had not wanted to enter the town, for any extra attention was unwanted attention; there would be enough eyes already tracking their progress.

Since Roman times, Burgh had been one of the main crossing points of the river Hymbre from Jorvik to the shire of Lindsey. Large ferries, almost as big as sea-going vessels, traversed the river from dusk until dawn, with even the occasional night crossing. It had been chosen as a departure point, for both practicality and deception. Practical, for it offered easy access to the ships that would take them down the eastern seaboard to East Anglia and Ængland. It would also let the party send ahead a bogus retinue that would cross the river by ferry and travel through Northland by road. A deception that would no doubt be short-lived, but any advantage that could be gained, any chance of remaining hidden, was invaluable.

Adelise was sitting at the campfire, animatedly retelling her adventures of the past several weeks to Abbot Arnewulf. Thurstan listened in, laughing and squirming in embarrassment in equal measure at her exaggerations of his fights. Arnewulf followed her tale with benevolent amusement, not interrupting her even when her stories clearly veered into the realms of fantasy.

"Two hundred men you say? Ten against one? Brought you back from the dead?" His eyes twinkled and he laughed at the young girl's enthusiasm and invention. He could only be thankful to the Lord and Thurstan that the girl had survived. Whatever the exaggerations, Arnewulf knew that but for the slightest difference in fortune, the queen would have been long dead.

Ceolwulf was sitting away to one side, hurriedly writing letters on the scraps of parchment that he had acquired from one of Arnewulf's entourage of priests. Before departing on the boat the following morning, he was to write several coded messages containing false information of their movements and plans. These would be taken by the bogus retinue on their trip to East Anglia.

As far as Ceolwulf knew, nobody outside of the Northlandic council would suspect that Arnewulf's companions were anything other than Sigtrygg's official envoy to the coronation. Yet it would be an optimistic, if not downright foolish, man that thought that no-one in Ængland would discover some part of their plan over the next two weeks.

Ceolwulf looked up from the parchment, cuffing at a drop of ink with his sleeve and stared at his future queen. From here, devoid of any jewellery or finery, she could just be another girl, a merchant's daughter or even a serving maid. Or, so they hoped, a boy. That the future of two nations, something of such paramount import, depended on an innocuous and insignificant group of travellers seemed unreal. He shook his head and returned to his writing, wiping the quill on the edge of the inkpot before deciding how to phrase the request for men. Just as he put the nib to paper, the sound of hurried footsteps caused him to glance up.

One of Arnewulf's entourage had scuttled over to where the priest was sitting with Adelise and was whispering into his ear, his gestures and agitation indicating he was in some state of distress. Arnewulf listened to the younger man, then nodded and stood up, leaving the fireside and disappearing into the gloom where tents had been set up.

Ceolwulf stood up and walked over to Adelise, who was now chattering excitedly to Thurstan. The Northlander nodded at him and he returned the greeting.

"Are there problems?" Ceolwulf asked.

"It appears that one of Arnewulf's monks has been taken ill, quite severely too," Thurstan answered.

"Not some sort of camp fever, I hope," Ceolwulf said. The dreaded flux that turned a man's guts to water, draining him of energy and life, was a killer whenever men camped in the same spot for more than a few days. It killed more soldiers on campaign than any battle would.

"Similar symptoms, but surely too soon for that. I imagine some sort of ailment contracted in Jorvik? Possibly something he ate?" Thurstan asked.

Ceolwulf nodded in agreement. He thought he understood what the Northlander had said, but the young man had a tendency to speak quickly and quietly which made it difficult. They sat in silence, watching the flames throw sparks high into the night sky, waiting for Arnewulf to return.

The quiet was broken by a single, low-pitched yet delicate voice suddenly bursting into song. On the far side of the campfire a young monk, whose name Ceolwulf believed to be Gamal, had taken out a lyre and started singing a melancholy lament. The words told of a love lost to the waves, which caused Adelise to blink back tears and Ceolwulf and Thurstan to exchange glances.

"That doesn't sound like a religious song to me," Ceolwulf commented.

"It isn't," Thurstan replied. "Abbot Arnewulf, from what I can gather, recruits monks from unusual backgrounds. Usually monks enter the Church at a young age as novices and are brought up there. Abbot Arnewulf, however, is a believer that God can find man, or man can find God, at any age. He accepts men of all backgrounds, whatever age; often young men from poor farming communities who would otherwise have been forced to work on the land."

"I thought the Church liked rich, younger sons who lacked land to inherit or military leanings?" Ceolwulf asked, half jokingly.

"I don't think it's quite the same with monks," Thurstan replied. "As such, some of the monks with Father Arnewulf are not quite the usual innocent, unworldly youths you would perhaps normally expect to see. Not that they are less devout, he tells me."

"So someone who doesn't look like a monk, or talk or act like a monk, could be passed off as one of Abbot Arnewulf's entourage?" Adelise asked, almost immediately.

"Yes," Thurstan answered slowly, suspicious of where the young girl was trying to lead the conversation.

"So," she started, a grin spreading across her face. "If Abbot Arnewulf is expected to attend with five monks, and one of them was to be taken ill, then there could be said to be a place available to come to Lunden? And that person doesn't have to look like a monk?"

Before Thurstan could reply, Abbot Arnewulf returned with a concerned look on his face.

"It would appear that one of our monks has been taken quite ill. Nothing catching, I can assure you; it is no pox or the flux, I feel, but serious enough for him to have to stay here."

"So one of the monks cannot come?" Adelise asked, her cheerfulness confusing Arnewulf.

"Sadly not, my child," he replied, unsure as to why she found such pleasure at the news.

Ceolwulf knew what she was about to ask and smirked at Thurstan.

Thurstan returned the look ruefully at Ceolwulf, in acknowledgement of what was about to be asked of him. He knew he could not refuse Adelise's request and he doubted Arnewulf could either.

Adelise blurted out the question, clapping her hands together in supplication to Abbot Arnewulf. The priest rubbed his brow and stared questioningly at Ceolwulf and Thurstan. Ceolwulf simply shrugged, leaving Arnewulf to address Thurstan.

"Can you read, Thurstan?"

"Yes, Father."

"Can you write?"

"Yes, Father. Not neatly, but yes."

"Do you know your Bible?"

Thurstan paused and gave this some thought.

"More than most, but not thoroughly. It's been explained to me. I think."

The reply did not seem to inspire great confidence in Arnewulf, who shook his head in bemusement.

"Why am I not surprised by this request?" he asked aloud. He stared into the fire's flames for several seconds, toying with the intricately carved ivory crucifix he wore around his neck.

"Ah well, I suppose one able swordsman more in Lunden will do us no harm. You, my lady, can explain to King Hakon though, why we have decided to kidnap one of his personal huskarls. They say the Lord acts in mysterious ways, so perhaps poor Bodin's sudden illness has been sent down on him for a reason," Abbot Arnewulf said, standing up and clapping his hands at a monk emerging from one of the tents. "Brother Matthias! A razor and a pair of scissors, if you will!"

Adelise jumped up, laughing with delight, pulling Ceolwulf to his feet, causing him to shake his head in weary amusement. Only Thurstan remained seated, staring into the fire and sadly stroking his long hair for one final time.

10th June 1166
The East Anglian coast, Ængland

"My lady!" Ceolwulf shouted across the barge. "My lady! Please be careful!"

Adelise was leaning over the low sides of the boat, stretching her arm down to see if her fingers could touch the snapping tops of the waves. She turned around and grinned at Ceolwulf. On seeing the concerned look on his face, she straightened up and ran over to him.

"Sorry, Ceolwulf," she said, picking her way through the outstretched legs of the sleeping Abbot Arnewulf. "I am bored, if I may be honest." This was the third day of sailing and now her initial excitement and seasickness had passed, the slow journey was becoming tiresome.

"I know, the wind does not seem to be favouring us today, does it?" Ceolwulf admitted. The boat rocked gently side to side on the waves, the distant shoreline appearing to move neither left to right, nor nearer or further away. They had been sailing for five hours now and Ceolwulf doubted whether they had travelled even ten miles.

"Where are we stopping tonight?" she asked, sitting down onto a coil of rope.

"I had wanted us to be at Herewic by nightfall, but I don't know if we'll make it now," he answered. "We are meant to be meeting some of my uncle's men, loyal to you, who will provide us with horse and carts."

"Is that in East Anglia?"

"Not quite, it's part of Eastseaxe, but it means we don't have to pass through Gipeswic and makes our journey much quicker," Ceolwulf replied.

"Then what happens?" Adelise pressed.

"Well then, hopefully, we ride into Lunden dressed as monks

visiting the capital for the coronation, just us three, Father Arnewulf and his companions."

"No armed guards?" Adelise sounded worried.

"No, none. Well, apart from Thurstan, I suppose. We go as holy men, attending the religious celebrations of the coronation," Ceolwulf said.

"And then we attend the coronation, pretending to be priests?"

"Yes, that is the plan, more or less. Or was. Still is, I think. The nearer we get there, the less sure I am. It seemed bold and daring in Jorvik, it now just seems foolhardy, but we have to get you inside Westmynster Cathedral," Ceolwulf conceded.

"Do you miss your father?" Adelise asked suddenly, catching Ceolwulf completely by surprise.

"Well, yes. Of course," he said hesitantly.

"You don't talk about him. You can talk to me, if you want, as I lost my father too," Adelise said, giving Ceolwulf a look of such intense and sincere concern that he was left in two minds whether to laugh or cry.

"Thank you, my lady. I genuinely appreciate your offer. I suppose at the moment I am filled with such anger about it, such hatred for Swegen that I have not thought about my loss. The events of restoring you to the throne have taken precedence of course, but I suppose my hunger for vengeance is such that I have not really taken on board that I have lost my father. My queen and the earldom come first, and then I can worry about my loss," Ceolwulf said, in what was possibly the longest conversation he had had about his father since the night of his death.

"Thurstan's father is alive, but does not speak to him or want to see him. He sent Thurstan away," Adelise said, picking at the frayed end of the tar-dipped rope by her feet. "I'm not sure whether I'd prefer a loving but dead father, or an unloving alive one."

Ceolwulf gave the young girl's observation some thought and shook his head.

"The dead can no longer be harmed nor do us harm. They will always live on in our memories in the most perfect state that you can remember them in," Ceolwulf replied. "The poets say that it is better to have been loved for a day than to live a lifetime alone and I think, for once, they might have a point."

He looked up to see Thurstan walking over to them. He had been below deck, where Arnewulf's monks were trying to sleep or allay the effects of seasickness.

"My lord Ceolwulf, my lady," Thurstan greeted them. He gripped the mast and took a deep lungful of sea air. Ceolwulf watched the Northlander as he stretched his back and let out a large yawn. Thurstan's hair, although now cropped much shorter, appeared to flap in a sudden breeze.

"Is the wind now up?" Ceolwulf asked.

Thurstan turned around, trying to gauge the direction of the sudden gust. Looking behind him, he froze.

"That," he announced, "is not good."

Confused, Ceolwulf got to his feet and stared at the eastern horizon.

Where just ten minutes previously the grey water had clearly stretched into the distance, there now towered a wall of black cloud that obscured the point at which sea became sky. The wind flicked at the hem of Ceolwulf's tunic and the air suddenly began to feel heavy. After a day sitting in almost totally still water, the barge's sails snapped into life and billowed. Ceolwulf stared hard at the horizon, shuddering at the sight of the wall of cloud closing in.

"No," Ceolwulf agreed. "Not good. Not good at all."

No matter how close he sat to the fire, Ceolwulf could not seem to get his clothes dry. It seemed impossible to have got this wet without having actually fallen into the sea. He had taken off what he could in an attempt to release the seemingly endless amounts of water that were trapped between layers, but the company of a girl queen and holy men made a man reluctant to strip.

Adelise was sitting next to him on the stony beach, huddling her knees up to her chin, shivering. The evening air was mild enough, but the hours of rain had seemed impossibly cold.

Had it been hours? The squall that had taken them had seemed interminable. Perhaps it had only been half an hour, an hour at most. Yet when the clouds had overtaken them, they had been plunged into a maelstrom of torrential, horizontal rain, vicious winds and a sky that had been as dark as midnight.

On the other hand, as Thurstan had helpfully pointed out, they had finally made good progress. By risking shattering the mast and keeping the sails raised, the barge had fair ripped along the coastline and they had finally landed, once the seas had calmed, not far short of their original destination of Herewic. A series of inlets and channel-laced marshland had offered them somewhere suitable to camp for the night. They had dragged the boat onto the shale beach as a group, panting and gasping, seawater in their eyes and mouths, burning their lungs.

Now they were all huddled around a makeshift fire in a large hollow in the grassy sand dunes, just a few metres from the shore. It had taken some time to find any wood suitable for a fire that was not drenched by the rain, but the blue-green flames had finally sparked into life and now offered some warmth to the drenched travellers.

They were still several miles away from their agreed meeting point, but they would travel no further today, Ceolwulf had decided. They would sleep here, by the beach, and rest, waiting for their clothes to dry. The rendezvous with their contact would have to wait until the following day, in the hope that the man his uncle sent would not abandon them for having been just one day late.

"How far away is Herewic from here?" Thurstan asked

Ceolwulf, stretching his bootless feet out, as close to the fire as possible without blistering them. Of all the Aenglisc in the group, Thurstan found Ceolwulf the easiest to understand, his accent not totally dissimilar to the Northlandic of Hoiland or Kestevan.

"An hour, possibly two by foot. We are on marshland though, so no doubt you would have to loop around all sorts of creeks and pools," Ceolwulf replied. "I don't even imagine there's a decent road to the town from here."

"And your uncle will have sent men that you trust?" Thurstan asked.

Ceolwulf snorted in wry amusement. "I don't think I trust anyone at the moment. Is anyone trustworthy at such times? When all values and authorities that you have held dear your whole life are trampled on and destroyed? Burnt to ashes? Yet we are left with little choice, Thurstan. If we could afford the luxury of choosing our company and manner of arrival into Lunden, then we would ride with ten thousand men on fine, white steeds, stopping at every tavern to sip the finest wines and ales."

Thurstan stared into the copper-edged flames that crackled loudly as a fresh split in the wood caused more salt water to sizzle out. Adelise appeared to have nodded off to sleep in the sand and he drew a light blanket over her. The sound of the outgoing tide was a calming, soporific background to the muted conversation around the fire.

Abbot Arnewulf's monks, as amiable as they were, kept themselves to themselves for the most part and appeared to be in quiet prayer. The abbot himself was snoring loudly, having lain down on his back, closest of all to the fire and promptly dropped straight off to sleep.

"We are essentially committing suicide, with a slight chance of success, aren't we?" Thurstan asked quietly.

Ceolwulf did not reply immediately, but poked at the fire with a long twig. He caused the logs to throw golden sparks up into the ever-darkening sky, watching them fade and disappear before they could fall back down to earth.

"I wouldn't put it quite like that," Ceolwulf said. "I think, perhaps, that we could say that we have very little to lose at this point."

"The girl does. She could lose her life," Thurstan said, carefully keeping his voice as quiet as possible. "Are we doing the right thing taking her to Lunden?"

Ceolwulf sat back and looked at Thurstan's earnest face. He had heard from Adelise about how he had taken down dozens of men, exaggerations he was sure. Yet to have brought her this far, he must have killed and, if the more trusted accounts were to be believed, he was rather good at it. It seemed difficult to reconcile that with the open, trusting face that was awaiting an answer.

"I have thought about this, and asked myself the same question," Ceolwulf said. "I suppose that yes, we could take her away. But then what? Swegen becomes king, and what becomes of Adelise? Could she ever live a normal life? We know Swegen has no qualms about sending men into Northland. Would she ever be able spend a day without looking over her shoulder for the next assassin?"

"Do you think he knows that she is still alive? Does he know about us?" Thurstan asked.

"I would be very surprised if we could get to Lunden, pass through Ængland from Northland without anything being noticed. Something seen, something suspected, something that eventually is passed from person to person until it trickles into Swegen's ear."

Thurstan nodded and seemed to accept this. He took his almost dry cloak from beside the fire, rolled it up and placed it behind his head, before closing his eyes and trying to sleep.

Ceolwulf stayed awake, listening to the sound of the waves lapping on the beach. He turned onto his side and looked at the sleeping figure of the girl Adelise. She seemed so at peace, so content, despite the hand that fate had dealt her over the last three months. To think that it could all end so suddenly and violently made him shiver. They could sail tonight, he thought, if the seas calmed. These boats were not really sea-going, but they could surely make it to Flanders if the weather held. They would no longer be in danger, no longer be hunted.

One of the patrolling sailors stifled a loud sneeze and Adelise's eyes flicked open. For a moment, there was a pang of fear in her eyes, but then she saw Ceolwulf staring at her and her face broke into a tired smile.

"We're going home, Ceolwulf," she murmured. "Going home." Her eyes dropped shut and before Ceolwulf could answer, he could hear her high-pitched snoring.

Ceolwulf remained awake until daybreak, watching the rising sun's first rays dapple the waves with pale yellow light. Thurstan joined him as the crimson arc grew steadily into the morning sun, sitting in silence as the rest of the party slept.

"We are alone in the world, Thurstan," Ceolwulf said quietly. "No-one must know of us, no-one will be able to help us once we're within the city."

"I know, my lord," Thurstan replied, amusing Ceolwulf with the rarely used epithet.

"Let me ask you something," Ceolwulf said. He squinted as the sun broke free of the distant sea and hung low in the morning sky, bathing the sleepers in a golden haze. "If you knew now that you were facing certain death and it would all be in vain, would you still do this? Would you still go, simply because you knew it to be the right thing to do?"

"Absolutely," replied Thurstan with no hesitation. "A thousand times over. I would gladly die tomorrow for the right cause, rather than live a lifetime of betrayal and misdeed."

"As I thought," Ceolwulf turned to the Northlander and gripped his shoulder. "Unfortunately for us, that may well be what tomorrow brings, my friend."

11th June 1166
Nr Herewic, Eastseaxe, Ængland

Ceolwulf and Thurstan were lying flat on their stomachs, peering out from the undergrowth towards the ruins. The warm sun was making their newly tonsured crowns prickle in the heat.

"Are you sure this is the place?" Thurstan asked, shifting his leg away from a nettle bush.

"Quite sure, quite sure," Ceolwulf reassured him.

The ruins had once been a Roman fort, built many hundreds of years previously to defend Britain against the Saxon invaders. It was now a sprawling collection of ruined stone buildings; nature had reclaimed half the buildings with weeds and grass, and the remainder was used by local builders as a source of free masonry.

Ceolwulf had visited the site dozens of times as a younger man when visiting his uncle in Gipeswic, or when he was with his father on business in nearby Herewic. Despite the derelict state of the buildings, it was a beautiful spot. The headland on which the fort had stood looked out onto the Arewan estuary and the North Sea beyond; the dawn sun would drench the landscape in amber on a clear morning.

The two men had been lying in the undergrowth for the best part of an hour now, waiting for any sign of the carts Ceolwulf's uncle had meant to send. He had requested that they be met by nightfall of the tenth, but the storm had put paid to those plans. They could only hope that the contact would return today. Ceolwulf estimated by the sun that it was now already well past midday.

"Do we go back?" Thurstan asked.

"No, no," Ceolwulf said, irritably.

They had left the rest of the party half a mile away, hidden in a small copse, away from prying eyes.

Thurstan turned over and reached over for a water pouch tied to his waist. His forehead was dripping with sweat, which ran into eyes already filled with midges and pollen. He was about to suggest to Ceolwulf that they change their position when he heard the telltale sound of hooves coming along the single dirt track that ran to the ruins. Ceolwulf must have heard it too, for he waved Thurstan into silence when the Northlander tried to alert him.

A few minutes later and two rather sorry-looking wooden carts, being led by equally sorry-looking horses, rattled into view. The lead driver stood up and raised an arm, bringing both carts to a stop. The driver, a tall man with shortly cropped blond hair and a long braided beard from his chin, stepped forward and cupped his hands around his mouth. He took a deep breath and emitted a shrill, barking call that sounded like an animal in distress

Thurstan gave Ceolwulf a puzzled look, but the Ænglander did not seem to be surprised.

"A small owl cry," he said quietly, with a grin on his face. "Our greeting call."

Ceolwulf stood up and stepped from out of the undergrowth.

"Lyfing! My friend! Gods be praised, it is good to see you here!" he called out, before almost breaking into a run towards the carts.

The bearded man shouted a greeting and leapt down from the cart, before embracing Ceolwulf in a bear-like hug.

"Earl Ceolwulf, it is good to see you still alive," he grinned, before checking himself, when he saw Ceolwulf's face. "I am sorry that you have earned that title through the death of your father. You shall no doubt one day avenge him."

Ceolwulf nodded, before beckoning Thurstan out from the bushes and introducing him to his uncle's steward. Lyfing courteously greeted him and then seemed to gaze intently at the two men's pink faces and freshly shaven crowns.

"An interesting manner for an earl and a warrior to wear their hair," he said. "Is this the new fashion in the north now?"

"A necessary deception," Ceolwulf replied.

"I know," Lyfing laughed. "Your uncle has told me every-thing, but not, I hasten to add, anyone else. We are, for the time being, able to move freely around Eastseaxe. The closer we get to Lunden though, the greater the risk we put ourselves in."

"I understand. Thank you, Lyfing," Ceolwulf said gripping the man's shoulder. His uncle, though, hadn't told him every-thing. As far as Lyfing was concerned, Ceolwulf was to be taken to Lunden to be reinstated and help overthrow Swegen; as Ceolwulf had requested, he knew nothing about the presence of Adelise. "We will never be able to repay the favour you are doing Ængland."

"Oh, I don't know," he said with a wink towards Thurstan. "Five big-titted whores and a hide of land wouldn't go amiss."

"Lyfing has been in my uncle's service for nearly fifteen years, Thurstan," Ceolwulf said, with what the Northlander considered a rare smile.

"Before that, I had some rather interesting experience of adventuring abroad, let us call it, which might well prove useful over the next few days." He delivered the last sentence with another chuckle and a wink.

"Who is the other driver?" Ceolwulf asked Lyfing.

"Bodo, a young lad from your uncle's service," he replied, before calling the boy over. "Bodo! Get your lazy arse over here and let's start unloading these wagons."

As the four men removed the carts' apparent cargos, Lyfing explained how they had left Herewic carrying barrels, filled with nothing but rotten vegetables and old rags, to give the impression of travelling merchants.

"You have not met with any trouble then, I pray," Ceolwulf asked Lyfing, once they had cleared the carts and were riding back to the copse where Adelise and the rest of the party waited.

"None, my lord, thank God," Lyfing replied. "However, on the road from Byrig to Herewic, we did pass soldiers coming the other way."

"Soldiers?" Ceolwulf asked.

"Yes, and lots of them. Mostly from Coleceaster, but some East Anglian ones too. Heading northwards, towards Grantbrygscir and the Northlandic border. Under orders from Lunden, from what I could gather."

Ceolwulf spat over the side of the ground, cursing Swegen's name.

"Those are not his men to order. They are my men," he snapped.

"I understand, my lord," Lyfing replied.

Less than half an hour later, they reached the copse where Abbot Arnewulf and Adelise had been resting. Ceolwulf introduced Lyfing enthusiastically to the party. The steward did not bat an eyelid when Adelise was introduced as Æthelweard, a young novice boy. Ceolwulf saw no reason to let him know otherwise at this point – the fewer people who knew the truth, the better.

With heavy hearts, the sailors who had accompanied them from Burgh were bid farewell, leaving just Abbot Arnewulf's monks as their only companions to Lunden. Ceolwulf shuddered as the men disappeared into the distance, feeling as if the last link to their sanctuary in Northland had now been shorn off.

"I hope they get home safely," Adelise said from under her newly donned monk's habit. She was riding in the second cart with Abbot Arnewulf and Thurstan, leaving Ceolwulf to catch up with Lyfing in the first.

"Not as much as they'll be hoping we make it safely to Lunden, I'd wager," Abbot Arnewulf said ruefully.

"We will be safe, won't we, Father?" Adelise asked him.

"We will, my son, we will. Just try to keep calm, speak some Latin once in a while and place your trust in God," Arnewulf replied, winking at her.

"I will, Father. In God and in Thurstan," she replied, grinning at the Northlander, who was trying to get comfortable in the monk's itchy garments.

"Not without a weapon, I wouldn't," Thurstan muttered to himself. They had chosen to leave all their arms with the sailors, for a sword-wielding monk would no doubt be the first character to arouse suspicion on the road to Lunden.

Their pace was slow at first, wary of being seen, but the countryside seemed empty, save for wildlife and flocks of gulls. After two hours of winding, narrow, rutted mud tracks leading away from the coast, they joined the wide, partially paved, west road to Lunden. Lyfing liked to pass the time singing folk songs, the lyrics of which Adelise did not quite follow, but seemed to upset the two monks in the lead cart.

They camped that night near Maeldune, by Ceolwulf's reckoning. Far enough away from the port to avoid the risk of encountering other people, but close enough to the road so as to not lose time. Ceolwulf had fallen to sleep with the sound of Adelise's laughter still in his ears as she recounted the funny things that Lyfing had said during the evening. The steward had amused the camp all night with his stories and tales, which were long-winded but humorous. He would pull all manner of faces and speak in the strangest of voices, mimicking accents and dialects, leaving Adelise rolling around in the grass with laughter.

Even Ceolwulf had chuckled to himself as he fell into a welcome and refreshing sleep. Being back on Ænglisc soil had not appeared to have held great significance for Adelise, for she had not commented on it. Ceolwulf was not sure what he had expected her to do, once she was back in her realm, but as Thurstan had pointed out, she just seemed relieved that no-one was actively trying to kill her.

Long may it stay that way, Ceolwulf thought.

12th June 1166

They awoke early the following morning, pausing only to eat a small portion of bread washed down with water, before setting off again. They encountered little traffic on the road, benevolently nodding in greeting to anyone they passed or encountered. No-one appeared to take much interest in two carts of monks, Ceolwulf surmised, for the roads must have been filled with visitors to Lunden for the past week at least. Short of interruptions, Lyfing said, they would arrive at the city walls at around noon the following day.

They stopped only once during the morning, to relieve themselves and to refill water bottles from a freshwater stream that ran alongside the road for a short stretch. By mid-afternoon, they had crossed the border from Eastseaxe into the shire of Middelseaxe. The road had turned westwards, away from the coast, and they were now travelling through open expanses of rolling, pleasant, green hills. Ceolwulf had climbed into the back of the cart to rest, leaving Abbot Arnewulf to talk with Lyfing. Their pace was steady, if not particularly rapid, and Ceolwulf found himself being rocked to sleep by the gentle jolting of the cart.

His dreams were filled with images of his father – his father ill, his father trapped in a burning house, his father dead. He tried to wake him, shouting his name, but his father just slept, never stirring, and his voice echoed and multiplied into a cacophony of infinite cries.

He was brought back to unwelcome consciousness by the sound of the carts clattering to a standstill and muffled voices calling out in greeting.

"Why have we stopped? Are we camping here?" he asked the monk who had accompanied them the lead cart. The pale-faced man, a novice named Simon, shook his head and glanced fearfully down the road. Ceolwulf stood slightly to peer between Lyfing and Arnewulf at what had brought them to a stop.

He was greeted by the sight of several men guarding a wooden bridge across a small river. They appeared to be stopping every cart and traveller hoping to cross, inspecting bags and possessions with great interest.

"Is it too late to turn back?" Ceolwulf whispered softly.

"I'm afraid so," Lyfing replied. "We just rounded the corner and there they were, we had no way of knowing. Sorry."

"Is there no other way?" Ceolwulf pressed, even though he knew it would be folly to turn and flee.

"This is the only road across the river for twenty miles," the steward replied.

"Just stay calm, keep quiet, and there will be no problem. They're not likely to ask you questions about your knowledge of theology," Abbot Arnewulf said, laughing weakly. "Besides, no-one is armed. Are they?"

Ceolwulf turned and stared back towards Thurstan.

"Are they?" Arnewulf asked again, this time with a tone of concern. The Northlander had been reluctant to give up his weapons, despite the understanding that travelling unarmed was a necessary risk in their disguise as monks. Arnewulf had pleaded with him to cast aside all weapons, but Ceolwulf suspected that the huskarl had kept at least one blade hidden upon him somewhere.

Yet Thurstan was nowhere to be seen. He could quite clearly see Bodo, Adelise and the monks, Gamal and Matthias, but the Northlander was conspicuous by his absence. Bodo gave a bemused shrug by way of an explanation and nodded towards the woods that lined the road towards the river crossing.

Ceolwulf cursed Thurstan's name as the carts were urged forward by the armed men for inspection. There were five men, one of whom also wore a large purse at his bulging waist and an avaricious grin that spoke of self-assured and petty officialdom.

"Greetings, brothers!" the man called out walking slowly towards the first cart. "On our way to Lunden?"

"That we are, my son," Abbot Arnewulf replied amiably. In the back of the cart, Ceolwulf stared at his feet and pretended to be deep in prayer.

"For the coronation?" the official asked, walking past Arnewulf and casting a curious eye over the carts' passengers.

"Indeed, my lord?" Arnewulf replied, letting the question hang in the air. "Forgive me, I did not catch your name."

"My name is not important to you, monk," the official snapped. The four other men had formed a line across the road and three had already drawn their swords. "You need to know only that I hold authority in this hundred and that my duty is to make sure no undesirables enter Lunden."

Arnewulf seemed unperturbed by the man's aggression.

"You are the sheriff?"

"I hold his authority here, as one of his deputies," the man replied, returning to the front of the cart and inspecting the horses' harnesses. *The assistant to a deputy's deputy, more likely,* Ceolwulf thought, but for now, he was the man with the armed men.

"We are here by invite of the Archbishop of Cantwaraburg himself," Arnewulf declared, fishing out the document that bore the late archbishop's seal as way of proof.

The official snatched the scroll of parchment from Arnewulf's hand and gave it a cursory glance. He spat onto the muddy road and tossed the paper back towards the abbot

Ceolwulf sank his head deeper into his hands. His brow had broken into a profuse sweat and his fingers felt numb. Unarmed and surrounded by monks; *Lord save me,* he prayed.

"I care not if you were sent by Saint John the Baptist himself. I have orders to stop unwanted peoples from entering Lunden," the official sneered. "Especially Northlanders."

"We are men of the cloth and, although it should not matter, I am Ænglisc born and bred," Arnewulf replied patiently.

"A traitor then," the official smirked. "I don't care where you are from, or who sent for you. I decide who enters Lunden on this road." He patted his belly, causing the coin purse tied to his waist to clink dully.

"I see," Abbot Arnewulf replied, sighing. "How much is this going to cost?"

The man laughed openly at the priest and stroked his fingers across his expensive looking tunic.

"Oh no, no, you misunderstand me," the official said. "We've been expecting you, Abbot Arnewulf. This is going to cost you much, much more. Get off the carts."

Reluctantly, Ceolwulf and Arnewulf climbed down from the carts. Lyfing helped them down, gently lifting Brother Simon out of the cart, as the monk's knees were trembling so badly with fear that he was unable to walk unaided.

Lyfing turned to Ceolwulf and embraced him. "I'm sorry," he whispered in his ear, before stepping backwards and walking slowly past the line of leering soldiers.

Ceolwulf stood for one moment dumbfounded as the realisation washed over him.

"I'm sorry, Ceolwulf," Lyfing called out, "but you were meant to be in exile. Your presence here is not wanted. I did not want it to end like this, but I could not let you get to Lunden. We need a strong king."

"Burn in hell, you traitor!" Ceolwulf shouted.

"Traitor? Lyfing?" the grinning official interrupted, his smile becoming ever broader as his soldiers stepped forward. "Oh no, my Lord Ceolwulf, I think you'll find that you are—"

The man's voice was cut off by an explosion of leaves from the side of the road. A blurred mass of robes and flashing blade enveloped him before he could finish his sentence. Thurstan sprang from the undergrowth and in one swift movement had sliced the official's throat. One hand held the dagger that opened the man's windpipe, the other relieved him of his sword. Thurstan stepped away from the gargling official as he sank to his knees, giving the sword a quick flick to test its weight, swapping it from one hand to the other.

The armed men stopped in their tracks, momentarily taken aback by the apparition of a killer dressed as a monk. The two nearest men struck out at Thurstan, who skipped backwards, his sandaled feet splashing on the muddy road. One lunged forward, bringing his sword around in a sweeping arc from above, aiming for Thurstan's neck. Thurstan dashed forward, ducking under the man's arm, flicking the sword blade up to open the man from groin to shoulder.

The second did not wait his turn but struck down at Thurstan's unprotected head. Thurstan took the sword on his with a metallic crash, jarring his hand and notching his blade in a burst of sparks. Thurstan gripped the man's swordarm by the wrist, before stabbing his blade forward and running the man through, spinning to avoid any counter strike.

The remaining two men were now hesitant, having seen three men fall to this monk's blade in a matter of seconds. They faltered, each one waiting for the other to strike first, hoping they could then land a killer blow whilst the monk was grappling with their companion. Without waiting to see who would strike first, Thurstan rushed them.

In his eyes, they were statues, frozen in time. Their movements were as slow and cumbersome as his steps were as light and quick. The first man swiped at Thurstan's side, trying to eviscerate him. His sword whipped through the air, the aim true and deadly. But Thurstan was no longer where the man expected him to be. Instead, he was already past him and easily parried the man's blow with a casual flick of his sword.

The other man saw his chance, for Thurstan was trapped, it seemed. He stepped forward and swiped low at the fighting monk. The man was surprised to see this blow parried too, for it appeared as if the monk had not even been looking at him.

Thurstan leant back, resting his weight on his heels and parried another blow from each man. The sword was dancing in his hand, darting from side to side, parrying the blows before Thurstan had even registered they were incoming. In the background, Ceolwulf was shouting something, but he did not, could not hear the words. Thurstan did not care.

A second parry, a third, a leap over a low, arcing swipe, and then one of the swordsmen swung high and Thurstan took his chance. He spun, having batted the man's sword upwards, seized the man's arm and stamped his boot down onto the man's leading foot.

The other swordsman attacked and Thurstan let his companion parry the blow, with his arm. The man screamed as his hand and sword spun away, leaving a gushing stump. Thurstan, his sword arm free, lunged forward and stabbed his sword into the other man's open mouth, before wrenching the sword out and stabbing backwards to silence the final, shrieking, swordsman.

Thurstan stepped away from the gore and bloodied mud, the five men killed in less time than it would have taken to say their names. He took a few paces forward, and then slowly let the world come back into focus. Colours flowed back into his vision and confused noise became words and sentences.

Thurstan looked up to see Lyfing backing away from the scene of the carnage. He quickly sprang after him, leaping onto the steward's shoulders, hauling him to the ground and into the mud. Gripping him by the collar, Thurstan hauled his face up into his.

"Why did you do this?" Thurstan shouted into Lyfing's now panic-filled face.

"I, I," he stammered, trying to back away. "I'm sorry, I had no choice."

"Why?" Thurstan shouted. Ceolwulf appeared over

Thurstan's shoulder, standing over the cowering steward.

"I received the message you'd sent to your uncle, about you coming back to claim the throne. There was no way it would work, Ceolwulf, Swegen is too powerful," Lyfing said, tears starting to roll down his cheeks. "All that would happen is that East Anglia would be punished. Your uncle has no part in this, he does not know."

"And no doubt Swegen would have rewarded you handsomely," Abbot Arnewulf said.

"Stay back, don't come over!" Ceolwulf shouted suddenly, turning to look behind him and seeing Adelise climbing down from the rear cart.

"Lady Adelise!" Brother Gamal shouted, revealing her identity and condemning Lyfing to death. The steward's eyes widened on hearing the name and he stared incredulously at what he had believed to be a young boy running towards him. He turned back to Thurstan and realised immediately that his fate was sealed.

"I'm sorry," Lyfing said quietly. "They know. They know you're coming." He closed his eyes and tilted his head back.

"I'm sorry too, Lyfing, but you cannot live," Ceolwulf murmured, tears in his eyes, before nodding to Thurstan. The Northlander whipped his sword blade across the man's neck twice, in quick succession, trying to make his end as quick and painless as possible. He cursed then stepped away from the limp body and stalked into the trees.

"*Requiescat in pace*," Abbot Arnewulf intoned over the man's body, before turning to grasp Adelise before she could see the full extent of Thurstan's swordwork. Ceolwulf walked over to Thurstan, placing an arm around his flinching shoulders.

"You had no choice, Thurstan. I would have done it if you hadn't," he said through tear-filled eyes.

"I know," Thurstan said quietly, staring at the blood on the blade, before tossing it into the undergrowth. "It is one thing though, to kill a man with a sword in his hand in combat. It is another to slay him in cold blood. One day, I will have to answer for this."

"We all will have blood on our hands, come judgement day. You have not done anything that a minute before they wouldn't have done to you," Ceolwulf said.

Thurstan nodded, and then looked back at the road. "We must move the bodies out of sight as soon as possible."

Ceolwulf agreed and between them, with the assistance of the monks, the bodies were laid to rest in the undergrowth, ferns placed over them and blessed by Abbot Arnewulf. Bodo, who had been driving the second cart, had disappeared. He had leapt from the cart and dashed into the trees the second Lyfing had betrayed them, Brother Gamal said, and no-one had seen hide nor hair of him since.

Thurstan retrieved his dagger and, without saying another word, walked back to Adelise. She had wept at the sight of Thurstan fighting, at the bodies, at the thought that men were still trying to kill her and that a man she had liked as much as Lyfing could have tried to betray them. Brother Mathias had tried to console her, but she did not stop crying until she buried her face into Thurstan's shoulder and hugged him tightly.

The entire episode had taken less than five minutes, yet it felt to have lasted a lifetime. Five long minutes during which their only piece of good fortune had been that no other travellers had encountered them on the bridge.

"What did you make of Lyfing's final words?" Ceolwulf asked Abbot Arnewulf as they returned to the carts, after having set the soldiers' horses loose.

"Well, possibly something good, possibly something bad. It would appear that Lyfing did not know about Adelise. Whether he concealed his knowledge, or it has been concealed from him, I do not know. It is possible that no-one in Ængland knows of her existence at all," Abbot Arnewulf said. "It may be they were only concerned with you."

"And the bad?" Ceolwulf asked.

"Alas, someone, somewhere knows we are coming and Bodo is on the loose," Arnewulf said, before sighing deeply. "I don't think we could turn back now though, even if we wanted. Of course, this does now pose a problem on how to enter the city."

"We can think of that later," Ceolwulf said, climbing up onto the cart and taking the reins. "For now, I suggest we get as far away from here as possible."

"Agreed," Abbot Arnewulf said, joining Ceolwulf on the cart. "Although I think it necessary that at the first possible juncture, we change into lay clothing."

"And I suppose we have spare garments with us, do we?" Ceolwulf asked incredulously as urged the horses forward, followed by Brother Mathias in the second cart.

Arnewulf chuckled. "It just so happens that I had foreseen the need to disguise our disguises, as it were. One of the sacks we have with us contains some lay clothing, so that we may pass for pilgrims, and yes, it does include hats to cover your tonsures."

"Do you always travel with spare clothing?" Ceolwulf asked, as Brother Simon started rummaging around in the sacks.

"You would be surprised just how many times it comes in handy when travelling from city to city," Arnewulf replied.

Five minutes later, the remaining members of the party were back on the road to Lunden. The carts trundled up the other side of the hill from the river crossing, emerging from the trees into open grassland.

"These are quite fine garments, Father, if you don't mind me saying," Ceolwulf said, trying on a richly dyed cap. Although of the highest quality, it was already making his tonsured head itch and sweat.

"Hah!" Arnewulf laughed, bouncing in his seat as the cart struck a particularly deep rut in the road. "I've chests full of fine clothes back at the monastery, which usually end up being handed out to the needy. One of my sisters, done well for herself, married a Scottish laird, and keeps sending me clothes, for she thinks I live in poverty. I think she does it out of ego more than charity, but I can't stop her, for she clothes half of Jorvik's Cheapeside."

The sun was starting to set as they passed the ten-mile marker for Lunden. There was no singing anymore, no conversation between the carts. At the first small wood they encountered on the road, Abbot Arnewulf ordered the carts to pull over, so that they might change out of their habits. Just as they were about to climb out of the carts to get undressed, Arnewulf waved his arms and ordered everybody to keep still.

"What is it?" Ceolwulf whispered.

"Listen," Abbot Arnewulf said, cupping an ear. "Horses and carts."

"Do we hide?" Ceolwulf asked, craning his neck to look between the trees, towards the road. "No," Abbot Arnewulf replied. "Just keep quiet and wait."

Just a few seconds later, from the same direction they had come, several large carriages and horsemen appeared, trailing a cloud of dust. The lead carriage was ornately decorated in pendants and red and gold banners.

"Well, there's an interesting development," Arnewulf whispered.

Then, to Ceolwulf's horror, Abbot Arnewulf jumped down from the cart and stepped out into the road.

13th June 1166
Lunden, Ængland

Adelise peeked between the canvas sheets that now covered their cart to see the gates of Lunden City close behind them. Ceolwulf hissed at her to come away from the tiny gap and let the carriage plunge into darkness again. The passengers of two carts were now huddled into one small, covered carriage, the last in a convoy headed by Hereman, Earl of Grantbrygscir. Adelise turned back and joined in with the murmured prayers of the monks, hoping the other passengers could not see her excitement at finally arriving in the city.

They had sat, trembling, listening as the city guards had investigated the carriage's occupants. They had heard the earl talking, almost arguing, with the men, explaining why his wife's illness had caused him to bring extra monks, more than had been expected by the gate's guards. The men had appeared to be highly suspicious of the surplus holy men, but the Earl of Grantbrygscir was a man of power and nobility and a city guard could not argue for long with such a figure.

Adelise had listened intently, excitedly, at the background noise of a bustling city, a city filled with voices similar to her own, speaking her language. She also listened to the sounds of scurrying footsteps and a whispered conversation taking place somewhere near their carriage. She could not make the words out, but the discussion ended with an order from the captain of the guard to let the caravan in, followed by a hurried apology to the earl for any offence or delay caused.

Adelise breathed a sigh of relief and offered up a prayer in thanks to Earl Hereman, the second time in less than a day. Yet again, he had saved them from being stranded outside the city, or worse. The first time had been the previous evening, when they had encountered the earl's party on its way to Lunden. Father

Arnewulf, having terrified Adelise's party by stepping into the road, had disappeared to speak at length with Earl Hereman.

Several long minutes later, Earl Hereman had appeared and introduced himself to both Adelise and Ceolwulf, away from the rest of his entourage. He had not said anything, save for the subtlest of bows and the declaration that they had found themselves a new escort into Lunden.

Less than a day later and they were now within the city's walls, watching the glimpses of the bustling streets flicker past them from between the canvas sheets covering the cart. The smells of burning wood, human filth and the general stench of thousands of people living within such a small area permeated the air. She ought to have found it repellent, but Adelise was excited by it, by the activity and vitality of the city.

The cart rumbled along the narrow roads, further into the city. It seemed incredible to Adelise that one could ride so far in a town and to still not have traversed its entire width. The wheels bounced over a succession of cobbles, dirt and mud, the surface depending on the age of the road or the importance of the buildings that it served.

The cart took a series of sharp turns and the light became dull, the smells more fetid. They had turned down one of the myriad of warren-like back streets that filled Lunden. Their carriage lurched to a halt and Adelise heard Arnewulf talk quickly to the driver, before jumping down and opening the canvas flap sheltering them from unwanted eyes.

"We leave here," he said to Ceolwulf, beckoning to the other occupants to get out. Adelise followed Ceolwulf closely down from the back of the cart, whose driver did not say a single word before disappearing off into the gloomy back streets.

There they stood, looking for all the world like seven lost country priests on their first trip to the city. Ceolwulf was trying to make out the direction of the sickly sun, before turning to Abbot Arnewulf.

"Are we near Cornhill?" he asked. The priest nodded.

"Follow me," Arnewulf announced, before turning and striding off down the narrow, filth-ridden street. The others hurried after him, trying to avoid the eyes of curious watchers lurking in alleys and doorways.

"Where are we heading?" Adelise asked, once she had caught up to Ceolwulf.

"Earl Hereman owns a house in the north of the city, which we may use as a base over the next few days," Ceolwulf replied.

"It's not another trap, is it?" Adelise asked.

"I doubt it, my lady. His family and ours go a long way back. It is no longer safe to use any of the houses owned by my family or Abbot Arnewulf anymore, nor can we stay in a tavern," Ceolwulf replied.

"Are they good friends of your family?" Adelise asked, as she scuttled out of the way of a passing mule, laden with timber.

Ceolwulf gave this some thought. "No, not particularly. I wouldn't say friends. I'm not sure if close friends are the people whose help we need at the moment. Good friends would most certainly be under surveillance. No, they are people whose family are in debt to mine, for some favour one of my ancestors did for them a hundred years ago or so. Possibly more," he added, with some element of amusement at how naive his words sounded.

"It must have been a big favour for them to still feel indebted to you a hundred years later," Adelise said.

"Oh believe me, if it were a grudge, they'd hold it against us for twice as long. No, let us say there are many families out there who I cannot say we are close to, but that we can trust. In times of need, trust can become more important than friendship and Swegen has been gaining neither," Ceolwulf said, sidestepping what he hoped was simply animal dirt. "Since leaving Lunden last month, I've been doing little apart from preparing letters calling in old favours. My uncle has been doing the hard work, or at least I hope he has. We shall see tonight when I meet our contact."

Abbot Arnewulf stopped at a junction and looked up and down what appeared to be identical streets, both lined with huddled wooden houses, leaning against each other for support and filled with people whose filthy clothes blended into the background of dirt and smoke. He scanned the skyline for a church spire. Seeming to find what he was looking for he turned north, checking behind him to ascertain the party were still all together.

"So the plan is still that we enter as the Northlandic Church's representatives?" Adelise asked, prompting a glare from Ceolwulf for having asked such a question aloud on the street.

"It is, brother," he replied, somewhat tersely.

"So we walk from Lunden town, out the gates, through Ealdwic, and follow the river to Westmynster? Is that not two miles that we have to be part of a procession, being watched by guards and soldiers and other noblemen?" Adelise asked.

Ceolwulf nodded, but did not reply. The girl was right. He did not like the plan, for it left them too open. Too much time had passed, too many incidents had happened, for no-one to be suspicious about the Northlandic priests.

"Don't worry, my la—, brother. Abbot Arnewulf and I have this under control," he replied before turning and giving a clumsy blessing to a crippled man on the street into whom he had nearly stumbled. Adelise fell back to walk with Thurstan who was at the rear of the group. He was swinging a short but sturdy length of timber as if it were a walking stick.

"Where did you get that?" Adelise asked.

"A couple of streets back. There was a cooper who didn't need it anymore," Thurstan replied casually. He used the Ænglisc words for cooper and streets, rather than the Northlandic, Adelise noted with amusement, something he was doing more and more.

"You stole it?" she asked, trying to sound shocked.

"I'm a monk now. I cannot steal. I appropriated it for the Church," he replied with a smile. Despite trying to not draw attention to themselves, Thurstan was walking upright, his head held high, his eyes darting from side to side, taking in everything around him, every flicker of movement, every smell or sound. He seemed to enjoy the mass of humanity surrounding him, the noise and clamour of thousands of men and women going about their daily routine.

"It's still theft," Adelise said, chiding him gently.

"I'm sure no-one will miss a bit of wood in a city such as this."

"The owner might," Adelise replied.

"Put it like this," Thurstan replied, lowering his voice. "In two days time you will either be queen or I'll be dead. I'd be much happier if it's the former. That means protecting you with my life; and a stick of wood never comes in handier than when you need to crack some skulls."

Adelise appeared to mull this over, then agreed.

"And anyway," Thurstan continued. "I tossed him a coin for it. An Ænglisc one as well, don't fret."

Adelise beamed at the admission that Thurstan had not become a thief.

"Whatever happens, Thurstan, Brother Thurstan, that is, whatever happens, I am glad you were here with me," she said, looking up at the Northlander.

"Do you know what?" Thurstan asked, as they finally arrived outside a large wooden house that looked to be in some state of disrepair. "So am I."

Abbot Arnewulf fished out a key from within his robes and, glancing around him, scouring the street for any prying eyes, opened the door and stepped into the windowless room. The group of seven priests quickly disappeared inside, leaving behind them a street filled with people that for the most part had not noticed, nor cared about them.

And the small boy that had been following them since their arrival disappeared into Lunden's alleyways.

Ceolwulf sunk further down into his seat, pulling the leather cap he had found in Arnewulf's bag of clothes as far down as possible without looking ridiculous. The smoky tavern was near to full, a combination of visitors to the coronation, merchants finished work for the day and those who appeared to have substituted work for the alehouse on a permanent basis. He had arranged to meet his contact in Lunden in this particular tavern before leaving Jorvik. The contact would be unknown to him; a man known to a man known by his uncle, which after the previous two days, was of little comfort to him. They would be mutually identifiable by a sprig of genet carried either about them or placed on a table.

Ceolwulf had seated himself in what he hoped to be a discreet position. He was at a table towards the back of the tavern, not immediately visible from the front door, but facing the bar so that the contact would not have to hunt around and stare at each patron. He rested his head in his hand and pretended to be maudlin, in his cups, twisting the spring of genet in his fingers, hoping that his apparently miserable demeanour would put off any unwanted drinker from wishing to share his table.

There was no way of knowing how long he had been waiting. An hour? Was it possibly two? Perhaps not even a half hour, but Ceolwulf's nerves and apprehension were stretching time out, rendering the slightest hint of tardiness out into an agonising wait. He was all too aware that he was sitting alone, his future depending on a scribbled note from two weeks ago and that he risked a simple dagger through the ribs should he be betrayed.

"Is this seat taken?" a quiet voice asked.

Ceolwulf looked up to see a young, round-faced man, with a sprig of genet pinned to his tunic, offering him a friendly smile.

"I think it may well be now, friend," Ceolwulf replied,

picking up the small flower he had laid on the table.

"I think we need not introduce ourselves," the young man said, in conversational tones. "At least not openly. Save to say that I am a loyal Ænglander and East Anglian. You should refer to me as Wiglaf, that would be best." He reeled off the sentence as if he were discussing the weather.

"You were not followed, I take it?" Ceolwulf asked.

"I would not be here, if I thought for a minute that I were not completely alone," Wiglaf replied. "Very few people know of our existence, my friend. Even fewer know that we meet. But rest assured, our cause has many friends, in many high places."

Ceolwulf smiled at the man's confident assurances. He took a sip of his ale and straightened up in his seat, the seated Wiglaf now shielding him from the most of the tavern's view.

"So, here we are," Ceolwulf said finally.

"Yes, my lord," Wiglaf replied cheerfully.

"My friend," Ceolwulf corrected him. "Our plans remained unaltered?"

"I believe so," Wiglaf said. "You are here with the Northlandic delegation of priests invited by the late archbishop?"

Ceolwulf nodded.

"So you will enter the cathedral on the coronation. The earls that support you will have armed men within the building, just waiting for your signal," Wiglaf continued. "Is this still your plan? You have not encountered any difficulties so far?"

"No, none at all. Does anyone know about our presence here, anyone who ought not to know?"

"No, not at all," Wiglaf replied, leaning in towards Ceolwulf, across the table. "No-one suspects that the exiled Earl of East Anglia has returned to take the throne of Ængland." The young man beamed and leant back in his chair. Ceolwulf took another slow sip of his ale and scanned the other occupants of tavern. Absent-mindedly, he flicked the remnants of the genet across the table and onto the floor.

"You are a contact of my uncle, then?" Ceolwulf asked.

"Let us say I am a friend of a contact of your uncle," Wiglaf replied. "It does neither of us any favours to be in too close contact. If I need to contact you though, where should I find you?"

"If you need to contact me, then there is a problem. If there is a problem at this stage, then we are lost," Ceolwulf said, reluctant to reveal any more information. He drained his ale and placed the wooden tankard down with a thump on the table. "There is little more to be said. It is best if we are not seen together."

"What will be the signal?" Wiglaf asked.

"Oh, you will know. I shall, let's say, make a scene," Ceolwulf replied, standing up. Wiglaf, instead, remained seated. "You are staying here?"

"It would be for the best if we are not seen leaving together," Wiglaf replied quietly, before raising his voice and bidding Ceolwulf farewell. "See you at the market tomorrow, cousin!"

Ceolwulf nodded and then strode out of the tavern and into the night. Wiglaf remained at the table for several minutes, before standing up and walking over to the bar where the tavern keeper was breaching a new barrel of ale.

From the opposite corner of the room, Thurstan lowered his mug and watched Wiglaf speaking quickly to the man behind the wooden counter, who then disappeared into a back room. He had been watching the evening's proceedings from deep within the cowled woollen cloak he had wrapped around him.

He had argued with Ceolwulf for some time about following him to the meeting point, for he had not wanted the Northlander let loose in Lunden. Arnewulf had pointed out that it was perfectly normal for foreigners with a poor grasp of Ænglisc to be found in the city's drinking spots and that Thurstan's presence would not arouse suspicion. When Adelise had all but ordered Ceolwulf to take Thurstan with him, he had finally relented.

Thurstan had arrived a good hour before Ceolwulf and had nestled himself into a corner where he had hoped not to be disturbed. In the end, he had struck up a conversation with a drunken ex-sailor. The man was innocuous enough and appeared happy just to have someone to talk to, giving Thurstan ample opportunity to gaze past him and watch Ceolwulf, all the while appearing to be in company. The old drunkard did not notice Thurstan's accent, or was not surprised by it, for Lunden's taverns truly were a mix of voices and dialects.

The barkeeper returned to the counter, in the company of a small boy. The child appeared to know Wiglaf, for they immediately started talking animatedly. At one point, the young man leant down and whispered something in the boy's ear, before ruffling his hair and giving him a coin. The boy thanked him then scurried out of the tavern. The door slammed shut behind him, the rush of air causing the smoke to swirl around Thurstan's table.

Thurstan took a final sip of his ale and stood up. He thanked the sailor for his company, then strode out of the tavern before the old man could bid him farewell.

The narrow cobbled street was almost in total darkness, but there was just enough light from the waning moon to allow Thurstan to see the boy from the tavern disappear round a corner at the bottom of the road. Staying in the shadows created by the cramped, two-storey houses and buildings, Thurstan ran lightly to the street corner, and then peered around. He saw the boy making his way, at a leisurely pace, down Bread Street towards the river. Casting a quick glance behind him to check for anyone following him, Thurstan put his head down and pressed forward.

He followed the boy through what appeared to be most of southwest Lunden, always keeping his distance, always making sure he kept in the shadows. The boy weaved his way through the web of narrow streets and alleyways. Not once did he appear to check behind him, even though Thurstan was sure his route had purposely doubled back on itself several times.

Despite the late hour, Thurstan could not help but wonder at the number of people on the street. People staggering out of alehouses, merchants selling wares in the street; more people were to be found at this hour in Lunden than in all of Lonborg or Kirkby during the day.

The streets were covered in a mix of straw, earth and filth, some of it animal, but, Thurstan feared, a lot of it human. He did not have the luxury of avoiding it though, as he dared not look down lest he lose the boy from view. Taking care only to avoid walking into other people and drawing too much attention to himself, Thurstan walked from doorframe to alleyway, from street corner to shadow. Then, just as Thurstan turned into a narrow street that he was certain he had already been down several times, the boy stopped in front of what appeared to be an abandoned building. Thurstan immediately stepped into an alleyway, the stench of which nearly made him gag.

The boy knocked on what must have been a door, though it appeared to be nothing more than several planks of wood nailed together. Glancing around, he waited several seconds before knocking again. Thurstan stepped back, a little further into the shadows, careful to keep out of view.

"If you have the coin, you can have me here," came a rasping voice from just behind Thurstan's ear. He spun round to see a middle-aged woman, her bare breasts on show, smiling peg-toothed at him, rubbing her fingers together in a way that left little doubt about her occupation.

"I, er..." Thurstan mumbled, before turning back to glance up the street. The door had opened and the boy was talking to someone stood in the doorway. Thurstan could not see the person's face from where he was standing, not without stepping into the street. He quickly turned back to the whore and fumbled for a coin from his scrip.

"Here," he said, handing her the piece of silver, which she snatched from his palm. She took him by the hand, trying to lead him further into the shadows, but instead Thurstan dragged her into the street. She seemed confused, but once on the street Thurstan took her in his arms and kissed her forcefully, as a lover would do to his paramour.

The stench of the woman's breath and greasy hair almost caused Thurstan to heave, but he was rewarded with a view directly into the doorway. A view that only lasted a few seconds before the boy disappeared inside and the wooden slats slammed shut. It was, however, a view that confirmed what he and Ceolwulf had feared. The view of the rotund face of Bodo, alive and well in Lunden.

Adelise awoke with a start. A noise from downstairs had abruptly stirred her. Someone at the door perhaps? There had been several comings and goings all night, ever since Ceolwulf had left to meet with his contact. She had gone to bed, but had not been able to sleep very well. The old wooden house could not be said to have a second floor as such, but a wooden platform that extended across half the building, supported by thick beams and reached by a rickety staircase. It was smokier in the rafters and she was sure there were at least two families of mice keeping her company, but it had offered her some privacy.

She turned over and squinted towards the door. Abbot Arnewulf had gone to open it, taking the precaution of keeping a hooded shawl over his head. The door swung slowly open, letting in a draught of cool night air that swirled into eddies of soot and straw. After a few, brief mumbled words she saw, with great relief, Ceolwulf step into the room. Arnewulf quickly peered out into the street, and then closed the door behind him.

The two men sat down at the house's sole table and Abbot Arnewulf indicated to Ceolwulf to speak quietly. Gamal and Mathias were already asleep, finding whatever corner they could, using their habits as blankets. Ceolwulf kept his voice low and spoke rapidly to Arnewulf.

"We are not safe here," he said.

"Your contact is compromised?" Arnewulf asked.

"He didn't know of our true purpose and wanted to know where we were staying. The opposite of what any real contact of my uncle's would," Ceolwulf replied.

"You are convinced of this?"

"Enough to not consider ourselves safe here. Nor, I should say, is our plan. The one thing the contact did know is that we had been travelling as monks. This is all futile," Ceolwulf said, slapping his hand down hard on the table, causing Gamal to briefly stir.

From where she lay, Adelise could see between the floorboards to the table below her. If she pressed her face to the floor, the ill-fitted boards gave her a clear view of Arnewulf's tonsured head and Ceolwulf's flustered state. Arnewulf did not respond immediately, but waited for Ceolwulf to calm down. The small hearth in the far corner of the house crackled as the small branches they were using for firewood twisted and snapped in the heat.

"Were you followed back?" Arnewulf asked. At that moment, a knock came at the door, causing the Ceolwulf's head to whip round in surprise.

"Not Thurstan already?" he asked. Abbot Arnewulf, who seemed unsurprised by the knock, stood up and shook his head. He disappeared from Adelise's view and she turned again, trying to look down at the doorway. Abbot Arnewulf opened the door and in quickly stepped a tall, bearded man dressed in filthy clothes. Ceolwulf sprang to his feet at the sight of such a large stranger, but Abbot Arnewulf waved a hand to pacify him.

"Do not worry, my Lord Ceolwulf, this is Bucca, a trusted retainer of the Earl of Grantbrygscir. The man responsible for the upkeep and cleaning of this house when it is not being rented,"

Abbot Arnewulf explained.

Ceolwulf tried desperately not to look at the cobwebs and filth covering every surface in the house. Abbot Arnewulf shrugged at the incredulous Ceolwulf and continued.

"Well, occasionally looks in, I assume. Most importantly though, he is an ex-soldier and the man who tracked you through the streets tonight, making sure you were not followed. I trust there were no problems."

"No, Father. No-one that I could see," Bucca replied, his voice flat and oddly quiet for such a big man.

"You will stay here tonight?" Arnewulf asked him.

"I will take some food, then sleep. I will leave tomorrow," the large man replied simply in a monotone.

"Very good," Arnewulf replied. "I may yet have another errand for you, if you do not object. There is soup in the pot by the hearth."

Bucca nodded and helped himself to a bowl. Adelise rolled back from the gap in the floorboards for a moment, the smoke seeping up making her eyes water. She was worried that Thurstan had not returned yet; she thought he was meant to be looking after Ceolwulf. The image of Thurstan, after having trekked the length the country to protect her, lying dying in a gutter somewhere in Lunden, flickered in her mind, causing her to rub her eyes.

She rolled over to face the rafters, hoping to fall asleep quickly. The sooner she slept, she reasoned, the sooner Thurstan would be back. She would not sleep though, she knew that. Father Arnewulf was trying to reassure Ceolwulf that all was not lost, but she no longer wished to listen to how hopeless their situation was.

In two days, all would be resolved, she thought. In two days' time, after the planned coronation, she would be either proclaimed queen, or she would be dead. The thought sent a wave of nausea through her. She wiped away tears from her eyes, this time not caused by the smoke.

Why could she not have stayed in Scotland? She had been happy there. Could she not have just stayed with her uncle forever? She shook her head to herself, for she knew she had had no choice. It was a duty, but then another pang gripped her; this time of guilt. Guilt, for at times, even though she had told no-one, she would sense a flicker of excitement at the prospect of becoming Queen of Ængland. Queen Adelise. As soon as she sensed that flicker however, she immediately snuffed it out. Eagerness to assume the throne felt wrong; it seemed selfish and childish and she had always been told that a desire for power did not make for a wise monarch.

Just as her mind started to wander, images of castles and courts mixing with scenes of shouting soldiers and blades, another knock came at the door, this time hurried and loud. Bucca walked over and opened the door just a fraction.

"Who are you?" came a familiar voice. Adelise scrambled to her feet and hurried down the stairs, as Arnewulf instructed Bucca to let Thurstan in. The Northlander stared at the big man with a mix of confusion and mistrust as he stepped inside.

Adelise rushed down the stairs and flung her arms around Thurstan the second he entered the house. He simply picked her up, as an adult would with a young relative, and then perched her on his knee as he sat down at the table. A disapproving Ceolwulf seemed about to say something, but held his tongue, for even he knew that now was not the time.

"Bodo," Thurstan said simply.

Arnewulf nodded and Ceolwulf swore.

"He is alive and here in Lunden. I followed a boy from the inn, a boy who spoke to your contact once you had left. I followed him to a house near the river where I saw Bodo. We are compromised."

"It is as I said then, we are lost. We cannot possibly hope to enter Westmynster now," Ceolwulf said.

"It is true. If Bodo knows of our plan, then surely so do the rest of our enemies. Nor, I should imagine, are we safe here. Perhaps they even know about Adelise and are simply waiting for us to present ourselves?" Thurstan asked.

Abbot Arnewulf leant forward on his stool and placed his head in his hands, pressing his fingers to his temples.

"I feared this might happen. To place our hopes in subterfuge and shadowy contacts, to travel from Jorvik to Lunden, by land and sea, and to not have any enemies learn of our plans did seem optimistic," he said. "It is for that reason, you understand, that I have kept certain things, such as our friend Bucca here, to myself. I am sorry for not telling you previously, but there are certain things I though best not to mention beforehand, for the sake of all involved," Arnewulf added, for the benefit of both Ceolwulf and Thurstan.

Mathias and Gamal had joined them at the table now, for the constant knocking and opening of the door had rendered any sleep impossible. They looked nervously at the faces around the table and found no comfort in their expressions.

"Then we are truly lost?" Ceolwulf asked.

"Not totally so," Arnewulf said wryly.

The priest beckoned Bucca over and whispered a few brief and hurried words in his ear. The big man nodded and immediately took his leave, disappearing into the night, much to the confusion of the house's other occupants. Adelise looked up at Thurstan, hoping that he had an answer, but he simply shrugged at her.

"There have always been alternative arrangements. Did I ever tell you," Abbot Arnewulf asked, straightening up and cracking his fingers together. "About my sister, Osgyth?"

15th June 1166
Westmynster Cathedral, Lunden

Swegen stepped through the large double doors of Westmynster Cathedral and turned to wave at the crowd. Hundreds of people, mostly from Lunden, but many from much further afield, had accompanied his cortege along the two-mile route from the city. They had left the city by the western Lud Gate, past the scattered houses of Ealdwic village, following the river along the Strondway, through the fields to Thorn Island, site of the great cathedral.

He raised his arms to salute the congregated well-wishers, displaying the rich cloths and furs draped around his shoulders. He stood there for several moments, soaking up their adulation, their shouts of support, letting the sun glint off the finery with which he had adorned himself. Godric had argued against the display, saying that he should enter the cathedral a humble man and leave a crowned king, but Swegen would not hear of it. Today was his day.

Swegen turned and started the long and slow walk down the carpeted nave. He nodded benevolently at the faces he recognised, bestowing the odd wave at those he deemed worthy of particular attention. He even smiled at the guests of whose identity he had no idea. There were countless foreign dignitaries, all of whom had decided to bring family with them. All at Ængland's cost no doubt, but the majesty of his nation ought to be seen by as many of Europe's nobility as possible.

From the beyond the transept, the voices of the choir rose higher. Singing God's praises, singing Ængland's praises and singing Swegen's praises. Although they were in a house of God, Swegen knew which of those three was the most important today. He could see his throne waiting, raised on a small dais, beckoning him forward.

A familiar face raised a smile and a flicker of a nod; the Earl of Sumersætscir and his hideously ugly wife, all red face and pockmarks. His daughter, on the other hand, might be worthy of special attention at the festivities later. A smile and move on. He passed several Cymric princes; he was sure only two had been invited, three at most, but an entire horde had arrived it seemed. A slight smile, then move on.

Ahead, he could see Godric waiting, dressed in his finest robes. The wily old fox was wearing a mask-like expression of solemnity and piety. Swegen chuckled inwardly, for a more devious and avaricious snake of man could not be found in Ængland, but here he was today, for all the world looking the part of the holier than holy churchman.

He walked by various foreign noblemen, hardly pausing to acknowledge them. Flemish, Frankish or Frisian? He wasn't quite sure; the only thing he could establish by their odd dress was that they were certainly not from these isles, all strange hats and clean-shaven.

Swegen reached the final rows of guests before the transept. Here stood the most important earls and dignitaries from Ængland's closest allies. And enemies, if truth be told; Normans, Kernewek, Scots – no Northlanders, obviously. Particularly no Northlandic monks; only this morning the captain of Lunden's city guard had arrested a group of five monks claiming they were from Lindisfarne; he would deal with them later. Things were, finally, as he would put it, tidy. As he passed the final row, he let a broad grin spread across his face, invisible to the congregation, but not to Godric, if his look of disapproval was anything to go by.

Straightening his face into a solemn visage, Swegen turned, bowed to the congregation, then turned back to kneel in front of Godric. The voices of the choir faded away and Swegen was left with a view of the archbishop's feet and a nose full of the incense that the churchmen insisted on burning copious amounts of at these ceremonies.

The coronation started with Godric's voice ringing out around the large cathedral, echoing off the high stone walls. Even though Swegen's rudimentary understanding of Latin was more than enough to understand the proclamations, his mind was elsewhere. This religious charade could not be over with quickly enough; every minute spent waiting, listening to sermons and rites was a minute longer he would have to wait to be crowned.

Swegen did not need to thank God for becoming king; it was not divine providence that had given him the throne. It was himself he had to thank; his cunning, his guile, his ambition and courage.

Godric appeared to have reached a prayer, for the assembled priests were repeating lines after him, followed with less certainty by the congregation. He glanced up for a second at the throne. The old chair did not look quite as impressive from up close. The gold leaf was flaking from the wooden legs, the silken cushion threadbare in places. It was still the coronation throne, however; the one used by his uncle over thirty years previously, the one used by his grandfather and great grandfather before him.

He let the history and majesty of the occasion wash over him. As Godric droned on, his mind drifted, tempted away by the thoughts of the glory and power that would be bestowed on him today. His name would live forever, joining the list of his royal ancestors. From Edward I, who had built the cathedral to Swegen. King Swegen. Swegen the Just. Swegen the Wise. Swegen the Great.

He felt Godric's hand touch his head and he looked up to see the archbishop commanding him to stand. On legs that suddenly felt as if the blood had drained from them, Swegen slowly raised himself to his feet and turned to face the congregation. Trying desperately not to break into a smile, he sat down on the throne.

He let his fingers clasp the arms of the chair and he inhaled deeply. He could palpably sense the power being given to him. It washed over him, making his spine tingle and his shoulders twitch.

From one side a bishop stepped forward with a cushion, upon which lay the crown. Swegen could just make out from the corner of his eye the glinting golden shape, but he did not turn his head. He kept his gaze focused on the far end of the nave, at the doors through which he had entered.

Godric's voice wittered on, holding the crown aloft and reciting what seemed to be interminable prayers. Swegen closed his eyes and bit back the urge to scream at the archbishop to hurry up. *Good God*, he thought, *he is getting as bad as old Eadric.* From the pews he heard the sounds of muffled footsteps; even the congregated guests were getting impatient to see him crowned, he thought.

He opened his eyes to see that one of the noblemen, one of those odd Flemish ones, had stepped out into the aisle of the nave. Swegen didn't recognise him, although he appeared to be the husband of Lady Osgyth of Flanders. He noted only that the rude idiot had seemingly brought all his children with him; one of whom, a small boy, was now walking towards the transept. Swegen glanced around to see if anyone else had noticed, but everyone seemed as shocked as he did.

Two more young men, other sons of the bearded noblemen, Swegen assumed, had followed the boy down the nave. One of them seemed oddly familiar, Swegen thought. Before he could gather his thoughts, the small boy turned and called out in a high, reedy voice.

"Stop the coronation!"

Godric halted mid-sentence and stared at the intruders into the transept. Swegen glared around to the edges of the cathedral, where armed men were stationed. He gave a quick nod and several figures detached themselves from the shadows and moved towards the boy. Seeing the men advancing upon him, the boy called out again, this time so quickly that his words were almost garbled.

"Stop the coronation! I am Queen Adelise and I have returned!"

The armed men stopped in their tracks and the cathedral echoed to the boy's impossible words. The two younger men stepped forward, each one placing themselves between the child and the confused soldiers.

"I am Adelise!" the child cried again, then turned and stared at Swegen.

It was her. It was. He felt bile rise in his throat and his euphoria swept away by a wave of nausea and dizziness. He recognised the face, the eyes. It was the dead girl. Ricmund's failure had been real.

"Guards!" Swegen called, finally finding his voice. It sounded oddly distant and high-pitched. "Seize this demented creature."

The soldiers stepped forward, prompting the two male intruders to step closer to Adelise. She turned to the congregation, removing her hat to afford them the best possible view.

"I am Adelise!" she called again, this time her voice rising in panic. The soldiers advanced on her, swords drawn. They were no more than ten paces away, when an earl in the front row stepped forward. Earl Hereman of Grantbrygscir glanced swiftly at Swegen, before dropping to one knee in front of the child.

"I see you, my lady, and I recognise you as my queen," he said simply. He would die for that, Swegen decided.

"No!" Swegen shouted. "She is not the queen. She is an impostor! Guards!" The armed men had all but stopped when the earl had stepped forward. Swegen waved his hand wildly, gesticulating at the girl, but the guards were looking as confused as the rest of the cathedral. Even Godric seemed dumbfounded and had stepped away from the throne.

"I see you, my lady, and I recognise you," came another voice. The Earl of Wireceasterscir had also stepped out the rows of pews and had dropped to one knee. Then another, the Earl of Sciropscir, of Suthrie and another and another. Only Suthseaxe and Wiltescir seemed unwilling to move.

"No!" Swegen screamed. This time his voice came loudly, almost a shriek. Any semblance of calm had completely gone and his cry was verging on the hysterical. "It cannot be her. It's not her. She's dead!" The last cry came almost as a plea, desperate for it to be true.

"Archbishop Godric!" one of the young Flemish noblemen shouted. "You recognise the Lady Adelise, Queen of Ængland, do you not?" His voice did not sound Flemish, Swegen thought. He stared at the man, trying to place his familiar voice, waiting for the Archbishop of Westmynster to sort out this nonsense. The conspicuous lack of an answer from Godric caused Swegen to turn to face the flummoxed archbishop.

The man had gone as pale as milk, his mouth opening and closing, uttering only gasps of breath.

"Godric!" Swegen hissed. "What are you doing, man?"

The archbishop stared at Swegen, then at the girl, then back to Swegen, before staring at the various earls who were still kneeling in acquiescence. He coughed then spoke clearly and loudly for the entire cathedral to hear.

"I do recognise her, and acknowledge her claim, my Lord Ceolwulf," he said, drawing an anguished cry from Swegen. The king-to-be screamed in rage, in recognition of the traitor and in horror at the thought of his throne slipping away though his fingers.

"Kill her!" he shrieked at the guards. But they did not move. Earl Hereman had clicked his fingers and even more armed men appeared from one of the side chapels where they had been concealed.

"Swegen, Earl of Berrocscir, you are a murderer. You are a liar,

D A V I D   H A W O R T H

a killer and a traitor to Ængland. You have tried to kill Queen Adelise, you murdered my father and you acted as if it was all in the interests of our nation, when it was purely to sate your greed. I denounce you, here, in the eyes of God and in front of all Ængland. I will not permit you to be king," Ceolwulf called out, his unblinking gaze not leaving Swegen's trembling, twitching face for one second.

"You denounce nothing, traitor!" Swegen shrieked. "You have no authority here! You're an exile and the girl here is an impostor!" He took a step forward.

The young girl, seeming to react to a gesture from the other young man, who was certainly no Flemish nobleman, turned to the congregation and held a hand up to the back of her neck. Lifting the hair at the nape of her neck, she displayed an angry red birthmark, visible from a distance to the congregation, before turning to show it to Godric.

"The Queen Adelise is alive and claims her throne," Ceolwulf called. "I support her and I denounce you. As the heir to the Earl of East Anglia, I call a bloodfeud between us, for the murder of my father."

Swegen snorted in disgust, and stepped slowly down from the dais on which the throne stood. He walked towards the assembled group of intruders, clapping his hands slowly. His bottom lip was twitching uncontrollably, as was his right eyelid.

"Very well," he called out, his voice light, tinged almost with laughter. "Very well. So be it. You have decided to ruin my coronation with this farce, this charade that appears to have taken my good earls in. And you would be?" The last question was addressed to the mysterious other young man who had stepped up with Ceolwulf.

"Your enemy," Thurstan replied simply, his Northlandic accent as strong as he could possibly make it.

Swegen shook his head in mockery at the answer, repeating the words over to himself.

"My enemy, really?" Swegen turned full circle, sweeping an arm around in a scythe-like manner. "You are all my enemies today, it would seem."

"My lord Earl," Godric called out from behind him. "Perhaps it would be wise…"

"It would be wise for you to shut up!" Swegen screamed, cutting him off. "No, no. There would appear to be only one solution here." He turned back to the congregation, flashed one of his serpentine smiles and then lunged at Adelise, drawing out a dagger from where it had been secreted in one of his heavily draped sleeves.

Adelise was transfixed in fear. All the courage and bravery she possessed had already been spent on stepping into the nave and proclaiming herself to the cathedral. She opened her mouth to scream, the blade arcing down towards her face, Swegen's face contorted by hate. The blade was inches from her eye, the cry just about to leave her lips, when a shape leapt between the dagger and the girl.

It was Thurstan. He made no attempt to deflect the blow, no attempt to disarm the broken-minded Swegen. He knew he simply had to stop the blade from reaching her. His body took the blade, along with the weight of Swegen behind it. Adelise was knocked to the ground, unharmed. Swegen tumbled to one side, screaming in frustration that he had not managed to harm his cousin. Thurstan saw all this and sighed with relief before the shock and pain of the blade hit him. He glanced down to see the dagger's hilt protruding from his breast.

Adelise was left lying on the stone floor, screaming Thurstan's name. Swegen picked himself up and scrambled backwards away from the encircling crowd of earls, from the armed guards and from the wild-eyed Ceolwulf.

"Godric, save me, or I'll tell them about your part," Swegen hissed at the archbishop as he stumbled towards him. Godric stepped away from the earl, shaking his head slowly.

"Give me a blade!" Ceolwulf called, to which Earl Hereman responded by taking a sword from the unresisting hands of a nearby guard and handing it over.

"You are going to pay! Pay for everything, by my hand, or so help me God," Ceolwulf shouted, advancing on the retreating earl.

"What are you doing?" Swegen cried, backing away, looking desperately around for any support. "I demand a trial at least. You cannot kill me in cold blood."

"Then fight me, you worm," Ceolwulf shouted.

"I am unarmed," Swegen whined, finding his way to the back of the cathedral blocked by a newly formed wall of armed men.

"Then find a sword," Ceolwulf snapped.

"This isn't Normandy; we're not going to duel. I demand a trial," Swegen, some of his usual venom starting to replace his panic.

Behind them, the congregation had either surged forward to watch the spectacle, or had fled the cathedral, fearing a bloodbath. The first few rows had formed a circle around Adelise and the limp, bloody shape of Thurstan.

"Godric!" Swegen snapped. "Tell him! I shall stand trial for whatever sins I have committed. Tell him and these soldiers to put their swords away. This is a cathedral, he cannot kill me here!"

Godric seemed to consider this for a moment, before Swegen snapped at him again.

"Godric! You need me! After all we've been through!"

This time the archbishop paused to give this some thought, and then leant towards Ceolwulf who was now standing, trembling in front of him.

"Kill him. God will understand," he whispered to the young man.

Ceolwulf nodded. "Oh I understand, Godric. I understand perfectly."

He exhaled deeply and lowered his sword.

"I will not kill you, Swegen. You will face trial for your sins, and when they are through, I hope they hang you high, you murderer," Ceolwulf said calmly, before handing his sword to a confused-looking Godric. He stepped backwards and gave the archbishop an expectant nod, urging him to speak.

"Ah," Godric started. "Arrest the Earl of Berrocscir?" The order came out sounding more like a question than an instruction. The armed men surrounding the altar closed in on Swegen. As Ceolwulf turned to run back to the injured Thurstan, he heard a cry of rage from the man who had been seconds away from being king.

"You Judas, Godric, you liar! I'll cut you down like the dog you are," Swegen erupted, rushing towards the trembling churchman who was limply holding Ceolwulf's discarded sword. He made to grab the sword, wanting to prise it out of Godric's hands and to strike him down.

Swegen's face was contorted into a snarling mask of hate; Godric's one of wide-eyed fear and confusion. Right up until the point when Swegen was less than a yard away and the archbishop suddenly gripped the sword and flicked it upwards. The blade ripped into Swegen's abdomen and sliced upwards, Godric's hold suddenly becoming vice-like.

Swegen's expression abruptly became that of fear and surprise; Godric's that of steely determination. He gripped the rushing earl, pulling him onto the sword, skewering him like a yuletide hog. To the shocked congregation, it looked as if Godric was embracing, perhaps even forgiving his attacker. Then the blood came, and the high-pitched whimper from Swegen. Godric stepped back, the look of fear and confusion quickly restored for the benefit of witnesses.

The sword clattered noisily on the stone floor as it fell from Godric's hands. Swegen's partially eviscerated body sank to its knees, spurting thick jets of blood onto the cathedral floor, before toppling over to a mix of screams and cries.

Godric turned to face Ceolwulf behind him.

"It is over," he said simply, almost to himself, for his voice was now lost in the maelstrom of voices. Ceolwulf nodded and then quickly ran back to where Thurstan was being attended to by Adelise.

The queen was weeping, gripping the hand of the Northlander. Abbot Arnewulf shook his head sadly at Ceolwulf as he knelt down to his friend's side. Thurstan's face was white and even though two earls' wives had managed to stem the bleeding, by tearing a woollen cape into strips, his lips had taken on a worryingly blue tinge.

"Please don't die, Thurstan," Adelise cried.

He turned his head weakly and focused on the girl with moist eyes.

"I am content. I've done what I set out to do," Thurstan said, a slight smile breaking across his pale lips. "I am complete. You are safe now. I can go home."

With that, his head fell backwards and his eyes closed, leaving Adelise to cry out in grief as the crowds outside the cathedral started to celebrate the miracle that their queen was still alive.

Epilogue
29th June 1166
Westmynster Cathedral, Lunden

The cathedral erupted into a chorus of cheers and applause as Queen Adelise stood up from the throne. Steadying the large crown with one hand as she half stepped, half jumped down from the large chair, she smiled with what she hoped was regal reserve and not childish enthusiasm.

In the front row, she saw Ceolwulf, now Earl Ceolwulf of East Anglia, the man to whom the hastily assembled witenagemot had entrusted her guardianship. He, along with Archbishop Godric, would be responsible for guiding and advising her until she was an adult or married: whichever came first. She hadn't been sure what difference having a husband would supposedly have on her decision making, but she knew that nine-year-old queens definitely needed some help.

For the time being, her close friend would help her become a good queen, along with the Archbishop of Westmynster. Godric seemed a nice enough man, although a little strange. Ceolwulf said he was a very clever man, that it was best to have him with them rather than against them. She hadn't quite understood what he had meant by that initially, but she could see that Godric seemed to think a lot about things. For now, he was being very helpful and didn't even appear to mind very much when he had been told by Ceolwulf that Cantwaraburg would have a new archbishop appointed.

Six maidens ran forward and took the hem of Adelise's long dress, holding it as she made her way down the nave towards the cathedral doors. In front of her, two blond-haired twin boys threw rose petals as she walked along the aisle. They laughed as they got in the way of the less-amused priests who led the way out, singing hymns, but no-one seemed willing to object today.

As she neared the main doors, she glanced to the side and beamed broadly. There stood the King of Northland himself, Hakon, who had been requested to attend by Adelise.

And next to him was stood poor Thurstan. Adelise slowed and gave her broadest, most childlike grin to him. Poor, poor Thurstan; never again would he wield a sword, or be able to ride a horse as he once did.

She felt desperately sorry for him; his dream to become a royal huskarl in the service of King Hakon had been taken away from him in a flash. Oddly though, he did not appear to mind. In those first few days he had not awoken once, but then he had come to speak to her one night. He explained to Adelise that he had achieved his life's ambition. He had given his best service to his monarch and made a sacrifice for the noblest of causes; what more could a man wish for? She thought he was just saying that to make her feel better, or possibly himself.

She gave him a final grin before stepping through the open doors, and into a warm summer sun. As she walked out of Westmynster cathedral, the crowd cheered and called her name. They surged forward, trying to get a sight of her pearlescent white silk dress, forcing soldiers to hold them back, lest they swamped the newly crowned Queen of Ængland.

She scanned the happy faces and struggled to think of a time that she had been happier. Well, there was little to compare to a coronation, was there? Her memories flicked back to that first moment that she had seen Thurstan. She had been convinced that she was about to die, in pain and fearful, and then a wild, longhaired Northlander had picked her up and carried her off. She smiled at some of the memories, tinged with both fondness and sadness; she flinched at others. She decided not to think about any of them for the time being, instead telling herself to enjoy the moment of her ascension to the throne.

As she stepped into the carriage that was waiting to take her back to Lunden and the newly named Queen's Hall, she permitted herself one final indulgence

She turned back to where Thurstan was standing and beckoned him over. He walked to her slowly, the crowd not wishing to part to let him through. She gestured for Thurstan to lean in and whispered into his ear.

"I want to say thank you, before I go. Thank you for all you have done. I am sorry that you didn't make all these sacrifices for your own king," she whispered, staring first at his pale face and then back at a bemused-looking King Hakon.

"I think I did, in an odd sort of way. Time will tell. But do you know what, Adelise?" he replied, using her forename, as so few people did nowadays. "I am a Northlander and a proud one at that. I will go back to my family and live the rest of my days in Northland."

He took her hand in his one remaining good one and gave it a gentle squeeze.

"In the end though, the country doesn't matter; you will always be my queen."

With that, he turned and melted into the crowd, leaving Adelise to ride to Lunden, to her future and to her Ængland.

The Anglo-Saxon Chronicle records

1166 (extract) In this year passed away King Æthelgar on 7 April at Oxnaforda and he is buried at Lunden. His granddaughter, Adelise, succeeded the kingdom, for his only son Edmund had departed this world some four years previously.

Hereafter Adelise was waylaid and kidnapped by a heathen host whilst riding through Northland to her coronation in Ængland. Earl Edgar of East Anglia and his son, Ceolwulf, were dispatched by the steward, Earl Swegen of Berrocscir, to rescue the unfortunate queen.

Earl Edgar made great slaughter of the heathens but received a grievous wound, to which he succumbed, once returned to Ængland. Thus his son, Ceolwulf, succeeded him to the earldom and delivered the Queen Adelise safely to Lunden.

Thereafter on 29 June Queen Adelise was crowned amid great rejoicing, save for a treacherous attempt by an assassin on the queen's life. The Earl Swegen sacrificed himself to save her and died with honour, as befits a Great Lord.

Then it happened that in the autumn of the same year, Godric, the Archbishop of Westmynster, died by drowning in the Temes river, falling from a boat at night.

1167 ......(continued) And in this year Ceolwulf, Earl of East Anglia, married Alice of Bruges, the daughter of a wealthy Flemish nobleman.[1]

1. It is unclear as to whether Alice's father was truly a nobleman of Flanders or a wealthy merchant, but it is generally agreed that he must have been a man of some significant standing.

**TOP HAT
BOOKS**

Historical fiction that lives.

We publish fiction that captures the contrasts, the achievements, the optimism and the radicalism of ordinary and extraordinary times across the world.

We're open to all time periods and we strive to go beyond the narrow, foggy slums of Victorian London. Where are the tales of the people of fifteenth century Australasia? The stories of eighth century India? The voices from Africa, Arabia, cities and forests, deserts and towns? Our books thrill, excite, delight and inspire.

The genres will be broad but clear. Whether we're publishing romance, thrillers, crime, or something else entirely, the unifying themes are timescale and enthusiasm. These books will be a celebration of the chaotic power of the human spirit in difficult times. The reader, when they finish, will snap the book closed with a satisfied smile.